# CONFESSIONS
# OF A GAMBLER

# CONFESSIONS
## OF A GAMBLER

## RAYDA JACOBS

THE OVERLOOK PRESS
Woodstock & New York

This edition first published in the United States in 2007 by
The Overlook Press, Peter Mayer Publishers, Inc.
Woodstock & New York

WOODSTOCK:
One Overlook Drive
Woodstock, NY 12498
www.overlookpress.com
[for individual orders, bulk and special sales, contact our Woodstock office]

NEW YORK:
141 Wooster Street
New York, NY 10012

Cataloging-in-Publication Data is available from the Library of Congress

ISBN-10: 1-58567-897-X
ISBN-13: 978-1-58567-897-6

Manufactured in the United States of America
10 9 8 7 6 5 4 3 2 1

COBS
ayda)

I would like to acknowledge Deepak Chopra's
*How To Know God,* and
Clarissa Pinkola Estes' *Women Who Run With The Wolves,*
from which I have quoted generously.

The first thing I have to confess is that I'm a Muslim woman. I'm forty-nine. I wear two scarves. An under scarf, and a medorah. I've raised all my sons with the Word of God. When you pass me on the street, you won't even glance my way. I'm one of those robed women who appear to be going nowhere.

The second thing I have to confess is that I like risk. I don't know where it started. It could have been at school when my Christian friend, Merle, and I liked the same boy. He had already written me a note, asking if I wanted to go to a matinée. But then Merle let him look down the front of her blouse, and he went with her. Ever since, I've been trying to get back the things that I've lost. This is what the counselor says. I don't know if it's true. I don't even know if it's the money. I don't lack for anything. My four sons provide. One of the very good things about my religion is that mothers don't have to do the guilt thing so many Jewish mothers are accused of. Right in our Book God tells us that heaven lies under the sole of a mother's foot. You can pray a hole in the ground, fast till you drop, but if you disrespect your mother, you can be assured of what awaits you. My sons know this. They grew up without a father, but not without the Qur'an. They all have good jobs. One gives more than the others, but then the one who gives the least, understands me the best and he is my favourite. Despite what the experts tell you, a mother can have a favourite. She just can't admit it. But I have good sons. The eldest one discovered my secret. The youngest one protected me from the twins in the middle. With twins you have to be prepared for double of everything. I will come to the names of my sons. Now, I just want to tell you how it all began.

It was January 2002. My friend Garaatie, who has a bastard of a husband, had just come and told me the latest cruelty. Why her mother had given her such a name, I don't know. People grow into their names. *Raatie taatie, 'n visgraatie*, they called her. Garaatie looked exactly like what her name conjured up, except she was no fish bone; she was dik.

Anyway, Garaatie had found in her husband's pocket, a phone number with the name, Moena, next to it. Garaatie sometimes surprised me with her creativity – pretending that she was from the municipality, she had called the number and got the address. She got into her blue Volksie, and drove to Woodstock.

She was shocked when she got there to see a girl in her twenties. Garaatie felt she had made a terrible mistake. She was about to turn around and leave, but the girl's expression stopped her. It was as if the girl had seen her before.

"Are you Moena?" Garaatie asked.

"Look," the girl said, "speak to your husband."

Garaatie was like someone possessed by the devil. Right there on the threshold she grabbed the girl by the neck, and smacked her. Garaatie is a big woman. I could imagine the marks on the girl's face. The mother came running out when she heard screams. She looked at the two of them. It dawned on her why Garaatie was there. She ordered Moena inside.

"Tell her to stay away from my husband," Garaatie shouted.

That night when Mahmood got home, he asked Garaatie straight out why she'd gone to the girl's house. He wasn't even one of those husbands who took a second or third wife for the wrong reasons. He just cheated right in your face. So when he asked the question, and Garaatie didn't answer, he knuckled her against the head. Garaatie then made a serious mistake. She quoted God, something she was fond of doing.

"Do you know what God says about marrying more than one woman?" she asked. "If you can't be fair, you must only have one. Do you think you're a prophet?"

"Don't talk nonsense to me," he shouted. "I can have four wives. I've not wanted to marry another woman before, but now I've found someone who meets all my needs, and maybe it's time to do it."

Instead of throwing a suitcase at him, Garaatie ran from the room crying. If there's one thing you can't let a man see, it's this. Cry in the toilet. Call a friend. Spit in his tea. But don't break down in front of him. Garaatie's eldest son, Sulaiman, lived five streets away. She called him on the telephone. He came over. Father and son sat in the kitchen a long time talking. When the son came to seek out his mother in the bedroom, he told her the bad news.

"Daddy has a right, Mummy. I'm not happy about it, but there it is."

For two days Garaatie lay in bed. She didn't brush her teeth, she didn't wash, or cook, or clean herself. She only got up to pee.

On the third day she came to see me. I knew nothing of what had happened. All she said, was, "Why don't we go to the casino?"

I looked at her, not understanding.

"The casino," she repeated, as if I should've known all about it. "You know we now have a casino in Cape Town, don't you?"

I didn't know. I read books, I didn't read newspapers. I had never been to the races or bought a raffle or lottery ticket in my life. I wouldn't know about a casino unless it was right across the street or people I knew spoke about it.

"Let's just go," she said. "We don't have to stay long."

"Have you been there before?" I asked.

"Yes. I went with Shariefa."

"Really?" Shariefa was the biggest fitnah. If you wanted bad news to reach Port Elizabeth faster than bad air, you just had to tell Shariefa, and tell her not to tell anyone about it.

"Shariefa's okay," she said, sensing my skepticism. "She's had a disappointment."

"Shariefa's disappointment had everything to do with her big mouth. Did you gamble?"

"Only fifty rand, which I lost. But it takes your mind off things. And it's a lot of fun."

The word *fun* coming out of Garaatie's mouth was another surprise. Garaatie was old school and tartiep. It was community work, the dinh, and her husband. That was her life.

The word fun wasn't in her vocabulary. She didn't know how to treat herself to an hour of pleasure. How many times I'd invited her to come out with Nabeweya and me on our Sunday morning walks at Muizenberg beach, or to my Tuesday night movies with Rhoda. She always claimed she was busy. What she was busy with was searching through her husband's pockets for evidence. It wasn't because Mahmood was Indian that I didn't like him for Garaatie. It was that old Indian-Malay thing that'd been going on for years. The Malays were never going to be easy about their daughters marrying Indians, and the Indians were always going to think they were better than the Malays. The term Malay is of course another carbuncle, but that's a story on its own. Let me just say this. My forefathers might've come from the islands around the Indian Ocean, but I'm no Malay. The government did a terrible thing in the nineteen forties when it made meat of the Malays, and fish of the Indians. And that's how it's been since. There's a rift. Not a big one, but occasionally you'll hear a story.

Like the one Garaatie told me about when all the sisters-in-law had to make a dish and a dessert when the fifty relatives got together for a family lunch on Eid. She made prawn curry and tiramisu from a recipe she'd tried out three times before on her own family. First the men ate and, according to custom, the women had to wait on them. When it finally came to the women's turn, she watched with disappointment as they passed around the chicken breyani and sosaatie, and her prawn curry stood untouched. I felt for Garaatie and had told her once to leave the marriage if she were so unhappy. She'd given me such a mouthful, I never told her again.

So, off I went to the casino with Garaatie. To protect myself from all the fun I was going to have, I only took fifty rand. I had money stashed away in a savings account at the Perm, but definitely wasn't going to touch it.

We arrived at the grand entrance. I was surprised by the size of the building and by the size of land it occupied. The parking lot was as big as a golf course. People looked like they were on holiday in slacks and shorts and colourful shirts. The security we had to pass through surprised me, but the moment we stepped through the great big glass doors into a marble foyer, I was mesmerised. It was like the time Rhoda and I went to Istanbul, and the tour bus came upon this enclave of shops – hundreds of them under one roof – and we told the driver not to wait for us. Stepping into the casino was like that. I was completely swept up by the lights, the hum and the atmosphere.

Garaatie and I walked around for a bit. I was amazed by the number of people milling about. Even women with scarves on, like me, and a few men with fezzes.

"God, Garaatie, there're Muslim people in here."

"I know, but we're not going to gamble," she said. "We're just going to have a little fun."

"Okay." I had been completely unaware of this side of Garaatie.

We found two machines. They were in the same row, but not next to each other. Garaatie chose the one with the wonder bars, and I went for the frosty white sevens. I watched Garaatie insert a fifty-rand note into the machine and start to play.

I hesitantly did the same and the worst thing that can happen to anyone who goes to a casino for the first time happened to me. I was on a machine I'd picked simply for its looks and knew nothing about how it worked or what you could win. I was down to twelve rand when suddenly I heard – *zing, zing, zing!* – in rapid succession, and saw three white sevens lock into place.

"She won the jackpot!" someone behind me exclaimed. "Four thousand!"

"Beeda!" Garaatie got up from her seat to come and see. "Oh my word, you are lucky."

Everything happened at once. The lights went on, the bell rang, people started gathering about me.

"How much did you start with?" a woman asked.

"I came with fifty," I answered.

Turning to the man next to her, the woman said, "She came with a fifty. Can you believe it? I was on that machine for half an hour and nothing happened. You won with my money, lady. I pumped four hundred rand into that machine."

"It's always the people with twenty rand who win," someone else said.

A girl with a striped uniform appeared and asked whether I wanted the four thousand rand on my card, or a cheque. I looked at Garaatie. Garaatie had lost her money. She'd said she was only going to play fifty, but had stuck in another fifty. I noticed something else, Garaatie's crooked smile.

"It's a large sum," she said. "You can't use it to buy food."

"I'll take a cheque," I said to the attendant. I knew I'd have to give Garaatie some. Why, I don't know. If I could figure that out, I'd figure out why I have such a soft spot for my youngest son.

His name's Reza. I gave him a bit of a fancy name. I'd read somewhere that the Shah of Persia had a son, Reza. It sounded princely, and I needed something, anything, to brighten up my life after finding myself alone in my ninth month. When my husband left, leaving me with three children and one in the belly, I cried till my head hurt. I was so distraught that my eldest boy, Zane, only seven years old at the time, went to call the neighbour. Mrs Petersen sat with me on the edge of the bed and appealed to Jesus to take away my pain. The next day I couldn't look the woman in the eye. I lined up my three sons at the supper table and told them, "You still have a father. He's just not going to live here any more. And Mummy's got to get a job now."

Zane took it hard. He was a broody kind of boy, serious. The four-year-old twins, Munier and Marwaan, ran off to their room. They thought it was some kind of game.

Garaatie and I took the cheque to the cashier. I gave her two hundred and fifty rand. "You can play some more," I said. "We both have two-fifty. I'm putting the rest in the bank."

"Thanks," she smiled. "You didn't have to."

"You brought me here. I wouldn't have had this if it weren't for you."

"O, Allah," Garaatie said. "I hope God's not listening. Bringing you to a casino. That's not good."

"And Mahmood doesn't have to know about this," I added. For if there was one thing about Garaatie that I didn't like, it was that no matter what cruelty she revealed about her husband, the first time he said a few nice words and drukked her vas, she blurted out all kinds of things.

Which brings me to my friendship with her. Garaatie's not a bad person. She's just weak when it comes to men. She knows her rights, but doesn't exercise them. It's like she looked in the mirror and wondered how she'd even landed a man. I'll tell you how.

When she was eighteen, Garaatie had a boy coming to visit her on Friday nights. One day her father asked the boy outright what his intentions were. Fathers did this. Three visits, and they told the boy there was no sitting the seats warm if he had no intentions. The boy hakked and takked, but managed to utter that he did have intentions. When? the father wanted to know. The boy said something about a long engagement. The following Friday he didn't show up. Garaatie phoned him. She left messages with his sister. He was never there. Garaatie went to his job in Paarden Eiland, where he worked as a carpenter. It finally came out that he had a girlfriend, and was getting married the following year. Right there in the workshop in front of everyone, Garaatie begged him to give her another chance. No dignity at all. No shame. Shortly after that incident she met Mahmood at a family braai. Those were the days of smooching on the back seat of the car at Rhodes Memorial or Signal Hill. Garaatie fell pregnant. And there was no sob story to tell her mother or father after that. Mahmood had to clean up his mess.

But Garaatie has a good heart. Once, she loaned me two thousand rand – a big sum for a woman who had to account for every cent she spent.

Reza wasn't the only one to have given me headaches. The twins, from about the time they started matric, frequently got into trouble. Garaatie had helped me out with lawyers' fees. The twins' trouble had been with the law. Reza's was with the Almighty. But I won't speak about Reza now. I have to be in a certain mood to speak about him. The mood I get into is a strange one. I become weepy. I blame God. But I've become one of those understanding mothers you see on television who read up on things, and see psychologists. The truth is, I don't really understand. There are times when I can handle it, and times when I can't.

I'm a woman of secrets and great sin. Some of the secrets will go with me to my grave. The sin I will come to. But first about my two friends. One plays the victim, the other does the victimising. Rhoda is my other good friend. She's about the same age as Garaatie, forty-five, younger than me, and the only one of the three who'd made it to Matric. I only went as far as standard eight, but have a Master's degree in real life. My father taught me from an early age to read. I can't tell you what's the world's tallest building, or longest river, or how many presidents the United States have had, but I can meet someone for the first time and know right away what I'm dealing with.

Rhoda, on the other hand, had a job as a teller before she married Rudwaan. She had an education, she would remind us, Matric. Not like the children of today who have to go to university and beyond before they can even think of looking for a job. Rhoda's own son, Shafiq, is in Australia now, on a two-year contract, as a result of his fancy education.

Then there's Rhoda's husband, Rudwaan, not a very strong man. And the way Rhoda sometimes bullies him is embarrassing. I know why she's like this. She's frustrated. But she won't make changes. It's that pebble-in-the-shoe thing. It hurts your foot, it's aggravating, but you don't want to stop to take it out. You keep walking. This is Rhoda's marriage. Cut a bit here, paste a bit there, keep the blink kant bo. Her real love had been a boy called Sadick, when she was nineteen. The problem was that Sadick was a motorbike hunk, and girls liked motorbikes. He had a whole string of girls fighting over him. Rhoda would write him off, then take him back, and so it went on for years. Finally the news broke that Sadick had got a girl pregnant and was getting married. Two months later, Rhoda married the nice boy at the bank where she worked.

My friendships with these women are long-standing. One I know from high school, the other from the time she married and came to live next door to my mother. Still, there's a jockeying for position to be the number one friend. When I'm alone with Garaatie, she says, "That Rhoda really doesn't know how to treat a man." And when I'm with Rhoda, Rhoda says, "I don't know why Garaatie doesn't kick that Indian out on his arse."

And so it goes. I agree with Rhoda about not taking scraps from a man, but Rhoda can go too far. I know why she married Rudwaan. Waanie, she calls him, a big man like that. Rudwaan goes along with all her schemes. Once she actually got him to join a time-sharing thing, and they lost money. It was unbelievable. People who don't take holidays, buying into a resort in the Eastern Cape. Who wants to go there? You want to go to Thailand or Jerusalem or the Holy Land. But that's Rhoda. She's like a piranha. Once she gets hooked on something, she hangs on. And if she doesn't want to cook, or iron his shirt, or some silly thing that men like women to do for them, she asks him if his hand's been in an accident. In front of me. And she hates sex. The poor man has to fight to get his hand between her legs. This is from her own lips. I feel sorry for Rudwaan; he's not a bad guy. He's good natured, and easy on the eye.

He just has one quirk. I came there one Saturday afternoon, and he had no teeth in his mouth. I asked Rhoda what the deal was with the no teeth. She told me that Rudwaan only wore his dentures during the week. On weekends he liked to give his gums a rest. Now that, I tell you, would be enough to keep me on my side of the bed.

Teeth is a big thing in the Cape. Almost everyone my age has removable teeth. Even my eldest sister, Toeghieda. She has two little gold slits stuck in between them. But not Zulpha, my youngest sister, and not me. We had both wanted to be like Toeghieda when she came to visit the first year of her marriage with a gap in her mouth. My mother said no. What Toeghieda's husband allowed was his business. She wasn't going to have daughters with four missing front teeth. Today I'm glad I didn't do it. There's no way – then and now – I would stick my tongue into anyone's mouth where there was food trapped under plastic.

But I enjoy my friends. We attend functions, we go to movies, we discuss our lives. Still, I don't tell them everything. I hardly ever mention my youngest son.

"I think we should try the spinning wheels next," Garaatie said.

I noticed a change in Garaatie's mood. She had a nice stash to play with, she had a new confidence. Me too. I was a first-comer, but was walking about the place like I owned something.

I followed Garaatie to the wheel-of-fortune machines.

"You should get an MVG card," the attendant had said when I'd collected my cash. Both Garaatie and I filled out forms. We stuck our red cards into the machines. What happened next wasn't a nice thing. Poor

Garaatie. It just wasn't her night. The machine she picked swallowed her money in minutes, while mine gave me three hundred and fifty rand. When Garaatie's money was all gone, she looked at me. "You're lucky," she said. "You not only won the jackpot, you're up three hundred. You got back the money you gave to me."

The way she said it made me feel bad. I was just about to dip into my bag for another hundred to give to her, when she just slumped down in her seat, and the whole rotten story of the note in the pocket and the smack in the face came out. It was the end of my playing. We ended up in the back of the fish restaurant drinking coffee while Garaatie told me over and over again what a bastard she was married to. I listened like I usually did. I didn't give any advice.

That was my first night at the casino. I left there with a very depressed friend, and a whole lot of rands. It was hard to feel happy and sad at the same time. But I must've been more happy than sad, for I lay in bed the whole night thinking of how the three frosty white sevens jumped into place, and how I was going to spend my money. But there was a problem with this money. It wasn't two or three hundred rand that I could pay an account with and think no more about. It was four thousand. A lot of money. And it was dirty money. I would have to keep it in a separate account. Maybe buy a vacuum cleaner, or a new oven. Or take a trip. I'd always wanted to go to India. One thing I couldn't do was buy food with it. Before drifting off to sleep, I thought of my late friend, Abdul. Abdul had been my sounding board for issues I needed clarified from the Qur'an, and would've been the first person I would've consulted. Abdul would've told me what to do with the money, then advised me not to go to the casino again.

I remember when he was at my house years ago and my son Zane, and his wife Rabia, were also there. Rabia asked him about the scarf. She said the Qur'an said you had to cover your bosoms, and dress modestly. It didn't say that the scarf had to be on your head. It made sense in those days, she said, to cover your head in the desert – you would boil your brains if you didn't. But we didn't live in Makkah or Madina. We lived in South Africa. And why hadn't God told the Christians and the Jews to also wear scarves?

It was clever what she said. I hadn't always worn a scarf myself. Abdul listened respectfully. He had a way of listening, and then responding in the gentlest manner. He said that the injunction was clear that we had to protect our au'rah, and our hair was part of our au'rah. But we didn't have to be wrapped up like a mummy. God understood that we lived in a Western society.

Some women, of course, take this Western thing too far and you see them with big scarves on their heads and in tight clothing. Or you see the scarf in the neck. The neck scarf is the thing with the young generation. What is it doing in the neck, I want to know. Is it to keep the neck warm?

Anyway, there's a movement towards covering up. I don't know if it's since the new government and people feel more comfortable, but it's become fashionable now to wear robes. Robes in the house, robes to go shopping, robes to visit friends. Wearing a robe is a blessing for some women. The pressure's off for those few extra pounds that show so easily in a dress or a skirt. And the scarf's a great protection. No one looks at me on the street.

The morning after I'd been to the casino, I was surprised to get a call from Garaatie. Usually when I saw Garaatie, I didn't see her again for a week or so. But I had just hung up the telephone from speaking to Rhoda, when it rang again. When I heard her voice, so early in the morning, I thought she was going to tell me some new tragedy. I was therefore surprised when the first words out of her mouth were, "I have two hours free this morning. I feel lucky."

I had just spoken to Rhoda about my winnings, and decided what to do with my money. I was going to put it in a fixed deposit for six months and use it with my savings, together with the money I would get from the sale of my red Toyota, and get the maroon Mercedes I'd always wanted to buy from Ali Gamieldien. I'd driven in that car. It was well kept, had low mileage, and was a real beauty. When Rhoda suggested it, I couldn't believe that I hadn't thought of it myself.

"Do you want to go to the casino?" Garaatie asked.

"But we were there just last night."

"So what? Who's going to know? We can have breakfast there. Have you had breakfast already?"

Garaatie surprised me. The night before she had sat in a pool of snot and tears, vowing to give herself over to God. Now she wanted to go back to the machines.

"What time?"

"I'll pick you up in thirty minutes."

"I have to go to the bank. I want to make a deposit."

"We'll stop there on the way."

We never stopped at the bank. My big mistake getting into the car was telling her that Rhoda had called. "What did she want?" Garaatie asked.

"I was supposed to go with her to the Waterfront yesterday. I forgot."

"She didn't tell you about Gafsa's break-up with Muhaimin?"

I knew all about Rhoda's daughter's difficulties, but never discussed one friend's secrets with the other.

"It's not really a break-up. They're working out things. You know how young people are."

"Muhaimin went home to his mother."

"How do you know?" I knew, but wanted to know how she had come to hear of it.

"In the mosque, from a friend of mine." She changed from fourth gear to third to slow down. "I'm surprised you never told me."

"I don't tell Rhoda about your private affairs either. Come on, you know some things are off limits."

Garaatie pouted all the way down Klipfontein Road. We turned left on Vanguard Drive. "Damn," she said, "I forgot to stop at the bank for you."

"It's all right. I'll go tomorrow. It's a cheque anyway, I won't spend it."

"And the extra three-fifty?"

"I left two hundred at home."

She smiled. "So you're only coming with a hundred and fifty? That's wise."

"And you? How much are you planning to spend?"

We were slowing down for another red light. Garaatie almost kicked her foot into the clutch. "I took five hundred from the safe."

"You took the shop's money?" I was surprised by both the amount she had taken and the deed. I was also curious to know what had transpired since Mahmood's declaration to take another wife. I didn't ask. One had to be in the right mood for a Garaatie-Mahmood episode. I wasn't.

"Let him count his riches and see it's missing," she said. "If I lose, he counts even less tomorrow night. If I win, I might put it back."

Garaatie got like this after a punch in the gut. The last time Mahmood got into trouble over a condom she found in his pocket, she cut the legs off his new trousers. Mahmood made no big stink about it. He just went away for five days to Sun City. That's how he gets back at her. The silent strike. When he came back, Garaatie was like a meek little lamb. I don't understand it. Sometimes I think she has a secret desire to be beaten. He's never done it, but I think she wants it. And then there's that thing that happens when Mahmood gets angry. She'd told Rhoda and me about it once. When Mahmood got angry, he got a helluva houter. I'd never even heard that word until she told us what it meant. The cobra would skiet and skop and afterwards Garaatie was all contented again. We looked at her differently after that graphic bit of information. We'd never thought of her as a sexual animal. I know women my age. They fall into two categories. The ones who like sex and the ones who don't. I'd always had Garaatie in the dried-up category. And she wasn't on patches or anything.

We stepped into the casino at ten-thirty in the morning. The floor was already abuzz with early-morning activities. Attendants walked up and down with wires dangling from their ears. Waitresses were busy taking orders and serving drinks. In some spots it was so busy, people had to wait to play on machines. There were no windows, no clocks. No night and day. One day blended into another.

"I want to go back to the same machine where I won," I said to Garaatie.

"Okay," she said. She came to sit next to me. We each started with fifty rand. After our fifties were gone, we put in a hundred. I had nothing left in my purse. Garaatie still had three hundred and fifty rand. I got a few ten and twenty rand combinations. Garaatie got nothing.

"Let me play a little on your machine," she said.

I thought it a bit of a nerve, but swopped seats. This became a pattern with me. I would know a machine was going to pay, and would tell people to play there. They would win the jackpot, and I would stand there grinning. The grinning was a hard thing to watch on people's faces when you won, especially when they had no money left. But it was even harder when you were the one doing the grinning. But not that morning. That morning the gods were still smiling.

I started to play on Garaatie's machine. Slowly but surely my money went down. Not even a ten rand coming my way. On the last four rand, just as I thought that my playing time was over, the machine spluttered suddenly, and two break-the-bank symbols and a yellow five locked into place.

"Oh my God!" Garaatie exclaimed. "And I just got up from that machine! How much did you win?"

"I don't know." How the heck would I know what I'd won? But I was immensely relieved that I had won something and that I could continue to play. I took out a cigarette and lit it, drawing the smoke deeply into my lungs.

The attendant arrived. "Congratulations," she said. "You've won two thousand rand."

I looked at Garaatie. This time there was no mistaking what I saw. She smiled and said I was lucky, but her hand stabbed at the button on the machine that she'd asked to play on. By the time the attendant had written out my cheque, Garaatie was down to twenty rand.

"This machine gave me nothing," she said. "I should've stayed where I was."

Right there, I decided never to come with her again. It hadn't been my idea to swop machines.

"Do you want to have coffee?" I asked.

"Are you finished playing?"

"Aren't you?"

"No. I feel like playing some more."

I knew what that meant. I had given her money the day before. She knew I had a cheque for four thousand in my bag, plus the one I'd just received.

"I don't think this casino thing is a good thing, Garaatie. Let's go and have something to eat. It's my treat."

"I'm not hungry," she said. "Let's just go home."

I didn't argue. We left without having anything to eat or drink. We had been in the casino for less than an hour.

"You don't have to stop at the bank for me," I said. "I have other things too I need to do. I'll get my car."

"You're not upset, are you?" she asked.

"No. Perhaps we shouldn't have come today."

"Why not? You won. Anyway, Ramadan's on our doorstep. In two months we're fasting. I don't want to come here again."

Garaatie didn't know it at the time, and neither did I, but her losing two days in a row had actually been a good thing.

After she had dropped me off at home, I quickly went to the toilet, then into the kitchen for a cup of tea before leaving to go to the bank. The answering machine was on a small table next to the counter. I saw by its flickering light that I had two messages. I switched on the kettle and listened to the first one. It was from my eldest son, Zane, reminding me that it was Rabia's thirtieth birthday, and that they were expecting me for tea after eight. The second one was from my youngest son, Reza, asking if I was going to be home that evening, and whether I could come to the flat in Sea Point.

I sat down for a few minutes. The morning had left me hungry and a little depressed. The thing in the casino had disturbed me. Then there were the telephone calls. Rabia wasn't my favourite daughter-in-law, but I couldn't not attend the tea. It would hurt Zane, and give Rabia more to talk about. And attending the tea was also an opportunity to see my twin sons and their wives and children. But Reza wouldn't be there. He wouldn't have been invited. And he also wanted to see me.

The kettle boiled. I poured water over a rooibos teabag and waited for the colour to change. As always, when I thought of my youngest son, a great heaviness came upon me. I have this recurring image of that wintry afternoon long, long ago when Reza was eleven years old, and I'd come home early from work. Zane had started work as a shop assistant in a de-partmental store and didn't get home until seven. The twins had gone to a soccer practice. I remember it, as if it was yesterday. I'd come to the gate and discovered I'd left the house that morning without the keys. When that happened, the last person to leave had to put the keys under a stone in the yard. I walked along the side of the house, past two windows. Before I came to the second one, I heard laughing. I thought the twins had come home early. But the laughter was different, and I stopped. I don't know if it happened in my head first, or my heart, but something told me to stand very still. I didn't recognise the voice, but I recognised what was happen-ing. I peeped through the window. On the bed was my boy with another boy, naked as the day he was born.

I moved back from the window. I suddenly needed to pee. But I didn't go to the yard, or into the house. I stood there, looking about as if I was in a strange place. Then silently went back the way I had come, out of the gate, and down the road. Until today I don't remember where I went. But I came home at six-thirty, like I'd been at work the whole day.

I said nothing for five years. I watched the boys that came to the house in their Marilyn Monroe and Lana Turner hairdos and pretended they were all just his hairdressing friends. Moffies, my son Zane said about them once. But they were friendly boys. I liked them. They were funny and talented, and I laughed a lot in their company. But at night when I was alone, I had long conversations with God. I asked God to change him, to make him like his brothers. I shared many things with my two friends, but not this. Once Rhoda spoke to me in a very roundabout way about a man who could cure things. We both pretended we didn't know what she was referring to. I went to see the man, but the man's bottle of holy water didn't do anything.

Shortly after Reza's sixteenth birthday, his father, Braima, gave me a call. "Beeda, how are you?"

"I'm fine," I said. "And you?"

"I can't complain. I just wanted to talk to you about something."

"Something serious?" I was surprised to get a call from him.

"I don't know – well, I – Reza came here the other day. I don't know why I – anyway, I had some people over, and he showed up here with this friend in a green sports car, much older than him. They were acting strange like."

I was supposed to know what he was trying to tell me. Still, I was glad that he'd called. In the years we'd been divorced, we'd spoken about school fees, clothing, child support, but never about the feelings and speculations around this son.

"What do you mean?" I asked. "You've just noticed now that he's different?"

"No. He's always been – special."

I didn't say anything.

"What's wrong with him, Beeda? He's there with you every day."

"You know."

"What do I know?"

"You know. As I know."

"What do I know?" he asked again.

"There's a word for it."

"Stop talking in riddles," he said, "Speak."

"Queer." It was the first time I'd said it out loud. "He likes boys. Not girls."

There was silence. When he spoke again, his voice had changed. "Did I hear what you just said? You're saying Reza's – God, I can't even say it."

I didn't help him. He came to see me the same afternoon. The children were always the ones who talked to their father if there was anything they needed, but this necessitated a face-to-face talk between him and me. We sat in the kitchen. I made him tea, and a toasted sandwich with butter and thin slices of tomato. I told him what I'd seen through the window when Reza was eleven years old. He sank deeper into the chair as I spoke. He leaned forward with his elbows on the table.

"You never told me."

"We never spoke. And what was there to discuss? I didn't want to believe it myself."

He lowered his head into his hands. I looked at the top of his head. Sleek, black hair pulled back with an elastic band. Javanese features. All his own teeth. Good to look at. As I sat there I wondered whether he still had any feelings for me. The thing that still hurt was why he'd left me for another woman.

"What did we do to deserve this?" he asked.

"It's no one's fault."

"Maybe we should talk to an imam," he suggested.

"Imams have wives. At night they lay next to each other and talk. I don't want the whole world to know my business. And what can an imam tell us, except that it's wrong?"

"Maybe there's a ruling."

"There's no ruling. It's not permissible. There's no ruling any imam can make to make it all right. But I've been to see a psychologist. A Jewish man."

He looked at me. He wasn't someone who would ever have dreamed of going with his problems to a stranger and have that stranger ask him about his childhood and his relationship with his mother or father.

"What did he say?"

"You can't take a pill and fix it. All he can do is help you accept it. Our people don't talk about stuff like this. When I go and see him I can talk about how I feel."

"When was this?"

"About two years ago, when he was fourteen."

"Do his brothers know?"

"How can they not? His friends come to the house. They sit in the lounge and play records. They make salads and food in the kitchen. There's always a lot of laughing going on. Munier and Marwaan are okay with it, but not Zane. Zane gets aggravated with them. He brings the girl-friend over on Saturday afternoons, he doesn't want her to know. But how can you hide something like this, and how can you change it?"

He lowered his head. I felt sorry for him. He was confronting his son's truth for the first time. I'd lived with it since that afternoon when I'd looked through the window.

"You have to accept it. He's not like his brothers."

"I won't accept it. I'll never accept it. A child of mine like that. Never."

He finished his tea and got up. He sighed heavily. I walked him to the gate. There he stood for a moment before opening the door of his car.

"I'm sorry that you had to carry this by yourself, Beeda. And I'm sorry about us."

I couldn't believe it. He was sorry. I can't tell you what that meant. He'd never said that before. No one had ever said sorry to me. Not Toeghieda, who let me take the blame for her when we were children and she stole money out of my mother's purse, and my mother gave me a hiding, telling me she would never trust me again. And not my mother, who always favoured her eldest and youngest daughters over me. Toeghieda, for being her first born and her white child, and Zulpha, for being her little lost Annie whom she wanted people to like.

I had been a lonely child. Toeghieda had been friends with the children next door, and never included me in their games. When Zulpha came, Toeghieda was eight years old, and Zulpha became the new toy. I was always left standing by myself in doorways, and learned from an early age how to occupy myself. My father, who was the one who paid attention to me, bought things for my birthday that he thought I might like; books, puzzles, word games, a doll that said, mummy, when you pulled the string in her back. He also did other things for me, like tying my shoelaces in the mornings before I went to school, and plaiting my hair. That was our little thing. Then my father died, and I was alone again. When I met Braima six months after I left high school, I didn't know it then, but I wanted something that belonged only to me, something that I could love.

Not long after Braima's visit to my house, Rhoda and I went for coffee at Cavendish Square. Rhoda and I both had teenage children. Her nineteen-year-old son, Shafiq, was causing her a lot of concern. He was in his second year at university and involved with a white girl.

"He's changing right under my eyes," she said. "He doesn't come home on Friday nights, he doesn't bring her to meet the family so that we can see what she's all about. And he did poorly this last semester. Does he think this money we're paying for his fees grows on trees? We didn't let him take a loan, we paid for it so he wouldn't have debt when he graduated. This is how he thanks us."

The real fear, though, was that Shafiq's head would be turned by the girl and that he would step out of his faith. But Rhoda had a plan. Her eldest sister, Malika, lived in Houston. Rhoda arranged for her son to go on holiday to his aunt. What she hoped for, happened, but not in quite the way she wanted it to. Shafiq fell in love with America, and asked if he could complete his studies there. Rhoda sent money for lawyers and visas, and it was four years before Shafiq returned home. He had long ago forgotten the girl whom his mother had worried about, and now told her that he was in Cape Town only for a short holiday before taking a post in Canada. This was a different problem all together.

Then there was Rhoda's daughter, Zaitoon, who had got pregnant in high school the year before. I was the only one who knew where Rhoda took her. Not even Rudwaan knew about the woman with the syringe in Hope Street. In hindsight, it was a terrible thing, because today Zaitoon is married and can't have children.

And so mothers will do what they must and tread where fathers fear to go. For our children we will do anything. It's easier to face God than to have the community know your business. God forgives. A community never forgets.

I told Rhoda about Braima's visit to my house.

"He's not a bad egg," she said. "He's got a conscience. And he's always supported his kids."

Garaatie had a different response when I told her. "It's a bit late to say he's sorry. Where was sorry when he left you pregnant, with three kids?"

They were both right.

That evening I went to Zane's house for tea. I had two lovely silk scarves I'd bought at the Waterfront earlier that year. I chose the plum one with the gold design, and thought it would be a good match for Rabia. Rabia was dark-skinned. The scarf would go well with her complexion and eyes. I wrapped the scarf in pink tissue wrapping, dressed it up with a silver bow, and stopped at the bookstore for a card.

When I arrived at their house, Rabia was still putting chocolate peanuts and dried fruit on the table. I had come early purposely so that I could leave at a reasonable time to go and see my youngest son.

"Happy thirtieth," I wished her when she opened the door, kissing her on the cheek, and hugging her. "May Allah give you many happy years Inscha Allah. Good health and prosperity." I handed her the gift. "Just a small little something."

"Thank you," she said. "You shouldn't have."

She never called me mummy or ma like my other daughters-in-law. Munier and Marwaan married twins, Sawdah and Sadia. The four of them did everything together. They even lived on the same street.

"Sit down," she said, "I'll get Zane. He's just busy with something in the yard."

She disappeared down the passage and I sat there like a visitor in my own son's home. There was no asking me to join her in the kitchen, or letting me feel comfortable to roam about on my own. At Munier or

Marwaan's house it was totally different. Sawdah and Sadia and I often baked together for functions, and sometimes I visited there on a Saturday afternoon and we watched movies while the men watched cricket or rugby in the other room.

Not here. You didn't touch, you didn't make suggestions about couches or curtaining, and you didn't come without being asked. She invited the family once a year for tea when it was Zane's birthday. She asked you not to bring presents as she didn't buy presents for anyone. We brought gifts anyway. She wasn't going to change the way we'd always done things. And she's tight with the rand, for all the money she earns as an admin assistant, and the comfort my son keeps her in. On the rare occasion when she does bring a dessert to a birthday or anniversary party, it would be a little tennis biscuit thing with caramel and a few chocolate sprinkles. For Sawdah's baby shower a few years ago, she'd brought a tube of cream for diaper rash. She said the big present would come when the baby was born. It did; a packet of Pampers with twelve diapers.

One must always trust first impressions. I don't know why we ignore them. We see the thing for what it is, and we still bite into it. I had my first impression of Rabia when Zane brought her to the house on his twenty-first birthday. He'd invited friends over for a little party; a get-together we called it in those days, where there was music and dancing, and the mothers allowed the lights to be switched off for a blues. There were lots of girls. Zane was a good-looking boy. It wasn't even ten o'clock when Rabia, standing dik-bek next to the hi-fi, said to Zane, "I've had enough of this party, I want to go home."

It was his party. She was supposed to be the girlfriend. We were still waiting for midnight, for the big speech and the presentation of the key. She knew about twenty-firsts, and how special the event is. Zane had to leave his own party and take her to Salt River. She had no thought that she was hurting him. When he told me a few months later that he wanted to marry her, I said all the right things a mother says to a son, but was disappointed in his choice. Not long after they got married, Sawdah told me of an incident at their house when she overheard Rabia telling him that all the things he did for the family must come to an end. I don't know if this referred to me too, and never asked my son.

As I sat there waiting for him in his lounge, I looked at the eats on the table. Rabia's high tea was really a low-key milk tart affair, with a chocolate cake, peanuts and sweets. There would be no savoury snacks or samoosas. Rabia ate samoosas when she came to visit you, but didn't make them for her guests. Sawdah and Sadia were the ones who would bring pizzas and quiches and fresh cream trifles and éclairs.

My seven-year-old grandson, Shaheed, came into the room. I knew his mother had sent him in to come and greet me.

"'laikum, Granny," he said, kissing me.

I gave him a squeeze, and a big kiss. "Not 'laikum. Salaam alaikum."

"Salaam alaikum, Granny." He looked at me with his big eyes, and said, "Did Granny bring me that computer game Granny said Granny was going to buy for me?"

I hugged him again. He was the first grandchild, and so precious. "Did Daddy say you could use his computer?"

"Yes, Granny. I'm allowed two hours a day. On weekends I'm allowed four."

"My, that's a lot of time to play games for a little boy like you."

"I'm not little, Granny," he gave me a serious look. "I'm going to be eight in five weeks."

"Five weeks. Oh my." I reached for my bag. He stood close, watching me take out the disk, still in its cellophane wrapping.

"Granny! Thanks Granny!" he hugged me. "Thanks!"

"Mummy, you're spoiling him," Zane said, coming in quietly.

I got up and we hugged. "You look nice," I said. He had on a green shirt and beige pants with suede boots. Rabia had changed his look completely. It suited him. Even the hair, cropped short, with gel to make it stand up.

"I promised him," I said.

Rabia brought in a tray and offered me a drink. "He mustn't get everything he asks for, or he'll think it's his due."

I took out my cigarettes. Let her tell me now to go and stand outside, I thought. I turned to my grandson. "Why don't you go and try out your new game?"

"Okay, Granny. Thanks again." He was only too glad to be gone.

Rabia brought me an ashtray. "I knew we'd need one today," she smiled.

"Mummy looks well," Zane said.

"Thank you. I've cut out red meat and potatoes. I've lost two kilos."

"What about chocolate?" Rabia asked.

"That's never going to go. Chocolate and cigarettes."

"Thank God, Zane quit smoking."

I drew a fat lot of smoke into my lungs. "Smoking will kill you," I said.

She gave one of those disdainful smiles. "When you tell a smoker that, he says he has to die of *something*. He's cheeky about it. And you can't tell a Muslim he's a drug addict. How can it be? It's not dagga, it's only cigarettes. My car was at the service centre the other day, and I had to take a bus to Mowbray. I sat in front of these two women with big scarves on their heads, smoking like they were at an open-air carnival. I turned around and pointed to the no smoking sign in the bus. 'Dis my liggaam,' one of them said. 'Zuma moet huise bou vir die mense. Hulle moet die katiene toemaak. Ek het nog nooit gehoor van 'n man wat 'n accident gemaak het met 'n cigarette in sy hand nie.'"

I laughed. It was funny. But I could tell from Zane's expression that he was worried the conversation was going to turn ugly. He needn't have worried. I wasn't going to let anything ruin his day. He was my firstborn, the one I'd waited for with a new mother's wonder and expectation. But first children also got hit the hardest. When his father left, Zane was seven years old, and had to forgo many things in order to help out. I got him a bike and he sold packets of masala for me. He helped with the washing of the school clothes and the cleaning of the house. On Saturday afternoons, when his friends were out playing in the park, he had to help with the frying of koeksisters, and on Sunday mornings had to deliver them to the neighbours. All the little bits helped.

Today he's a successful businessman and has two shops. Rabia doesn't know it, but on the first of every month, Zane gives me six hundred rand.

"Listen," I said, "I came early because I have to leave early. Reza wants me to come over and see him. I'm leaving around eight. I hope you're not going to mind."

"Not at all," Rabia said. "He's also your son."

I wanted to ask then why he hadn't been invited to the birthday party. But I knew why. They'd had an argument once and he'd called her a naai. An ugly word, I admit, but there it was; he'd said she was a cunt. We had to accept the reason for the ban although we all knew that it was much more than that. He wasn't welcome because he was gay.

"When last did Mummy see him?" Zane asked. "I heard from Munier that he wasn't well."

"I saw him last week. He has some kind of flu. You know him. He hardly eats."

"I suppose we can call it that."

I looked at him. He looked right back at me without wavering.

"So he's ill. We all get the flu. Next week he'll be all right again. Let's not spoil Rabia's birthday with all this talk of sickness."

"You're not spoiling my birthday," Rabia said. "I think it's important to talk about these things. Munier and Marwaan also saw him last week. They said he has Aids."

I got up. I walked over to the mantelpiece to rearrange my scarf. I had to do something or I was going to hit her. I came back to where she was sitting. "Listen, Rabia. I don't want to hear from you that my son has Aids. Do you understand?"

She blushed. "I was just saying. Some people can't bear to . . ."

"No, you listen to me. I don't want to hear anything from you. Was he invited to this party? Do you have contact with him? You're the last person I want to hear say anything about him." I picked up my purse and started to walk to the door.

"Where's Mummy going?" Zane asked.

"To my other son. The one who wears his own pants."

"I don't wear his pants for him," Rabia retorted.

I stopped. "Listen," I said, turning slowly to face her, "I can say something to you now, and the day will end badly." I brought my face closer to hers. "I don't like you. I'm never going to like you. Are you satisfied now?"

I got into my car and drove away, not even noticing Munier's jeep as he passed me on the street. But I didn't drive to the flat in Sea Point. I made a detour. I felt angry and disturbed. How dare that bitch tell me that my son had Aids?

I went to the casino. I don't know how much money I had with me that night, or how much I smoked, but I know I lost. It was ten o'clock before I left.

I got into my car and drove without stopping. Speeding along the N1, I wondered what it would be like to jump the hill and drop into the oncoming lane.

I arrived at the flat and rang the doorbell. Patrick opened the door. Patrick was the friend.

"Hello, Patrick, how are you?"

"I'm fine. How's Mrs A?" He always called me Mrs A.

"I'm fine, thank you. Well, I'm not that fine, but what's the use of complaining?"

Reza appeared behind him, in his pyjamas already. He kissed and hugged me, and walked me into the flat. "Mummy's late."

"I know. I had other commitments."

Patrick disappeared into the kitchen to make tea. I looked at my son. He was thin, with dark circles under his eyes.

"I brought you some chocolate peanuts," I said, "with some chocolate raisins mixed in between, just how you like them."

"Thank you." He sat down next to me on the couch, and put his right arm round my shoulder. I sensed that he had asked me there to tell me something.

"Are you all right?" Suddenly I knew in my heart that what Rabia had said was the truth. There was no other explanation for his gauntlike appearance. His mouth smiled, but his eyes were large and birdlike. He was dreadfully thin. Why had I seen it and not seen it?

"I have Aids, Mummy."

The words chilled me. He had said it. And confirmed my fears. I became aware of the traffic sounds through the window, the tinkling of crockery in the kitchen where Patrick was making tea. I couldn't speak.

He turned to look at me. "Did you hear what I said, Mummy?"

"Yes."

"I didn't want you to hear from anyone else that I'm ill. I thought it was time that we talked. I'm sorry I never told you before, and I'm sorry if I've embarrassed you."

"You've never embarrassed me. Don't ever think that."

He smiled. "I've never been able to talk about this. Can I say how I feel?"

"Tell me." I didn't trust myself to say too much, for fear I would burst out crying.

He closed his eyes, and after a while started to talk. "I know God loves me."

"Of course God loves you. You're a good person."

"But I also know that I've done wrong. From small I knew I wasn't like my brothers. I liked to play with Hafsa and Koelie next door. Remember them? I wasn't interested in running after a ball with my brothers. And I didn't think there was anything wrong with it – not until other children made fun of me. I liked cooking classes and sewing, and always thought I was going to be a dress designer. Then when I was about nine or ten, this new teacher, Mr Hartzenberg, came to our school. Mr Hartzenberg took us to Kirstenbosch, and when the term ended in November, a few boys got to go with him to Boulders Beach." He paused. "Everything changed after that."

I felt a spasm in my chest.

"It was the worst time of my life. I knew I had done a terrible thing, but at the same time as I thought that, I also knew I couldn't stop. And I couldn't talk to anyone about it. Even the boys who were like me. They had their own demons to deal with. That was when I started to talk to God. I pleaded with God. I prayed. My head would be down on the muslah so long, I was dizzy when I came up. Every day I would wake up and think this is the day it's all going to be different. But every day was the same. My feelings never changed. God gave me these feelings, Mummy. I was born with them."

And there it was. All nicely wrapped up and handed to me. He hadn't chosen it. God had created him. The thing I'd battled with during my visits to the psychologist. If God was the Creator, the Planner, the Knower of Everything, what chance had he had? This was my grey area. My anger. We can talk about genes and genetics, or some long dead uncle who liked boys, but it all came down to God.

"Prayer is the only thing that can help you," I said.

"To help me live, or to help me die?"

It was the only indication he ever gave of his anger. But he was a believer. He never would've rallied back and forth with God the way I had.

"I know this is hard for Mummy. Mummy's friends. The family. Things like this don't stay a secret. One other thing I wanted to tell you, was that I took out a life insurance policy two years ago. It's not a lot. Twenty thousand. You and Patrick are the beneficiaries."

"A policy? What for? Nothing's going to happen." I was surprised that he had done something like this. Money had always been scarce. I had sat with them enough times watching their films to know what their money was spent on.

"We have to talk about these things. I'm only telling Mummy now, but I've lived with Aids for some time."

My hand dropped from around his shoulder. "How long?"

"Almost a year." He paused. "I never even told the twins, until just recently. I didn't want to believe that I was sick, and couldn't drag anyone else into it. But I accept it now. I know I'll get worse." He turned his head to look into my eyes. "Did Mummy know I was gay?"

"Yes." I didn't want to go into how and when I knew, or my feelings about it. I had another question, one that suddenly popped into my head. "Would you like to come home?"

He didn't answer.

"Did you hear what I asked?"

"Yes. I did think about it once. I thought if I got really sick, I wouldn't mind being back at home with my mother."

His words touched me. "And why can't you be?"

"No reason. But not now. Patrick will be lost without me."

"Patrick can come too."

His eyes widened. "Really?"

"There're three rooms, remember? You can have your old one back. He can have the other one."

He hugged me. "I love you, Mummy."

"I love you too."

I'd never said these words to any of my children. I don't think mothers of my generation said these words. But we felt them. As we boxed their ears, we loved them more than words could express.

Patrick must've sensed that we'd finished our mother-son talk. He came through the door and set down a tea tray with refreshments on the coffee table, handing two pills to Reza. It moved me to see this tenderness between them. I'd always told myself that Patrick was just the flat mate. It had made it easier. But he was much more than that. My son had a safe place to fall.

I left the flat after midnight. I felt restless. Patrick had told me things when he walked me out to my car. Things he'd said he was concerned about. I listened and said goodbye and drove straight to the casino. I had no money in my purse, and went to the ATM machine and withdrew three hundred rand. The casino was packed. No one paid any attention to a woman dressed in loose cotton pants and a black scarf.

I looked around for a waitress, ordered a large Coke with slices of lemon, and made myself comfortable at a Double Treasures machine. I inserted my card, loaded a hundred rand onto it, and pushed the button. On the third hit, a red seven and two double treasures came up. I pressed the spinning wheel. It stopped on three. I sat staring at the machine. I wasn't one bit excited. Did it think it was just going to take and take and not give?

I was standing already when the attendant came back with a cheque for fourteen hundred and forty rand.

I had been in the casino twenty minutes. I had blustered in, and left there with the same fury. I couldn't pray that night when I got home.

I brushed my teeth, and went to bed. Sleep wouldn't come. I tossed from one side to the other, my conversation with Patrick going round and round in my head.

"His tablets are expensive, Mrs A."

"Does he have medical aid?"

"No."

"I also have to tell you what the doctor said. Reza didn't tell you, but his condition's advanced."

"What do you mean advanced?"

This was where Patrick got stuck for words. I didn't push him.

The next afternoon I called my ex-husband at work. "Braima, can you come over? It's about Reza."

I was amazed at my calmness when he arrived, and came straight to the point. "I went to see Reza at the flat last night. He has Aids."

He looked at me with his mouth hanging open. "Ya Allah, Beeda, that's a helluva way to start a conversation –"

"He's known for a year, but only decided to tell me now. And it's bad. His condition's advanced."

He walked around the table. "Are you serious? He has Aids?"

"Go and see him. You won't need to be convinced." I poured him a cup of tea and offered him a biscuit.

He sat down. "Where does he live?"

"Where he's always been, on High Level Road, in that beige building on the left just as you come up from Strand Street. There's parking right on the shoulder."

"He lives alone, or with someone?"

"He lives with Patrick. They make documentaries."

"Patrick?"

"Patrick's the friend."

He looked up at me from his tea. "This is disgusting."

"Well, get over it. You need to pull yourself together."

"Do you think it's going to be easy for me to go there and see my son living with another man?"

"This is not about you, Braima. It's about him."

"It's about God, Beeda."

I wanted to scream. "Always it's about God – isn't it? Well, there's no time to play the holies. He has Aids. That's real. I need you to help, not make it worse."

"What do you suggest?"

"I don't know. Try and understand what he's going through. He needs us. He told me a lot of things last night. He talked about God, how it's been for him. He didn't ask to be gay. He wouldn't have chosen this life for himself. God had created him. He spoke about his feelings."

"He said all these things to you?"

"Yes. When Patrick walked me to the car, he talked to me further. He brought up Reza's medication. The pills are expensive. There's no medical aid. I'm thinking of calling a family meeting."

"You're going to ask the children for help?"

"It's their brother."

He took a few sips of his tea. He was silent for a long time. The words came out in a groan. "Tell me how I can help. You know, in all these years, he's never invited me, or called me."

"Have you called him?"

"No."

I could've said a little something there, but decided to stay on his good side. "I also had difficulty with it at the beginning, but I kept in touch. I didn't wait for him to call me. He came here more than I went there though. You know how boys are. They have that thing with their mothers. Maybe they think their fathers will judge them."

He looked down at his hands. "Could we have avoided this? I mean, you see so much on television. You see them on the street. Is our son like that?"

I let him feel what he had to feel, and let him talk. I'd felt the same helplessness many times. I went out with him to the car. "It's nothing we could've avoided, Braima. It's no one's fault. He's a good son."

The third thing I have to confess is that I felt so guilty about where I was going in my spare time, that I came up with a name for the casino. "I'm going to see Auntie," I would say laughingly to Garaatie or Rhoda when I was ready to leave them for an hour of fun. Auntie became the new buzzword. Let's go to Canal Walk, Rhoda would suggest. No, let's go to Auntie. One mustn't neglect one's relatives. No man, Auntie only wants your donations. This is one auntie you should stay away from.

I noticed a few things starting to happen. A friend asks how much you've lost, and you say a hundred, when in fact you've lost five or six. Or they have that worried look and ask how many times a week you go to Auntie, and you reply once a week, when in reality you're finding your way there almost every other day. The odd time when you win five or six thousand rand, you tell yourself that you got all your money back. Which might be true for the money you've lost that past week, but doesn't begin to address the thousands you'd spent since you first started. I thought several times of sitting down and adding it all up, but wasn't brave enough to do it. To confront my losses was to confront my addiction.

*Concerning wine and gambling. In them is great sin. And some profit for men, but the sin is greater than the profit.*

These words nagged at me, but I paid no heed. When I saw how much I liked visiting Auntie, I decided to educate myself. If I were going to do it, I would do it right. I went to the library and took out a book on defensive gambling by a Las Vegas gambler who'd been banned from all the casinos, and another book on the psychology of gambling. I read the one on defensive gambling first.

If you insist on gambling, it stated, be smart about it. The casino is a business. They're there to make money. The idea is to provide fun, and make the departure of your money from your wallet as painless as possible. The only winners were the ones who stayed away.

I read every word with great interest. The book promised that I would still lose, but would lose less after following its advice. It had many valuable tips. Like if you had been planning to see a movie or a show at the casino, it suggested that you buy those tickets first so that if you lost at gambling, you at least had something to show for your evening. The tip worked. I saw *Lord of the Rings, Moulin Rouge, The Mexican*, two films with that Australian actress and the American actor husband, who now had a new love interest, and many other films. But I often ended up paying five hundred rand for a movie, for that's what you end up paying to see a show at a place like that.

Another tip was to leave all credit cards at home, to bring no cheques, and not to borrow from friends. Better yet, not to come with a friend. The book also warned not to play the slot machines near the tables. Casinos don't want roulette and blackjack players to drift off to the machines when they lose, so the machines in those areas are turned down.

There was also advice not to play a machine at the same speed for long periods of time as the machine spun at so many milliseconds, and soon got used to a rhythm. It was good to alternate the speed now and again by taking a break or changing the rhythm of the play. This had to be true, for I'd seen people get up from a machine, then someone else sitting down and getting lucky right away.

But one of the best things the book recommended was to check the computer on the floor for pay-outs, and to choose high-traffic areas as the casino liked to show off where there were lots of people. This was true and not true. I don't know about the Las Vegas casinos, but this one was so full of people, there was traffic everywhere. The wheel of fortune machines, especially, had daily pay-outs of a thousand, fifteen hundred, and two thousand rand every few hours, and had players waiting in line for a turn.

Rhoda had heard so much now about Auntie, she decided to come with me one Wednesday afternoon to see what it was all about. To make sure no one would recognise her, she wrapped her scarf around her head like a mummy, threw another scarf over it, and kept on her sunglasses.

"Are you getting a card?" I asked, as we walked through the wide doors.

"A card? For what? I'm not going to play," she said. "It's haraam."

"I have two cards, if you change your mind."

"I don't think so. In any case, I only brought twenty rand with me." She stopped for a moment to look about. "My God, this place is like a shopping mall. Where are you going to play?"

"The wild sevens. I want to try out this new strategy I read about."

"You read a book about gambling?"

"You know I read. I can't afford my psychologist anymore. You can save a lot of money on doctors if you buy the right books. I believe in them. And I read two on gambling. One gave tips. The other examines why you do it. Don't worry, I'm not a gambler."

"I don't know," she laughed. "You come here too much if you ask me."

We stepped down onto the floor. In front of us the machines hummed and purred.

"Can't I buy an ice cream or something nice first?" she asked.

Ice cream was the last thing on my mind. Did she think we were in Sea Point, strolling along the boardwalk, admiring the ocean? This was a casino. I wanted to get down to the business of playing.

"How much do you think an ice cream costs in this place?" I asked her. "I'll buy you one later. You only have twenty rand."

"How much did *you* come with?"

"Two hundred," I lied. I had two hundred in the wallet part and three hundred stashed in with the ATM and library cards. "Let's go," I said, leading her to a long row of machines, where as luck would have it, the only one available was the one with the wild sevens I wanted to play on. I inserted my card and a hundred-rand note.

"Bismillah," I said, touching my hand to the button.

"Haai! Don't say Bismillah to gamble."

I started to play. Rhoda stood like a watchdog behind me. The money disappeared three rand at a time from my card every time I hit the button.

"You're losing your money," she said after a few minutes. "You're down to ten rand. I would never waste my money like this."

"Ssshh," I said, beginning to regret that I'd brought her along.

She watched as the money went up and down on my card. When it seemed like my last ten rand would be swallowed up, the machine would give me a consolation prize of twenty or forty rand which would allow me to play a bit longer, then take it all back again. I played for half an hour with the same hundred rand.

"As long as it holds steady," I said. "It's when it takes more than a hundred that you have to worry."

"You mean you allow yourself to lose that much before you stop?"

I wanted to laugh. Sometimes it took three or four hundred to dislodge me from my seat. One thing I forgot to tell about Rhoda. She wasn't stingy when she invited you to her house for a tea or a supper, but she was tight with the rand. She would stand and argue with people in a shop that the rolls had gone up three cents. It wasn't the fault of the person behind the counter, and it was still cheaper than making your own rolls if you considered the cost of electricity. Once she bought a Magnum ice cream at a Seven Eleven, and said to the cashier, "Eight rand? My God. Are there rubies in this ice cream that it costs eight rand?" I'm not like that. If I want something, I buy it. I don't care how much it costs. And I'm not one of those who go shopping just to look. This is Rhoda and Garaatie. They can walk up and down in a mall looking at things, feeling the fabric, trying on shoes. I never go shopping with them. I'm a need-and-buy person. I don't wear out my shoes and patience trolling from shop to shop, comparing prices, to save five rand. So I wasn't surprised at all by her murmuring. She could go on murmuring. And she wasn't wrong about what I was doing. I was pumping money into a greedy guts with no guarantee of any kind of return.

"Do you know how many loaves of bread that could've bought for the poor?" she asked.

"A lot," I said, "especially if you buy white bread. Poor people mos don't like brown bread. They like white bread. Isn't it funny? When we were children, we also just liked white bread. Brown bread was the poor person's fare. Now it's almost criminal to have white bread in your house."

She laughed, but her eye was still on the happenings on my card.

"Go to another machine," she said.

"No. I put money in here."

"This doesn't look like a good machine."

"It's not bad. I'm back up to sixty rand."

She nodded her head. "I don't understand the fascination," she said. "I would go nuts sitting on a machine watching my money go up and down like this."

The worst thing you can have with you at a casino is a motjie imam. I already knew what I was doing was wrong, and didn't need to be made to feel like a bad little girl. I opened my purse and took out some change.

"Why don't you go buy yourself an ice cream? The Magnums here are nine rand fifty, but I'm paying."

"No," she said. "I want to see what's going to happen."

"Go and buy the ice cream."

"No."

"Okay, but don't nag me." When my money was down to nine rand, I took out my card. "I'll just let it rest for a minute. That book I read says you must pause in between plays, give the machine a rest, then play at a different speed."

The man on my left got up. I raised myself up slightly, and leaned over to stick my card in for three hits.

"Can I have your other card?" she asked suddenly.

I was surprised. "You want to play?"

"Yes. I'll play here while you're playing on that one."

"I'm not playing there. I just stuck in my card to play out the nine rand. I'm still playing here," I said. "I want to rest the machine."

"Can't I have a turn then?"

"I'm resting the machine, Rhoda. I put money in this machine. You can see I'm still sitting here. Play on this one," I said, indicating the one next to me.

"I don't want to play on that one. And I only have twenty rand. It won't take long."

I felt bad. I had already lost my nine rand, and was ready to stick my card into my own machine with a fresh hundred.

"Okay. Use this card then," I said, handing her the one I'd just played with.

"How do you put the money in?" she asked.

I inserted the twenty-rand note for her.

"Can I sit down?" she asked.

I got up. She positioned herself on the seat like she was going on a long trip to Mars. Finally, she touched the button. All three wild sevens jumped into place.

I looked at the machine. I couldn't speak. She'd won ten thousand rand! Money I would've won if she hadn't insisted on playing on my machine.

"Ya Allah, Beeda, I won! I won!"

I didn't know what to say. The lights flashed. The bell rang. A fat woman who'd been standing there all along waiting for the machine, turned to the man next to her and said, "Huwa haa, daai vrou het die hele tyd hier gespeel, toe sê dié een sy wil net gou haar kaart insteek, en daar wen sy tien duisend rand op daai vrou se machine!" Shame, that woman was playing here all the time, and this one said she just wanted to stick her card in, and she won ten thousand on that woman's machine.

I couldn't have said it better myself. I looked at Rhoda. She was bright-eyed and excited, and kept asking over and over again how much she'd won. The fat woman told her. I was too disturbed to speak.

People started to gather about. I waited for her to turn to me and say something. But she was gesticulating with her hands, telling onlookers how she'd just stuck her card in and won with twenty rand.

The attendant came. "Congratulations!" she said to me. The card was in my name. "It's a big amount," she said. "You'll have to take this cheque to the cashier. They'll give you cash or a bank cheque."

This was the moment. I would soon know now what Rhoda was going to do. I sat with the cheque in my hand, fully expecting to hear her say that she owed me for insisting to play on the machine I'd still been busy with.

"I have to take this to the cashier," I said. "How do you want it?"

"I'll take a cheque."

And that was it. As God is my witness. Not a word about how she'd won, and not five cents to me. I couldn't believe it. She'd stepped in on my turf, and like a jackal was standing there with a dripping mouth, too greedy to share. In that moment I recognised the full evil of gambling. My resentment towards her was toxic, and more poisonous than anything I could've said. And she was supposed to be the good one, the one who made all her salaahs on time, the one who'd been to Mecca three times. And she couldn't understand the fascination? She wasn't a gambler? She was worse. At least there was honour among gamblers who exercised some kind of ethic on the floor. What irked me further, was that I still had to drive her home and listen to her drivel in the car. It was the longest twenty minutes of my life. When I finally dropped her off at the gate, I forced a smile, but knew that I never wanted to see her again. When I'm finished, the door's shut squarely in your face. I don't talk about it, I don't make a party out of it. I just don't put on the same shoes again.

But I was depressed. My body felt heavy, and I could hardly walk into my house without almost immediately sitting down again. It was five in the afternoon and I felt like someone who'd worked the whole day with a pickaxe in the sun. How had I ever allowed something like this to happen?

I sat at the kitchen table for a long time, staring through the window at the branches of a tree. Eventually I got up and searched through the drawers. I was looking for a blue pamphlet I'd brought home from the casino long ago. I found it in the drawer with the accounts, under the spoons. I read the information, and went to the telephone and dialed the 800 number. A woman came on the line.

"A terrible thing happened to me at the casino this afternoon," I said. "I need to speak to someone."

She listened. At the end of our conversation she gave me a number to call.

"You'll get six free sessions," she said. "John's very good."

"I have to pay for this?" I asked.

"No. The casino pays."

I thanked her for listening, and said I would call the number. But I didn't. I would do this on my own, I said. I would go into the shower and take my ablutions, and turn to God.

For two weeks I stayed away from the casino. I took on orders for cakes and pies, and kept myself busy. I went to the library. I like mystery stories and nonfiction, and took out two Ruth Rendells and a Liberace autobiography. I don't know why I chose that book. Liberace had died long ago, and it wasn't like it was his mother talking about her gay son who'd written the book. But that was another thing sitting in the back of my closet that I had to take out.

As far as what had happened at the casino with Rhoda, I mentioned nothing to Garaatie. But I knew she knew. She kept asking me on the phone when last I'd seen Rhoda. Finally, she came to my house one afternoon as I was busy rolling out pastry for chicken pies, and said, "Did something happen with you and Rhoda at the casino?"

And there it was. Rhoda had told her. But what had Rhoda told her? The thing of it was, Garaatie wasn't direct friends with Rhoda, but friends with Rhoda through me. Rhoda had never invited Garaatie alone to her house.

"Did Rhoda say something happened?"

"She just said that you two went to the casino. She won on the machine that you got up from."

I put down the rolling pin. "That's what she said?"

"Yes."

"Well, then, we'll leave it like that."

Garaatie took off her scarf and put it over the back of one of the chairs. Picking up a salaah timetable from the dresser, she sat down and fanned herself.

"Wasn't it so?"

"Not quite." Garaatie was a good friend, but I had to decide how much I was going to tell her. I was also confused at that moment as to who really were my friends.

"What happened?"

"No, Garaatie, I'm going to leave it. But greed did this."

"You're not going to tell me?"

"No. I'll tell you one thing though. I'm ever sorry I set foot in that place."

"And I'm sorry I took you there. It's my fault. Now look what happened. What are you going to do? You've been friends for years."

"For me it's over. I mean I'll greet her when I see her, but I can't be the same with her again."

"Don't say so. You don't know what lies ahead. Rhoda's feeling bad about it. And you know her. Can't go out the door without making a dua'h. She doesn't know what to do with that money. She didn't tell me how much it is, she just said she couldn't tell Rudwaan."

"She didn't tell you it's ten thousand rand?"

"What! Ten thousand! Oh my word. I didn't know that."

"Oh yes. With a twenty rand on a machine I told her I was still busy with. And as far as Rudwaan; he'll lecture her about the evils of gambling, then think of a way to invest it."

Garaatie laughed. "It's true, hey. Money can do that. But now what? How is this going to be resolved?"

"It can't be. The damage is done. Right away when she won, she had to do the right thing."

"It's never too late, Beeda. You can't chuck away a friendship of thirty years. You've known each other since high school."

I admired her determination to have peace.

"Rhoda's the last of my worries, Garaatie. I don't care about the money now. Money destroyed what we had. I have other stuff going on in my life. I have a meeting with my sons here tonight."

"How much money would it take to fix things?" she persisted.

I knew then for sure that Rhoda had put her up to this. "Listen, Garaatie, don't force me to talk figures with you. It's not about how much, it's about what happened. And I don't want to talk about it any more." I washed my hands at the sink and switched on the kettle for tea.

She picked up the rolling pin and continued where I'd left off. "You're doing a lot of baking," she said. "For tonight?"

"Yes. Braima's also coming. Not the wives. Just Braima and the boys."

"Oh my. It's a family meeting then, a big one."

"It's about Reza. He's not well."

Garaatie didn't know how to handle this bit of unexpected information. I never spoke of this son. She and Rhoda knew he was gay. I never confirmed it.

The cell phone rang in her bag. She took it out and spoke into it. "Hello?"

I watched her. "Yes," she said into it, glancing at me. "No. I'm at Beeda's house."

I knew from the way her face lit up who it was.

"Okay then," she said. "I'll look in the paper." She said goodbye and put the cell phone back in her bag.

I waited for her to tell me.

"Mahmood," she said. "He wants to know if I want to go to a movie tonight."

"Aah." I had wanted to know long ago what was happening on that front, but hadn't asked.

"Don't say aah like that," she said. "I know what he's up to."

"What's he up to?"

Her expression changed again. "He's been hinting that something big's coming up, that he may have to go away for a few days on business."

"Aah."

"Stop it, Beeda. I hate it when you get that way."

"What did I do?"

"You're being sarcastic."

"Okay," I smiled. "So how are things at home?"

"It's okay. Nothing wonderful. It's a wait and see thing. But Ramadan's next week. Even he behaves during this month."

"I can't believe how the time's flown. Just the other day we celebrated Eid. A whole year's passed. When you're twenty, a year seems like ten years. When you're forty-nine, it seems like three months."

"I'm thinking of helping out at the old age home," she said. "It's a good month to do it."

"It is," I agreed. "Maybe I'll join you."

"They say it's good to give of yourself to other people when you're in pain. Oprah did a whole show about it."

"Did she? I missed that one. Did she have Dr Phil on? What's it they call him? A life strategist?"

"I think so. No, he wasn't on."

"I can't stand him. He's so rude to people. I'd like to look in *his* closet, and see what *he's* hiding."

"He's right, though."

"Bugger it, Garaatie. You can be right. You don't have to hurt people."

"Sometimes they have to be hurt."

I looked at her. She was right. I'd hurt her once or twice myself trying to make my point.

Garaatie left well before maghrib. I tidied the kitchen after my baking and got things ready. I knew the moment I heard the double rap on the door that my night was about to be spoiled. Only one person knocked like that. I opened the door and saw Zane and Rabia on the doorstep. I'd specifically told my sons not to bring their wives.

"Salaam alaikum," Rabia greeted me. I greeted her back and looked at Zane.

"Rabia's going to her cousin on Haywood Road," he said. "She just came in to greet."

"Okay," I said, much relieved. I walked them into the lounge. There was another knock, then the twins came bounding in. Naughty boys when they were young, and still naughty, although their energies were channeled now in a different direction. Even though they lived in different houses, they still dressed the same most of the time, and both had on jeans and cream cable jerseys. It had always been like that. With how they dressed, and the mischief they got up to. They'd given me lots of trouble in their teens. One would have the thought, and the other would already have written the script. If you don't know about twins, they're joined at the hip. They did everything together. Even when they dated, they looked for sisters. They found twins. But long before they discovered girls, they pulled my chain and gave me double of everything. My friend Abdul had worked wonders with them. Today they're high school teachers, and on Saturday mornings teach Islam in the townships.

"Salaam everyone," they greeted, kissing everyone in turn. "Hello, Rabia."

"I just popped in for a few minutes," she said. "I'm going to my cousin, Fawzia." She got up and adjusted her scarf. "Oh," she said, turning to me as if she'd just remembered something. "I heard about that thing with Auntie Rhoda."

I knew then why she had come.

"Zaitoon and I go to cake decorating classes on Saturday afternoons," she continued. "She said you and her mother had been to the casino. Auntie Rhoda won quite a lot of money. The two of you aren't talking now because of what happened."

Her statement hung like a bad smell in the air, and if looks could kill, she would've been a dead mossie on the floor.

"If you heard it, then it must be so," I said.

She looked at her watch. "Well, I must go," she said to Zane. "What time should I pick you up?"

"I'll call you on the cell," he said.

I didn't walk with her to the door. And my expression warned my sons to dare talk about what they'd just heard. But my night was ruined. Zane, I knew, wouldn't say anything. But I would hear from the twins. Their shocked expressions told me that they had never expected to hear that their mother had been in a casino. I was glad Braima hadn't arrived yet. She wouldn't have spared me in front of him. At least I'd been saved that embarrassment.

After Rabia's departure, I went to the kitchen to switch on the kettle for tea, and left my sons to their discussions. I readied the tray with biscuits and pies, and heard the doorbell.

Let them have a few minutes alone with their father, I thought. How long had it been since all of them were together in this house? For no reason, I felt weepy. But I needn't have worried. My sons had a good relationship with their father. When I carried the tray into the lounge, they were watching the highlights from the rugby game and conversation was lively.

I greeted Braima. I noticed the quality and cut of the suit he was wearing. He was still a good-looking man, with all his own teeth and a full head of hair. I wondered if he was happy at home. His wife, Zainap, was three years younger than me, but looked older. I'd heard from someone that she'd had her uterus out. Braima had three daughters with her. All three were married.

They all got up from their seats in front of the television and came to sit at the table. My eyes went round the group. I thought of that night, long, long ago when Zane had stood in the doorway, one foot on top of the other, watching his father put money on the table and leave the house. There had been three of them then – one was still in the womb – and three of them now. The memory made me feel sad. My baby was sick and an outcast, and the man at the head of the table belonged to another table at another house.

I poured the tea and listened to Braima talk about how as a child he'd always wanted to be a rugby player and how he had to leave school early to get a job. My boys listened with interest. I hadn't raised them with animosity. They had aadab and respect, and today they can sit at the same table with the father who'd abandoned them.

When Braima was finished with his story, I started to speak.

"Your father's here because I wanted us to sit down together and talk about Reza. We hear about Aids every day, but we don't really want to know anything about it until it strikes someone in the family. And even then, we don't want to face it. Whatever our feelings are, we have to put them aside now. God alone judges. Reza's ill. He's going to need us."

Looks passed around the table. Zane took a sip on his tea.

"Has Daddy seen him?" Munier asked.

"I'm going to do that soon. Your mother says he has no medical aid, but this meeting's not about money. I'll take care of his pills. This is about trying to understand what is happening, being together in this, and not abandoning Reza."

"He's abandoned us," Zane said.

I glared at him. "This isn't the time, Zane."

"Mummy's right," Munier said. "I don't have a problem with Reza. He's my brother, and that's it."

"And we've talked to him," Marwaan added. "We've talked to him many times. And he talks to us. We've told him that God doesn't condemn you because you're gay. God doesn't condemn the *feelings*. You just can't act out on those feelings. It's hard when you love someone because you want to consummate that love, and I don't know how it feels to abstain because I've not been there, but we've talked to him, and he knows. He's cried about it. He prays a hole in the ground begging God to forgive him, and can't change how he is."

I noticed Braima's expression. His twin sons were far more liberal and understanding than he was. He was trying hard to understand.

"Munier and I always go and visit him," Marwaan said. "He lives in two worlds. Sometimes he's happy, and sometimes he can't even hold a decent conversation with you he's so down. Did he talk to Mummy about it?"

"Yes. Two weeks ago. He was very emotional, and told me quite a lot. But the thing I came home with was that he hadn't chosen to be this way. It's good that we're talking about it. It's out now, we don't have to talk around it. That's why I called you all together. We're used to doing things as a family. This is about your brother. It could've been any one of you."

"Why doesn't he come home now and put his spiritual life in order?" Zane asked. "He has time. Until the roggel comes, he has time."

I didn't like this talk of death. "He *is* coming home. I suggested it."

"Really?"

"But not now. He said Patrick will be lost without him."

"Patrick will be lost without him? He tells this to his mother?"

"Ssshh. I told him he could bring Patrick."

"What?" Zane was almost out of his seat. "How can this man come and live with him in the house?"

"Zane's right, Ma," Munier said. "Patrick's a nice guy, but you can't have him here. It's wrong, and people will talk. I'm surprised that Mummy would suggest such a thing."

I turned to my former husband to see if he had an opinion also.

"I agree with them, Beeda. You can't have him in the house. You can't create fitnah. Whether or not we care what people say, you mustn't give them something to talk about. You can't hide Aids, but you don't want people to say that you've encouraged his lifestyle."

"You haven't seen him – right?"

"Right."

"Then you haven't seen what I've seen. No one invites him to their houses. Not for a supper or a tea or for any family function. Only one person cares. Patrick gives him his pills, he comforts him, he's there when Reza's sick and no one else is. Is it fair for us to disrupt what they have?"

"We can't think about such things now, Ma."

"We *will* think about them. Patrick can come here. He'll be in the spare room. There'll be no nonsense going on. But he'll be near. I want Reza to have his family and his brothers around him. And I'd rather have him here, *with* Patrick, than have him dying alone in a flat."

Braima looked away. My sons didn't meet my eyes. They were quiet because I'd silenced them. But they didn't agree with me. For all their modern ideas, they still went by the Book. But the Book also talks about compassion. I'm a mother. I carried my son under my heart. I wasn't going to rob him of his last moments with his companion and friend.

*Punish me, God, if it's wrong. I only have good intentions.*

The meeting ended at eleven-fifteen with pledges about contributions and support. The twins would spend more time with Reza, and Braima would build up his courage to go and see him. He asked if I would accompany him. I said yes. Zane said nothing. When they were gone, I sat at the table looking at the empty plates and teacups, replaying some of the conversation. The telephone rang. I went to my bedroom to answer it.

"I drove past your house an hour ago and saw cars," the caller said. "Are your visitors gone?"

I stood with the phone in my hand, my heart beating a little faster than usual. "Yes."

"Is it too late to come and see you?"

I had visions of the jeep driving past my house, and of the man inside. "Yes."

There was a moment's silence. "I still care for you, Beeda. You know that."

"I know a lot of things, Imran. It's too late."

I'm ashamed to tell what I did after I put down the phone. I changed my clothes, got into my car, and went to visit Auntie. I'd decided not to go there any more in my regular clothes, and had been to Mr Price recently and asked to be fitted for a pair of jeans. "Not tight ones," I said to the salesgirl. "Something comfortable I can wear with a long shirt." She looked me up and down, and brought out a size 34. God had blessed me with straight legs, good teeth, and a great figure. It fit perfectly.

I was gliding towards the arches already, when I realised I didn't have my MVG cards. No matter, I thought. I would buy one. It was just on midnight when I parked the car, and got out.

I forgot all my troubles when I stepped through the door. It felt like a world removed from the real world, a place where I could escape. Even at that hour the floor was busy. I headed towards one of the stations to buy a card. I inserted a hundred rand into the slot, and received a white card. But where was I going to play? I would never go near the wild sevens where Rhoda had won the ten thousand, and which I felt had betrayed me. I stood for a moment behind a woman at a Double Treasures machine and watched her lose two hundred rand. When she got up, I took her seat and inserted the card I'd just bought. It said I had two thousand credits. There was a mistake, I thought. I'd only put in a hundred rand. The card had to register ninety credits after withholding ten rand, which it reimbursed when you returned the card. I took the card out, and reinserted it. It still showed two thousand credits. I took the card to a different machine. The same thing happened. I decided to see what would happen when I played. The amounts went up and down, but still registered the high credits. I took it out and walked to the cashier. I had lost only thirty rand.

"I want to cash out," I said, careful not to mention an amount.

"All of it?" she asked.

"I drove past your house an hour ago and saw cars," the caller said. "Are your visitors gone?"

I stood with the phone in my hand, my heart beating a little faster than usual. "Yes."

"Is it too late to come and see you?"

I had visions of the jeep driving past my house, and of the man inside. "Yes."

There was a moment's silence. "I still care for you, Beeda. You know that."

"I know a lot of things, Imran. It's too late."

I'm ashamed to tell what I did after I put down the phone. I changed my clothes, got into my car, and went to visit Auntie. I'd decided not to go there any more in my regular clothes, and had been to Mr Price recently and asked to be fitted for a pair of jeans. "Not tight ones," I said to the salesgirl. "Something comfortable I can wear with a long shirt." She looked me up and down, and brought out a size 34. God had blessed me with straight legs, good teeth, and a great figure. It fit perfectly.

I was gliding towards the arches already, when I realised I didn't have my MVG cards. No matter, I thought. I would buy one. It was just on midnight when I parked the car, and got out.

I forgot all my troubles when I stepped through the door. It felt like a world removed from the real world, a place where I could escape. Even at that hour the floor was busy. I headed towards one of the stations to buy a card. I inserted a hundred rand into the slot, and received a white card. But where was I going to play? I would never go near the wild sevens where Rhoda had won the ten thousand, and which I felt had betrayed me. I stood for a moment behind a woman at a Double Treasures machine and watched her lose two hundred rand. When she got up, I took her seat and inserted the card I'd just bought. It said I had two thousand credits. There was a mistake, I thought. I'd only put in a hundred rand. The card had to register ninety credits after withholding ten rand, which it reimbursed when you returned the card. I took the card out, and reinserted it. It still showed two thousand credits. I took the card to a different machine. The same thing happened. I decided to see what would happen when I played. The amounts went up and down, but still registered the high credits. I took it out and walked to the cashier. I had lost only thirty rand.

"I want to cash out," I said, careful not to mention an amount.

"All of it?" she asked.

"Well, now and then, it pays you to hit maximum."

My eyes glanced at the buttons on the machine. "That's ninety lines."

"That's right. Forty-five rand."

No way, I thought. The fifty cent machine was going to turn out to be more expensive than my one rand machines where the maximum was only three rand. But as luck or circumstance would have it, I accidentally hit the maximum button, and forty-five rand came off in one shot from my card. I almost screeched, but what was happening on the screen in front of me, made me watch in fascination. Three pirates suddenly appeared with shovels and started to dig. One hundred, two hundred, three hundred, all the way to two thousand six hundred credits. I couldn't believe it. It was a fifty-cent machine, and I had won thirteen hundred rand!

"See there?" the woman said. "I told you."

"It was a mistake," I said. "I hit that maximum button by accident."

"Well, that's a lucky accident."

"You don't say," I said, waiting for the credits to load onto my card.

"Where are you going?" she asked. "You should play on."

"No way. It's going to take it."

I went back to the cashier and cashed out, asking her to leave a hundred rand on the card. I now had three thousand one hundred rand in my wallet, besides my own money, which I hadn't even touched. By the fourth machine, I had eight thousand rand. One more, I said to myself, and then I'm going home. I had hardly stuck my card into a wheel of gold machine, when I got a spin and won a thousand rand.

I left the casino. Strangely, I felt depressed. I couldn't explain it. My bag bulged with notes, but I wasn't happy. I had just got tired of winning.

Garaatie came by the next afternoon and found me sitting at the kitchen table with two piles of notes in front of me, a stack of accounts to the side.

"Ya Allah, Beeda, where'd you get all that money? Don't tell me you went to the casino?"

"I did."

"You won all of that?"

"Yes. I just counted it out. Almost ten thousand rand."

"Ya Allah."

"This is the clean money," I pointed to the thinner pile on the left, "and this is the dirty money."

"That's a lotta dirty money," she said. "What are you going to do with it?"

"Well, I have some accounts. I can pay the electricity and the phone, and call up the insurance company, and tell them I just want to pay my car and house insurance in one shot, and not have monthly payments. I'll save some money on the premium if I pay annually."

"What are you going to do with the rest? Are you still planning to buy that maroon Mercedes?"

"Yes. I was thinking of using some of it towards that. I would have to sell my Toyota."

Garaatie looked skeptical. "I don't know if it's a good idea to buy a car with it," she said. "Just now you have a bladdy accident. It's not good money, Beeda. I wouldn't. Jy gaan straight na die jahanam se vuur as daai gebeur." You're going straight to the hell fire if that happens.

"I know. I was thinking the same thing."

"And you know you can't use that money to go to Mecca – if you're still planning to go next year. How much in the clean pile?"

"Only five hundred. That's the money I had on me, my own money. I tell you, Garaatie, I couldn't stop winning. By the time I won that thousand on the last machine, I was thinking the strangest things. I thought maybe it's all those vitamins I'm taking. I've been taking those soya isoflavones for almost a year now. I have no hot flushes at all. I thought, maybe there's something in my system, or my skin, or some magnetic thing, that when I play, the machine responds. Isn't that stupid?"

Garaatie laughed. "That's funny," she said. "You're losing it, Beeda. But you can test it. Go back and see if you win again."

"No way. I'm not giving that money back. And what if I win another ten thousand? And another? How many cars can I drive? I'll be the only Muslim in Cape Town with a hundred thousand in a bank account, who can't afford to go on hajj. I go to the casino for the fun, Garaatie. Three hundred, six hundred. If I win a thousand I'm happy. It means I can come back and play again. I don't want to lose, but I don't want to burn in the jahanam fire either."

Another thing I'm ashamed to confess, is my weakness for things physical and attractive. I used to keep my hair in a bob. It's easy to blow-dry, and manageable under a scarf. I was particular about how my hair looked. In the house I was bareheaded, in the street I covered up. I wasn't one of those women who washed their hair only twice a week. I liked it springy, silky and smooth.

And so I discovered a new look quite by accident. I never usually stare at my reflection in the mirror. From the neck down, I am blessed, and can actually take off my clothes and look at myself. Not many of my friends can do that. Garaatie undresses in the dark. She doesn't want to see the puckers and ripples. Rhoda also told me once that at night she gets into bed first before pulling her clothes off over her head. Not me. I have always been a strutavarian in my own home. Beeda Boude, they used to call me in school for my great legs. But my face wasn't going to make a man miss his supper. He might pause, like one who's suddenly discovered something interesting on his dessert plate, but not ask for the recipe.

People always asked my eldest sister, Toeghieda, to be flower girl and maid of honour, being fair like our father, with green eyes, and some Muslims being very made up with white complexions. My younger sister, Zulpha, was black as a panther and had that same kind of agility. But because she was so dark, no one had ever asked for her to be in a wedding party, and in my opinion she was the real beauty. I got the in-between colour and looks. Sultry, but not outstanding.

So quite by accident I discovered this thing with my hair. I had just dried off after a shower, and found the hairdrier broken. My hair was longer than I liked to have it, almost to my shoulders, and I brushed out the tangles and shook it once or twice. I was going to go out and buy a new drier, when the phone rang. It was Garaatie giving me an update about the movie she and Mahmood were supposed to have gone and seen, and how she waited and waited for him to come home and he only arrived at ten-thirty, giving the flat-tyre-on-the-road excuse. By the time Garaatie had finished her lament, my hair was half-dry.

I looked at my hair in the mirror. I had never seen it like that. My hair was soft and fine, with a natural wave, and the way it had dried, with locks and wisps about my face, it gave me a completely different look. I liked it, and for the hell of it put on some lipstick, dusted some brown shadow onto my eyelids, and stood back to examine myself. I couldn't believe this wild woman staring back at me.

I threw my head this way and that way, scrambling my fingers through my hair to fluff it up even more. I was on such a high, I went to the cupboard to see what I could find to offset this look, and found a fitting, plum-coloured satin dress with gold dragons, and a high mandarin collar – a Chinese outfit I'd worn for my thirtieth birthday.

I looked at the dress under the cellophane wrapping. Did I dare? Could I stand to be disappointed? I was slim and watched what I ate, but had a more mature body now. I removed it from the thin plastic cover, and searched in the shoe boxes at the bottom of the cupboard for a pair of black pumps. Stepping out of my gown, I unzipped the dress and pulled it over my head. I couldn't believe it. Except for a little snugness in the armpits, the dress fitted. I had blossomed a bit in the top section, but had slim hips and great legs.

I looked at myself in the mirror, teetering on the stilettos. I looked and looked. The woman with the wild hair and slinky outfit was a far cry from the scarved one out on the street.

Who was the real Abeeda Ariefdien? Was she a good girl? The woman in the mirror smiled, but the smile faded slowly.

I sat down on the edge of the bed. Reza's image rose before me. I saw his thin face and his large eyes. I saw Patrick. I saw my other sons with their families. I saw the bleak landscape of my own existence. A million and one things kept me busy during the day, but at night I got alone into bed.

The sound of the doorbell jolted me back to reality. I looked out of the window. My sister Zulpha's husband's jeep was in the driveway.

"Zullie?" I called from the window. "Are you alone?"

She came to the window. "Yes. Open up. I'm carrying a tray."

She could only see my face through the blinds, but I could see all of her. Zulpha liked her loose cotton pants and matching tops. And she knew what colours looked best against her dark skin. Pale pink and white were her favourite colours. I'll never forget the dress she'd had made for her twenty-first birthday; a shocking pink organza with a bow that took your breath away. But even at forty-three, there was no scarf, and when she absolutely had to wear one, it was always in the neck, or she wore a turban.

I went to the front door in the black pumps and slitted dress.

"Ya Allah!" she exclaimed when she saw me, laughing suddenly. "You look – ravishing!"

We hugged one another.

"What's going on?" she asked.

"Having some fun. Going a little crazy."

She stood back and looked at me. "That dress must be from the seventies."

"My thirtieth birthday. Don't you remember? It was a present from Rhoda."

"And the hair? Did you have it done?"

It was my turn to laugh. "No. I washed it, then Garaatie called. You know Garaatie and her stories. By the time she was finished, my hair had dried like this. Not bad, eh?"

"I like it." She followed me into the kitchen, and put the tray on the table. On the tray were two small pots.

"I was thinking of you this morning, and thought I'd come and visit you. I brought something for us to eat. Hot custard and stewed prunes."

I lifted the lids to look inside. "Thanks. Just what I feel like."

"How're you?" she asked.

"Good. And you? Have you lost weight?"

"A little. But I'm okay. How's Reza? Imran said he saw him at Century City a few weeks ago; he looked thin."

I sat down, still in the black pumps and the satin dress. I had never discussed Reza with my sisters. They knew, of course, but no one said anything. Toeghieda completely avoided asking about him. Of my two sisters, I liked Zulpha the best. Nothing shocked her, and when she listened to you, she was all ears. Toeghieda, again, you would talk to her about something, and right in the middle of your sentence, she would cut your words, and say to her husband, don't forget to call so and so, or do this or that, or she fiddled with something, or got up to feed the cat. She always interrupted you and in some way trivialised your story.

But was I going to tell Zulpha? If it weren't for the guilt I still felt, Zulpha would've been my best friend. But how can you be best friends with someone you'd betrayed?

The words came out on their own. "Reza's dying," I said.

"Oh no." She came and put her arms around me. "Oh, my sister."

"He's gay, Zulpha. I've never said it out loud. My son's gay."

"I know," she said.

"He has Aids."

She held me tighter. She smelled like spring flowers. Her teeth sparkled white against her dark skin. Her sleek black hair tickled my cheek.

"You must be strong for him," she said. "Does he have a good doctor?"

"Yes. He's on medication. But he's very thin. When Imran saw him he still looked good."

"I know it's easy for me to talk," she said. "I come here with custard, but I'm so busy with my own life, I've hardly come to see what's going on with you. You must ask for strength. Ask, and it will come to you. I know it's not going to be easy."

"How do you accept it when it's a child? A parent can't bury a child. It's not right."

She looked at me. She had no children of her own. I knew of the miscarriages and the fertility pills. "I'm not a mother," she said. "But I know how I felt when Mummy died. I imagine, when a child dies it's much worse. It's not in the order of things for a child to go before the parents. And he's so young. Remember what Booia always used to tell us? He said we only have the moment. Not even the next day's promised to us. You've always stood by and toughed it out with your kids. I'm here, don't forget."

Right there I wanted to burst out and tell her what a rotten sister I'd been. That I'd taken from her, and that even now, the man who shared her bed, carried me around in his heart. But I could never tell her. I had to live with the shame of my past. It was almost twenty years ago when it all happened, but the memory of the pain never died. I console myself. I was young. I was vulnerable. I'd just been deserted the year before.

How it all started, is as clear as if it had happened yesterday. The twins had played cricket in the yard and smashed one of the windows. I mentioned it to my mother and my sisters during Sunday lunch when we all got together. Zulpha was still living at home, and was engaged to a builder.

"I can ask Imran if he can fix your window," Zulpha offered. "He's coming here this afternoon."

I had met Imran once or twice, and said, fine. He came to visit Zulpha on Wednesday nights and Sunday afternoons. On Saturday nights they went out. My father had died already by this time, and my mother was strict on how often a boy could come and sit the seats warm.

On the following Wednesday night, Zulpha and Imran turned up at my house. He took measurements of the window and said he would come back the next day to fit it. We had tea in the kitchen while my son Zane put his twin brothers to bed. The baby was in my arms, getting his last bottle before being put in his crib for the night.

"Beeda's moving to Rondebosch East at the end of the month," Zulpha said.

"Really?"

"I need a bigger place than this one," I said. "The house I found is a nice house, off Kromboom Road, but it needs work. The good thing about it is that the owners are leaving for England and are prepared to rent it to me for two years, and use the rent money as a down payment towards purchasing the house. I could never afford to get a house otherwise."

Imran, dressed in a blue shirt and jeans, was leaning against the kitchen sink, listening to me. It was probably the first time I really looked at him. Tall, lean, shirt sleeves rolled up, strong brown arms. His hair was curly, and cut close to the scalp. He had piercing brown eyes, and had a habit of looking at you intently. I saw what the attraction was for my sister. Imran wasn't a talker. He listened, he assessed, and said six words at the end.

"Who's going to do the work?" he asked.

He was only twenty-six, but had a team of labourers, bricklayers and carpenters working for him. I didn't know if he was offering. "The work at the house, you mean?"

"Yes."

"No one. I can't afford it right now. I have to look for a job closer to the house. I'll also have to think of something extra to do to bring in some money. I just have to get into the house first."

"I went with Beeda two weeks ago to sign the papers," Zulpha said. "I liked the garden and the back yard, and two of the rooms are nice and big, but I hated the smell of the house."

He had an easy smile. "Smells are easy to get rid of," he said. "A fresh coat of paint. Are there carpets?" he asked me.

"Yes. And they're old people living there. You know how they accumulate things. Everything's got that musty smell about it. But the smell will be gone once the carpets are pulled up. There are oak floors underneath.

And it's got the most beautiful wooden window frames and oak doors. They've painted over it, can you believe it?"

"I can come and have a look," he said. "See if I can help you with anything."

"How much will you charge?" I asked.

"We'll talk about it. Let me see the place first."

And so it started. Innocently, like that. At the end of the month Zulpha and Imran and two of Imran's friends helped me move. They came with two open vans and made three trips. I didn't know how much stuff I had until it all stood out on the lawn waiting to be loaded onto the vans. I didn't have money to give Imran's friends, but baked a hundred mince pies a week later and had Imran deliver it to them.

By my third week in the house, I was getting used to Imran dropping by during the day. He was either at a job up the road and could easily drop by, or had a spare hour to quickly strip the wallpaper in the back room, or seal up some of the nail holes the previous owners had made in the walls. The furniture was stacked in the living room. The boys slept in one room while the second room was being stripped and prepared. I was in the main bedroom with the baby, which would be done last. The most important thing was to get the children settled in their own rooms. The twins would share and Zane would be in the other room. When Reza was old enough he would be either with his twin brothers or with Zane – whoever was going to make the least fuss about it.

One afternoon, after some weeks of coming on his own to do work on the house, I noticed a strain between us. He had finished varnishing the skirting boards, and was having a sandwich with me. We were sitting on the top step of the stoep in the backyard, watching some birds flittering about in the trees. We laughed, and then we looked at each other, and then he looked away. I felt something flit through me. I dismissed it.

When I still hadn't found work and a babysitter after a month, Zulpha suggested that I bake pies for a living.

"Pies?" I said. I was surprised that she would suggest such a thing.

"Yes," she said. "You can sell it at Cars 4U where you worked. They have auctions once a week. I've been to one of those. It takes all bladdy day. They sell things to eat there for the customers. I'll also see if I can get orders for you at the office. What do you have to lose? And you can make pies."

She was right. And I would be at home looking after my own baby and be there when my sons came home from school.

"I'd have to sell a helluva lot of pies for it to be worth it."

"Don't worry about the numbers," she said. "Just start. You'll see, it will all happen. You'll come up with other ideas too. Mummy can look after Reza when you take the pies away. Or she can sit with him in the car. And Mummy can maybe even help you if you get really busy. Maybe she'll have customers for you too."

I decided to give the pies a try. I called my old boss at Cars 4U and told him what I was trying to do. He was encouraging and told me I could come and set up for the auction on Wednesday.

I started with a hundred pies, worrying all the way in my Volkswagen Beetle whether I'd made too many. But people sampled my pies, and every last one was sold. I used real butter, not margarine, and lots of meat. I sold the pies for seventy-five cents. My profit, after expenses, was fifty rand. Not bad money for those days.

"The pies are expensive," one of them said, "but lekker. What about rooties? Some mince rooties would be nice."

"I'll see," I said, already working out in my head how much flour and ground beef I would have to buy, and left there feeling on top of the world. The pie idea had worked. My rent for the house was six hundred rand a month. The support my ex-husband paid just covered that and the electricity bill. If I could get extra orders and earn two hundred rand a week, I could pay for food and clothing and school things, and perhaps even save two or three hundred rand. I didn't allow myself to get excited. I had to get the orders first. And there was also Imran. He hadn't told me yet what he was going to charge me for all the work he'd done, but it weighed on my mind that I owed him.

I told Zulpha and Imran about my success at Cars 4U when they came to visit me the following Wednesday night. Zulpha was thrilled that it had worked out for me. She said that she didn't know if there was enough business at her office to warrant a trip all the way to town to sell fifteen pies, but that Carol in the office was planning her mother's thirtieth wedding anniversary, and wanted two hundred.

"Two hundred! That's great."

"And she wants to know if you also make fancy cakes. I said yes."

"Oh my word. What does she mean by fancy?"

"I don't know. But think of something you can make, then I can tell her."

"You know what you do," Imran said, "go to the bookshop, buy a cake recipe book, pick one that looks really fancy, then make one here for us to try out."

I liked his idea. And I liked reading, and doing things out of books. I could add my own touch to it. "I'll do that. I'll make one for us for Saturday."

Zulpha had more ideas. "And when you get really busy, you get a helper. You need one anyway with four children."

I agreed. Washing and ironing for five people was a lot of work, and standing in a hot kitchen all day rolling out pastry wasn't fun if you still had to do the cleaning up afterwards.

The next day I went out and bought three books on cakes, one specialising in chocolate delights. I made a sample white chocolate one for us to try out on the weekend, and Zulpha took a slice with her to the office on Monday. Two days later I got the order from Carol for five cakes, as well as the two hundred pies. On the day of the anniversary party, I got a last-minute call from Carol asking if I could also make fifty chocolate éclairs. I had never made an éclair in my life, but said yes. I called my mother, who agreed to help me if I picked her up. I had everything ready for Carol at six o'clock when she collected the order. I made two hundred and seventy five rand that weekend.

One afternoon I was making tea for Imran to have with his sandwiches he'd brought from home. The twins' room and Zane's room were finished, and looked really nice.

"I like what you did with the boys' rooms," I said. "You haven't told me yet what all this is going to cost me."

"Nothing," he said. "I'm engaged to your sister. We can be friends."

"You did a lot of work. It can't be for nothing," I said. "It's your time."

"I'm not losing time. I have people working at the site. I like talking to you."

"We haven't really talked about anything."

"We have. We talked the other day about your father, how strict he was, and how you used to hate it when he woke you up at faj'r, but today you don't miss any of your salaahs. It was helpful to me to hear something like that."

"Really?"

"Yes. I'm an only child. My father was a trawler. He drowned at sea when I was ten years old. My mother gave me the right upbringing – so she says," he said smiling, "but I didn't have that father thing in my life.

I'm not firm in my salaah. I make faj'r and maghrib, but that's only two out of five."

"Better than nothing. And the fact that you're aware of it."

"Do you think so?"

"Of course. If I tell you how neglectful I've been, you won't believe it, especially when Braima left. Three children, nine months pregnant. Think about it. He didn't die, which would've been traumatic enough. He left me for another woman. It was hard for me. There I was, clumsy and overweight, and he was leaving me. I was so hurt. And I was angry with God. I started to neglect my prayers. What was there to be thankful for? What prayer could get my life back to the way it had been? Reza was born and I became worse. I didn't pray at all. It was like I was challenging God to punish me further. You think stupid things like that, as if the prayers are for God and not for you. Anyway, that's how reckless I was. But God had his hand on my shoulder. He never let go of me. I started to feel guilty. There was something missing in my life. I missed my little communications. I decided to go back on the mat. I said, 'God, are you angry with me? Why are you angry with me? What have I done that you're angry with me?' Even then, I couldn't take the responsibility. And of course, God doesn't answer with words, and I still don't know why Braima left me. But here I am, a year later, in a new house, excited about my future."

My tale surprised him. "You obviously still think of him."

"Yes, but not like before. The edge is off. I still feel a little pang when I remember how he left me, but I don't need to understand it any more. I'm not violent in my thoughts like before. Besides, I've seen his wife."

He laughed. "You have a sense of humour."

"She was pregnant too, but she lost the baby."

"Did you love him?"

It was something I'd thought about many times. Yet it was something I couldn't answer with complete honesty. I'd thought Braima had loved me, and that I'd loved him. I'd thought that what we'd had was enough. When it blew up in my face, I had no feeling.

"I was comfortable. I don't think I was *in* love."

He looked at me directly. "You're a good person," he said.

"How do you know?"

"I don't, but you're good to me. It's easy talking to you."

I didn't see Imran for a week after that conversation. He and Zulpha didn't turn up on the Wednesday night or the weekend either. The work on my house was nearly complete. Only the kitchen had to be painted, and that had to be done on a day when I wasn't busy with pies. Friday was the best day for this, when I went to Cars 4U to deliver, but Friday was jum'ah prayers, and a short day for those who went to mosque.

When I returned from my deliveries at about three, I saw Imran's bakkie in the driveway. He was inside the house with my mother who'd been looking after Reza while I was gone. A Friday was my mother's day at my house now. Zulpha dropped her off at seven-thirty in the morning on her way to work, and I took her home. My mother helped with the baking and the rooties that were now also on my list.

I can still remember on that specific day wearing jeans and a T-shirt. I was a very fashionable girl. After my father died, I started to wear stove-pipes and sleeveless dresses and this didn't change even after I got married. My mother complained and said the things mothers had to. I paid no attention. I knew what I looked like in jeans and a T-shirt with my long hair trailing down my back. I parked my Beetle behind the white bakkie and went inside.

"I was just going to leave," Imran said. "Mummy made me some tea." He called my mother mummy already. "I came by to tell you that I'll do the kitchen on Sunday, if you're not busy."

"I don't bake on Sundays," I said. "That's good. Thanks. I'll be so glad when the kitchen's done."

He said goodbye to my mother, and I walked him out to the van. He opened the door and turned to me, handing me a piece of paper folded into a small square.

"Don't read it now," he said.

I looked at the thick square in my palm. My heart pounded. What was it? An invoice for the work he'd done? But I knew from his whole manner, and my own reaction, that it was a letter to me.

I went inside and put it under my pillow. I would read it that evening after my children were in bed and I had the house to myself. I went back to the kitchen. I noticed my mother looked a bit pale.

"Is Mummy okay?" I asked, taking the baby from her.

"Yes. I felt a bit tight in the chest earlier on, but I'm fine now." She was a handsome woman for forty-seven, but had asthma and had had one or two serious attacks in the past.

"Where's Mummy's pump?"

"It's in my bag, don't worry."

I relaxed. "Was Reza cranky?" I asked.

"No. He slept while you were away. He only woke up about half an hour ago. Did you sell everything?"

"Everything. I just put petrol in the car. Braima came to see the children last night and paid their support. I stopped at the agent's office on my way home and paid the rent."

"Good," she said, satisfied that things were going well for me. "And Imran," she said out of the blue, "what do you think of him?"

"What does Mummy mean?"

"I mean, do you think he's good for Zulpha?"

"Of course. I got to know him quite well now. He's hard working, respectful. They make a good couple."

She was quiet for a while, then looked at me in that way that told me she knew she was treading on dangerous ground. "Zulpha's never been married," she said.

I waited for her to continue.

"You've got four children already."

"I don't understand this conversation we're having. Where's Mummy going with this?"

She turned her face away from me. "I can see far, my girl."

"What does that mean?"

"Your sister hasn't had a turn yet."

I looked at her, the forlorn way she sat with her head bowed, looking down at her hands.

"Imran didn't visit Zulpha on Wednesday night," she continued. "And he didn't come on Saturday either. He hasn't called."

That explained why I hadn't seen them. But it was news to me that there was a break in communication. "And Mummy thinks I have something to do with that? What is this all about, Ma? Say it."

She turned to me with a worried frown on her brow. "I'm not accusing you of anything. I'm just asking. He's here a lot. Maybe he said something to you. Zulpha's a good child, but she hasn't been lucky with men. I would like her to have a chance."

*I would like her to have a chance.* I hadn't done anything. I didn't even know what was in the letter. Already my mother was making her plea for Zulpha. She suspected something. What? It was hard to be honest with myself. But deep down I knew, as I knew vinegar doesn't mix well with oil, I knew that Imran was attracted to me. I had known before getting the letter. I had felt it in the way he took care always not to stand too close or to stare, or from the way he worked vigorously with his sandpaper or paints not looking at me. I had felt it and smelled it. You know when something like that is happening to you. No words need to be spoken. The feeling is one of lightheadedness. The body speaks. The brain is on a long break.

My children arrived home from school. I piled them all in the car and drove my mother home. I didn't talk much. My mother's words had unsettled me. Mothers could indeed see around the bend when it came to their children.

When I returned home after dropping her off, I got out the rolling pin and the pastry from the fridge. I had two hundred pies to get ready by seven o'clock. I didn't turn down orders, no matter how fatigued I was.

"Zane!" I called out to my nine-year-old son.

He came out with a textbook in his hand. "Yes, Mom?"

"What are you doing?"

"I'm studying. I have exams on Monday."

"I want you to change Reza's nappy, and give him his supper. Mash the carrots and potatoes in the small pot, and put a little mince with it. I don't have time now to feed him. I have to get this all done and baked by seven."

He put down the book and went to fetch Reza. I stared after him, feeling bad that I gave him so much to do. He had a lot of chores for a nine-year-old.

I started to sprinkle flour on the pastry sheet. As I rolled and cut out circles of dough, I thought of what my mother had said about Imran not seeing Zulpha. I was disturbed to hear it. I didn't want my sister to be hurt.

After the pies had been collected that evening and the children had been washed and fed and put to bed, I made Reza's last bottle for the night, and put him down in his crib. The house had quieted down. An old Dinah Washington tune was playing softly on the radio in the living room. I sat down on the edge of the bed and took out the folded note from under my pillow. I looked at the small square, with the words, *For my friend*, written on it. I unfolded the paper. It was a page torn out of an exercise book, handwritten.

Abeeda,

Probably you are shocked that I am writing you this letter. I would've told you in person if I had the courage, but I don't. A terrible thing happened a long time ago and I thought I would share it with you. We had talked about mothers and fathers, remember? I told you that my father had drowned when I was ten years old. He did drown, and my mother did take the best care of me, but what I didn't tell you was that my father had jumped off the boat. I didn't know this until I was about sixteen or seventeen, and met two of the fishermen my father had trawled with. They were far out in the ocean, and were heading back as there was a fierce gale and the sea had turned rough. My father had climbed up onto the edge of the boat, and just stepped off. They reported to the captain that he had fallen in.

I was stunned. My father had committed suicide. I wanted to know why. I went to see one of the men at his house. I begged him to tell me anything he could remember about my father, and promised that whatever it was, I would never talk about it. Eventually, he told me. He and my father had been friends. He couldn't say if what he was about to tell me had anything to do with it, but my father had caught my mother with another man just a week earlier.

This is my struggle, Abeeda. I treat my mother with respect, and give her everything she needs, but she robbed me of my father. And I can't get it out of my head – her with another man. I talked to someone about it once. He told me it's in the past and to let it go. I've tried, but I find myself being short with my mother, and I feel bad about it.

My other struggle is a new one. I'm engaged to one sister, and have fallen in love with the other. Don't be shocked, Abeeda. I am more shocked than you. I can't sleep at night. Every living moment I think of you.

I'll see you on Sunday to finish your kitchen.

Imran

The morning after Zulpha's visit to my house, I got a call from Garaatie. "Beeda, it's bad news. Prepare yourself. Shehnaz died this morning. She had a stroke right on the muslah."

"What?" Shehnaz was Rhoda's only sister. She was forty-two. "What happened?"

"She and Moegsien got up at four. They made salaah together. When she was down with her forehead on the ground, she fell sideways. Moegsien got such a fright, he stopped his salaah to see what was wrong. But she couldn't answer him. He lifted her up and put her on the bed and called Dr Salie. He said when he called the doctor, she was gone already."

"Oh my word. And so young. And Rhoda?"

"Rhoda's taking it hard. She called me at five-thirty this morning. I'm on my way there now. I couldn't get away earlier. I had a helluva thing here with Mahmood. I found the airline stuff for his trip to Malaysia scheduled for after Ramadan. There were two tickets. I wanted to know whom the other ticket was for. He won't tell me. Anyway, enough about that. The janazah's at two o'clock. They're waiting for Shehnaz's son, Taliep, to come down from Jo'burg. His flight's getting in at twelve."

"And Rhoda's son?"

"Shafiq's in Australia. She called him."

My head spun with questions. It was interesting, I thought, that Rhoda had called Garaatie, and not me. But what was I to do now? There was this gambling thing between us, but there was now also a death.

I went to the bank and deposited the money I'd won a few days ago. I put it in a special account. I couldn't go to Mecca with it, or buy food with it, or even use it towards my son's medication, but would use it to pay my electricity, rates and taxes. After the bank, I popped in at the supermarket to pick up some items for Ramadan, which would start in two days' time. I had also asked Reza and Patrick to come and have supper with me that evening. Under different circumstances, I would've cancelled the supper and spent time with Rhoda, but I had no feeling for it.

I arrived at the janazah just as the toekamandies came out of the room. I noted who they were. Rhoda, her daughters, Zaitoon and Gafsa, and the well-known toekamandie, Amina Toufie. Anywhere you saw death, you saw Amina. She came with a crew of toekamandies; women who prepared the kafan – the white linen cloth – cut the linen strips, and sectioned the cottonwool to be flattened on the inside of the burial garment.

I wondered how Rhoda had fared in the room. She was squeamish and hadn't been able to participate when her aunt died. I had washed my own mother, the face and the hair. Toeghieda had washed the right side. Zulpha had done the left. The toekamandie had done the private parts and the loosening of the joints and the feet. When the time came to put our mother in the kafan – quite a maneuver as the body had to be rolled on its side while the kafan was slid in underneath – I slipped the little ring my mother had given to me when I was a child under the covers and put it under her hand.

I went up to Rhoda and consoled her. It was our first meeting since the casino. Her eyes were red, but she seemed strong. There was nothing in her demeanor to indicate that there was anything wrong between us. "It's a big shock," she said, "but it's Allah's Will. What can we do? She was so young, she's never been sick."

"You have to be strong," I said. "She was a good sister."

"Yes. Life is short. We take so much for granted. It can happen to any one of us."

I went over to Zaitoon and Gafsa, and gave my condolences. I noticed Muhaimin also in the crowd. Things had to be all right again between him and Gafsa, I thought. I hadn't spoken to Rhoda so I didn't know the latest news. I went up to Moegsien, and listened to him tell a friend how his wife had stood next to him on her muslah that morning, prostrated herself before God, and collapsed.

"She was alive when I lifted her up onto the bed. But I knew when I set her down . . . her eyes opened for a moment, then she slipped away."

I sympathised with all the members of the family, then went to sit on a bench next to another friend, Nabeweya. I hadn't seen Nabeweya since she'd had her uterus out four months earlier, but we kept in touch on the telephone. In a way, phone friendships were less toxic, and distance worked wonders. But it was good to see her again. One thing about death – someone died in the morning, and an hour later you saw people you hadn't seen in ages. There were fears and tears, but a janazah was also a social event.

"How are the boys, Beeda?" she asked. "Everywhere I look, I see Zane has another shop opening. He's doing well."

"Alhamdu lilah. And they're all well."

She looked at me. She didn't ask about Reza. No one asked.

From where I sat in the corner facing the door, I saw everyone who arrived. My sons, and their wives. Rhoda's relatives. My ex-husband, Braima, and his wife, Zainap. Braima's unmarried sisters, Rugaya and Jaweier. Neighbours and friends, and a lot of other people I knew. I had taken care with my appearance, and had on the robe with the gold trim I'd bought in Mecca years ago. My scarf was black silk, wrapped African fashion, with a narrow gold twine weaved in between the folds. I knew I was going to see and be seen.

Rabia saw me next to Nabeweya, and came to greet me. I greeted her back. The astounding thing about Rabia, and I give her credit for this, is that she was so thick-skinned, that she behaved as if nothing had happened between us.

"Mummy looks nice," she said.

"Thank you. You too." She was friendly and endearing and calling me mummy.

The imam arrived and the proceedings got underway. People started to file into the room where the mayyit was, to pay their last respects. Rhoda stood with her daughters at the head of the katel, crying into a handkerchief. Finally, the men lifted up the mayyit and put it on the bier. The wailing got louder. I stood with my daughters-in-law and watched the men file slowly out of the house. They would walk with the mayyit to the St Athan's Road Mosque, then go by transport to the cemetery.

When the men were gone, the kitchen got busy. Lamb curry and rice and milk tart were served. An acquaintance, Shariefa, came to sit next to me at the table in the lounge. She was a big woman with wheezing problems and gasped a little when she talked. For a few minutes we bemoaned the fugitive nature of life and the suddenness of Shehnaz's passing, then I almost choked on a piece of potato pudding when she leaned close and whispered in a conspiratorial tone that she'd heard I'd been to the casino with Rhoda.

"How'd you hear that?" I asked.

She had her fingers on a piece of grisly meat, trying to bite around the fat. "I can't remember," she said. "I just heard you were there."

"Bull dust. You know. You just don't want to tell me." But it didn't matter. What concerned me, was that the story was out. And in Shariefa's hands, it was dangerous. A ten thousand rand casino story would be the biggest scandal in the community. I could hear the imams on their mimbars talking with fresh gusto about the evils of gambling.

"I heard it on the wind." She smiled to let me know it was her secret. "So *have* you?"

On the wind was her favourite getaway. It spared her from having to divulge her sources while she knowingly damaged a reputation.

"I've been to the casino, yes." With someone like Shariefa, you give them all the ammunition just to see how dead they'll shoot you.

She gave a breathless little laugh. "Everyone who goes there says they go for the restaurants, or to see a movie."

"I go to play," I said.

She had a small mound of rice left, and moved it around the plate with her fingers to soak up the last juices. "It's haraam, you know."

I smiled at her, a smile that told her just how I felt. "I'm not as good as you, Shariefa. I'm a sinner."

She hit my hand playfully. "You're not a sinner. But I think you like calling yourself that. It lets you get away with things. You just say you're a sinner, and that shuts everyone up."

I looked at the spot of grease on my hand where she'd tapped it. "There're lots of things that are haraam, Shariefa. Not only gambling. Fitnah's a big one. Spreading stories about other people. Remember what Jesus said about casting stones?"

"What?"

"Read the Bible, Shariefa. The Qur'an isn't enough for you." I got up with my plate, leaving her staring after me. I knew that story would travel, and I dared it.

In the kitchen I helped with the drying of the dishes, and said hello to Zainap. We had met many times before at my sons' functions. I had nothing against her. She was younger than me, but didn't have my figure, my spirit or my flair. I'd long ago forgiven her for taking my husband. What had she really taken? A man who was there to be had. I got over Braima ages ago.

Men, I can tell you, are different from women. They can promise undying love, they can tell you they can't live a moment without you, and would go to pieces if anything happened to you, but you die tomorrow – three months later they're married to someone else. I don't know how they get it right in their heads, but I know two men who've done that. They can't deal with sitting alone at the breakfast table or creeping alone into bed. After the hundred nights, the imam sommer came one time and performed the nikkah, and they picked up their lives and carried on.

Women don't do this. They've got this huge lay-by of love that's got to be very carefully laid to rest. They nurture the past. Women light candles and listen to music to help them cry. They talk to a friend. They're not in a rush to get over it. They go through all five stages of grief, and a few more, until their hearts are still again. A woman's sorrow is a last act of loyalty, an expression of love for the man who'd once shared her life.

But women are fools also. They give too much of themselves, and hold nothing in reserve. They believe entirely in this human being who's promised a lifetime of happiness. When the human being fails, they look at his failings and not at their own desperate need to be loved. They find out for the first time that no one can love them until they've done the job themselves. That's not to say that I have no longings. Many, *many* times I wished my life had been otherwise. I love men and love being in their company; I just don't want to be contracted to one again.

I watched Sawdah and Sadia set out plates for the men who would soon return from the cemetery. They're identical twins, and sometimes I have to go by the mole on the left cheek to know who I was talking to. They were pretty sisters in their early thirties, with slanted eyes, and a slightly Javanese look. Both of them worked for attorneys as legal secretaries. On Saturday mornings, Sawdah gave classes in floral arrangements and silk painting, and Sadia looked after the children. On Sunday afternoons, Sadia played Scrabble at a Claremont club, and Sawdah did the same for her. I was fortunate that Munier and Marwaan had found such wonderful girls. My children had done better than me in choosing a partner.

But then I hadn't really come to marriage in the ordinary way. It was a second date with Braima on the back seat of his blue Citroën that got me facing an imam after the doctor told my mother why I was vomiting every morning. There were no discussions. My mother told my father, who promptly called up Braima's parents who ordered their son to do the right thing. Luckily, not one of my sons had to face the imam this way.

I walked over to Sawdah and Sadia. "Where are my favourite granddaughters?" I asked, giving both of them a big hug.

"They're in the new after-care program at school," Sadia answered. "They're there until six."

"Is it safe to leave them there for so long? They're girls."

"It's safe," Sawdah laughed. "And they have friends there. All four of them are going to be in their first school play. I'll tell Mummy when it's on so Mummy can come too."

"I'm glad you didn't bring them here," I said. "I don't believe in little children going to funerals. Kiss them for me. And tell Huda and Rushda that I haven't forgotten what day the 23rd is." Huda and Rushda were Munier and Sawdah's children. They were turning six during Ramadan. Both Munier and Marwaan had a set of twins. Marwaan's girls, Firdous and Zuraida, were seven months older. The four girls moved in a pack and allowed no one into their circle, except their cousin, Shaheed.

"Is Mummy going already?"

"Yes. I have Reza coming for supper. I also have some other things to do. Don't forget Saturday night. Iftaar dinner's at my house."

"How can we forget?" Sawdah said. It was customary during Ramadan for the family to come over on the first Saturday evening of the holy month to break their fast at my house. On the following Saturday nights, they all took a turn inviting the family to come and eat with them.

I said goodbye and went looking for Rhoda, greeting people as I went along. I found Rhoda with her daughters in the room where the mayyit had been. I hugged each of them in turn. "Take care of yourselves and keep strong," I said. "I have to go. I have people coming for supper this evening."

"Don't forget the seven nights, Auntie," Zaitoon reminded.

"I won't."

Rhoda walked me out to the gate. "I haven't heard from you, Beeda," she said.

"I haven't heard from you either."

"Are you all right?"

"I'm as all right as all right can be. Thanks. You keep well," I said.

I drove down Belgravia Avenue and realised that I was going the wrong way. I was supposed to go left on Kromboom Road and then turn right down one of the avenues to my house, but was driving all the way down to Klipfontein Road. At Klipfontein Road I made a right and headed towards Vanguard Drive. I was coming from a funeral and heading straight to Auntie.

I had three hundred rand. I parked in the lot, took a hundred rand and left it under the mat in my car for petrol. I entered the casino, glancing at my watch. I had an hour for a quick smoke and a play before I had to go home and prepare supper.

Within twenty minutes, I had no money left. I walked quickly out to the parking lot for the hundred rand I'd left in the car. I tried a different machine. It took the whole hundred.

I glanced at my watch. It was five o'clock. Reza and Patrick were going to be at my house at seven. I found myself at the ATM machine withdrawing three hundred rand. One hundred for petrol, and two hundred to play with. I went to a different location on the floor and tried the machines there. At five-thirty I had lost it all, including the petrol money.

*Go home, Beeda. Cut your losses and go home. Tomorrow's another day.*

Desperation takes hold of you. You've got to get back what you've lost, and I'd lost six hundred now. Money I could've used to pay my rates and telephone account. Money I could've used towards a gym membership. Money I could've given to feed the poor. On and on I blamed myself. But back I went to the ATM machine for one more try. By the time I finally stopped playing, I was filled with recrimination. I went to the ladies room. There I sat with my bag on my lap in the small cubicle looking into the empty wallet, asking myself over and over how I could've done such a thing. I'd lost one thousand four hundred rand.

I was late getting home, and was just putting the potatoes into the pot when the Golf pulled into the driveway and Reza and Patrick appeared at the back door.

"Mummy?"

I went forward and hugged him. He was so thin, I took care not to squeeze him. "I'm a little late with supper," I said.

"Not a problem," he said, sitting down. "We had some paw-paw before coming here."

Patrick handed me a bunch of sunflowers. "To keep you in smiles," he said.

"Thank you. I need something right now to cheer me up." I turned back to Reza. "How're you? You look tired."

"I am a little, but I'm taking these new vitamins. It's supposed to increase your energy."

"Can these vitamins cure you?"

"Some people swear by it. I've just started to take them."

"Reza must open his mind to it," Patrick added. "Two of our friends have been positive for more than five years. They're taking a lot of alternative medicines and vitamins. They're still going strong. Reza must give it time."

I noticed Reza's clothing. It was a warm evening, but he had on a shirt, a jersey, and a windbreaker. "Are you cold?" I asked.

"Yes," he hugged his jacket about him. "This afternoon I sat for a bit on the balcony in the sun. It was nice. But now I feel cold again."

Patrick changed the subject. "So? How's Mrs A?"

"Fine. I was at a funeral today. A friend of mine died at dawn this morning, of a stroke."

"Who?" Reza asked.

"Rhoda's sister, Shehnaz."

"How old was she?"

"Forty-two. It was a total shock to everyone. She's never been sick."

"How tragic. I remember her. Were there lots of people?"

"Yes. Your father and Zainap, your brothers and their wives. Do you remember Shariefa? One of the spinster sisters?"

"The one who had the disappointment with that man from Jordan?" he asked.

"Yes," I laughed. "That's her claim to fame, that he was a Jordanian. Actually, he came knocking on the door selling tablecloths, and saw a way to stay in the country."

"That's naughty, Mummy."

"I know," I laughed. "Anyway, she'd heard that I'd been to the casino, and just had to let me know that she knew." I don't know why I brought it up with my son, but was beginning to believe that everyone knew what had happened, and didn't want him hearing it from someone else.

"I also heard the story," he said.

"You did? How?"

"Munier and Marwaan visited the other night."

I was surprised that the twins had discussed me. "What did they say?"

"Rabia told them that you frequented the casino."

"Frequented?"

"Don't worry about it," he laughed, "she's not one of your fans. But apparently something about a machine that you or Rhoda had played on, and Rhoda won, and now the two of you are bad friends."

"My, how things go around. Do you want to hear what happened?"

"Tell us. Patrick and I can do with a good story. We've had bad news all week. We've just had our documentary on the teen mothers in the Cape Flats rejected."

"The one you worked on so hard?"

"Yes. But we're taking it overseas. Tell us the story."

"Okay. First, Rhoda never wanted to play. She only came along to watch and only had twenty rand. I was playing on a machine and took my card out for a moment to stick it into the machine next to me when all of a sudden she asked if she could borrow my card and play on my machine. I told her I had pumped money into that machine and was still playing there, and was just sticking my card for three quick hits into the machine next to it. She insisted on playing on my machine. I didn't want to be mean, and thought, well, she only has twenty rand. So I let her. She stuck the card in and on the first hit won ten thousand rand."

"What? That's not fair!" Patrick exclaimed. "What happened next?"

"That's just it. Nothing. She took all of it in a cheque. She didn't say one word to me about what she'd just done."

"I don't believe it."

"Believe it. A friend of thirty years. When I saw her today at the funeral, I acted like nothing had happened, but something did, and she knows it."

"For damn sure. She insisted on playing on *your* machine. She should've given you half the money."

"That's what I also think," Reza spoke for the first time. "That would've been the fair thing to do – even though you let her play on the machine."

"I know."

"Money brings out the worst in people. Do you go often?" Patrick asked.

"Once every two weeks or so," I lied.

"I don't see anything wrong with it now and again," Reza said. "But that's a bit regular, Mummy, don't you think? How much do you play with?"

"A hundred rand," I continued my lying. "The first time I went I won four thousand five hundred."

"You're joking!"

"I'm not. Garaatie was with me. In fact, she's the one who first took me there. I never even knew we had a casino in Cape Town."

"Garaatie gambles? Good grief. It gets more interesting."

"She doesn't go any more. She only went two or three times."

Reza got up and took a glass from the cupboard and poured some cold water from the fridge. "I think it would be good if you also stopped. Gambling's not good for the soul. Even if you're winning."

"I agree," I said. "But it's not a danger to me. I'm thousands up on the casino."

"Thousands?" His eyes rounded in surprise.

"Yes."

He came to stand next to me at the stove and put his arm around me. "I like you to be happy, Mummy. You're all alone in this house. I'm glad you have friends and go out to the movies and have fun. But you know the pitfalls of gambling. And it's dirty money. You don't want it contaminating your life. Look what it did to your friendship with Rhoda."

"I know, and I don't want you to worry about me. I can stop any time I wish."

"Okay. Now where's that food you promised us? I didn't even ask what you were making. What do you think it is, Patrick? Chicken? Breyani? I smell coriander."

"Lamb curry and rootie," I said. "Your favourite. And it's almost ready." Patrick helped me set the table, and we started to eat.

Reza tore off a piece of rootie and dipped it into the sauce on his plate and tasted it. "Mmm, this is good. My mother really makes the best rootie. So fluffy and crispy."

I smiled. It was always a pleasure to cook for him. "You know everyone's coming over the first Saturday night in Ramadan for iftaar?"

"I know. I usually come in the week."

"This year I want you to also be here."

"What?"

"And I want Patrick to come too."

"Mummy's not serious?"

"I am. Things are going to be different this year."

"But Mummy knows what it'll be like sitting at the table with all of them. It'll be awkward and uncomfortable. No one will know what to say. It'll spoil everyone's evening. I'm surprised that Mummy would suggest such a thing."

He turned to Patrick. "Would you come to a dinner here with all my brothers?"

Patrick finished chewing the food in his mouth. "Well, Munier and Marwaan come to the flat. I don't think that's a problem."

"You haven't met my eldest brother. And his wife."

"It's up to you," Patrick said. "I don't mind. I've already gone through this with my own family. I just don't even try to explain."

"Talking about family," I said, "I called everyone together the other night. Your father also. I told them what was happening."

"You talked about me?"

"Yes. I wanted everyone to be informed, not only the twins. I also brought up the subject of your medication."

He turned red. "How does Mummy know about my medication?"

I had the good sense not to look at Patrick. "Aren't you on medication? One only has to read the papers or listen to the news to know how expensive it is in South Africa."

He glanced at Patrick. "Oh Ma, I can't believe you did this. They won't understand."

"They understand better now than before. They all offered their support. So I don't want you to rule out coming here. Think about it. It's a start to get the whole family together. For years there's been this separation. I want it to end."

Patrick nodded that he agreed.

"I'll think about it," Reza said.

"I don't want my presence to unsettle the family," Patrick said.

"So what if it unsettles the family? We have to start somewhere."

"We'll think about it, Ma. I'll let you know."

The sound of a car pulling into the driveway got our attention. Minutes later, the twins came striding through the back door.

"You've timed it perfectly," I said. "I was just going to serve dessert."

"We know when these things happen in the neighbourhood," Munier laughed.

"You're not in the neighbourhood. You're out of your territory."

They kissed me and sat down. "We just knew something was happening," Marwaan said. "My mother's playing favourites again, I see. You guys get invited for supper and we don't."

"You're all coming on Saturday night," I said.

"I see. That's how it works."

I cleared the dishes and set out dessert bowls. Conversation at the table turned to the American president's preoccupation with war in Iraq. Here all four of them spoke the same language. I listened with half an ear. I watched the news, I read the papers, I knew the arguments. Bush was going to do what he wanted irrespective of world opinion. But I had my marching shoes in case there was a protest. What I was more concerned with at that moment, was the real reason my twins had come around. It soon became apparent.

"So, Ma," Munier, turned to me, "are you all ready for the big month?"

"I've been ready for weeks. Just the other day it was Ramadan. Here it is Ramadan again. The time flies."

"And it goes by faster the older we get."

"I agree."

"Do you know the significance of Ramadan, Patrick?" Marwaan asked.

"Yes. Reza's explained it to me. An annual spiritual overhaul."

"Absolutely. It's a really good time for Muslims, a chance to make real changes in our lives. We all need to do that. We service our cars. Why don't we do the same with our souls?" His tone changed. It became more respectful. "I'll be honest, Mummy, I didn't like hearing about this casino thing that happened with you and Auntie Rhoda. This casino is the worst thing to have hit the Cape. People are losing their life savings, their homes, marriages are being destroyed. I believe there's even a bus that picks pensioners up on pension day and brings them to the casino. It's shocking what this government's allowed. And our own people are going there."

I tried to make light of it. "So you came here to lecture your mother a bit."

"We know you're not a gambler, Mummy, but it starts out as fun and next thing you know, you're going there all the time. I mean, that ten thousand rand story's an ugly story. You and Auntie Rhoda have always been friends. And how can we go and do daw'ah work and our own mother goes to a casino? You've been to Mecca. You know the sin. Gambling takes you away from Allah."

"Mummy's only been there a few times," Reza said. "And that thing with Auntie Rhoda's unfortunate, but they went out for a little jol and it didn't turn out to be so. It's not like Mummy makes a habit of it."

The twins looked at him. "Are you saying it's all right for Mummy to go to the casino?" Munier asked.

"Of course not, but I don't think we should make it such a big issue. Mummy's not a child. And we all sin."

"We don't have to add to our sin," Munier continued. "It's not good to be seen in a place like that. People talk. Remember, Tapie Salie who had a heart attack at the race track? People never stopped talking about it.

They forgot about the work he did with old people in the community, but they never forgot where he was when he died."

"That's true. People remember what they want. Anyway, I've talked to Mummy about it. I believe you're all coming for supper next Saturday?"

"Yes. Are you?"

"I'm not sure. Mummy wants me to come."

"I think you should. It would be really nice for all of us to be together. Our children don't know you. They know they have an Uncle Reza, but they never see him."

I knew Reza's feelings on the matter. "Whose fault is that?" he asked. "You visit me. You don't bring them. You don't invite me to your homes." He sounded easy about it, but it was actually a sore point.

"Well, it's not that we didn't . . ."

It was an embarrassing moment. "Listen, guys," I interrupted, "let's not go off the track here. Reza's coming to supper. Let that be a start."

It was close to midnight when they left, conversation having returned once more to American politics. It was hours to Ramadan. My sons were hardly down the road, when out came my jeans and my gold card. I'd already lost thirteen hundred rand that day and was going back. I vowed as I drove to Goodwood, that it was my last time at the casino – my last throw before the holy month.

I had five hundred rand and an amazing burst of energy for that time of night. I wasted no time deciding where I would play. I selected a machine and lit a cigarette. I ordered a coffee with hot milk and settled down to play. I can't explain the feeling I have when I'm there – the thrill of not knowing, the expectation, getting a hit. This time, however, something very different happened.

I had chosen a good machine and within twenty minutes had eight hundred rand on my card. That, together with the four hundred in my wallet, amounted to twelve hundred.

I got up. I'd never deluded myself into thinking that a machine would just give and give. I went to another machine. Again I'd chosen a good one, and by one-thirty I had two thousand three hundred rand. I would choose a machine by watching people play, then get on after them. A terrible, terrible thing, for in effect, I'm waiting for them to lose, so I can take it.

I was starting to feel tired. I was up a great deal of money, but just couldn't tear myself away and go home. I went to the Golden Anchor, and ordered a latté. I'd seen a woman order this at a machine once, and asked what it was. When it arrived, I lit another cigarette and relaxed back against the soft cushions. My eyes closed for a moment. I saw my sons' faces flash before me. I opened my eyes and looked about. I saw Johnny, one of Zane's drivers, at the next table, looking at me. I got such a shock. My first reaction was to pretend that I hadn't seen him, but I knew that that would only make matters worse. Zane would know in the morning – it was morning already – that I had been to the casino. And that after they'd left my house discussing their sick brother just the other night.

"Hello, Johnny," I said, going up to his table, noting the woman next to him. "Are you winning tonight? Hello, Mary. Is this your wife, Mary?"

Johnny changed colour. "I don't really gamble," he said. "We come to watch. This is . . . my cousin, Jo-Anne."

"Okay. Hello, Jo-Anne. This place is busy, hey, for this time of the night?"

"It is," Johnny said. "But I have to take Jo-Anne home now. Work in the morning."

"Don't worry, I haven't seen you."

"Okay, Mrs Ariefdien."

*Hell, Beeda, that was low.*

I said goodbye and walked off. My wallet bulged with notes. It was my last fling, I told myself. Was I ready to go now? If my feet carried me to the exit, I would go home and leave a winner. If they didn't, well . . .

I wound up at the wheel of gold machines. These were the big gluttons on the floor. There were ten of them – five back to back – with big glittering heads, which made a helluva racket when you got a spin. Jackpots ranged from R15 000 to R72 000, and the machines gave R1 000 spins and R1 500, R1 800, R2 500 and R3 000 combinations daily.

The trick was to get on the right machine at the right time as they spun at a heck of a speed and gobbled up your money. I'd stood behind a woman once with R1 300 on her card. Within forty minutes the whole amount was gone. I stuck in my card immediately after her, and on the third hit, won R1 800.

And so it goes. One man's tears is another man's cheer. And there I was standing again at the spinnies at this ungodly hour of the morning. I noticed three of the machines gave regular R100 and R200 spins, but a woman at the end with R400 on her card, got nothing at all. When the money on her card was down to R56, she got a spin for R25. I went to check the pay outs on the computer. A summary showed that the machine had paid R1 000 six hours earlier, but nothing since. It was time for it to turn around.

I waited. If the woman got a spin, and the machine turned, I could forget it. She would never get up. The earringed man next to her got a spin, and her eyes went longingly up to the wheel, then dropped again when she saw him win R1 000. It was horrible to see what happened to people's faces as they watched other people win, and their own money disappear.

The amount on her card reached zero. I waited to see what she would do next. She sat for a moment staring at the machine as if waiting for something to happen, then opened her bag, and took out another hundred-rand note. This went as fast as the four hundred before it. After taking out and losing another three hundred rand, she finally got up.

I took her seat. Taking my own time to insert my card, I looked around to see if I could spot a waitress. I ordered another latté and lit a cigarette. I glanced at my watch. It was just after three in the morning. In an hour and a half it would be faj'r.

When the machine took the first hundred rand, I didn't panic. I put in another. When it took that one also, I still didn't worry. It had taken all of the woman's money, and two hundred of mine. Soon, it was going to give something. By the fourth hundred, I was beginning to feel a little down. All around me the machines were spinning. Only my machine was asleep.

"Daai machine's af," a voice said behind me.

"Honestly," I said. "Not even a twenty or fifty."

"Get off lady, I'm telling you. I won that R64 000 jackpot the other day. I know these machines. This bastard's not going to give anything until morning. The other machines are all paying. Your machine's paying for them. Get off."

I smiled at him and when he smiled back I noticed he had a gold tooth. "The woman before me put in over eight hundred. It has to turn."

"It doesn't have to," he laughed. "I watched that woman. She didn't put in eight hundred. She put in more than a thousand. The machine should've turned long ago. You're on a naaier, lady, I'm telling you. But stay if you want to. I won't watch."

What did he know, I said to myself. He was a gambler like me, full of theories and strategies. I took a moment to take in my surroundings. The wheel of fortune machines attracted a lot of bystanders. I became aware of a woman with a flaming red bouffant behind me, waiting for me to get up. I took another hundred-rand note out of my purse. The machine gobbled that up also. I took out another. And another.

When I'd lost a thousand rand, I heard someone say "Daai vrou's mal. Nogal 'n slamse vrou. Wie't jy hoeveel het sy ingesit?" That woman's mad, and on top of it, a Muslim woman. Do you know how much she's put in?

I didn't turn around to look. I was too embarrassed. I was losing at a reckless rate, but wouldn't get up. Determination to get my money back urged me on. How could a machine be so absolutely relentless and give you nothing?

Twenty minutes later, I sat back in my seat and dared anyone behind me to ask if I was finished playing. People get edgy when they see you sitting there doing nothing. They want you to get up so they can have a go. I looked around for a waitress. Maybe if I gave the machine a few minutes to cool down, it would turn around.

The man with the gold tooth materialised out of the crowd. His eyes glanced at the amount on my card. "Anything?" he asked.

"Nothing. Not one spin. How about you?"

"I won twelve hundred at the Cash Attack. That's it for me. I'm finished playing. Are you getting up?"

This was the big question. But how could I and let someone else have all the money I'd pumped into the machine? This was the heartbreaking part. Running out of money and having to get up. I had dared to look in my wallet, and counted only five hundred rand remaining. I'd given the machine one thousand, eight hundred.

I won't give you a long story about disgust. You can't describe disgust when you're feeling it. But, I still had my original five hundred that I'd come with. If I got up now and went home, I wouldn't have lost any of my own money – just what I'd won.

The woman with the big hair tapped me on the shoulder, "Are you still playing here?" she asked.

That decided me. "Yes."

She gave me a nasty look. I ignored her, and because she'd been cheeky, I asked the man with the gold tooth if he would mind sitting in my seat while I went to the ladies room. He was only too happy to oblige and tell everyone around him how he'd won the jackpot of R64 000 and paid off his bond.

I returned to the machine after a few minutes. Now, I thought. The machine had had time to resettle. I would get a big combination and go home. Surely, now, my luck would change.

I sat down and started to play. The machine next to me got a spin. I looked up to see what amount it would settle on. It stopped on a thousand rand. It had paid out over four thousand rand in two hours. Mine had done nothing. As I sat there feeding the machine one note after another, I heard the woman with the big hair behind me tell someone that I'd just saved her four hundred rand.

I had a hundred left. Gold tooth stood next to me and shook his head sadly as he watched me take my last note from my purse. At that moment I still believed that something would happen.

"Good luck," he said.

I smiled, a hollow little smile. "You should play here after me if I don't get it."

"No," he said. "I've won enough," he patted his pocket. "I'm a professional, lady. I know when to stop."

Well, I won't make a party out of it. I lost. All the money I'd come with and all the money I'd won. And I ignored yet another piece of my own advice, and that was not to watch after you'd lost at a machine. But I watched the woman with the big hair take my seat. She put in a fifty-rand note. She stabbed the button three times. On the fourth stab, three diamonds locked into place, and she got my two thousand rand.

The drive home was painful. As I passed the Epping market, I understood for the first time what made some people drive their cars off bridges.

The sun was up when I walked through my door and switched on the kettle for tea. While I waited for it to boil, I looked for the blue pamphlet with the telephone number I'd been given some weeks ago. I found it mixed up with some of my accounts in the second drawer.

The kettle boiled. I filled the pot and then dialed the number. It was just after seven in the morning. The call was answered on the second ring.

"I'd like to speak to John, please."

"This is John."

"John? You don't know me . . ."

I mran's letter shocked me. I sat on the edge of the bed with the page in my hand and felt hot. I read it again. And again. I looked at the handwriting to work out how it identified its writer. The words were round and decorative, with flourishing edges, creative in its design. But it had been hurriedly written. I could see that from one or two ink blotches, and a sentence, which had been scratched out and rewritten.

I looked over at my son making cooing sounds in his crib, drifting off to sleep, insensible of the world about him, the future that beckoned. I read the letter a few more times, then folded it up and put it in my jewelry box in the third drawer of my cupboard.

The next day was busy. My mother's moulood jam'aah were celebrating their fifteenth anniversary on Sunday, and had ordered six cakes and six coconut tarts. I had to go out and buy the ingredients. I had to pick up my mother to help with the tarts. I also had to take the twins to be fitted for new shoes.

As I went about my day trying to juggle the children, the baking, the shopping, I thought about the letter. The letter had changed the order of things. Imran hadn't seen my sister, and hadn't called her, and he had fallen in love with me.

How had I contributed to this? I thought about it all day. I had been conscious of my appearance when he was around. I had teased him a little, laughed a little too much, said things designed to make him notice me. Had I done it to nab him or just to test my attractiveness?

As soon as I'd read the letter, though, I knew what my response should be. To laugh it off and make him feel easy about it. To tell him that I understood he had a little crush on his future sister-in-law, and that it was all right, but that I didn't feel the same way. I could do it. He would feel a little embarrassed, but then it would be all right again. I would never mention it or remind him in any way about it. That would be the right thing to do. But was it the truth, and the right thing by me? I had felt his heat, and was attracted to him also. The letter confirmed what I believed.

It was a good feeling to know that someone you had feelings for felt the same way about you. But as I savoured this deliciousness, another part of me revolted. It was my own sister I would take from. How could I do it?

After maghrib prayers that evening, I replaced the telephone receiver in its cradle. I had left it off the hook all day. The phone rang almost immediately.

"Did you read the letter?" he asked.

I took a moment to gather myself before responding. "Yes."

"I hope it didn't disturb you. I've been thinking about you a lot."

Right there I had my chance. The words were ready, I'd gone over them all day. But the words that came out were completely different. "I've been thinking about you too."

There was a moment's silence. "I took such a chance," he said. "You could've rejected me. It was such a risk writing that letter. I want you to know that I had nothing like this in mind when I offered to come and help at the house. I had no idea this would happen."

"I believe you."

"I think the night I varnished the skirting boards and we spoke about our parents, and you told me about your husband – I realised I was coming there because I liked talking to you. We sat on the couch afterwards and watched the news. I came so close to touching you."

I felt a shiver of pleasure. I remembered the night.

"How about you?" he asked. "When did you first know?"

"I think that time when we were having sandwiches on the stoep. I felt something. But I thought, no. You're engaged to my sister. I'm imagining it. I just put it out of my mind."

There was a long silence. Both of us knew the next question.

"And now, Beeda? What do we do with this? Zulpha and I are supposed to get married in three months."

It wasn't something I could answer. Zulpha had been in my thoughts all day. I had no solution. "Don't you love her?" I asked.

"Not like this. I love her, but I'm *in* love with you. I don't know if you understand. If I had never met you I wouldn't have questioned my feelings for her. But now, I don't know. I feel something different for you. I lie awake at night thinking about it. It's everything about you. Your spirit, the way you laugh, that little giggle you have, the way you tend to your kids. It's your fire. I'm attracted to it. Jy's 'n lekker Slamse meit."

His words shot like hot mercury through me.

"I'm comfortable with Zulpha. We get along and have fun. It was just natural to take it to the next level. I don't know if I can do it now."

I didn't want to know more. Already I had asked and said too much.

"Tell me to stay away if you don't want to see me," he said. "Tell me now, and I will."

"I can't tell you what to do."

"So you also want to see me?"

I was too cowardly to answer.

"If only you weren't sisters. Anything else, but sisters. But there must be a solution."

"There isn't. My sister will get hurt. And I'll be the one responsible. I couldn't live with myself."

"What does that mean?"

I responded with a question of my own. "Are you going to see her? I believe you haven't been there for a while."

"I can't see her. Not the way I feel now. I've already betrayed her by writing that letter."

"She doesn't know. Just go to her. This thing with me is just a little crush. You like your future sister-in-law, and that's okay. It happens. Don't mess up your life. Go and reassure her that things are all right."

"I can't. Even if nothing happens with you and me. And knowing how you feel about me. No way. I can't sell my soul, Beeda. I also have a right to be happy. The marriage hasn't taken place yet. We don't have to make a mistake."

"Are you saying the wedding's off?"

"It has to be."

"Oh my God. Think about what you are saying. My sister will be devastated."

"Do you really want me to go back to her?"

Again I had the opportunity to set matters straight. I remained silent.

"Are you there?" he asked.

"I'm a divorced woman, Imran. I have four children."

"You're not answering the question."

"I don't want to answer your question."

"All right, then. I'll see you tomorrow to finish your kitchen. I'll come early."

I didn't fall asleep easily that night. I hadn't heard from Zulpha, and imagined that she was probably worried about what was happening with her relationship with Imran. I didn't know if Imran knew the story about the medical student Zulpha had dated for almost three years. Nazeem was from Port Elizabeth and came to live in residence at Groote Schuur. Zulpha took him food on the weekends and put up with all his moods. He worked grueling shifts at the hospital and was often fatigued to the point where he had to cancel their plans at the last minute, leaving Zulpha sitting by herself on a Saturday night. It was always understood that one day they would marry. One Sunday afternoon Zulpha went as usual to take him some lunch, and was told by another student that Nazeem had left for P.E. Zulpha was shocked. Nazeem had been with her just the previous night and had said nothing. She was further informed that Nazeem was coming back for his graduation the following week, after which he and his younger brother were leaving for Australia. Zulpha came home and locked herself up in her room and didn't come out for a week. The doctor put her on antidepressants. She lost thirty pounds. It took her years to get over the rejection. When Imran came on the scene, my mother was vigilant as a fox and watched for any sign that her daughter might get hurt again. But Imran was the kind of boy mothers liked for their daughters. He was steady, from a good family, and hardworking. When the two of them got engaged, my mother relaxed for the first time.

The next morning Imran arrived with hot koeksisters – coconut-covered doughnuts – for our breakfast. I sat with him and the boys at the table and smoked three cigarettes. I'd cooked lunch early that morning so he would have a clear kitchen to work in. He finished his coffee and got started. I went outside with the children to keep them out of his way. The phone rang. Zane went to answer it. He asked if he and his brothers could go to Steenbras for a picnic. His cousin Dickie was on the phone and wanted to know if they should pick them up. They had finished their homework and I said yes. The twins, just six years old, jumped up and down with the news, then ran back inside for things they would take along on the trip. I went to sit with Reza on the grass under the avocado pear tree. I had a magazine on my lap, but had to keep my eye on Reza who was crawling everywhere, stuffing things into his mouth.

The twins came out with their sunglasses and hats. "Can we have some of the money daddy gave us, Mummy, to buy ice creams?"

"Yes," I said, smiling at them. They chose their own clothes and always picked the same things to wear. "Zane knows where the jar is with the pocket money."

Zane stood behind them looking sheepish in long pants. It was new pants, only for special occasions – not for a picnic – but I said nothing. My mind wasn't on my children's attire that morning. I was too aware of the man in the white overall on the ladder painting the kitchen ceiling. I had a perfect view from where I sat. I watched him. He had a handkerchief tied about his head for protection against the paint spray. He worked quickly, a roller in one hand, the pan in the other. The kitchen radio was on. I could hear him whistling along with a Chicago tune.

The scene was idyllic – children playing on the grass, the daddy painting, the mummy looking after the baby. As long as no one said what this was, it didn't exist. But it did. In the silences. In the way we stole glances. In the way his eyes would find mine, lock into them, then look away. As I sat there under the tree, I dreamed of a life with a house full of kids, and a man who came home at nights with cement stains on his pants and lust in his heart. I'd always liked the silent, work-with-the-hands type.

A silver Mercedes pulled into the driveway. It was Toeghieda and her husband, Mylie, and their two children coming to fetch my boys.

Toeghieda got out of the car. She was dressed for a picnic, in a pink sleeveless dress, and a scarf around her neck. My children ran up and kissed her. Toeghieda saw Imran on the ladder in the kitchen and called out to him. Imran wiped his hands on his pants and came out.

"How's the work coming along?" she asked.

"It's done after today," he said, smiling. "Well, it's never done. There's always this and that to be fixed, but the house is livable now."

She looked around. "Where's Zulpha?"

"She must be at home," he said.

She looked at him, then at me. "Well, maybe we'll make a turn at Mummy's later. We'll see you there then," she said.

"Maybe. Although I don't think so. Someone has to be here while the doors and windows are left open for the paint smell to leave."

Imran and I walked her back to the car. Mylie was smoking a cigarette and leaned his head out the window to greet us. My three kids and their eldest son were in the back. The youngest would have to sit with Toeghieda in front. A long silver fishing rod protruded from the side window. Toeghieda and Mylie liked picnics by the sea. Often my children went with them.

"I didn't pack in anything for them," I said. "Can I give you some fruit to take with you? Drinks?"

"We have enough," Toeghieda said, getting into the car. "I'll see you later, when I drop off the kids."

Imran and I stood around in the yard for a bit after they had left. We looked at each other, aware that, apart from Reza, we were alone.

"I just have to do that piece above the cupboard," he said. "You can go in if you want to do something in the kitchen."

"I have to feed Reza. Are you hungry?"

"I will be when I'm done. In about half an hour."

"Okay. I've got roast chicken and potatoes. I'll just see to Reza. He usually has a nap after lunch. I want to make a small salad. Do you eat mushrooms?"

"I'm a Grassy Parker. I eat everything."

I smiled. "Okay then."

I went about the kitchen with my son on my hip, washing greens and setting out plates. While the food warmed, I made Reza's bottle, aware of Imran working behind me. Finally, he was done painting and went outside to stand under a cold spray. When he came back in, he had changed out of his working clothes, and was in jeans again. By this time Reza had finished eating and was in his crib. I dished up a platter of chicken and potatoes, and brought the salad from the fridge. We carried the food out to an old wooden table in the yard.

"It looks great," he said. "I don't know what was the matter with that husband of yours that he didn't appreciate your cooking."

"He appreciated my cooking. It was me he didn't appreciate."

"He was stupid."

"I suppose he had his reasons."

We sat down. Imran dug in right away. I dished up a little salad and watched him enjoy the food. It wasn't like before. There was an awareness now. A static between us.

"Six cents for your thoughts," he said.

"It'll cost more than that."

He kicked me under the table. I kicked back. We laughed.

There was silence again.

"What are we going to do, Beeda?"

"We can't do anything."

"I want to be with you. Don't tell me I can't be with you." He got up and came around to my side of the table, and drew me out of the chair. He held me up against him. My heart beat like a frightened rabbit in my chest.

"I've fallen in love with you, Beeda."

I was swept up by the moment. My body felt weak, my head swam. I could hear children's voices on the other side of the wall, the hum of traffic further away on Kromboom Road. His mouth was inches from mine. He kissed me. To tell you about that first kiss . . . oh God. I had never been kissed like that.

"I love you," he said.

I kissed him again.

"Can we go inside?"

He led me into the bedroom. Reza was asleep in his crib. I was wearing a peasant skirt with fringes that was popular at the time. He drew me towards him and nibbled at my ear. His breath was hot in my neck, his hands weaving through my long hair. He tweaked the tip of my nose with his teeth, nibbled my lips, and ran the tip of his tongue along the inside.

"Take off your top," he said, releasing me.

I moved my hair out of the way and untied the string at the back while he sat on the bed and watched. There was nothing hurried about my movements. He watched me slide the top over my head, watched me unclasp my bra. Then he reached forward and touched one of my breasts. It was like I'd waited my whole life for his touch.

The rest of what happened that afternoon belongs to me alone. I call it up when I want to remember and feel again what it was like to float over the edge and be taken outside of myself. But I betrayed my sister that day.

Later, when we were outside waiting for my children to come home, we were respectable again.

"Zulpha called last night," he said.

"What did you tell her?"

"My mother took the message. I haven't called her back."

I thought of my sister, who'd always been good to me. "Do you know what my mother said to me on Friday? She said that Zulpha had never been married before, and I had four children already. I can't be with you, Imran. Go to Zulpha and forget me."

"I can't." He reached forward to pick up one of the children's toys. "Things have changed. How can I go to her now when I feel like this about you?"

John's office was tiny – a small round table, two chairs, and his briefcase at his feet. There were no books, no pictures on the wall, nothing to take away from the sterility of the lemon walls. It was in a treatment centre and probably a room used by counselors for all kinds of substance and emotional abuse. John was in his early forties. I, a Muslim woman of forty-nine, was going to talk to a white man about my gambling.

"You are probably shocked to see a woman like me in your office," I said.

"Not at all. I see all kinds of people in here." He had an easy manner and sat back in his chair, waiting for me to talk.

"It was hard for me to come here," I started. "Do you know anything about my religion, John? Our Book says clearly that it's a sin to gamble, yet I do it."

He nodded.

"I've won more than I've lost, but I don't like the thought that I might be a gambler."

He smiled at my use of the word might.

"I go because I have fun. The casino is like an amusement park for me. I have a smoke and a coffee, and I forget my troubles on the machines. Is there such a thing as normal gambling?"

"There is, but usually the people who come to see me aren't normal gamblers. A normal gambler is someone who can go to the casino, spend a hundred rand, and go home. They can take it or leave it. Does your religion make allowances for normal gamblers?"

"No. Gambling is gambling. But I think once you hear what I have to say, you will come up with a new kind of gambler."

"I doubt it," he laughed.

I liked John and found it easy to talk to him. And no one was going to know what we talked about. I told him about my visits to the casino, the thing that happened with Rhoda, and what had just happened that morning.

"So you have lost a friend already," he said.

"She lost me."

"Was she not a worthwhile friend?"

"She was."

"And you have lost money. You've discovered you have no control."

"Is that what you call it?"

"Yesterday you lost thirteen hundred rand. This morning you lost over two thousand. That's three thousand three hundred rand that you've given to the casino. That's compulsive gambling."

His words hurt.

"Tell me how it felt after you lost your last hundred."

"Do we have to talk about that?"

"Yes."

"Horrible. I was disgusted with myself."

"You felt worthless," he added.

"Yes. At that point it wasn't money any more, just numbers on a card. I wanted to make the numbers go up. It didn't."

"And you couldn't stop. Anything else?"

"I felt dirty. Like a loser. I hate losers."

He didn't say anything. He only looked at me. Finally, he deemed it the right moment to say something again. "Do you want to stop?"

"I think so."

"You have to be sure."

"Yes."

"All right. It's not going to be easy. Gambling's an addiction. But this is how it works. You get six free sessions of one hour each. You'll do an inventory of all the money you've borrowed, cheques you've written, money you've lost."

"I haven't borrowed any money, or written cheques."

"That's good. I will ask you to write out four incidents that have affected you as a result of gambling. I want the incidents and I want the consequences. In other words, you went with two hundred, you lost it, you went to the ATM machine and took out more money. You lost that too. In the end you couldn't pay your telephone account. That's a consequence."

"That sounds like homework, John."

"It's confronting your weakness, making you see what you've done. Compulsive gambling is a disease, and it's progressive. That means it gets worse with time. You can't cure it, but you can arrest it. The only way to beat it is to stop. You need to replace it with something else. Do you have a spiritual life?"

I laughed. "I wouldn't be dressed like this if I didn't." It was a silly thing to say because spirituality had little to do with how one dressed. But I was sure he understood what I meant.

"I will ask you to go to your higher power. I'll also ask you to consider going to Gamblers Anonymous."

"I don't think I can do that," I said right away. "It's one thing sitting here talking to you, we're alone. It would be a shocking shame for a woman like me to be seen there."

"More shocking than being seen in a casino? Already you're telling me what you don't want to do, Abeeda. Is the embarrassment greater than how you feel after having lost?"

"No, but I don't think I'm so bad that I have to go to Gamblers Anonymous. Maybe I should be sitting in a psychologist's office, finding out *why* I'm gambling. There must be a reason for it. I've never bought a lottery or a raffle ticket in my life."

He shifted his position in his swivel chair to look even more intently at me. "Let me tell you the difference between going to a psychologist and coming here. The approach is completely different. At a psychologist's office, the patient is under the bed and the psychologist is coaxing him out, asking him about his feelings, his childhood. Here, you're *on* the bed, and *you're* doing the work. You don't have six years to find out why you're gambling. It doesn't matter why you're doing it, you have to stop."

I fidgeted in my chair. "Perhaps I was in too much of a rush to come here. Ramadan starts tomorrow. I'm very good during this month. The casino won't see me at all."

"Your religion is a serious matter to you?"

"Yes."

"Why isn't it enough then to keep you from the casino at other times?"

"I don't know."

"And you don't have to know. All you have to know is that you're a compulsive gambler. You're addicted to gambling. Stopping for a month is not a victory. It's like the alcoholic who says he can abstain for a month, and the day after, goes on a binge. That's not stopping."

I got up. "Look, I'm glad I came to see you. I've taken the first step. I appreciate your time and what you've told me. Can I see how I feel after Ramadan? If I can stay away from the casino for a month, maybe I can stay away forever."

"By all means. Staying away will be the only way."

I walked to the door. "What do I do when I get the urge?"

He smiled. "Don't have the conversation. You know the one. Should I go, shouldn't I go, I only have a hundred rand, I'm just going for fun, I won't go to the ATM. Stop having the conversation."

I left John's office, glad that I'd made contact. But the thought that I might be a compulsive gambler, and that it would get worse, scared me. I was so disturbed by the thought I vowed never to set foot in a casino again. Besides the money I lost, I didn't want to be seen as a gambler, and end up like those pathetic losers one saw hanging around the track.

I spent the afternoon in bed, and started my devotions in the evening by going to mosque. It was the night before Ramadan, the first night of tarawih prayers. The mosque was full. I saw a dozen women I knew. The imam's talk on the holiness of the month was inspirational. I drew strength from my surroundings and emerged from the mosque feeling hopeful and renewed. I went home, set my alarm for 4.15 a.m., and slid into bed. At dawn I was up and started my first day of fasting.

The day went beautifully, and that evening I broke fast by myself. It was a long-standing habit I had, to be alone the first night. I had a quiet and simple supper, after which I went to mosque. By the third day of Ramadan, I had put great distance between myself and my addiction.

On the Friday, I got a frantic call from Garaatie, asking me if I was busy, she wanted to come and see me.

"Of course," I said. "Come around four, then you can stay and eat with me. Just butternut soup and samoosas. We can go to tarawih together."

"I need a place, Beeda. I'm leaving Mahmood. I need a place to stay for a few days."

This got my attention. I told her to come over right away. Garaatie arrived with an overnight bag. I couldn't make her tea or offer her anything because we were fasting. I led her inside to the lounge where the sofa was comfortable and it wasn't too hot. "What happened?" I asked, taking a seat opposite her.

"The airline tickets," she said flatly. "I called the travel agency. The other ticket's for Moena. When Mahmood came home from work, I told him what I'd found out." Garaatie put her hands to her face and started to weep. "He told me he was getting married. He was going to Malaysia for his honeymoon."

"What?" Even I had not thought that he would actually do it.

"Just like that. I'm taking a second wife, Garaatie. You must think about what you want to do."

The worst words a woman could hear from a man. I went to sit next to her.

"I have such a headache, Beeda. All morning I've been crying. I didn't want to call you and didn't want to call any of my children. My sons will feel sorry for me, but will tell me that their father has rights. What about *my* rights? What about my right to feel safe, and protected, and loved? Is this love?"

I felt sorry for her. I knew what it was like to lose out to another woman. And for it to happen during Ramadan.

"What're you going to do?" I asked.

"I don't know."

"Are you going to stay with him? Be a first wife?"

"I don't know. I want to leave."

"You want to leave, or you just say you want to leave? You're not going to win this one with him, Garaatie. He's talking marriage. And if he's going for his honeymoon after Ramadan, that means he's getting married in the next three weeks. That means her family knows. And maybe your children too."

"My children? Don't be daft. They would've told me. How can you say such a thing?"

I didn't want to comment on Garaatie's sons. They were good boys, but were very much their father's children. This was the difference between my sons and hers. Mine had been raised with a single set of rules. Hers had been raised with conflicting opinions. Sulaiman, the eldest, had the same single-mindedness as his father.

"Do you know what he said to me when I asked him if he really believed that God didn't take women's feelings into account? He had the audacity to say that God had created women differently from men. Our hormones made us weak and irrational. I said that that would be an unfair God, and God wasn't unfair. I said, let's assume that I was allowed to have another husband and went off four nights a week. Are you telling me that your emotions are different, and that you won't feel rejected and hurt? He laughed and said, God knew that men needed a lot of sex. That's why the Book talks about adultery. So to avoid adultery, you marry the woman. Men have healthy appetites and need more than one woman to satisfy them."

"What a load of shit." I had listened to Garaatie's stories about her husband for years and had never said outright what I thought of him. "I don't believe this man can be so stupid. You married an asshole, Garaatie. It's idiots like him that give Islam a bad name. What did you say?"

"I threw my jewelry box at him. Bangles and necklaces and pearls rolled all over the floor. That was just the excuse he needed. He left the house saying I was mad. I spent an hour picking up the beads and lay in bed the whole night crying. This morning he came home before faj'r to have a shower, and told me to think about what I was going to do. I'm scared, Beeda."

"What're you scared of?"

"I don't want to be alone. I'm not tough like you. Look how long you've been alone. You like the way things are. I don't know if I can live like that. Your relationship with your children also. They visit you. Adiel comes, but he doesn't come often enough. The other one again, comes once a year with his wife and children to do his duty, like on Eid, or my birthday. Otherwise I don't see him. I don't want to be like one of those overlooked women that other women feel sorry for. I'm too old to start over."

"For God's sake, Garaatie, a man isn't the answer to everything. You're younger than me, there's a whole life out there for you still. You have a lot of things going for you. And your community work – doesn't that give you satisfaction? You came here with your overnight bag. Have you changed your mind already?"

"I've never been alone," she wailed. "I've not been with another man. I came straight from my mother's house to his. He can't do this to me. What are people going to say?"

I realised that Garaatie was never going to change. For all her suffering, she needed a man to validate who she was. She had no identity of her own. She was nothing if not someone's wife or mother. She'd come with an overnight bag, but it was only a show for Mahmood. It was her last card. This was supposed to make him regretful, and change his mind.

"Worrying about what people are going to say, should be your last concern, Garaatie. And stop saying, he can't do this to me. He did it. Stop comparing his integrity with yours. The man has no conscience. As far as staying with me, you can stay with me as long as you want, but you have to be careful now that you don't lose your house."

"I thought you would be glad that I'm leaving him."

"You're not leaving him, Garaatie. You came here with your bag, but you're crying about being alone. Leaving him doesn't mean a physical separation only. And this isn't about me, what I would be glad about. It's about you. What you think of yourself. What you want. How you want to spend the rest of your life now that you know. All I'm going to say is, don't lose your house. Mahmood's going to marry that girl. You can't change that. But you don't have to drop to your knees and spread out your goods like a beggar for him to pick from. What I'm saying is, you can stay here, but if you leave your house now, you'll end up living with one of your sons. Think about it. He's told you his intentions. Lose *him*. Don't lose perspective."

Garaatie stayed with me until maghrib. By the time we broke our fast, I had her headache. We talked some more. She decided not to sleep over, and returned to her house. She was hardly home when my phone rang again.

"He was here while I was gone," she said. "His cupboard's empty. And three of the suitcases are gone."

"That was his move, Garaatie. What's yours?"

"I'll have to call Sulaiman and Adiel."

"That's a good start. Talk to your boys. And remember, you can't blame them for what their father's done." I was about to invite her to break fast with me again the next evening, but remembered that my own children were coming, and didn't want her there with Patrick and Reza.

I said goodbye to her and promised to speak with her again in the morning. Garaatie's troubles had unsettled me. I didn't go to mosque. After my last prayers, I ran a bath, put lots of apricot bath salts into the hot water and soaked myself. I had been up since before dawn and was exhausted. From the bath I stepped into the shower, then climbed wearily into bed with a book Rhoda had given me. I didn't get to the end of the page.

The next morning I was woken up by the telephone.

"Beeda, it's me."

"Garaatie? Oh my God, what time is it?"

"It's ten past eight. Didn't you get up for faj'r?"

"I forgot to set the alarm."

"I'm depressed, Beeda. I've decided I don't want the house. I mean, what would I do in the house by myself? I'd rather live with a friend."

I groaned. I had overslept and had had nothing to drink or eat. Garaatie was going to aggravate me on an empty stomach.

"How can you say you don't want the house? Are you nuts? You're forty-five, Garaatie. Your life hasn't ended. Get a grip."

"I'm scared, Beeda. I didn't sleep at all last night. It's lonely in this big house."

"I know, and I know how that feels, but you can be lonely in a house full of people too. Think, please. You can always get someone to stay with you. A boarder, a friend. Make this work for you. Don't do something you'll regret. You might even be happy. Did you think about that? Husbands are good to have if they're good husbands, but women can be happy on their own too. Are you scared to be happy?"

"Don't be silly. Who doesn't want to be happy?

"So there. You have three options. You take the easy way out and beg him to come back, and maybe he does, and maybe he doesn't, but you're always going to have him sniffing around after other women. It's his nature. Or you allow him to take this woman as his second wife, and share him. Maybe he'll be fairer to you than he was when he had to go behind your back. Maybe you'll even be fine with this arrangement. Or you walk away and cut yourself off completely. You know nothing, and you ask nothing, and you move on with your life."

There was silence.

"Are you there?"

"I'm listening. Are you going to be home today?"

"I'm going out this morning to pick up a few things. My kids are coming for supper. I always have them over for iftaar the first Saturday night in Ramadan."

"You're lucky to have these get-togethers with your kids," she said.

"You can have them too, Garaatie. Call up your sons. Invite them. If I have time, I'll pop in at your house after the supermarket for a few minutes."

"I'm going to wait. I want to discuss something with you."

When Garaatie wanted to *discuss* something with me, it was usually something she didn't dare bring up on the telephone for fear I would lose my patience and hang up.

"What do you want to discuss?" I asked.

"We'll talk about it when you get here," she said. "Remember that man I told you about, who helped Rugaya?"

"For God's sake, you're not going to a doekoem."

"He's not a doekoem, he's a herbalist."

"If he did that thing for Rugaya, he's a doekoem. You know what I think about doekoems. Jy willie hoor nie. Have you forgotten what happened to your cousin in Salt River? She went to the doekoem to fix that boyfriend who couldn't make up his mind, and in the end she married the doekoem."

"If you're going to be like that, I'll drop it."

"Drop it, Garaatie. A doekoem can't fix your husband. Your husband has to fix himself. Let him go, for fuck's sake. See there? You made me swear during the holy month."

"You just like to swear, Beeda. Don't say I made you do it. Anyway, Rhoda wanted me to remind you about the seven nights on Monday."

Mention of Rhoda's name changed my mood further. I couldn't think of her without thinking of the ten thousand rand. "Did you tell her your troubles?"

"She has her own. There're problems with Shehnaz's will."

"What do you mean?"

Garaatie was reluctant to talk. "Well, the bulk of it goes to Moegsien and the son, but Shehnaz had other property. She and Rhoda, being only children, had inherited two properties in Constantia from their father. Rhoda had sold hers and used the money. Shehnaz had renovated hers and rented it out. The property's to be sold, and a big chunk is to go to Rhoda. On Saturday it was discovered that the will hadn't been signed by two witnesses."

"Oh my word."

"Basically she died without a will. Moegsien can take it all for himself and his son."

"Not if he has a conscience. Surely, you're not suggesting – and as the executor he can instruct the lawyers to do the right thing. It's clear what his wife wanted."

Garaatie didn't respond.

"Life is strange," I said. "Talk about poetic justice."

"What do you mean?"

"Nothing." But I was thinking of how Rhoda had gypped *me* out of money.

"I also spoke to my sons last night. Their father *had* said something to them. Sulaiman said I had to accept it. He's very cut and dried about these things. Adiel was more understanding. He also said what you said, that I mustn't leave the house."

"See? There'll always be that one who'll have his mother's interests at heart. Did they say when he will be getting married?"

"After Ramadan. But if it's only after Ramadan, where's he gone now with his clothes?"

I didn't want to voice my opinion, but what I thought was, skunk that he was, he wouldn't go and live openly with the girl, especially during the holy month, and was probably married already.

I said goodbye to Garaatie and told her that if time allowed, I would drop in. Oversleeping had messed up my system, and made me grumpy. A whole day without water wasn't going to be easy, and Garaatie's call hadn't helped. The phone rang just as I was about to leave the house.

It was Reza, sounding very tired. "You won't believe me if I tell you, Mummy . . . we were going to come, both of us . . ."

"What's wrong?"

"I'm feeling very weak today. I hope you're not going to mind."

"I'm disappointed. I was looking forward to it. Are you fasting?"

"I did yesterday."

"You mustn't fast if you're not well. God doesn't want that. Do you have food?"

He gave a little laugh. "There's always food, Ma. Not your wonderful delights, but there's food. Patrick's quite handy in the kitchen."

"I'm making roast lamb and potatoes for supper," I said. "I'll bring you some tomorrow."

"Thanks, Ma. And Patrick says hi. He wants to speak to you."

Patrick took a few moments before he came on the line. "Mrs A? How are you?"

"I'm fine, Patrick. And you? Is everything all right there?"

"Everything's all right," he said. "I'm talking to you from the other line. Reza! Put the phone down!" he called out.

I heard the line click in my ear. He came back to me. "I just wanted to tell you that Reza couldn't stand up this morning."

I felt a jolt to my heart.

"He tried to get out of bed, and he couldn't. I've called the doctor. We're waiting for him to arrive. He can stand, but he can't stand, if you know what I mean. He's weak."

"I'm coming through now."

"Please. He's saying to you that he's not feeling well, but it's more than that."

I said goodbye to Patrick.

*Please, God, let there be nothing wrong.* My whole schedule had been interfered with. There was the shopping to be done, the food to be prepared for that night's supper, and I hadn't had a drop of water since the previous night. I felt dehydrated and moody – not a good combination – and sorely missed my helper, Margaret, who'd gone home to Somerset East for a month to tend to her son who'd been shot.

I got in the car and drove to Sea Point. I couldn't get there fast enough.

When Patrick opened the door to the flat he told me immediately. "You just missed the doctor. Reza's got a chest infection."

"Is it pneumonia?"

"He didn't say so, but I think it is. He's coming again tomorrow."

"But Reza was fine when I saw him."

"Not really. He pretends. He's lost twenty kilos."

"I didn't know it was as much as that. This infection is serious, isn't it?" He looked at me.

"You mustn't keep anything from me, Patrick. I'm his mother."

"I won't. I don't know anything more. But, yes, it's serious."

I followed him down the passage to the last room on the right. The flat was quiet. A room I passed was taken up with computers, monitors, tripods and lights. Another man was sitting there working on the computer.

I entered the bedroom. The room pulled me right into my son's life; a photograph of him and Patrick on the dresser, two nightgowns over the back of a chair. A king-size bed.

Reza was curled up on his side on the left side of the bed. I stood looking at him for a few moments – the full lips, the sunken cheekbones, the bony shoulders poking through the pyjamas. A thought came to me cold and calm, without panic. My son was going to die. His life was going to end as quietly as it had begun. He was going to leave me.

All my children were special to me, but this was my baby. The only one of my sons who'd never sat on his father's lap. His father hadn't been there, and Reza, even as a toddler, had never wanted to go with his brothers to visit him. He was the one who sat with me in the kitchen at night, when I was baking my last batch of pies or icing that last cake, when the house was quiet and his brothers were asleep. He was the one who'd gone shopping with me, who'd let his friends practise haircuts and hairstyles on me, and who'd always, when coming home after his parties, come and talked to me in my room. I never went to sleep until all my children had arrived home from wherever they'd been.

"Tell him I was here," I whispered to Patrick. "I'll bring him some food tomorrow."

Patrick walked with me to the front door. He looked at me awkwardly.

"Is something wrong, Patrick?"

"I don't know how to tell you this."

"What?"

"He told me this morning that when the time comes he doesn't want to leave from here."

I drove back to Rondebosch East with a heavy heart. My enthusiasm for the family get-together that evening was gone. I went to the fruit and vegetable place, the supermarket, and ran into an old friend, Mymoena, at the bakery who'd just got the news that her husband who was in Mecca, had died of pneumonia. He was a healthy man, there had been nothing wrong with him. Her brother-in-law had told her it was the cold air-conditioning, then going out into the sweltering heat, then coming back in again. I felt sorry for her, losing her husband like that. People wanted to die in Mecca, but no one wanted to lose a loved one.

By the time I arrived home it was close to six. Iftaar was at a quarter to eight. I put a leg of lamb into the oven, and got busy. I made savoury rice, put the chicken pies out on a pastry sheet, fried the spring rolls, set the table in the dining room. I was crying. My life wasn't exactly the way I'd told Garaatie. There were moments when I was contented and happy with things the way they were, and then there were times when I needed very much for someone to be there and love me. I wasn't different from any other person when it came to the need to be loved. But the love I'd had, I could never have, and would never find again. I had used my faith to learn to accept it.

By the time my sons arrived with their families at seven, my smile was back, but my spirit muted. We broke our fast with dates and spring rolls and chicken pies and made salaah together in the front room.

"Is Mummy all right?" Sawdah asked.

"Yes," Munier added. "Mummy's quiet tonight."

I looked at my sons around the table. Sawdah and Sadia had just set down platters of masala fish and seafood breyani. Everyone brought a dish with them to iftaar, and the table brimmed with food. I glanced at the smaller table nearby where my five grandchildren had their own platters and their own conversation. They couldn't hear us talk.

"I went to see Reza this afternoon," I said.

"How is he?" Munier asked.

"He couldn't stand up this morning."

"But Marwaan and I just saw him here the other day, he was fine."

"That was then. This morning he couldn't get out of bed. He's got a chest infection."

"A chest infection? That's not good. Is it pneumonia? That's what usually happens."

Looks passed around the table. "I'm hoping it's not," I said. "I didn't speak to him. The doctor had been already when I got there, he was asleep." I turned to Zane. "He misses you."

Zane looked down at his plate.

"I wouldn't like you to leave things the way they are."

"We've never been close," Zane said.

"That's a reason not to see him? He needs his brothers now. Can't you be a brother to him?"

"He's never allowed Zane to be a brother to him," Rabia chimed in.

I looked at her. She just didn't know when to keep quiet. "This is family business, and between the brothers. Ssshhh."

Rabia picked up the serviette next to her plate and dabbed at her lips. The others didn't look at her.

"It's not that I don't care," Zane answered. "He's never really come to me for anything. When he was small, he was more with Munier and Marwaan than with me, they were the brothers. And he's Mummy's favourite. Everything that was wrong with him, Mummy attended to. And always there were excuses for him. The trouble he got into when he bunked school. When he took off to Port Elizabeth without telling us. The fuss when it was his birthday. Even his condition, if you want to call it that. Yet, I was the one who had to give up a lot of things. Who made a fuss of me?"

His words drove a knife into my heart. I looked around, at the other faces at the table. They were as surprised to hear these emotions come pouring out. Zane had never voiced any of this before. I never knew of these feelings. And it wasn't entirely true. I *was* guilty of some things, but Zane was my first born, and first children were much awaited. You waited for months for this first experience, this first child that was going to have ten fingers and ten toes and look like you. He was my most reliable son, and I loved him in a way that perhaps was different than my love for my other children. I looked at him now, so young still, just turned thirty, and so responsible. How had I missed these feelings? I wanted to throw my arms about him, and say how utterly sorry I was that in my zealousness to protect his younger brother, I'd sometimes overlooked him – that I loved him, and that he'd always been my pillar of strength. But the words were stuck in my throat. I was close to tears.

"The lamb's good," Munier said.

"Yes? How about some mint jelly to go with it? I have some in the fridge." I got up and went to my room.

I sat on the bed and looked at myself in the mirror; a tired woman. I lay down and buried my face in the pillow.

There was a knock on the door. "Can I come in?"

"Yes."

Zane came in and sat next to me. "I'm sorry," he said. "I didn't mean for it to come out like that. I'm so sorry."

"You had to say it." I put my arm around him. I hadn't held him in ages. "And you're right. I was overprotective of Reza, and sometimes forgot that you needed me too. The twins had each other. You were always the eldest brother, the boeta. We all took you for granted. I'm so sorry. Mothers too make mistakes. They don't come with a manual, they just do and hope for the best. I'm sorry if I've neglected you, my baby. Can you forgive me?"

"There's nothing to forgive, Ma. It all just came out like that. I didn't know it was going to." He took my hands into his. "I love Reza, even though it doesn't look that way. But I also wanted him to come to me sometimes, to include me. I know that he can't help what he is. I know all that. But it doesn't make it easier for me to deal with. Many times I wanted to see where he lived and what he did, but I couldn't bring myself to do it. Long ago I saw one of his films and was proud when I saw his name at the end: Reza Ariefdien – Director. I've always wanted to be close to him, and have him talk to me, but he's never made me feel that he wanted to be close to me. It shocked me tonight when I heard that he missed me."

"He does. Very much."

"When's Mummy going to see him again?"

"Tomorrow. I'll go every day now. Your father's coming with me on Wednesday. And there's something else. I didn't mention it at the table. He told Patrick that when the time comes, he doesn't want to leave from there."

It took Zane a moment to understand. Then his arms went about me and held me tight. "Don't cry, Ma. I'll come with you tomorrow. Maybe it *is* time for him to come home."

I kissed him on the forehead. "I love you, Zane. You've always been my number one son. I mean it."

And I did mean it. I had a number one son, a favourite son, and double treasures.

I didn't see Imran until Wednesday when Zulpha called me from the office in the afternoon and said that she and Imran wanted to come and talk to me.

"Is something wrong?" I asked.

"It's Imran. I never saw him at all last week. He never called me, he never came to the house like he usually does, and he didn't return any of my messages. On Monday night I went to see him. He was having supper with his mother, and I asked him what was going on, if there was a problem between us. He said he'd been busy and was going to call me to discuss something. We went into the living room and he told me that he thinks we're rushing things, and that he wants to be on his feet financially before he takes on a wife. I couldn't believe it. This has never come up. And he is on his feet. He has contracts lined up until the end of the year, and his business is doing well. I make good money too. I reminded him of all of this. Money had never been an issue."

"What did he say?"

"Nothing that convinced me that we should wait. He had no real argument. And he seemed strange towards me. I think he's got cold feet."

"But the wedding's not off?"

"I don't know. I mean, we've got the hall booked for March. We've had the invitations printed. He went round and round in circles, talking about having a solid foundation before we start. It's not the truth. I know it isn't. I suggested to him that we come and see you. I know he respects your opinion. Maybe you can reassure him that he's worrying for nothing."

"Okay."

I replaced the receiver and put on the kettle for tea. I felt low. I was responsible for Imran's behaviour. He had cooled towards Zulpha. He had not gone to see her. And Zulpha had marched right over to his house and demanded an explanation. It wasn't wrong considering that they were engaged, but I would never have done such a thing. If a man had reservations and stayed away, that was what he had to do. It was better than

103

going through with something and getting hurt. I hadn't expected that my sister had it in her to do that. But I understood why. She feared being jilted again. It wasn't an experience anyone wanted. It was painful. Any loss hurt. You were undesirable if you got jilted. And Zulpha was far from that. She was educated, smart and quite stunning.

But with all my feelings of guilt and remorse, I also couldn't understand why I had to deny myself. Imran didn't love her. He loved me. Two people would be unhappy instead of one. Two people would pine forever for one another. And one would live in a contrived state of happiness. But how could I hurt my own sister?

The afternoon passed quickly. I dreaded the evening to come. When the doorbell rang at seven-thirty, I was apprehensive. I never wore a scarf in those days, but had just finished my evening prayers, and had one on, tied at the back of my head. I didn't want to be in jeans and a sweater when they arrived.

Imran came in behind Zulpha. One glance told me all I wanted to know.

I made tea, and put out some biscuits. Zulpha did all the talking. She seemed nervous, and went all over the place; from the office function that had made her late, to my mother's diagnosis at the doctor's that afternoon. Our mother was an asthmatic, and had now also been told that she had low blood pressure and had to watch her sugar.

Finally, she came to the point. "Imran wants to put the wedding on hold for a year," she said. "He wants the business to pick up before he takes on the responsibility of marriage. I don't understand. We have everything."

I looked at Imran. "Marriage is a big responsibility," he said. "Fixing a crack in the wall is better than having the whole thing tumble down."

Zulpha's eyebrows shot up. "A crack in the wall?" Her voice rose a little. "I didn't know we had problems. Maybe you want to explain that. We've had the invitations printed. I gave a thousand rand deposit for my wedding dress. Don't talk like a builder. Tell me what that means."

Imran opened his mouth to say something, then stopped.

"Say it," she insisted.

Imran looked ready to come clean with the whole thing. My heart sat in my throat, fearing his response.

"I feel bad about it, Zulpha, and that's the truth. But you want both of us to be happy, don't you?"

She looked at him. "You're not happy?"

"I didn't say that."

"Well, what is it then? Why don't you just tell me the real reason for all of this. You've been very distant these past three weeks. Is it another woman?"

I didn't dare look at Imran.

"I just need you to ease off a bit," he said. "The pressure is too much."

"Pressure?" She became quiet and looked down at her hands. "Do you want to back out of what we have?"

"Listen, Zulpha–"

"Answer me," she said quietly. Her voice had taken on a distant tone.

"I don't want to hurt you. I like you a lot."

"You like me?" She dropped her head like a broken little doll, and sat slumped in the chair. "We're engaged, and you *like* me?"

I looked at Imran. Imran didn't know where to look.

Finally, Zulpha turned to him. Her eyes had that look of someone who had just been dealt a devastating blow. "I'm releasing you from the engagement, Imran. You're free."

"Listen . . . "

"I don't want to listen," she said. "I don't have to listen any more." She got up to indicate that the discussion was over. "Don't worry about taking me home. Beeda will."

Imran glanced at me. I didn't walk him to the door. A few minutes later we heard the van pull out of the driveway.

"That's it," she said. "It's over. All those promises, all those feelings. All for nothing."

I was lost for words. I hadn't even poured the tea, and the whole thing had unraveled in five minutes, like a newly knitted bonnet.

Zulpha started to cry. I put my arms around her. What could I say? We had both lost. Only I had to live with the guilt. I made her a cup of tea, and we talked. I don't know what we talked about. When I took her home and she got out of the car, she turned to me and said, "I won't tell Mummy yet. When you see her on Friday, don't say anything."

I drove home with a stone in my heart.

The next afternoon, I was busy taking washing off the line, when Imran's bakkie pulled into the driveway. I stopped with sheets and pillowcases flung over my shoulder. I hadn't expected to see him, and had thought that after what had happened, he would stay away.

"How're you?" he asked, walking up to me.

"As you see. Not happy."

"Me neither. I feel dreadful about the whole thing. I couldn't sleep last night. I felt so sorry for Zulpha." He took some washing from me. "But I can't lie to myself, Beeda. I can't lie about how I feel. I'm not letting you go."

A rush went through me. "How can I be anything to you now? It would kill her. I can't continue."

"And I can't be with someone I don't love." He pulled a sheet over my head and drew me towards him. "I love you," he said, kissing me through the sheet. "Don't you feel anything for me?"

"You know the answer."

"Then tell me how I can have you."

The words had a bewitching effect. "You can't."

"I *will* have you, Beeda."

The washing dropped to the grass, and we kissed. The kiss had urgency and passion, and we knew as we stood there leaning into each other amongst the billowing sheets, that we were struggling upstream – that we would never be able to have a home together, that we would never be able to go out in public and hold hands. Yet, we couldn't stop. Logic has no chance against desire. While my sister's face faded before me, we tumbled around on the sheets on the lawn.

Afterwards, we washed off under the tap. There was no time for a shower. My sons would soon be home from school. We had coffee and a smoke, and he reached into his pocket and took out a small blue box. I watched him open it. Inside was a thin gold band. He took it out and slipped it on my right hand. "In friendship."

I looked up at him. "If we continue with this, we're both skunks."

"I fell in love with you, Beeda. How fair will that be to your sister?"

It was time for him to get back to the site. I watched him reverse the van out of the driveway. I thought of Adam and Eve, and the apple. This was the bite. Was I going to be doomed to a life of suffering?

When my mother came the following morning to help with the orders and to look after Reza, she told me that Zulpha hadn't gone to work. It was the second day now.

"Why not?"

"I don't know, but I know something's up. They came to see you on Wednesday night. What happened?"

"Mummy must ask her."

"Is the engagement off?"

"I don't know. Really. They haven't told me."

She was silent for a while, sipping on her tea. She turned to look at me at the counter preparing Reza's bottle. "Imran finished the kitchen."

"Yes."

"Toeghieda told me. She was here, she said. Have you seen him again?"

My mother was a trick questioner. No one could back you in a corner like her. "On Wednesday night, when they came here."

"Not since then?"

"No."

She helped me pack the pies, and wrap the rooties. "I don't want to be away from the house too long today. I want you to come back as soon as you can."

"Okay. The auction usually lasts until three, but I'll come back as soon as I've sold everything. What happened at the doctor's? Zulpha said something about low blood pressure."

"Yes. I'm always tired. The other day I was at a friend's house for supper, and I felt so tired, I couldn't keep my head up. I had to ask them if I could lie down. When I woke up, I felt better, but a bit weak. They gave me some Coke, and I had all my energy back again. I might be a diabetic. I'm waiting for the results. In the meantime I have to cut out those snacks I'm having, and take half a Disprin."

"Is Mummy taking Disprins?"

"Aagh. What can half a Disprin do? I don't have any pain. But I've cut out the crisps and the chocolates."

I packed the pies and the rooties in the car, and came back in for my bag. "Reza's bottle is ready for when he wakes up. Mummy can mix in a little mince with his mash."

"Don't worry," she said. "Drive carefully."

I was gone for three hours. My business was flourishing and I was asked to bring even more rooties the following week. I took orders, collected outstanding monies, and added koeksisters to my list.

I was back in my driveway at a quarter to three. The children weren't home from school yet, but I knew the moment I opened the car door and heard the baby howling inside the house, that something was wrong. I left the cake tins in the car, and went hurriedly in through the back. On the kitchen floor, blocking my way to the bedroom, was my mother, lying face down, with the baby's bowl and the food splattered on the floor.

My heart pumped in my ears. I kneeled down and felt for a pulse in her wrist. I couldn't feel anything. I moved one eyelid. Nothing stared back. Oh God, I begged. Not my mother. I didn't know what to do first. I ran into the bedroom and took Reza out of the crib, and tried to still him as I dialed my sister's number.

"Zulpha! Call an ambulance right away! I came home now and found Mummy on the kitchen floor! Now, please!"

An hour later, both my sisters stood with me in the yard as we watched Mylie and Imran carry my mother out of the house. She had come in the front seat of Zulpha's car, and was leaving in a blanket, in the back of a van. Imran was the one with a van. Toeghieda had wasted no time calling him. "My mother died of a stroke, Imran. We need a bakkie."

My children and I got into my Beetle and followed the bakkie to my mother's house. Toeghieda was in her own car with her sons and with Zulpha. Mylie and Imran were in the van.

My children were quiet as we drove away. It was the first time they had seen a dead body. Zane was in the passenger seat, holding Reza. The twins were in the back, looking out of the window with sad faces.

"What's going to happen to Granny now?" Munier asked.

I thought about how I should answer him. "Granny's going to be washed first, and dressed, and then she will be buried."

"Will she go into a coffin?" Marwaan asked.

"No. Muslims don't get buried in coffins."

"Will she go to heaven?" Munier asked.

"There's no heaven in the sky or hell in the ground," Zane spoke suddenly. He hadn't said a word yet about his grandmother's death.

I looked at him; my broody son, always so serious. "What do you know about heaven?" I asked.

"There're no rivers and gardens. There's nothing up in the sky. You don't go up there. The calipha says the soul goes into barzak. It meets other souls."

I was surprised that he knew so much. "And you, Munier? What do you believe?" Both my twins were naughty, but Munier was the most mischievous.

"When you die," he said, "you can meet Allah, and eat lots of chocolates, and Allah won't make your head pain."

They all laughed. I needed to hear their laughter. The shock of losing my mother hadn't hit me yet. Everything was happening in a vacuum. I was being swept along.

At my mother's house, Toeghieda took charge. The toekamandies were on their way already. Toeghieda also called one or two people in the family and told them to inform others. Malboets – people who went around knocking on doors, giving the news – were dispatched. Everyone had his job as things had to be done right away.

Imran went to pick up the death certificate. Mylie arranged for the kafan; the burial cloth, and the planks. Zulpha and I sorted out the food. Neighbours and friends helped in the kitchen. One of the women peeling potatoes, was twenty-something-year-old Garaatie, who'd moved in next door two years earlier. I already knew who she was, but it was then that we really first talked to one another and became friends. The house was busy. My sisters and I didn't have time to stand around and console one another. We had to be in the moment, and save our grief for when we were alone.

By four-thirty the house was packed as more and more people came in to pay their respects. By five-thirty my mother was washed and shrouded and put on the bier. An hour after that she was in the ground.

The men came back to the house. Food was served. More people came and went. By isha'i that evening, the mourners were all gone, the furniture was back in their proper places, and my sisters and I sat in the kitchen with Imran and Mylie.

"I can't believe Mummy's gone," Zulpha said.

I suddenly realised that Zulpha would be alone in the house now. It had only been her and my mother and Sophie, but Sophie had left a month earlier for a job in a factory.

As if reading my thoughts, Toeghieda said, "Zulpha can't stay here alone tonight."

"I was just thinking that," I said. "I'll stay here for a few days. I'll just go home to pick up some things for the children. It's Friday, we can stay for the weekend."

Zulpha was seated next to me on the bench. "Thank you. I know this is awkward for you."

"It's not awkward. I just have to go home first."

Zulpha became weepy. "Just this morning Mummy and I were sitting here, having breakfast. She had a soft-boiled egg, and a slice of toast. I drove her to your house. I never thought I wouldn't see her alive again."

Imran was seated next to her on the other side. He offered her a white handkerchief. The handkerchief was pressed, like in my father's day. He was attentive. And Zulpha seemed to have forgotten what had happened between them. I realised that the people at the table thought that they were still engaged.

"We have to decide if we're going to have only the three nights and the seven nights," Toeghieda said, "or if we're going to have reciting every night until the seven nights."

"It's not necessary to have it every night," Mylie said. "It's up to you sisters, but it might be too much for Zulpha, who's alone now."

"It's not too much," Zulpha said, "but I think just the three nights and seven nights."

"I agree," I said. "And just the family."

"That's settled then," Toeghieda said. "I'll bring samoosas. Maybe you can make a pot of boebe, Zulpha. And you can bring some pies, Beeda. That's enough."

That night, when everyone had gone home and my children were asleep, Zulpha and I sat alone in her room, talking.

"The house feels empty," she said. "I can't bear to think of Mummy in that hole."

There was nothing I could say to make her feel better. I had been thinking the same thing. My mother with the brown hair and green eyes and pretty smile, in a white winding cloth in a half-sitting position between four sand walls. My mother who had known in her heart one sister's temptation which would cost the other.

"Let's talk of something else," I suggested. "Did you see Mylie's sister, Fakhariah's new baby? Fakhariah says they're moving to Canada in three months. They just got their visas. But she's glad the child was born here. She doesn't want one child to be South African and the other Canadian."

"They won't last there," Zulpha said. "Fakhariah won't take that cold. People who've been there talk about how cold it's there in winter. I know her. And she'll be there two months, then she'll pine for her mother. You know that mother must go everywhere with them. Even to the movies. They have no privacy. If she's not careful, she'll lose that husband. But they're leaving now, so that should take care of the mother."

We talked until late, hoping to ease some of the pain with our chatter. When she finally put out the light, I couldn't sleep. I was in my mother's house, in my mother's bed. My children were in Zulpha's room. My mother's house belonged to the three of us now. Any one of us could buy it. Toeghieda and I had our own homes and would agree for Zulpha to be its new owner. Would she want to buy it? And who would live with her?

Zane came to pick me up at the house shortly after the midday prayers at one-thirty the day following the family meeting. My helper, Margaret, was back from the Eastern Cape, and gave me my scarf at the door.

"We're going now, Margaret. Don't open the door for anyone except family. You're in charge now. If my sisters call, tell them I've gone with Zane to Sea Point. And if people come knocking for food and ask for me, just say I'm busy. Don't say I'm not here."

"Eh-weh, madam."

"Did you understand what I said, Margaret?" Margaret was hard of hearing.

"Yes, madam. Not open the door. Madam's busy. And tell the sisters."

In the car driving to Sea Point, I spoke to my son. "You haven't seen Reza in a long time," I said. "Prepare yourself. And don't show your shock when you see him."

"We should talk to him about coming home, Ma. There's no need to prolong it."

"It's not that easy. There's Patrick. We can't ignore him. Whatever we think, we have to take him into account. And it's what Reza wants."

"He said he wanted to come home."

"When he's ready."

"Are we going to wait for him to tell us?"

"Yes."

We drove for a few minutes in silence. Then he said, "Johnny said he saw you the other day."

I stiffened. "Really?"

"At the casino."

I said nothing. I watched the trees flash by on the M3.

"He's not married to Mary anymore."

"Is that so?"

"They split up six months ago."

That was it. And that was my son, Zane. He let me know that he knew,

111

but said no more about it. He didn't have to add that I'd been there in the middle of the night.

We arrived at the flat. "Park just up here, on the road," I said. The conversation had disturbed me, but there was no time for recriminations now. I felt for Zane. He wanted the right thing for his brother, and the right thing by God. But the right thing by God also meant not hurting people, and Patrick had been good to my son. If I had to stand in front of God myself one day and beg his forgiveness for this action, I didn't have it in my heart to separate Reza and Patrick until they themselves were ready to do it.

We got out. Zane looked up at the four-storey building. "So this is where he lives."

"Yes. And be nice to Patrick. He's also someone's son."

Zane looked at me. We walked up a flight of stairs to the front door. I took his hand and squeezed it. It would be the first time he would see his brother in years. I was apprehensive. I never knew what I was going to hear when their front door opened.

Patrick answered almost immediately. I could tell by his scowl that things had not improved.

"Hello, Mrs A. I'm so glad you've come."

"Hello, Patrick, this is my son Zane."

They shook hands and greeted one another.

"Dr Shapiro's with him now," Patrick said. "He had trouble breathing during the night. He's taken a bad turn."

"Can we talk to the doctor?" Zane asked.

"Of course. You have to. Let me just go in and see what's happening."

Patrick excused himself and we sat down. "He had trouble breathing," I said. "That can't be good news."

Zane said nothing. His eyes were on the passageway waiting for Patrick to return.

Eventually Patrick and the doctor came out of the room. Patrick introduced us.

Dr Shapiro greeted us, and came immediately to what he had to say. "Your son has pneumonia, Mrs Ariefdien. I want to book him into Groote Schuur, but he's not keen on going to hospital. I've arranged for him to go on a drip and to have an oxygen pump. A nurse will be here in two hours to set it up."

It was too much all at once. "An oxygen pump? It's that bad?"

"Yes."

The question that had been burning in my heart for the past week found its way out. "Is he going to die?"

"He has Aids, Mrs Ariefdien. His condition is getting worse."

"He's going to die, doctor?"

"Yes."

I sat down on the couch, and let Zane speak. "We'd like to take him home, Dr Shapiro. My brother has expressed this wish. If he's this ill, he needs to be with his family."

The doctor looked at Patrick. Patrick put his hands to his face.

We all waited. I felt sorry for Patrick. I had gotten to like him. His little earring. His quirky ways. And he loved my son. He had cared for my son. I got up and put my arms around Patrick. Patrick sobbed into my scarf. Eventually he wiped his face. "I must let him go home," he said. "It would be better for him."

"Thank you, Patrick." I had never said thank you to anyone before and meant it like I meant it at that moment.

"When do you want to move him?" the doctor asked.

"Today, when we leave, if that's possible," Zane said. "The nurse might as well come to my mother's house and set it all up there."

"That would be better, yes, than to move him later and hook him up again."

I glanced at Patrick. Patrick looked away. After a few moments, he walked silently down the passage.

"Sad business," Dr Shapiro said. He took out a business card and handed it to Zane. "These are my details. I'll need yours."

Zane took the card from him, and gave him one of his own. "Here's mine. I've written my mother's address and telephone number on the back. The account can come to me."

"He's developed some sores. You will need a nurse to come to the house every day. You can speak to her. She's from a good agency."

"Whatever is needed, doctor."

The doctor went off to make some calls. I went in search of Patrick, and found him in the room with the computers and film equipment. He was sitting on a swivel chair, staring out the window. I went to stand behind him, and followed his gaze out the window, looking at the roofs of houses and palm trees sloping down the hill, at the ocean below it. The sea glittered silver in the sun. In the distance was a steamer heading for Cape

Town harbour. Children's voices flitted by in a haze of laughter, their footsteps growing fainter on the cement stairs as they ran on into life.

I put my hand on his shoulder. Patrick lowered his face into his hands. His grief spilled out in all directions.

"You understand, don't you?"

He didn't speak immediately. "I understand, Mrs A."

"My offer still stands. You can be there."

Patrick looked up at me through his tears. "Thank you. I appreciate the offer, but I won't come to stay. I'll come and see him."

"Come and see him, Patrick," I heard my eldest son say behind me. "Any time you want."

The doctor came into the room. "I've made the arrangements," he said. "A nurse will be at your house at four, Mrs Ariefdien. I have to go. You have my card. Don't hesitate to call me."

The doctor left and we went into the bedroom to see Reza. My breath caught in my throat. He was awake, lying back on the pillow, his big dark eyes sunken in his head. His breathing was laboured. His eyes went from me to Zane. He wheezed as he strained to lift himself up.

I leaned forward and kissed him. His skin felt clammy. "Your brother's here," I said.

Zane came forward and sat down on the edge of the bed. He hugged Reza, a long, brotherly hug. "I've missed you," he said. "So much."

Reza lay back with his head on the pillow. The embrace had exhausted him. "Me too. A lot. You haven't changed," he smiled. "How's your family?"

"Don't talk," Zane said. "They're fine. When the oxygen is hooked up we can talk."

"We want to take you home today, Reza," I said.

Reza looked around. "Where's Patrick?"

"I've asked Patrick to come too. He says he won't come to stay, but he'll visit you."

"He can't leave here. There's too much work."

"You will come back with us, then?" Zane asked.

His eyes closed a little. "Yes."

Patrick came into the room and sat on the edge of the bed. It was sad what Zane and I had to witness. We made way for him and stood back. The two of them talked. Patrick held his hand. Reza lay back with his head. Tears streamed out of his closed eyes and rolled down his cheeks.

Patrick took a tissue from the box and handed it to him. Then he got up and took a leather suitcase from a top cupboard.

"I'll pack in some of his things. When I come tomorrow I'll bring the rest."

"No clothes," Reza said. "Only the books we talked about. For my mother."

Zane and I went into the living room to let them say their goodbyes. When Patrick called us to come back inside, Reza was wearing a gown over his pyjamas, and had on socks and slippers.

"He's ready."

Patrick fought back his tears as he watched Zane lift Reza up and carry him down to the car. As we followed, a different picture played itself out in my head – my son being carried out on a bier – lowered into the hole where three men were waiting. The three men were his brothers.

The moment was dark, and unforgiving. The sky had turned purple and broody while we were inside. I got into the back seat with a plastic bag of pills and ointments and powders, and a large envelope Patrick had stuck in my hand. As we drove away down High Level Road into Strand Street, I felt grim. Zane was driving. Reza was lying back in the passenger seat. It started to rain as we got onto the M3.

When we arrived at my house, the nurse was there already, talking to my sisters in the kitchen. Zane had called Zulpha and Toeghieda from the flat and told them what was happening. Margaret had let them all in. They had changed the sheets and pillowcases on the bed in the guest room, put flowers on the dresser, and a floral duvet on the bed. Zulpha had also scratched about in the fridge and was at the sink cleaning vegetables for supper.

When Zane carried his brother into the house, Reza came into a warm kitchen, to family. I was grateful for the effort my sisters had made to receive him. They registered no shock at his appearance.

"The boy's back," Zulpha said, kissing him on the cheek.

"Tossing us all one side," Toeghieda added, pressing her lips onto the other cheek.

But the ride had weakened Reza, and Zane put him in bed. The nurse took his pulse and blood pressure, and hooked him up to the drip. She fitted him with an oxygen mask, and showed me and Margaret what to do. "He's too weak to sit on a commode," she said. "He'll have to wear a diaper. Who's going to change him?"

"I will," I said.

Zane went to the chemist, and brought back everything the doctor had ordered. "I have to go and see what's happening at the shop now. I'll be back after iftaar this evening."

"Call your father and tell him Reza's here."

"Who else should I tell?"

"No one," Toeghieda said. "People are biss. They just want to know what's going on in your house. Tomorrow your business is out on the street."

"Just your father," I nodded.

"It's the seven nights tonight at Auntie Rhoda's," he reminded.

"I can't go. It's Ramadan, and I have Reza."

"Just as well," Toeghieda said. "Don't let a whole lot of people come here, Beeda. And those who come uninvited, don't let them see him."

"Garaatie will probably call later. She's going through some stuff now, but she'll be along."

"She's always going through stuff. She should leave that man and get a life. But I like her, she's not two-faced. But that Rhoda – you can build her up all you want, I can't stand her."

"She's never been two-faced with me."

"Really?"

I looked at her. She knew something.

"It's damn disgusting what she did at the casino, if you ask me."

"You also know?"

"Yes. I ran into Shariefa at Woolworths. She's a fitnah, but there's always some truth to her stories."

Zulpha was cutting up carrots and stopped with her hands on the cutting board. "What really happened at the casino?"

"It's a long story."

"We have three hours to iftaar. Talk."

I looked at my two sisters. We had changed in appearance over the years, but not in spirit. Toeghieda, the fair princess, was now a big woman with a big scarf, who liked her knee-high stockings – passion killers, she called them – and belonged to the same mouloud jam'aah my mother had belonged to. She wasn't the most diplomatic, but was quick to be of assistance, and could be relied on in a crisis.

Zulpha, again, had got thinner, and was modern with her fancy turbans and baggy pants. She looked much younger than her forty-three years.

"Well, it's like this, I started. Rhoda didn't even want to gamble. She only had twenty rand. *I don't gamble*, she said. *It's haraam. I only came to watch*. But then . . ."

My sisters listened. I told them the whole story.

"I don't believe it," Zulpha said. "Rhoda? Religious Rhoda?"

"Believe it. I stood with her at the cashier's desk, and she told the cashier she wanted it all in a cheque. In other words, I'm not giving away any."

"How unfair," Toeghieda said. "She insisted on playing on your machine. That was *your* money. She should've given you half, if not bladdy all of it. I'd better not run into her."

"You mustn't say anything. Promise me."

Toeghieda hesitated. "That's hard, but I promise. When last did you see her?"

"At her sister's janazah."

"Well, you did your duty. And you're right not to go tonight." She looked at her watch. "It's past five. I'm going to make salaah."

Zulpha got up also. "I called Imran. I told him I was staying for iftaar. He won't come. He was invited out by some friends."

I hadn't expected Imran to come and break his fast with us. Imran came to the big functions, when he had to make an appearance, but hardly came to my house.

"But he's coming tomorrow to come and see Reza. He's very pleased that Reza's home."

It was still hard hearing Imran's name. My house was a very different one now from the one he had worked on all those years ago. There were wooden window frames, ceramic floors, a modern kitchen, and antique furniture and Persian rugs. My need to forget had made me change things. It had also led me to the discovery that you could be in love with one man, and be attracted to another.

I never told Rhoda or Garaatie about Imran. But I did share it with a bespectacled stranger in a room with a wing chair and a couch, for a hundred and fifty rand a visit. When the file closed at the end of the session, the story was contained. I knew no one would hear it. I still feel a little knot of sorrow when I hear Imran's name, but have come to terms with what had happened long ago.

Ten minutes before iftaar, my twins arrived with their families. They brought dates, chicken breyani, mince pies, and drinks.

"There's less than three weeks left of Ramadan," Marwaan said. "One of us will be here every night to have iftaar with Mummy and Reza."

"You don't have to," I said. "It's difficult during Ramadan, going to tarawih, and all of that."

"We want to. We've already discussed it. Mummy doesn't have to cook at all during this month. We'll bring whatever we have."

"I'll be here also," Zulpha said. "I haven't seen my nephew in years, I want to make up for lost time."

We all knew what she meant. Toeghieda didn't say anything. She wasn't one to make promises. She just showed up and got into the act.

It was almost time to eat. Sawdah and Sadia set the food out on the table. Everything was ready. Marwaan had set up chairs in Reza's room, and the men went to eat in there. Reza was awake. He wasn't hungry, but Munier fed him some soup.

Zane arrived in the middle of all of this with his son, Shaheed, and said that Rabia had gone to the seven nights at Rhoda's house. It was unusual for anyone to show up in the middle of a supper during Ramadan, but I was glad that he'd come. It was the first evening in almost twenty years with all my sons together. Not the happiest of occasions, but the best I was going to get.

After supper, the men decided not to go to mosque. They took turns reciting from the Qur'an in Reza's room, after which we all performed salaah together in the lounge. When they all finally left to go home, Margaret cleared away the last of the cups, and I was alone with my son.

I stood by his bed. I could see that the reunion had worn him out. He had left my house as a sixteen-year-old, and come back at twenty-three. With sores on his body. Struggling to breathe.

His eyes opened. "Would you like some Milo?" I asked.

He tried for a smile, and shook his head. He seemed uncomfortable.

"Is something wrong?" I asked.

"I'm wet, Ma."

I realised that this was embarrassing for him. "It's all right," I said. "So you're wet. Didn't I wash this stinky old bum many times before?" I went to fetch a basin of hot water, and washed him and dried him, and settled him back under the blankets. His eyes softened, and he looked at me, just like when he was little and I'd tucked him into bed with his teddy bear.

"I want Mummy to sit by me for a bit."

I smiled, and pulled up a chair. I sat with him and we talked. I talked, he listened. I had always read to him as a child. I told him about a new book I was reading, *Women Who Run With the Wolves*.

"Let me read you this wonderful opening . . .

*Wildlife and the Wild Woman are both endangered species. Over time, we have seen the feminine instinctive nature looted, driven back, and overbuilt. For long periods it has been mismanaged like the wildlife and the wildlands. For several thousand years, as soon and as often as we turn our backs, it is relegated to the poorest land in the psyche. The spiritual lands of the Wild Woman have, throughout history, been plundered or burnt, dens bulldozed, and natural cycles forced into unnatural rhythms to please others . . ."*

I sat with him until his breathing was even and he was fast asleep. I looked at him in a way I didn't dare to when he was awake. I touched his skin. It was warm. I picked up his wrist and circled it with my thumb and forefinger. His pulse was even. Everything about him looked dreamy and peaceful. But I knew it was a ruse. A lull before the storm.

My mother's brother, Uncle Joe, had been in his forties when he came home one afternoon from his collection rounds and told his wife that he was feeling so good. He went into the toilet, came out, and had an asthma attack. Right in front of her eyes he dropped to the floor and turned blue as he gasped for breath. He was dead within minutes.

In your last forty days, it was said, your deceased family visit you. Dying people often talked about an old aunt or grandmother whom they could see, while no one else could. I looked for signs with my own son, but he hadn't been in my house long enough for me to witness anything.

The night went by slowly. I sat by his bed long after he was asleep, reading the book I'd just read from. I was that wolfish woman with the keen sensing and playful spirit, intensely concerned with their young. The wolf stayed until the end. And then when it was all over it keened throughout the night and howled for the life that was. *They are experienced in adapting to changing circumstances constantly; they are fiercely stalwart and very brave.*

I went to bed at two, then got up again for faj'r just before dawn. I had a cup of tea, two rusks, and performed my prayers. I was ready for another day of fasting.

My first call, at ten that morning, was from Garaatie. She'd been to the seven nights, and heard from Rabia that Reza was home.

"How is he?" she asked.

"He's on a drip, and on oxygen."

"Oh my word. How are you coping?"

"Fine. Margaret's back from her family. Everyone was here yesterday.

Zane and I went to fetch him. They're going to come by every day. It's a full house. You know how it is."

"Can I come through? I have to talk to you."

"Of course. You don't have to ask. Did Mahmood come home?"

"No."

The second call was from Braima. Zane had called him. He wanted to know if he could come and see his son. I told him that he could come any time. I told him to bring his wife.

"How is he, Beeda? Zane says he's on oxygen."

"He's ill."

"God, I hate that word. It doesn't tell you anything."

"True. But it's good for now."

"What can I bring him?"

"Nothing."

The third call was from Shariefa. She'd also been to the seven nights and heard the news. "I'm so sorry to hear that he's sick," she said. "And he's back home? For good?"

"Yes."

"You must be happy to have him."

"What mother isn't glad when a child comes home?"

"That's so true. Anyway, I'm coming to Athlone this afternoon for some curtaining. I thought I would pop in. Are you home?"

"I'm home, but it's not a good time. It's Ramadan, I have the nurse coming. The family's in and out. You know how it is during this month. There're so many things to do."

"I understand," she said, sounding disappointed. "Maybe after Ramadan. Is it serious?"

"He's got an infection. He's on medication."

"I'll make do'ah for him," she said. "Take care."

"I will. And thanks for the call."


Garaatie arrived shortly after eleven. After spending a few minutes with Reza, I led her into the living room. With Garaatie, you either sat at the kitchen table where you could have tea to listen to her stories, or the couch. It was Ramadan so there was no tea.

"I know you don't believe in these things," she started, "but I went to see that man I told you about. He's not a doekoem. He heals people. He gave me a bottle of panaa water and said I must get Mahmood to drink it.

The water will make him come to his senses. The problem is, how I'm going to get him to drink it."

"I thought you said the man was a healer?"

"He *is* a healer. He's healing me."

"For God's sake, Garaatie, he's not healing you. He's giving you false hope. You can't have a man drink a bottle of water to come to his senses. That assumes he has a conscience to begin with. And why must he come to his senses? It's got nothing to do with logic. It's lust. Something young and exciting in his bed that he can say is his God-given right. Where's he now?"

Garaatie looked weary. "I knew you wouldn't understand."

"Don't try that misunderstood stuff with me, Garaatie. I understand very well. I told you I don't believe in this stuff. Go see a psychologist if you need help. You're too needy."

"You're my psychologist."

"No. I need my own head looked at. And you don't listen to me. You have a problem accepting what this man's done. Where's he? You haven't told me."

Garaatie looked down at her hands. "He's with her."

"What do you mean? They're living together? During this holy month?"

"They're married two weeks already."

"Wow. What a skunk."

"Yes. All this time we were fighting, he was married already."

"And now? Surely, you see now that you have to do something, or come to terms with it. You want him to drink a bottle of water, to do what? Give up the girl? Is he worth it? Even if the panaa water worked?"

Garaatie looked down at her hands. "He's never been worth it."

"Why then?"

"I love him."

"You love him?" I wanted to wring her neck. "What is it that you love?"

Garaatie looked up at me with woeful eyes. She had lost weight. Her scarf sat crooked on her head. "Sometimes you can be very cruel, Beeda."

"I have to be, to knock some sense into you. You're the one who needs the panaa water, Garaatie. Is it love, or fear of being alone? I'm the first one to say, stay together and work things out, but Mahmood's taken another wife now. When he was with you, he cheated on you. At least now you know where he is. If you can handle it, there's no problem. You know what goes with being a first wife. If you're not okay with it, for God's sake, a bottle of water's not going to change him. Go to God, Garaatie. There's your answer. See a psychologist. Join a gym. Get a hobby. If you want to know about love, I can tell you about love. This thing you have with Mahmood isn't love."

Garaatie looked deflated. "I'm sorry I burdened you with all this. You have your own stuff to deal with, and I come here with my problems."

"Don't be sorry," I said. "I'm your friend, but you have to start helping yourself. A psychologist will give you an unbiased perspective. More than that, you'll understand why you are in this situation. What it is about you, that allows a man to do this. It's about you, Garaatie. You've allowed it."

She gave a weak little smile. "I'll have to do some serious thinking. How're you handling things here?"

"Okay. I'm not thinking right now, just doing. It's more than pneumonia. He has Aids."

"Aids?"

"Yes."

She looked at me. I could see her brain working. Telling her he had Aids was telling her a lot more. It was admitting that my son was gay. Out of nowhere my eyes became full. I hadn't cried when I'd brought him home, and hadn't cried when I was alone, but was crying miserably now in front of my friend.

She came to sit next to me, and held me. "You'll come through this, Abeeda. You're strong. Don't give up hope. Trust in Allah. You have friends. I hope you know that. I'll always be here. If there's anything I can do."

"You don't know everything about me, Garaatie. I'm not that strong. You don't know the things I've done, and the things I've not done."

"You're strong, Beeda. You're the strongest one of us."

"I'm the only one without a man, Garaatie. Have you ever wondered why?"

"No. You never wanted to be with another man after Braima, you told us."

It was like something was loosening my tongue, and I couldn't stop. "That's not the whole truth. There *was* a man. I never told you. That man, and not Braima, took the last twenty-five years of my life."

She released me. "What?"

"Yes. My sister's husband, Garaatie. My own sister."

"Ya Allah, Beeda. I didn't know. Imran? You had something with Imran?"

"If you knew how it started . . . if you knew what I had to give up . . ."

That was the beginning of my tale, and the first time I trusted any friend enough to tell the story. In the end her coming to me for help, ended up with me being listened to. She sat like a wooden doll, blown away by my tale of love and betrayal.

"Now you know why I never married again."

"Do you hate her?"

"No. He was hers first."

"He loved you."

"Yes."

"Do you still love him?"

"I'll always love him. But I've accepted it. Do you think I did the right thing?"

"It's your sister. You had no choice. But I hope you didn't look at this as a rejection because it wasn't."

"I did look at it like that, and you're right, it's not. But I often wonder what would've happened if my mother hadn't died. If he would've married her."

"I don't think so. I think he felt sorry for her. And I think God loved you, and saved you from losing your sister. It was the only way, Beeda. Can you imagine the scandal? You would've had him, but been an outcast in your own family. Do you still have the letter he wrote?"

"No. I don't know what happened to it. I put it in my jewelry box. And then one day it just wasn't there."

She looked at me. "Before or after your mother died?"

I smiled at her through my tears. She was thinking the same thing I'd always wondered about. Whether my mother had looked for something in my jewelry box and found the letter, and if that's why she had the stroke.

"I don't know. I didn't look for the letter right after her death so I don't know when it disappeared."

"Do you think she found it?"

"I don't know. The body was on the kitchen floor when I found it. There was no letter."

"How do you know? Did you look?"

"No."

Her look was penetrating. "Who took off her clothes?"

"The toekamandies."

"Who was in the room with them?"

"Me and my sisters."

"Do you remember what she wore that day?"

"A cream skirt and a blouse."

"Pockets?"

"Yes."

"Who took the clothes?"

I couldn't answer immediately. "They were left at the house. I suppose Zulpha took care of them afterwards."

Garaatie let that last statement hang in the air between us.

"You're not suggesting, Garaatie, that my sister . . ."

"I'm not suggesting anything."

"We don't even know if my mother had the letter. I may just have misplaced it."

"You may have."

But the seed was planted. And if Zulpha had found the letter she had known all along about the affair, and had played the lost little orphan one more time, and won.

After my stay with Zulpha when I was to return to my own home with my children, Imran brought his mother, Latiefa, to the three nights. I had not been alone with him since the day before my mother's death, when he'd given me the ring. The ring was on a gold chain around my neck, hidden under my clothes. I had been with Zulpha for three days, and hadn't expected him to call me there. I did, however, think that we would find a few moments alone.

But Imran greeted me, and kept to the room where the men were reciting, and didn't come out. I didn't give it any credence as I knew we couldn't draw attention to ourselves. But I did notice his mother in quiet conversation with Zulpha in the bedroom.

The reciting ended. Toeghieda and I started to serve the cake and tea. While the men were still seated on the sheeted living-room floor, Latiefa came out of the bedroom with Zulpha. She found Mylie and Toeghieda and me in the kitchen. Imran had come out to help carry in the tea things and was also there. He stood next to Zulpha.

"I have an announcement to make," she said. "It's about the wedding. Zulpha doesn't want a big wedding, with your mummy just gone, and her being alone in the house. The big wedding's off. She and Imran have decided to get married ten days from now, on Sunday. Just a small ceremony; the imam, and the immediate family, after ish'ai."

It was as if someone had punched me in the gut. I listened to the words. I knew they were true. Things like this happened in real life. Only never to you. Or so you think. I didn't look at Imran. He was leaning against the doorway much like the time he'd leaned against my kitchen counter when he first offered to work on my house.

"What good news," Toeghieda exclaimed. "You didn't need that big wedding anyway, and you might as well do it now if you know what you want. Why wait? You shouldn't live alone in the house."

I felt something vibrate in my chest, and waited for it to stop. I discovered that I could act, and also turned towards my sister. I don't remember what I said, but I remember my performance. My smile, all the right words, my bleeding heart.

The hardest part was the next hour when I had to sit with them and discuss my mother's will. I agreed with Toeghieda that Zulpha could buy the house. I agreed to everything they said. At ten o'clock, I gathered my kids and told them to get into the car. Zulpha helped me out with their belongings.

"Thanks for staying with me," she said. "I couldn't have stayed here alone."

"What are sisters for?" I turned the ignition, and looked up at her through the window. "When did you two decide to do this?" I asked.

"The day after Mummy's janazah – after his mother spoke to me."

She had been home every day, but I remembered her telling me that she had to go out for an hour to pick up something at the shop. "It was *her* decision?" I asked.

"No. But she'd spoken to Imran. She asked me to speak to him too."

At home I put my children to bed, got into bed myself, but lay awake the whole night staring up at the ceiling. When I heard one of my sons cough in the next room, I looked at the clock. It was five-thirty. I switched on the light, and opened the cupboard to take out my jewelry box. I wanted to read again the letter that had started it all. But the letter wasn't there. I sat on the edge of the bed, wondering where I might've left it. I'd read it just a few days ago.

I went to the dining room and took out a writing pad and pen from the sideboard. I was a reader and a writer. No one knew I wrote poetry. I returned to my bed, and started a letter.

*Dear Imran . . . I can't believe that after all you've said that you could've . . .*

I balled up the letter, and started again. *My lover, my brother-in-law . . .*

I discarded that one also, and wrote another. I wrote and rewrote until the bed was strewn with crumpled paper. At last, I could take it no more, and burrowed my head under the pillow and cried.

I can't remember what I did during the next few days, but know that I didn't bake pies for Cars 4U. I'd decided not to have my hands all day in a flour bowl any longer. I would get a job where I had to get dressed up and wear lipstick, and be with other people. My mother was gone. I would have to get a babysitter, and find work. There was an urgency in me to get out into the real world. I was angry, defiant, and foolishly brave.

One night during that week I saw an ad for a receptionist in a small medical centre in the classified ads. I'd never had a job except for a brief stint as a cashier in a supermarket after Braima left me. I had no experience that I could speak of. But I had a good speaking voice, and a very presentable appearance.

On Wednesday morning I called the number in Claremont, and asked for an appointment. On Thursday morning, one of the doctors in the practice, Dr Akojee, interviewed me. I told him straight out that I'd never worked in an office, but that I knew how to talk to people, and wouldn't have to be told twice what to do. Dr Akojee called me back the following day to meet with one of the other doctors, a cardiologist, Dr Paul Lewinsky, who asked me two or three things and said I was hired.

I left the medical centre feeling both elated and terribly depressed. How could one feel both those things at once? But I focused my thoughts on the new job, and refused to think of anything else. I'd looked at the secretary who did the typing, and saw that I could wear pants. I bought two new outfits that same day. There was just enough money left for food and to pay the expenses for the rest of the month.

I told my children that I was starting work on Monday. Zane was happy for me. The twins didn't really understand. I called up another friend, Nisa, who also had moved to the Athlone vicinity, and lived on one of the avenues. Nisa had a six-month-old baby, and had a woman who lived in to do housework. I told her that I'd found a job, and needed a babysitter for Reza. She said she was home for a year, I could bring Reza on Monday morning.

"I'll also look for a woman for you," she said. "With four children, you need someone to do the washing and ironing and clean the house. I know two women who might be interested."

Enormously relieved that I had found work and would no longer have to bake pies, I toyed with the idea of telling my news to my sisters. Zulpha was getting married the following Sunday. As a sister, I should've called her long ago to ask how I might contribute, but I didn't. I didn't want to see her, or know her plans, or anything about the man she would marry. If I knew nothing, I would have nothing to think about.

But my conscience pricked me. She was my sister, and already it was unusual that I hadn't called. But before I could do anything to rectify the situation, she and Imran came to my house on Saturday morning with a bowl of koeksisters. My children rallied around the coconut-covered doughnuts like hungry wolves. Zulpha made coffee. Imran sat on the step outside with Reza on his lap.

I hated him. That he had come and disturbed my life, planned all this with Zulpha, and not said a word about it. And the nerve to come to my house.

"I got back some of the deposit for my wedding dress," Zulpha said. "That was lucky. And thank God the invitations never went out or I would've had to call everyone."

"How many people are coming?"

"About forty."

"Quite a few. Can I offer to make anything? I've been busy looking for work this week. I'm sorry I didn't call."

"If you can make three trifles, that would be excellent. Toeghieda's arranging the finger foods with Garaatie next door."

"I have some dough in the fridge. I'll make some mini pizzas also."

"You say you were looking for work?" she asked.

"Yes. I found a job. I'm starting on Monday. Receptionist for four doctors in Claremont." I was surprised that I could talk to her like this with all the resentment I felt.

"That's wonderful news! Did you hear that, Imran?"

Imran came inside with Reza, who had fallen asleep in his arms. Zulpha took the baby from him and went to the bedroom.

Imran was seated on the other side of the table. I didn't look up, but I could feel his eyes on me, his intensity. It was our first moment alone since the day before my mother's death nine days ago.

"I love you," he said.

The words knifed through me.

"I will explain it all to you. Can I come and see you this evening?"

Zulpha came back into the kitchen. "He's sleeping," she said. "What a sweet child. He never cries, does he?"

"Not much," I said. "He's starting to walk."

Her face became solemn. "I have to go through Mummy's things soon. I thought we could give her clothes to some of the old-age homes, and to charity. Do you want to sort through it with me? Toeghieda's coming down on Wednesday. We can do it together."

"I'll be working," I said, glad for a real excuse not to be part of the whole thing. "I'll leave it to you two to decide."

"There're some bags that you liked," she reminded me. "You should come and see what you want. And you liked that old mirror, the one from our grandmother."

"I'll take that."

"I know it's soon to be doing all this, but I have to clear out the cupboards to make room for Imran's stuff. Mummy also said you could have the silver tea set. Toeghieda's taking the oak sideboard."

"And you?"

"I'll take what you two don't want. I have the house. It was a good price."

I didn't say anything. The house was worth more than a hundred thousand rand, but Toeghieda and I let her have it for seventy-five thousand, which meant she only had to pay us twenty-five thousand rand each. Zulpha had ten thousand saved. Imran was coming up with the rest. They would have a house, fully paid up, to start their marriage. What had I had when I started? A few pieces of trousseau, an eight-week-old foetus, and an unwilling participant who stood before an imam in a new suit, cloaked in fear.

"If I think how Mummy built that house on weekends after Daddy died," she said. "As she got money from her rounds, she paid the bricklayers and carpenters. No money, no work. It took almost two years to finish. Mummy's sweat went into this house. It'll always be the family home."

I listened to her talk. She went on and on. After another coffee, she said they had lots to do, and had to go. My heart ached. In the midst of all this, I had to be civil. I had to contain my pain.

I sat at the kitchen table and watched my children chase one another up and down in the passage. I was too worn to tell them to stop. I love you, he had said. I'll explain it all to you. What was there to explain? He had made his choice.

Shortly after nine-thirty that evening, he came to my house. I took him into the living room.

"Here's your ring," I said, placing it on the coffee table.

He left it there between us, and looked up at me. "Do you want to hear what happened?"

"Talk."

"She came to see me the night after your mother died. She was simple about it. No histrionics. *I want you to give me another chance, Imran. Just like that. Plain and to the point. My mother's gone, I'm alone in the house. You told me once you loved me. Your excuse is invalid now, we have a house. My sisters will agree to sell the house to me. If I've done something wrong, I want you to tell me. I want to get married. You did ask me once to marry you.*"

I was shocked to hear that my sister had done this.

"And you agreed?"

"I told her I didn't love her."

"Oh my God."

I couldn't believe that he had actually said this to her. And I couldn't believe that my sister was going through with something as serious as marriage after hearing it. I waited for him to tell me more, but he said nothing else.

"That's it?"

He looked down at his hands, then back up at me. "I felt sorry for her. And you told me we couldn't – "

"I know what I said."

"Didn't you mean it?"

"Of course I meant it. But I wanted you to come up with a solution!"

"What was the solution, Beeda? She was sitting there crying. I couldn't bear her unhappiness."

"So you decided to sacrifice yourself?"

He lowered his head into his hands. "Tell me what to do, and I'll do it. Do you want me to cancel the wedding?"

"Now, after all this? How can you? It would be even worse now than before. She'll be little Red Riding Hood, and I'll be the wolf come to devour her."

I went to the kitchen to put on the kettle. He followed me. At the dresser, I took out two cups. His arms went about me. His mouth was close to mine.

"I don't love her, Abeeda. I love you. Do you want me to call it off? I'll go home now to my mother, and tell her. Right now I can do it. They'll hate us for a few months, and then it'll be all over."

"And my sister?"

"That's a hard one. I care for her, but in time she'll come to accept it."

I tried to convince myself that I could do it, that I had a right to be happy too, that my sister would eventually understand and forgive me. I burst out sobbing in his neck.

"Don't cry," he said, stroking my hair. "Do you want me to cancel?"

I felt the strength of his arms around me. It felt so good to be there.

"I can't tell you. It must be your decision. If you were broken up for a year, that would've been different."

"Do you want me to break it off, and we wait for a year?"

That also sounded like a possibility, but I knew it wouldn't happen that way. "They'll know, Imran. I have children. My children will see you. After a while, we won't care any more who knows, and then it will all come out."

He turned my face up to meet his. "What are you saying?"

"I don't know. The right thing."

"The right thing by you or by her?"

That was the big question. The right thing by my sister, was marriage. The right thing by me, was not to get married at all.

"I don't know."

"You know I'll come out in the open with you. I'm prepared to do that."

"I can't hurt my sister, and I can't tell you what to do."

"I understand. But do *you* understand? If I can't have you, I'm not going to look for anyone else. I don't want to love anyone else. I'll just go through with it."

It was a horrible situation. I understood, but the thing of it was, I didn't accept, and was deeply unhappy. How was it fair that Imran should be with someone he didn't love?

The days that followed were heady ones. I was at my new job only four days when Dr Paul Lewinsky called me into his office and asked whether I would mind taking a walk to the bottle store for two bottles of Cointreau. He was having a party at his house that evening, and wouldn't have time to pick it up.

"I don't mind going on an errand," I said, "but I wouldn't like to be seen entering a bottle store."

He slapped his palm against his forehead, "I forgot about that," he laughed. "Of course, I understand."

I stood in front of him at the desk in my dark pants and cashmere sweater, waiting. "Is that all, doctor?"

"Yes," he said smiling. "Maybe one day we can have coffee and you can tell me a bit about your religion."

I looked at him. Somehow I felt that it was more than my religion he was interested in. He wasn't much older than me – thirty-two at the most – and good-looking, with dark curly hair, blue eyes, and a dazzling smile.

"Sure," I said. "I'm not an authority, but I'll try."

I didn't delude myself that anything would happen between us. He was Jewish and married, and I had four children. But I liked that he had found me attractive. When he called me into his office on Friday and said he was running late for his appointment at the hospital, and asked me to go to the deli to pick up two bagels with smoked salmon and cream cheese, I obliged. When I brought it to him, he said one of the bagels was for me.

"Can I eat this?

"Yes, it's kosher. What I can eat, a Muslim can eat. I'm Orthodox. Sit down."

I was flattered by the attention, and knew by this time from Marion, the secretary, that the previous receptionist had fallen in love with the good doctor.

"Don't take him seriously," Marion said. "He's a tease, but he makes sure you know he has a wife. His wife's one of those arrogant and spoiled women with too much make-up you can't stand, but he's never going to leave her."

And so I sat down and bit into my bagel. I wasn't even hungry, but couldn't not please this good-looking man who was being so charming to me. He asked how old my children were. How I liked working there. He knew my mother had died, and asked how I was coping. I called him doctor, and answered his questions. I was very much aware of the laws of apartheid, and the white man's attraction to brown-skinned girls.

When we had finished eating, he thanked me for having lunch with him, and said he had to hurry. Marion was at her desk typing a medical report when I came out.

"You were in there long," she said.

"Doctor asked me to have some lunch with him."

"Oh my. So soon. He usually waits two or three weeks."

I laughed it off, but knew what she meant, and didn't forget the warning when I opened my car door in the underground garage later that day, and the headlights of a silver Mercedes Benz flashed and I saw him behind the wheel.

He'd planned it – parked his car across from mine, knowing that I left the office at five. He'd been at the hospital all afternoon, and had waited in the car for me to come out.

He beckoned to me. I walked over. "Your messages are upstairs, doctor. And a package from the clinic."

"Did Dr Kahn call?" he asked.

"Yes," I said. "He'll send over the report on Monday morning."

He got out of the car, and stood facing me. He smiled. "I like having you in the office, Abeeda," he said. "You're very refreshing."

I was reminded of the little girl, and the big bad wolf. I wasn't savvy enough yet for smart replies, and wasn't used to white men. So I just smiled, and said thank you.

"Do you have to hurry home?" he asked. "Is someone looking after the children?"

"My eldest son looks after the twins when they come from school. My baby's with a sitter."

"So you have to get home."

"Yes. Was there still something you wanted me to do?"

"No. My wife's in Johannesburg this weekend. I was looking for some-one to have supper with."

I felt something rush through me, something pleasurable. "I can't. My sister's getting married on Sunday. I have things to do."

"Too bad," he smiled. "Maybe next time."

I got into my car and drove away; flattered by his interest, but also a little burned that he could assume that when his wife was away the brown girl in the office would be only too thrilled for his company.

Still, I forgot all about him when I got home. Zane told me that Imran had called twice, asking when I was going to be home. He was coming at eight. I had to wait for him before going to Zulpha.

I couldn't imagine what it could be. I hadn't heard from him all week. I missed him. I longed to be with him. I'd also had time to think about my sister, and what she'd done. Always the one everyone felt sorry for, and always this pity worked in her favour. I remember several incidents as a child when our mother made me give up things for her. She wasn't such an innocent. She said little, but worked behind the scenes. I, on the other hand, was transparent and what you saw was what you got. I would never have dropped to my knees and declared my desperation. How could you be with a man you knew didn't want to be with you? I'd not even asked my own husband, who was the father of my children, to stay when he wanted to leave. But playing this last card had worked. And she'd been crafty the way she'd gone about it – not telling me where she was going that Monday evening when she ran off to see him. And telling me that Imran's mother had talked to her and told her to speak to Imran when she was the one who'd done the begging.

I set about making supper wondering what it was Imran wanted to talk to me about. It was only a week in the new job, I was still trying to get things organised with my children. Reza was taking his first steps. My twins wanted to tell me what had happened at school. Zane complained that no one helped him in the afternoons and that he was behind with his homework. Everyone clamoured for my attention when I got home.

Zulpha called in the middle of supper. "Are you coming through?" she asked.

"Of course. I just have to feed the kids." The night before a wedding, family and friends always congregated at the homes of the bride and the groom. They brought presents, they helped pack in the trousseau. There was cake and tea, it was a social event. Zulpha's wedding would be a small affair, but there would still be people who would come to the house.

"Imran's not here yet," she said.

"Is he supposed to come?" Usually the man stayed at his own house the night before the wedding to receive his own guests.

"He said he was, for a bit."

"Maybe he's not home from work yet. It's only six-thirty."

"He finished work after jum'ah. I spoke to him. He's supposed to bring over two pots for Garaatie. She offered to make the breyani."

"I'll be over soon," I said, wondering whether Imran not turning up at her house had anything to do with his wanting to talk to me.

I got my children ready, but didn't leave the house until after eight when I thought Imran would call. He didn't, and I left with my children to go to Zulpha's house. Toeghieda and her family were already there, with Garaatie and Mahmood, and a few friends. Zulpha didn't have trousseau to pack in as she was staying on in the house, but in one of the bedrooms she and Toeghieda had displayed all the nightgowns, outfits, linens, and gifts.

I didn't see Imran, and didn't ask. At nine o'clock Zulpha made a call to his house. She spoke to someone on the telephone and waited. Finally, she replaced the receiver.

"He's just gone out quickly. I left a message. It sounded like there're lots of people there. I doubt that he'll come now. What about the pots?"

I knew it wasn't the pots she was worried about, and again I felt sorry.

"It'll sort itself out," I said. "I'm going to start with the trifles. I brought the ingredients. I thought it better to make them here so they can chill in the fridge and save me from bringing them with me tomorrow."

"Good idea."

I took the ingredients out of the bag and discovered that I'd left the sponge cakes at home. I couldn't make trifle without sponge cake. I started with the jelly base, and set the bowls one side to cool. I would have time to get the sponge cakes before the jelly was set.

I got my car keys and told Zulpha I was going home quickly. "I forgot the sponge cakes, I won't be long. Keep an eye on Reza for me. He's with Zane."

I got to my house, just as Imran's bakkie was starting up at my gate.

"Thank God you're here," he said. "I came looking for you, and was just about to leave."

I could see from his eyes that he was stressed. "What's wrong?" I asked.

"Where are the children?"

"They're with Zulpha. I forgot something, and had to come back. Come in."

As soon as we stepped inside and the door had closed behind us, he took me into his arms, and kissed me. He picked me up and carried me into the bedroom. Buttons popped, clothes flew in all directions. We devoured each other like two ravenous beasts. Urgent and desperate. Finally, our bodies quieted down, and we lay for a few moments in silence. He was holding me, his face in my neck, his hands in my hair.

"I can't marry Zulpha," he said.

I looked over his shoulder at a picture frame on the wall – a watercolour painting of a ballerina taking off a ballet shoe. She was leaning forward on a chair, her right hand on her left ankle. Her posture reminded me of a tired swan who'd danced and danced, and after the encores, was a lonely figure in a dressing room.

I started to cry.

"Don't cry, Beeda. I came here for a purpose."

"It's all so unfair," I wailed.

"I know, and I don't want to do it. Tell me now, once and for all, what you really want. I've suffered this week. I thought I could stay away. Look at this. The night before my wedding. How can I marry someone I don't love?"

"I don't know, and I don't know what we can do. I love you more than anything, but if we do this no matter how long we wait, you'll be a bastard in everyone's eyes, and I'll be the one who betrayed my own sister."

His eyes misted up. "I love you, Beeda. I don't think you know how much."

"I know, and I love you."

"We could go away. To Australia. We could start a life there. After a while it would all blow over, and we could come back. Your sister will probably be married by that time."

The telephone rang. I cleared my throat so my voice wouldn't give me away. I lifted the receiver. "Hello?"

"Beeda, where are you?"

"I'm here, Zulpha. Is something wrong?"

"No. I just wanted to know if something had happened to you."

"Nothing's happened. I'll be there now."

I replaced the receiver, and went into his arms. "I'm never going to stop loving you, Imran."

"And I'm never ever, ever going to stop loving you."

Three days before Eid, Reza went into a coma. I called his father. Braima came immediately with his wife. Reza was hooked up to the oxygen tank, making gasping sounds.

Braima sat down in a chair by the side of the bed and cupped his hands in prayer. Zainap waited for him to finish reciting.

"The two of you have things to talk about," she said. "I want to go out and take a look at your vegetable garden. I saw some herbs when we came in."

I watched her leave the room; a big woman, immaculately dressed in a black dress and coat. I've never seen her in a robe. Braima got up, and came to stand next to me. He didn't say anything. We watched our son labouring towards death.

"It's a hard way to go," he said.

My heart was too full to respond.

"Do you think that . . . perhaps, if he'd grown up with both of us this wouldn't have happened?"

"No."

He took out a handkerchief from his pocket and wiped the corner of his eye. "I regret that I left you, Beeda."

The words came as a shock.

"I regretted it a week after I had left."

His words had a cataclysmic effect, but it was too late. I didn't ask him why, if he regretted it a week after, he didn't come back. I knew why. Zainap was pregnant. He married her, like he married me when I was pregnant. But Zainap had lost the baby. After that there were three girls in a row. Lovely daughters, I met them. One's a little plain, like Zainap. The other two have their father's spirit.

"We sometimes do things that we don't understand," he continued. "I was young. As Reza got older, I blamed myself. I wasn't around very much for him."

He wasn't around for any of them. Weekend trips to the zoo or to bioscope wasn't the same as being there for the homework, the day-to-day grind. And that only started after two years anyway.

"You're not to blame," I said. "It was put out that way."

"Is it put out when bad things happen?"

"I don't know. I think we create it."

"Did we create this?"

"No. That was how he came to us. Nothing you or I could've done would've changed things. Don't blame yourself for this, Braima. It's not you."

As I uttered the words, I thought how strange life was. Women, even after they'd lost and got hurt, still had to make men feel all right. I wanted to ask if he was happy, but didn't have to. There was no heady, romantic stuff, but there was compatibility and comfort. You ate together, you prayed together, you slept together. You reminded yourself daily of the fleetingness of life, and didn't cling to earthly love and transient pleasures. Tomorrow you die, you pause, and you continue. Reward wasn't in this world, it was in the next. That's what kept you going. That's what kept you satisfied.

"Is your life good?" I asked.

"Alhamdu lilah. We have our ups and downs like everyone else, but Allah's been good to us."

"I'm glad."

He looked at me, not sure of my tone. And he wouldn't understand. He couldn't. He didn't know about the hole in my heart, the loss, the abandonment. He knew nothing of what I'd gone through since our marriage ended so abruptly all those years ago.

The bell rang. We heard Zainap open the door to let the doctor in. I was familiar with the procedure already. Dr Shapiro checked the drip, took Reza's blood pressure, listened to his chest.

"What's your opinion, doctor?" I knew the diagnosis would be different.

The doctor finished his examination and looked up at the two of us. "His breathing is much worse. He's suffering. The drip's keeping him going, but it's not going to be long. All you can do now is make him comfortable."

"How long?" Braima asked.

"Maybe twenty-four hours."

Braima took Zainap to her sister's house, and returned that evening to break his fast with us. My sons and my sisters took turns coming for iftaar, but that night we were all together. It was a sombre affair. We had fasted all day, but no one really did justice to the food. After supper, the men went into Reza's room to recite at his bedside, and the women remained in the kitchen.

Rabia surprised me that evening. "I'm off this week," she said, placing a cup of rooibos tea in front of me. "I can stay here with Mummy one or two nights, with Shaheed."

The offer touched me, especially as it would be Eid in a few days. "Thanks," I said. "But you must have lots of things to do before Eid. And Margaret's here."

"Is Mummy sure?"

"Yes. Thanks. I appreciate the offer."

"Someone should stay here with you, though, Beeda," Toeghieda said. "What about this Patrick? I've heard so much about him, I've never met him. Wasn't he supposed to stay here?"

I didn't ask how she knew. Probably Zane had told her. He'd always been fond of this aunt. "I said he could, but he decided not to. He comes in the mornings, depending on his work schedule. He stays for quite a while. The other friends come also. Jonathan, Tolla, Mietjie, Bernie and Niefie. Niefie makes salaah in his room."

"All gay?" she asked.

"Whatever they are, they know their business. Mietjie sits by his bed and recites. I had a long talk with him in the week. I don't think he had that talk with his own mother, and I still don't know why he opened up to me. Maybe because I'm a Muslim mother with a gay son and he needs to feel accepted. But at one point, he had his head on his forearms on the table, and cried like a baby. I'd asked him a question I never could ask my own son. I asked him, 'What does it feel like, Mietjie, to be gay?' It was like the floodgates opened and all these emotions poured out. He wasn't from Cape Town, he said, but from Pietermaritzburg. He'd always known there was something different about him. But he'd kept his feelings in check, and at age nineteen even went out with a girl. He hated it. Then four years ago, he moved down to Cape Town, and was in this public toilet in Sea Point, where he heard sounds in the cubicle next to his. There was a hole in the wooden partition and he looked. And that was it. He couldn't control himself after that. 'I can't help it, Auntie. I struggle with my feelings. I pray and pray, I make all my salaahs, I love God, but I can't help it. Sometimes I sit for an hour on my muslah, begging God, but it hasn't changed how I feel.'"

They looked at me. I could see by Toeghieda's expression that the story had moved her. "Shame," she said. "It must be hard." But she was uncomfortable and changed the subject. "Has Garaatie been here yet?"

"Many times," I said. "She came yesterday with Rhoda."

"Rhoda was here?"

"Yes. Reza's home three weeks now. People know. He has Aids and that's it. You can't stop people from what they're thinking. No matter what the truth is, they still talk. And the truth is that he's gay, and he has Aids, and I'm not going to hide it."

"Beeda's right," Zulpha said. "She owes no explanation. We must all sweep in front of our own doors. That Shariefa, for instance, whenever she wants to know someone's business, she puts on that sorrowful face, and says, 'Shame, it's a pity about so and so, eh?' Then you're supposed to say, 'oh, I know', and fill in the gaps for her. She's so biss. But does she tell you about her niece who was involved with a married man, or about her own fatherless son who dated that girl who shot herself in a toilet in a nightclub? You don't hear anything about that. That's all top secret."

"I can't stand her," Toeghieda said. "She's a total fitnah. I don't know about some of these friends. Garaatie's not a bad egg. She's just dof when it comes to men. It's that Rhoda; so full of herself. And what's so great about her? Her great big weight, yes, and a man without teeth in his mouth on the weekends."

We laughed. We needed something to lift our spirits.

Braima came out of the room. He stood listening to us for a few minutes, then pulled up a chair. Somehow his presence comforted me.

"How are things in there?" I asked.

"His breathing's faster than this morning, more laboured." He looked around at the faces staring back at him. He knew his daughters-in-law well because the twins often visited their father with their families, but he hadn't really seen my sisters, except at funerals and other family functions, and hadn't really spoken to them in years. Toeghieda had hated him at one time.

"We were just saying that Beeda shouldn't be alone now," Toeghieda said. "Even though she has Margaret. Margaret also needs her sleep. Someone should be here, just in case."

Munier came out of the room. "I heard that," he said. "I agree. I'll stay here with Mummy. Someone has to sit up with him tonight."

We all knew what that meant.

Munier went home to fetch some things, then returned and set up in the spare room. We took turns sitting with Reza. When I got up at dawn to have something to eat before the fast started, Munier was already in the kitchen making toast.

He poured two cups of tea, and set a toasted cheese sandwich before me. We had two days left of Ramadan. We sat next to each other at the round table.

"Did you sleep?" I asked.

The cup seemed to shake in his hand. "No."

I knew then. I put down my cup, and went to stand at the sink. He came to stand next to me. We held each other. I couldn't cry.

"What time?" I asked.

"About an hour ago."

He walked me into the room. He had already removed the oxygen mask and the drip and drawn the sheet over the face. He pulled it back a little to show me.

I looked at the lifeless form of my son. The colour had drained from his face, he looked small. His mouth was open. I touched my hand to his cheek. He was still warm.

"We have to close his mouth. How did it happen?"

"I was asleep in the chair when I heard choking sounds. He was struggling to breathe, his chest going up and down rapidly. Then it dropped, like he was taking a rest, and I waited. It took a long time. Then it rose again, a last time, and a long, slow sound, like a low whistle, came from his lungs."

I turned to look at him. He stood with his face in his hands and cried.

It's unbelievable what you're capable of at a time like this. You move into the storm. You take hold of it. The brain makes allowances. Funny things come into your head. Elvis has left the building, I thought, as I put my arms around my son, and comforted him.

"He was a good boy. We must be satisfied."

"I'm so glad Mummy brought him back. He wasn't with strangers."

We held each other for a while, then he wound a band around the jaw and head to keep the mouth closed, and covered the face.

"Call your father," I said. "And the family."

While I sat in a chair by the bed and made du'ah for the safe passage of my deceased son, Munier got busy on the telephone. When he was done, I made my own calls. I didn't wake Margaret. She would have a busy day.

But I made it easy on myself and took a tranquilizer with a glass of water. It was only after I'd swallowed the pill that I realised that I should've stopped eating or drinking ten minutes ago.

My family arrived within the hour. Zulpha and Toeghieda took care of the phone calls and announcement on the radio. My daughters-in-law helped prepare the burial cloth and the cotton wool. Zane and his brothers made arrangements for the death certificate and the hole. By ten the house was filled with people. Braima and my sons washed the body, and wrapped it. Patrick and his friends stood in the yard. Silent and watchful. When they carried the mayyit out, they kept to the back and followed the procession to the mosque. Patrick didn't come and say goodbye to me. But I knew I would hear from him.

Reza was buried at two. His brothers were the three men in the hole who turned him on his side facing east, and placed the planks over him. Braima was there when they climbed out.

That night we were all together again for iftaar. How many times I've sat in kitchens after the toekamandies and the mourners had departed. Friends, relatives, a father, a mother. Only this time it was my son. Parents didn't bury children. Children buried parents. As I sat there listening to my children argue over who I should stay with for one or two nights, I was grateful for the family I had, but didn't think anyone really knew what was going on inside of me.

There was my ex-husband sitting with his wife, and there was Imran next to my sister. Both still being where they'd said they didn't want to be. They'd found a way to make it all work. Tonight, one could hold the other, and be the strong one. Tomorrow, it's the other one's turn. Who was there for me? I didn't need someone for a night or two. I needed someone to lean into, and to let go. Of all the people I felt I wanted to talk to at that moment, it was Garaatie.

"Come and stay with us for a few days, Mummy," Zane said. "There's a spare room, or even a bed in Shaheed's room. He would like that."

Even if I did decide to spend a night at the home of one of my sons, it wouldn't have been at his. As a guest I hardly felt comfortable. I couldn't imagine what it would be like to be on my best behaviour around Rabia for two days.

"Thanks, but I can't. And I have Margaret. It's Eid in two days. I haven't really prepared anything."

"Don't prepare anything," Sawdah said. "We'll bring Mummy some cakes and things for the table. Come and have iftaar with us tomorrow night."

"Thanks, but I want to be alone for the next little while. I'll see you on Eid."

Braima got up. "We have to go. Take care of yourself, Beeda. Let me know if there's anything I can do."

"Thanks."

"Are we getting together for the three nights?"

I looked at my sons at the table. "No. Just the seven, forty, and hundred nights."

He greeted everyone, and said goodbye. Zane walked them to the door. I had thought about him since his declaration to me at Reza's bedside. He was a good man. He had made some mistakes, and regretted it. One thing I hadn't expected to see at the funeral, was finding him in the yard consoling Patrick. Of everyone present, Patrick was the one I felt most sorry for. The overlooked mourner. The one no one knew about, and who suffered in silence. Even at the funeral, he couldn't really express his grief.

That night when everyone had gone, and Margaret was asleep, I went into the room where Reza had been. Everything had been moved back and in place, the bed had a new duvet cover, there were fresh flowers on the dresser put there by Margaret. But the oxygen tank in the corner brought a lump to my throat.

I sat down on the edge of the bed, where I'd sat for three weeks and spent time with Reza. Then I lay down with my head on the pillow. I don't know how long I stayed there, but the pillowcase was damp when I got up, and I knew it was ten past three in the morning when I got into my car.

I arrived at the casino and went straight to the machines where I'd lost all my money the previous time. I had a full pack of cigarettes, and a whole lot of misplaced vengeance. I waited for one of the five machines to become available. I didn't care who saw me, or reported that they'd seen me in the casino in the holy month, and on the same night I'd buried my son.

The man on the second machine from the right got up. I decided not to play there. An old woman with a thick cardigan and a doek on her head sat down, with thirty rand on her card. On the fourth push of the button, she got a spin, and it landed on a thousand. She was so surprised, she looked at the people next to her and asked what was happening.

"You've won a thousand rand," a woman with short blond hair said.

She got up after her winnings. I took her seat. I'd seen these machines give a thousand, then shortly after, give another. I sat down, lit a cigarette, and started to play. In less than twenty minutes, the five hundred rand I'd withdrawn from my savings account was gone. I turned to the woman on my left.

"Can you keep an eye on the machine for me? My card's in it. I'll just be a minute."

I headed for the ATM machine and withdrew another five hundred. My limit was one thousand for the day. If I lost this, I would have no money left, unless I took money from my credit card. But I'd taken two thousand five hundred rand from that card previously, and hadn't paid any of it back.

I returned to the machine and continued to play. This money went even faster, and as I inserted the last hundred rand into the slot, I knew it would give me nothing. I knew what unconscionable bastards the wheel of gold machines were, yet, I couldn't get up and play elsewhere. When this money was gone also, I turned to the woman again, who now looked sorry for me. She had fifteen hundred rand on her card.

"You shouldn't have played there," she said. "That other woman got a thousand. The machine won't pay again. But I'll keep an eye on it for you."

It was easy to give advice when you were ahead, but she had to be careful with that fifteen hundred on her card, I thought, or she wouldn't have it much longer either. I went back to the ATM and stood with my credit card in my hand. Was I going to do it? I'd lost a thousand already.

*Draw the money. You just need another hundred or two to turn that machine around.*

I withdrew five hundred rand. Surely, now, the machine would give me something. I returned to my seat and thanked the woman for watching my card.

"That man on your right just sat down and got a thousand," she said.

"Really?" I felt depressed. It wasn't the first time I'd chosen a wrong machine and overlooked one that paid repeatedly.

Still, I held out some hope. The machine had taken a thousand rand of my money. It couldn't possibly be this unrelenting. The worst of it was, you didn't want to get up and let someone else get what you'd put in.

I inserted a hundred-rand note. I lost it. I inserted another. I lost that also. On my last hundred, I got a spin. It stopped on forty. I couldn't believe it. Two minutes later, all my money was gone. I had lost fifteen hundred rand. I looked at my watch. It was 4.30 a.m. I had been in the casino less than an hour.

I sat there, not knowing what to do. Behind me a couple teetered back and forth on their heels, waiting for my machine. I smelled their eagerness to cash in on my loss. They were waiting for me to run out of money, and the longer I played, the better their chances to score big – unless I got a good combination or a thousand rand spin. But even if I got a thousand rand now, I would still be down five hundred.

I felt a tap on my shoulder. "Are you still playing here, lady?" the man asked.

I looked at him. A beefy creature, with a round blonde at his side.

"Yes," I said.

He pursed his lips as if to say, that's okay, we'll wait till you've lost everything.

Again I turned to the woman next to me. "I just have to run to the loo. Do you mind?"

"Not a problem," she said, putting her bag on my seat, flashing the couple a look. She knew where I was going, but knew what it was like to be down and have someone else cash in on your loss.

I found myself back at the ATM machine. I didn't allow myself to think. I just stuck in my credit card and withdrew another five hundred. With a tightness in my chest I returned to the machine. The woman took her bag off the seat and I sat down. The two onlookers hovered in the background.

I took my time. I lit a cigarette, turned around to see if there was a waitress. I'd lost fifteen hundred rand already and hadn't even had something to drink. I'd also read that it was a good thing to let the machine rest a few minutes every now and then.

With fresh hope, I inserted my sixteenth hundred-rand note. I got a spin after three pushes. It stopped on twenty-five rand. I played on. A few pushes later, I got another spin. Forty rand. The woman on my left turned to me. "At least it's going up," she said.

"It could be on a twenty-five, forty-rand cycle," I said.

It was. The only thing that changed was that it took a longer time to lose this hundred. But I did lose it. On the third hundred-rand note I got several spins – nothing more than seventy-five rand. I came to my last hundred rand. I could feel the devil's breath at my ear. If nothing happened with this hundred, I would've lost two thousand rand.

I watched my money go down slowly: seventy-five – sixty – thirty. On the last nine rand, a wheel of gold and two of the purple bars locked into place, and I won two hundred rand. I was so relieved, I lit a fresh cigarette, and told the woman to watch my machine. This time I really had to go to the loo. I sensed discontent behind me. The couple was getting agitated. Other machines had become available, but they wanted mine. They knew how much money had gone into it.

And so I prolonged their agony. I returned with a waitress and ordered a coffee. I sat down. An hour later, I was up to eight hundred rand.

*Get up, Beeda. Take that money and go home.*

I played on. I got a spin. It landed on five hundred rand. I had more than half my money back.

*Now, Beeda. Get up.*

I continued to play and got another combination. A wheel of gold and two of the yellow bars. Three hundred rand.

The couple behind me left. They knew that I wouldn't get up now.

I sat at the machine until 9.00 a.m. and at one point had three thousand two hundred rand on my card, and a crowd of people watching me get spin after spin.

At last I got up. I had been at it for six hours and was exhausted. I had my two thousand rand back, plus an extra thousand.

I went to have breakfast in the lounge reserved for members. After a toasted cheese sandwich I felt refreshed, and headed back to the wheel of gold machines. The couple had returned. The woman was playing on my machine. I watched her lose three hundred rand. She got up and someone else sat down. The same thing happened. I watched several people sit down and lose their money. They got small spins of twenty-five and forty, and eventually lost. I stood with my money bulging in my bag, feeling mighty good that it wasn't me. An hour later the machine had taken more than two thousand rand.

At ten-thirty I was still standing there, tempted to try again. But I let a few more people have a go. I watched with sadness as player after player lost their money. The machine had taken in over four thousand in the time I'd stood watching. Finally, the seat stood empty and no one wanted to go on.

"Why don't you try, lady?" one of them said. "You were lucky there. Maybe you'll be lucky again."

"I don't want to give it back," I said.

"Just give it a hundred."

*Don't, Beeda.*

I got on. I inserted my card and a hundred-rand note. On the first hit, two wheels of gold and a five jumped onto the screen, and the machine made a ticking sound.

"Holy fuck!" the man exclaimed. "You're lucky, lady! Four thousand rand!"

The attendant came and handed me a cheque. I left. It was only when I was in the car, counting out my money – six thousand eight hundred rand – that I realised I had eaten, that Ramadan was not yet over. My son was not yet twenty-four hours in the ground. My bag bulged with dirty money. Right behind the wheel, I broke down.

Eventually I went home, replaced the money I'd taken from my credit card and squared everything up again. I owed no one money. But my winnings didn't make me feel good. I didn't eat the rest of the day, and to punish myself, only had a cup of tea later that night. On Eid, I spent the day with my children, and the day after that returned to the casino. I didn't allow myself to think. To think would be to feel guilty. And I had the urge. Again I was lucky and won a thousand rand. I came home with the money. I wasn't too bad, I told myself.

After that I stayed away for a few days, until the seven nights was over, then returned. I would treat myself, I said, and had a thousand rand on me. I was a big spender now. My Auntie-allowance had shot up from three hundred to five hundred to one thousand.

In no time I lost the whole thousand. I went to the ATM and took out another thousand. I lost that money also. I went back and withdrew a thousand from my credit card, and went back to play. I had a few small spins, and lost everything.

I had exceeded my limit and had to leave. I could hardly concentrate on the drive home. My visit had cost me three thousand rand. Who did I think I was? I had no regard for the value of money. It had come easy and I had given it back even more easily. Three thousand rand was a luxury mattress. A new TV. A weekend at a spa. I had lost it so fast, it hadn't hit me yet. Over and over I berated myself. Something I'd done before and something I'd promised not to repeat. But here I was again, hating myself. I sought comfort on my prayer mat. It didn't help. I was a hypocrite. I couldn't pray with sincerity.

*Please, God . . . I promise . . .*

My promise was good for two days when the urge was upon me again. So you lost. That was the other day. This is a new day. A new cycle. Go back. So maybe you won't win it all back, but you'll get something.

I went back. Four mind-blowing days in a row. I won. I lost. I withdrew money. I replaced it. Two thousand. Three thousand. I lost count. Once I stayed from two in the afternoon until midnight, waiting for the day to change dates so I could withdraw more money and play on. I couldn't get enough of the casino. I hated the atmosphere, the greediness, the illusion of fun, the pathetic grins, and I hated that I was one of them. But, I couldn't stop.

By the time of my son's forty nights, I had lost all my money, had nothing left in my savings account, and owed the credit card company four thousand, five hundred rand. There was a small balance of five hundred left for that dire emergency, but if I took that, I would owe five grand.

I sat at the kitchen table with the telephone, water, and electricity accounts spread out before me. The amounts totaled more than eight hundred rand. Even if I withdrew the five hundred from my credit card, I couldn't pay all of them. And I still needed to pay the credit card, Margaret's wages, put petrol in my car, buy groceries and the ingredients for the cakes and pies I had to bake for that evening.

I couldn't believe what I'd done to myself. I was a sensible woman, I always had money, and had always known how to manage my wealth. But I had spent my time in a palace of losers, getting high on the sound of machines and lost everything. Not one thousand, not two thousand. More than twelve thousand, and I *owed* four thousand, five hundred.

What was I going to do? My sons gave me money, but it wasn't the end of the month yet. I didn't have three rand for a litre of milk. There was no money for bread. And I had a whole lot of people coming that evening for the forty nights. I felt a pain in my heart as I thought how disappointed my sons would be to know what I've done. A woman of forty-nine, a woman of ibadah, a woman who'd been to Mecca and knew the sins of gambling.

*You went there with your eyes wide open, Beeda. No one kidnapped you. You thought you were different. You thought because you were Muslim that you could control yourself. What a laugh. It's got nothing to do with what God you pray to. It's who you are. Who are you, Beeda? Who?*

It was 11.30 a.m. I was still sitting at the kitchen table, down to my last cigarette. I had people coming in less than eight hours. I watched Margaret through the back door talking to her friend, Evelyn, who worked four houses away. The two of them were deep in conversation, Margaret doing the listening, Evelyn the talking, a cigarette passing back and forth between them. When the cigarette was done, Margaret took another out of the front of her dress, lit it, and handed it to Evelyn. Evelyn was a younger woman, and from her woeful expression, the way she dabbed at her eyes with a wad of toilet paper – Margaret had brought out a toilet roll – and from Margaret's serious concentration, I knew there was a dirty rat of a husband somewhere in the tale.

Margaret's been with me for a while. I got her through an agency in Grassy Park; about fifty, stringy as a beanstalk – says two words when you speak to her, eh-weh, Madam – but a heart of gold.

"What does that mean, 'eh-weh, Madam'?"

Margaret didn't hear.

"Margaret, did you hear what I said?"

Margaret went on merrily peeling potatoes. She refuses to go to the doctor to have her ears seen to. People who called my house knew about Margaret already. They didn't bother to leave their telephone numbers. There was always a digit missing, or a letter in the name left out – like eith for Keith. Whenever I came home, and asked if anyone had called, I got the same answer.

"Eh-weh, Madam. I wrote down."

"Who called, Margaret?"

"Madam's brother."

"Margaret, I don't have a brother.

"Eh, Madam, haikona."

And so it goes. I like Margaret. She may be a little deaf, but she's not dof, and to look in her face when she's sitting on the bench outside in the yard smoking a cigarette, is to look into the face of someone who has waited her whole life for things. People who come to my house know they're not to order her around. Once I came home Margaret told me Nabeweya had been there in my absence. She couldn't get the name right, and said, "Madam se vriend met die goue tande." Madam's friend with the gold teeth. She told me Nabeweya had told her to go into the yard to pick avocados from the tree. She told Nabeweya that no one was to go into my garden while I wasn't there. Someone else had done it before and I'd been cross. Nabeweya told her to go out into the yard anyway. They looked up into the tree, the avocados were high up. Nabeweya made her stand on a rickety ladder, which she held, and told her to pick the fruit. Margaret picked four avos. Nabeweya told her to pick more. She went home with twelve avocados. When I got home, Margaret told me what had happened. I went out into the yard. The tree hadn't borne a lot of fruit that year, and there were maybe two or three avos, very high up, which even if you stood on a ladder and reached up with a rake, you couldn't reach.

I called Nabeweya. "Listen, Nabe," I said. "How are you?"

"I'm fine, Alhamdu lilah. I was at your place, you weren't there. Your girl gave me some avos."

"No, Nabe, that's not how it happened. She told me you told her to go out and pick avos for you, and she told you that I would be cross. Someone else also came here once and went into my garden, and just beat the avos off the tree. I mean, really. I don't go onto other people's property, and just help myself to their things. It's not the avos. Don't misunderstand what I'm saying. And you had her stand on a ladder. What if she fell? I'm pissed off, Nabe, and I don't know if I'm more pissed off with you taking twelve avos, leaving me three, or whether I'm ticked that you came here and ordered Margaret around."

She was so upset, she didn't walk with me for almost a year.

Margaret came in with the toilet roll. Her friend, Evelyn, had gone back to work, and Margaret switched on the kettle for coffee. Margaret always ate breakfast around eight in the morning, but didn't have coffee until around eleven. I could tell from her expression that she was concerned about something.

"Everything all right, Margaret?"

"No, Madam.

"Wat's verkeerd?" What's wrong?

"It's Evelyn, Madam. That husband of hers. He got another woman. The woman come to see Evelyn."

"Evelyn's husband lives with Evelyn on the premises?"

"Yes, Madam, in a room in the yard. But he don't come home for three days. The woman come."

"What did she want?"

Margaret took the coffee out of the fridge. She didn't answer right away

"She come tell Evelyn she must get her another man."

"Bladdy nerve. What did Evelyn say?"

"My friend, she's soft, Madam. She cry. She's pregnant. I tell her she must finish with this man. She must not blame the unborn child. She must have it. She must get rid of the man."

The very advice I would've given. Margaret, the listener, comforter, and giver of advice. My heart went out to them. Who can they turn to? And listening to them talk in their own language, is no different than listening to Rhoda, Garaatie and myself when we discuss our troubles. We judge people when they can't speak English or Afrikaans as well as we can. We think they are stupid, that they have no heart, no feelings, no longing, and no aspirations. Margaret and Evelyn had their own language. We had never had to learn theirs; they were forced to know ours. We would've fared far worse in their world trying to make ourselves understood. I felt remorse as I thought how I myself was often guilty too.

"That was good advice you gave her, Margaret. You can only be her friend, and support her through this."

"I know, Madam. She's my friend."

"Margaret, how much money do you have?"

Margaret had four children living with her mother in the Eastern Cape. In four months' time, she was going home for a holiday, and I would have to give her double pay.

"Madam?"

"Have you got money?"

"Eh, Madam. Madam needs?"

"I need five hundred rand, until next week. Have you got?"

"Yes, Madam."

"I'll give it back to you."

"I know, Madam. I don't need it now, but when I go home."

"Don't worry, Margaret. You'll have the money before you go home."

She went to get the money out of her cupboard, and came back with a brown paper bag, and counted out five one-hundred-rand notes. Margaret never wanted me to pay her in fifties or twenties. "I'm going to eat it, Madam," she said, meaning that change was a dangerous thing for her to have as she would spend it. She liked sweets, and I made sure I had toffees and licorice in the house. Margaret bought three cartons of cigarettes once a month, kept the change in a small little purse, and saved the hundred-rand notes in a brown paper bag. It had to be a crisis at home in the Eastern Cape for Margaret to open this brown paper bag, take off the elastic band around the little roll, and part with the money. She saved everything she earned to take home with her for her children. It made me sad to see how generous she was, knowing where I was going with that money.

But Margaret's five hundred rand was my last, desperate attempt to change the situation I was in. I went to the shop and bought all the things I needed for the savouries I had to make for that night. I put petrol in my car, and went to the casino with the balance of two hundred rand.

"Madam's going to Auntie?"

I smiled. "Yes, Margaret. I'm a sick woman. Maybe I should talk to you, Margaret, and you can tell *me* what to do."

I headed straight for the wheel of gold machines. I was apprehensive when I stuck in my card. Two hundred rand was suddenly a lot of money. If I lost it I would be in real trouble.

Immediately I got a hundred rand spin. I continued to play. The money on the card went up and down, until I lost the hundred I'd put in, plus the hundred I'd won. I inserted a fifty-rand note. I lost that also. I looked about, wondering if people could tell from my face how worried I was. I lit a cigarette, and inserted the last fifty rand. On the first push, I got a spin, and it stopped on a thousand rand.

I couldn't believe it. I was saved. I got up, cashed in, and left the casino.

Margaret's brows shot up when she saw me open my purse. She didn't say a word when I handed her back her five hundred rand.

"Thank you, Margaret."

"Eh, Madam. Madam doesn't need?"

"Not today, Margaret. Thanks."

"Because Madam can lend."

"Borrow, Margaret, not lend. You lend to, you borrow from. I don't owe you anything else, right?"

"No, Madam."

"And don't lend me anything if I ask again."

Margaret smiled. "Auntie was good today to Madam?"

I laughed. "Auntie was very happy to see me." I often gave her a hundred rand when I won, but not that day. I just had enough to do the necessaries. "You must never go there, Margaret, you must promise me. It's not a good place."

"Never, Madam."

"And before you start packing away the groceries, please go and pay this telephone account. I don't want them to cut the line."

When Margaret was gone, I phoned John.

"John, I don't know if you remember me. Abeeda Ariefdien. I saw you some time ago. The lady with the scarves."

He laughed. "Of course I remember you. How's it going, Abeeda? Have you been gambling?"

"I think we have to have that talk, John."

He was quiet for a moment. "All right."

"And I want the address for Gamblers Anonymous."

With a pain in my heart, I stood with my family and watched Imran put the ring on Zulpha's finger. She looked up at him through mascaraed lashes and smiled. My heart broke, and for a reckless moment I wanted to scream out, and stop the proceedings. He doesn't love her! I wanted to shout. How is this fair! I don't know how I managed to stand there and look happy and wish them.

It was the longest night of my life. I hated that I'd had to consider my sister. Would she have done the same for me? I who was always accused of being the brash one? No one thought a big mouth had feelings. Every time I thought of them, a pain swept through my heart. I thought of what he was doing with her. I thought of her in his arms, under him, receiving his love. I hated him for being able to do it. How could you do it if you didn't love? Then I would remember that he hadn't wanted to marry Zulpha, and forgave him. Then I hated him again. Over and over, round and round, the beginning of a vicious spiral of hate and forgiveness that knew no end. I couldn't bear the mention of his name. If I heard it in conversation, I left the room. I wanted to know nothing about him.

But I did my duty as a sister. I attended family functions. I baked, I brought presents, I sat with cousins and aunts and listened to all the stories about her wonderful life.

Imran started work on my mother's house soon after they got married. I still referred to it as my mother's house even after they'd bought it. He was always busy in the yard mixing cement, or fixing some piece of equipment. He would greet me, spend a few minutes in idle chatter, then stay out of my way. He made sure we were never alone.

I couldn't believe how it had all turned out. In my own convoluted little brain, I had thought he would marry her and love me. I had thought we would still have a loving relationship. I hadn't expected that he would cut me off like that. He didn't seem hard-pressed by the marriage he'd said he didn't want, and in fact, seemed to have settled in very well. Where was his suffering? If he had loved me, why was there no evidence of it?

The weeks passed. I started to make excuses for one or two family functions, and found reasons to stay away. Things also took a turn at the office. One Saturday morning Dr Lewinsky called me at home and asked if I could come in for a few hours. There were some reports he had to get out. I said I would ask my babysitter if she could look after Reza. I didn't remind him that I didn't type and that Marion did the reports. I knew well what the call was about. I told him I would be at the office in an hour.

I slipped into jeans and a T-shirt, and examined myself in the mirror. My hips were narrow, my legs long and strong. They didn't call me Beeda Boude for nothing in high school. I ran for my team in standard six. And with my hair reaching into my back, I looked like one of those mod girls with the thick eyeliner and black fringe and straight black hair you always saw in ads on Carnaby Street. Like Cher in the early days.

I arrived at the office and found him waiting for me in the reception area. He too was in jeans. There was no briefcase or files. The light wasn't on in his office. We both knew why he'd called and why I was there.

"Let's go to Sea Point," he said.

"Okay."

"And call me Paul. In the office you'll say doctor."

"All right."

I got into the passenger seat of the silver Mercedes. I didn't look at him. I wanted a bit of fun and attention, anything that could make me forget for a few hours.

He stopped on Beach Road at the ice-cream parlour and bought two huge cones with chocolate flakes. We didn't go for a walk, or for coffee. We couldn't be seen together; he lived in Sea Point. So we sat in the car watching the waves, licking our cones.

"I'd like to show you my house," he said.

"Sure."

"You know you're a very attractive girl."

I glanced at him. "Thank you."

"Do you have a boyfriend?"

"I thought I had."

"What happened?"

"He married my sister."

"Oh."

He took out two serviettes from the glove compartment, and handed one to me. 'I'm sorry to hear that."

"It's all right. She knew him first. I don't know why I told you."

"Maybe you just needed to say it. How do you feel?"

"Not good."

"I've been there," he said. "It's hard in the beginning, but you'll get over it."

I listened to him. What did he know? If he knew anything about love, he wouldn't be sitting with me in a car thinking of cheating on his wife.

"You're young," he continued. "You have your whole life ahead of you."

"I have four children."

"That's all right. When a man falls in love, he doesn't care how many children you have. Men give up their children for love."

"Really?"

"Yes. I don't mean they don't have a relationship with them. They do. They see them on weekends, they take them to parks and movies, and spend time with them, but they will leave home for a woman they love."

I thought of Braima who'd left a pregnant wife and three children. "I guess you're right. Do you fall in love when you're happily married?"

"You're not happily married if you look around."

I could've told him then that he wasn't, but didn't say anything. I was digesting what he'd said. It was almost two years since Braima's departure, but I still hurt when I remembered how it had all come to a crashing end. And it *was* for another woman. That was what hurt most. That it made you feel that you hadn't been good enough, or pretty enough, or exciting enough. That's how you felt irrespective of what the truth was.

We talked some more, then he started the car. "I won't take you to my house now," he said.

"That's fine."

He drove back to the office, and thanked me for coming with him. He waited for me to get into my car. "Take care of yourself."

"I will. Thank you."

But the outing had changed the dynamics between us. At the office on Monday he was flirtatious when we were alone, and I took even more care with my appearance. I wore pants instead of dresses and skirts, and wore my hair loose now instead of tied back.

On Friday, when the last patient had left, and I was picking up the cotton gowns from the doctors' rooms, and taking them to the front where the cleaning woman collected them, Paul Lewinsky followed me out, and spun me around. It happened so fast, one moment he was holding my hand, and the next I was up against the wall and his mouth was on mine. I stood trembling under his touch.

At last he let go of me. "I'm very attracted to you, Abeeda."

I was too shaken to speak. I snatched my purse from the counter, and ran. In the car I saw I was late for the babysitter. Traffic was thick, it was Friday. I arrived at Nisa's house just as she was getting ready to go grocery shopping. I thanked her for waiting, strapped Reza into the car seat, and drove home. When I took the corner into my street, I saw Imran's bakkie in the driveway. He was playing ball with the twins in the yard. My heart thundered in my chest.

The twins left the ball and came running up. "Mummy . . . "

I kissed them and handed Reza to Munier and told them to go inside.

"What're you doing here?" I asked.

"Is that how you're going to speak to me?"

"What are you doing here?"

"Beeda, please . . . "

"Fuck off!"

He turned to look at the back door to see if the children had heard. There was no one.

"Can I talk to you?"

"There's nothing to talk about. I don't want to see you."

"You told me to do this."

"I didn't tell you to throw me to the dogs. I didn't think you would slip right into your nice little marriage and forget about me."

"I didn't forget you. Do you want me to lead a double life?"

"What do you think this is, coming here? Are you here with your wife?"

"I wanted to talk to you."

"What about?"

"I'm not going to talk if you're like this." He started to walk away.

"No, talk to me! Don't come here and play with my feelings. What do you want to talk about? I wish you'd never written that letter, and come into my life."

He stopped and turned to me. "How do you think I feel? I'm with her, and I'm thinking of you. How is that fair? And when you visit, I stay out of your way. It's too hard for me to be in your company. If I'm to have any chance in that marriage I have to kill you off in my brain."

I wanted to cry when he said it. "Then kill me off. What are you doing here now?"

"I couldn't stay away another day. I miss you. I wanted to see you."

I started to walk away. He pulled my hand. "I didn't love you, Beeda. There's no past tense to this. I *fucking* love you. But what is this love, when I can't have you? You told me it was better this way."

My nastiness flared up again. "How does it feel to have sex with her?"

"Stop."

"How does it feel, Imran? You manage, don't you? You get it up?"

"I hate it when you get like this."

"You hate it? It's uncomfortable for you? I'm hurting!"

Zane came out of the house. "Mummy, what's wrong?"

"Nothing," I said. "Go inside. Do your homework."

"There's no school tomorrow," he answered. "Auntie Toeghieda's picking me up, remember? I'm spending the weekend with them."

"Go and get ready then." I turned back to Imran. His car keys were in his hands. I had moments left. On one side, my life was slipping away; on the other, it was going on furiously.

"I just wanted to see you."

"That's it? You just wanted to see me? What must I do with that?"

"Zulpha had a miscarriage. I have to pick her up at the medical centre."

It was a serious bit of news, but I was too angry. "A miscarriage? My. That means she was pregnant. You're having a hard time getting it right, aren't you?"

His eyes pleaded with mine. "Do you want me to leave her, Beeda?"

"And do you want to know what I did with the doctor an hour ago?"

"What?"

"Never mind. You couldn't handle it."

He lowered his head and walked away to the van.

"Don't come here again!" I shouted. "Don't fucking come here!"

And so began my torrid affair with Dr Paul Lewinsky. He was forbidden by all the rules, but I didn't care. It wasn't love, I didn't think of the consequences. I saw him on Wednesday and Friday nights at a flat in Bantry Bay, and knew that what happened on the fake leopard skin couch was all there was. Hungry bodies. Hurting souls. An office attraction that played itself out in a rented flat. I didn't expect more. He couldn't give more. I made no demands. When his wife called at the office, I brought tea and asked about the children. I had no feelings of guilt.

When I had worked for the good doctor for six months, Marion quit her job, and a new secretary started. Jennifer Fiedler was a stunning girl with blue eyes and soft brown hair. I could tell right away that she was smart, cunning and confident. She got on the pony right away, and was there two days when she told me Paul Lewinsky was cute.

Paul Lewinsky picked up the scent. His radar flickered like a beacon in distress. From Jennifer's very first week his manner towards me changed. He still asked me to get his lunch, but no longer invited me to eat with him, and asked a little too much about the new girl. He called her the new girl so I would think his queries cold and impersonal, but I'd never deluded myself that Paul Lewinsky would leave his wife and go Muslim.

First, he cancelled our Friday night appointment and said he had things to take care of at home. The following week Jennifer went to get his lunch. A week after that she came to work with two hickeys in her neck – much like the ones I'd sported a few weeks earlier.

I went home that evening feeling like a loose undersole, flip-flopping my way through this new development. I had two men now I was pining about. I didn't know which one I hated more. Both had been brutally honest, and both had betrayed me. And I had allowed it. I had set myself up. Imran had also called some time ago to ask what I'd done with the doctor. It was the day after I'd gone to Paul's flat the first time.

"I fucked him. I went to his flat and fucked him. Like you're fucking my sister. It's a fuck, isn't it? You don't love her."

He put down the phone. For a long time I never heard from him. Four weeks later I got a call from Zulpha who told me she was pregnant.

I cried. Zulpha thought it was out of happiness, but the news confirmed that I had to take stock of my life. A child was on the way. I had to let go. I spent the weekend in bed feeling sorry for myself and doing a lot of thinking. I decided that when I got to work on Monday, I would check the classifieds and look for another job.

It was at this time that I really came to know Garaatie. Zulpha had told me that Garaatie was going to Muslim school one night a week, and was raving about the calipha. I was in search of something. I didn't know what, and went to see her.

I had known Garaatie for about two years as my mother's neighbour, and had come to know her a little better after my mother's death, but didn't really know anything about her. That night I sat in her living room and got an inkling of the kind of man she was married to.

She'd been married two years. I told her what Zulpha had told me and asked how she'd come across this new Muslim teacher.

"I was interested in knowing more about polygamy, and someone told me to go see this mu'alim, Abdul Latief, who's very enlightened. He has a madressah. I joined, and found out what I wanted to know. He's not one of those die-hards who points a finger at you and says if you don't obey the Word, that this and that is going to happen to you. Everything has to make sense, he says, and he explains things in a way that's easy to understand. He's educated and modern, and tells you repeatedly that the Qur'an wasn't just for the desert."

"Where's his school?" I asked. "Can I come with you?"

"His house isn't far from here. He's in Penlyn Estate. Of course you can come."

Mahmood came into the living room, wearing a sports jacket. His hair looked freshly combed. I'd met him before, and greeted him.

"I'm just going to Faried quickly to pick up a gasket," he said.

"Are you going to be long?" Garaatie asked.

"Half an hour."

"Okay."

An hour later, Garaatie was starting to glance at the clock.

"I hope Mahmood didn't mind me coming here," I said. "Did you have plans for this evening?"

"He's never home long enough for us to have plans."

I could've asked – she looked like she needed to talk – but didn't. I didn't know anything about her personal life at that time. We talked for a while longer. Garaatie had a ten-month-old son, and told me that she had just found out she was pregnant again. She didn't look happy when she told me, and again I didn't pry. By the time I got up and said I had to go, I had been at her house almost three hours. Mahmood still hadn't come home.

I left her house glad that I'd gone to see her. She had inspired me with her talk about Abdul. I arrived home, had a shower, went on my prayer mat, and made a fresh attempt with God. I had made a mistake with Imran.

*Please, please, forgive me my trespasses, Allah. Please forgive me, and please be with me.*

On Monday morning I went to work early. I had some things to file away that I hadn't done the Friday, and wanted the desk to be cleared before the day started. I arrived at the office to find the door locked, but the light on when I entered the reception area. I left my bag on the front desk, and walked to the small kitchen area to switch on the kettle. I found Jennifer in the back office with Paul Lewinsky. I had such a fright, I just stood there, looking at the two of them. He was standing, with his pants dropped to his ankles. She was kneeling before him with her face in his crotch.

There was nothing more to think about. I didn't run, or make any utterances. I just turned around, and walked out. When I received a cheque in the mail two weeks later, I didn't question either the amount or the forms that came with it. My brief stint as a receptionist was over. I had no intention of working in an office again.

On Wednesday night I met Garaatie in front of Abdul's house.

"Did you hear the news?" she asked. "Did your sister call you?"

"What news?"

"She had a miscarriage this afternoon. She's in hospital. I was outside in the garden, when Imran got out of the jeep and told me."

Another miscarriage. I couldn't believe it. "I wasn't home today," I lied. "Maybe they tried to call me."

We stood at the gate for a few minutes talking. My mind whirled with the news of a second child lost, but I was in another place now, and wanted desperately to separate myself from my sister's life. I felt I was two people. The sister who cared deeply and wanted the best for Zulpha, and the rejected lover who hated the man who had started all this, and the sister who again was getting what she wanted.

We entered the house. It was a standard bungalow with a dining room and lounge. Twelve women ranging in age from twenty-something to older ladies in their sixties, sat on couches and chairs in the lounge. A young, fairish man with green eyes, and a neat beard, dressed in jeans with a beige top over it, sat at the head of the group.

Garaatie introduced me to Abdul, and to the women. Abdul asked a few questions, then Garaatie and I sat on chairs brought in from the dining room. Another woman and her daughter arrived, and the session started.

"Tonight I want to talk about the demands of the ego, and our preoccupation with me, my, I, and mine," Abdul said.

"I want to talk about jihad. The jihad with the self. The struggle against the open enemy, Satan. Satan who wants us to follow our desires, instead of the path of God. Satan who promised that he would mislead us. This is where the ego comes in. You can't be a slave to two masters. The ego believes in acquiring more and more. Pleasure, power, sex, money. But more and more doesn't make anyone happy. It leads to isolation, you start to fear loss, and worst of all, you start to identify with externals. When you've lost a husband or a child, or going through some painful experience, these things don't help you."

I looked at the faces of the other women. Were they there also because of the pain in their hearts? Abdul was young. I had thought the lecture would be about what to do and what not to do, but the words sin and punishment didn't pass his lips once. His talk was tailor-made for me, and coming at the right time. I wasn't there to learn how to behave as a Muslim. I wanted some nugget of light I could take into my heart and act on, something that could save me. I was looking for an effective way to end my pain. I was looking for God. I had realised that I put my forehead on the ground five times a day, but didn't know a darn thing about God.

"That doesn't mean that you can't be rewarded for hard work, or that you can't have that car you've always wanted, or nice things. These things are here also for us to enjoy, but these are not things we should aspire to. These are not things that will sustain us. It's the spiritual life we must seek out. We will leave this world with nothing except a level of spirituality that will continue in the next life. The next life is forever. We will not have a chance in the next life to change things. If we leave here thinly padded, without having learned anything after a lifetime on earth, we will wander there as we're floundering here. So let us talk about the ego . . ."

I was drawn in, and knew I'd be back. The lecture ended. I went up to Abdul. "I really enjoyed listening to you," I said. "That was an interesting talk, and I have so many other things I'd like to ask you. Is it possible to see you outside of this class?"

"Of course," he said. "I have classes three mornings a week at the university, but I'm free from three in the afternoons. Not Fridays, of course. Unless you want to come in the evening."

We agreed on a time, and I left with Garaatie. We sat in my car for a few minutes before driving home in our respective vehicles. "That was really great, Garaatie. I'm glad I came. Thanks."

"I told you. He knows all the scriptures, even the ones not mentioned in the Book. His approach is different. Not the way we were taught. He doesn't give you the party line. And he's progressive."

Progressive and modern were bad words in the community. "He's young," I said.

"He's thirty-three."

"That's young, for all this knowledge. Is he married?"

She smiled. "There's a story that goes with Abdul."

"What's the story?"

"Abdul's sort of the Muslim equivalent of a priest. He's given up earthly love to devote his life to the purification of the soul."

It seemed odd to me that anyone would do that. Monkery wasn't allowed in Islam.

The day following my visit to Abdul's house, Zulpha called to say that she'd lost the baby. She made light of it, but I could tell that she was disappointed. She said she would wait a few months, then try again.

"I quit my job at the medical centre," I said.

"You did? I thought you were happy there."

"I was. Anyway, I quit. I spoke to Garaatie. She says there's money in chocolates."

"There is. My friend Mareldia ran a thriving business from her home. She made all kinds of sweets. I can give you some contacts. She buys her chocolate from a special place. She has a lot of customers."

It had been Zulpha's idea about the pies in the beginning, and it was her encouragement again, to go into making sweets. And so I started a little business in my garage with one helper, Iris, a gas burner, and a lot of baking chocolate and nuts. I experimented with peanut clusters, truffles and fudge. While Iris worked at melting, mixing, and moulding the chocolate, I went around in my Beetle to the shops. In a few months I had so many orders, I couldn't keep up.

I was making more money now than at the medical centre. My children had two pairs of shoes each, new blazers for school, and also got pocket money. I didn't fret when Braima's maintenance payment was late. I was saving up for a bigger car and bikes for the children.

I worked hard at getting Imran out of my thoughts. I didn't sit at home and fret. I worked at my business during the day, but also took time for myself and my children. There wasn't only the pain of Imran. I heard about the birth of the baby girl of my ex-husband, Braima. You can be in love with someone, and still be hurt by a past loss. Sometimes the current involvement is because of a past loss. I heard from my sons, after a weekend visit to their father, that they had a sister. I said nice things, but I hurt. And I went on. My days and evenings were full. I went out, I read books, I took my three older children to a matinée once a month. I saw Abdul. After a while I was seeing him so much, I no longer went to madressah. I invited him to my house, made him things to eat, and had lengthy discussions with him. I shared his love for history, the past, and the old patriarchs, and found a new way of seeing things.

"I read this book," he said to me once, "that the God of pestilence and plagues was the God of four thousand years ago."

"What do you mean?"

"The author's implying that as man evolved, so had God."

"You mean the old God was harsher?"

"Yes. Man did evolve, you know. We have an understanding now to become highly spiritual beings. It's something to think about."

I did think about it, and went to the Bible and the Tawrah to read things for myself. I had always loved Bible stories, especially the stories about Jesus. These discussions with Abdul took me in a direction that helped me greatly overcome the shallow happenings in my life. I still don't know if I believe that God had changed, but from those early days with Abdul already, he showed me a different view of God.

One Wednesday evening, before I stopped going to madressah altogether, one of the women in the group brought along a friend. I recognised her immediately. It was Rhoda, a girl I'd known from my days in high school. When the lecture was over, I went up to her.

"I recognised you too," she said, "but I wasn't sure. How are you? You married Braima, didn't you?"

"I'm divorced now. Almost three years. He's married again, they just had a daughter. And you?"

"I married Rudwaan. I worked at First National for ten years. We met there. We live in Athlone now."

"My goodness. I'm in Rondebosch East. We're near each other. This is Garaatie," I said. "Garaatie used to live next door to my mother. She and her husband, Mahmood, just moved to Rylands. You must come to my house. We must chat."

This was the beginning of our teas, our movies, and our walks together. After four or five times with these two friends, I knew every little secret in their lives. Garaatie had thus far only been my madressah friend, but I got to know her much better now. She talked openly about her husband.

"I search his pockets, yes. It happened by accident the first time when

I was looking for money in one of his trousers, and found this folded up piece of paper with two numbers on it. There was no name or anything, but I just wondered whose numbers they might be that it doesn't even require a name. He goes out a lot by himself."

Rhoda told me about the squabbles with her mother-in-law. The woman lived in the same house with them, upstairs, and didn't like her because Rhoda didn't cook for her son the way she had. And Rhoda served rolls and viennas on Fridays, and didn't cook on Saturdays.

"But she won't be with us long. Rudwaan's sister, Fawzia, is moving to a house in the Bo-Kaap in six weeks – she was lucky to get it – and his mother's going to live with her. Fawzia lost her husband six months ago in a car crash, she's alone."

I told them about my failed marriage, and my short stint as a receptionist at the medical centre. I couldn't let Rhoda think she was the only one who'd worked in an office. I talked about Braima, but said nothing about Paul Lewinsky or Imran.

On my thirtieth birthday my sisters came to my house and surprised me with a cake. Rhoda and Garaatie had come for tea, and were also there.

It was the first time I saw Imran since his visit to my house a month earlier. Telling him about the doctor had made it easier for him to forget me, and I was sorry I'd told him. What disturbed me though was realising that, despite all my efforts at trying to forget him, my feelings hadn't changed. Even though he was with my sister. Even though his child had already lived in her womb. Even after all my soul searching, pleading and beseeching.

I remember what I had on that day. The plum-coloured dress with the gold dragons, the mandarin collar, and slits. My hair was pinned up Chinese style. The reason I remember the dress, was because it was a gift from Rhoda who'd seen me admiring it in a boutique when we'd gone out for coffee and cake the previous month. I had to put on the dress for my friends, and Rhoda had pinned up my hair. The visitors arrived as I came out to show them what I looked like.

"Wow, Beeda, you look smashing!" Zulpha said. "That style really suits you."

"It's a bit tight," Toeghieda said. "You can make the slits shorter. They don't have to go up so high."

"It's a present. I like it."

"And it suits you," Garaatie added. "You have the body."

"Don't tell her things like that," Toeghieda said. "She doesn't need any encouragement."

Everyone had something to say about the dress except Imran. But he called me the next day.

"So the lady in the Chinese dress. You looked divine."

My heart pumped in my chest. I didn't say anything.

"I won't ask if I can come and see you," he said.

"Don't."

"How are you?"

"As you saw."

There was a moment's silence. "I'm not okay," he said.

I refused to get into it. I said nothing.

"Are you not going to talk to me, Beeda?"

"What's there to talk about?"

"We can be friends, surely."

If he had been in front of me, I would've slammed the phone against his head. "Is this what you called me for? You want to be my friend?"

"Of course not. But it's all we can have. Are you never going to talk to me? I miss you."

"You don't know that you hurt me, do you?"

He didn't answer.

"Say goodbye, Imran."

I saw John twice before I was brave enough to drive myself to a school hall at Cairncross and Protea on a Tuesday night to attend Gamblers Anonymous.

"You won't feel uncomfortable at all, Abeeda," John told me. "Everyone there is just like you, they all want to stop gambling."

I raised my eyebrows when I walked in with my double scarves. A silver-haired man in his sixties came up to me, and introduced himself.

"I'm Gavin," he said.

"I'm Abeeda. I haven't been here before."

"Don't be nervous," he said. "Let me introduce you to Robin and some of the others. We have three newcomers tonight."

I met several people before the meeting got started, and spotted a man I knew from the Bo-Kaap, Achmat Samaai. I didn't know Achmat was a gambler and was very surprised to see him here. Muslims wouldn't be seen in a place like Gamblers Anonymous. The Qur'an said gambling's a sin. Muslims didn't gamble. They didn't commit sin. And they never would admit it by being there. I glanced at him. I knew he'd recognised me, but went along with the pretence. I wouldn't tell anyone, and he wouldn't tell either.

The meeting started and we sat in a circle facing one another. There were many addictions floating about in that room. The room soon turned blue with smoke.

"My name's Keith," a tall youth started, "I'm a compulsive gambler." He paused, rearranging his long legs in front of him, leaning back in the chair. "I've been clean now for three months and six days, and every day's a struggle for me. I'm a driver. I can't even go to the airport, or up the N7 or N1, without taking a turn at the casino. Any time I get close to that brown sign, I get the urge. My urges come every few minutes. But I stay away. I make a detour to avoid passing any of the exits. The mornings are the hardest. I have this terrible urge for roulette. To put my chips down on the table, and see if my number comes up. But I suffer through it. I smoke. I'm a heavy smoker already. You all know I kicked crack thirteen months ago. I'm still clean."

I looked at the other gamblers. Men in business suits, jeans, track pants, and women of all sizes, some with long cigarettes and mournful expressions. I recognised one or two from the casino.

Keith continued. "My problem started fourteen months ago when my friend Jeremy got a cheque from his grandfather's estate, and gave me five hundred rand. No one had ever given me money before, but he'd gotten a big cheque, and he felt generous. We decided to go to the casino. I had never been to a casino before, and was swept up by the atmosphere. Jeremy played roulette, and I watched. I didn't want to spend the money he'd given me. Two hours later, Jeremy lost the two thousand rand he'd come with, and I decided to give it a try. I knew nothing about roulette, or how people kept track of numbers, and had no strategy, but I'd watched for two hours, and decided to try my luck. I would only play a hundred rand. To tell you how naïve I was, I didn't even spread the chips around, I just put the whole hundred rand on a number. I couldn't believe it when the number came in. I still remember it, thirty-six."

I watched the faces about me. The expressions were grim. They knew what was next. I knew also, but still wanted the thrill of his win.

"I won't bore you with details," he continued. "We had arrived there at six in the afternoon. At midnight, I had everyone standing around me. I don't know what happened. I just chose numbers and they came up. I asked people to tell me what year they were born, and would pick the last two digits. By midnight, I had over sixteen thousand rand in chips. There was no place to stack them on the table, and I had them dripping out of my pockets. I gave my friend back the five hundred rand he'd given me and a thousand rand bonus. He went to play at another table, and lost."

I noted the smiles and the nods. Whatever the winnings, all the stories ended the same.

"At one in the morning, two of the bosses – I guess from upstairs – came downstairs, and watched me. They changed the dealer. My luck didn't change. By this time I had forty-three thousand rand. I could hardly stand on my feet so tired was I, and so giddy from the experience. I took my chips and cashed in. On our way to the exit, Jeremy suggested we go to the private room in the hotel, where the big dogs played. This room was even more intimidating. Here people placed five and ten thousand rand bets. I won another fifteen thousand rand."

He paused, rearranging his legs, his eyes focussed on a spot on the floor. I couldn't believe it. I'd heard many good-luck casino stories, but had never heard one like this before. And it was obviously true for the group seemed familiar with some aspects of the tale.

"That was the beginning," he said, looking up at no one in particular. "I went to the casino every night after that hoping to repeat my performance. I lost everything I'd won and everything I'd saved up. I had a job in a printing shop, earning five thousand rand a month. I quit that to gamble full time. I had the touch, I told myself. I was a professional. But I had no money now, no job, and had accounts to pay. I'd bought a new car the day after my big win, and given only ten thousand rand as a deposit. I had payments of eleven hundred rand a month. I had no income to continue the payments. I could give the car back and pay off what I owed them, but kept telling myself that things would change. I fell more and more in arrears, and the car depreciated further. I started to sell things. My guitar, a Gibson. It was worth about eight thousand rand. I sold it for seven hundred. I would win big, and buy it back. After that my drum machine had to go – a 505, worth about seven thousand. I sold it to a guy on the Cape Flats for a thousand. I'm a part-time musician. I had all my songs composed on it."

Keith's story was long. I wondered if everyone was expected to spill their guts like this.

"Eventually I had nothing left to sell, and they came for the car. I went to my mother's house and stole her gold bracelet." He turned to look at an older blonde woman with a severe haircut next to him, who I imagined was his mother.

"I took it to the coin exchange in Adderley Street, and got two hundred rand. It broke my heart that I stole from her, but I still did it. I went to the casino, in that last hope that I would hit it big again. You know the rest. I lost. I started to write cheques to the casino. There was no money in the bank. To cover the cheques, I went to a loan shark. The loan shark covered my eight-thousand rand debt, which made me indebted to him for twelve thousand rand. I couldn't pay. I borrowed money from other loan sharks to cover this one. I borrowed and I gambled and I lost. Finally, my indebtedness to them reached two hundred thousand rand."

I listened to this tale of horror and told myself that I didn't belong in that room.

"I now owed three loan sharks money. One of them had already started to make threatening phone calls to the house. I went back to my old job as a printer. They were good enough to take me back. I paid three thousand rand to the loan sharks at the end of the month. This didn't even dent the interest. The amount I owed them got larger. By this time I had lost ten kilos. I couldn't sleep and couldn't eat. One night Jeremy and I were on the highway, coming home from a club, and I flung open the car door to throw myself out. Jeremy had to hold on to me, while I sat crying hysterically. He drove me straight to my mother's house. My parents are divorced."

His mother took his hand into hers. "My mother called my father. He came right away. He listened to the story. When I was finished, he got up and paced around the living room. He was a boardroom guy and was used to making decisions, but this one silenced him. Finally, he came to sit in front of me, and said, 'I'm going to help you if you do exactly as I say'. He asked for the names and addresses of the people I owed the money to. He would phone me the next day and tell me where I was going to go for treatment. He was going to pay for it. After treatment, I was going to start work in his company, and pay back my debt. If I went to the casino even once, he was finished with me."

Keith's eyes squeezed shut. There wasn't a sound in the room except for a match being struck. The room was thick with smoke. I lit a cigarette also.

"The next day my father came back to the house. He had contacted the casino. There was one more thing he wanted me to do. He was going to pick me up the next morning and take me to the casino. They were going to take my picture. I was going to have myself banned. If I was seen anywhere on the floor, I would be arrested. And if I was seen even once in any casino or at a race track or place of gambling, he would disown me."

I looked at the woman next to him. She had a sympathetic expression, but there was a hardness also that said that she agreed with the father.

"It's been three months and six days now, and it's hard to stay away, but every day I manage not to go, is a victory. Going for treatment saved me. Being banned, forces me to stay away. I still have the urge to go, but I take it one day at a time. I haven't been desperate enough yet to disguise myself and sneak in, but I've thought about it."

I glanced at my watch. His story had taken almost fifteen minutes.

The group leader for the evening said a few words. "My name's Robin. I'm a compulsive gambler. We have some new people here tonight. Maybe we'll just go around the room and introduce ourselves."

A young man sitting across from me, said, "My name's Rob. I'm a compulsive gambler. I have multiple addictions. I'm a recovering alcoholic and a recovering drug addict. I haven't touched alcohol in five years and I haven't done crack in ten months." He took a puff on his cigarette. "I'm also a sex addict. I pay women for sex and do anything they want."

I looked at him. He didn't appear to be more than thirty; a good-looking boy, clean cut, and well dressed. I couldn't believe that he would have to pay anyone for sex. His story was even more bizarre than Keith's. It didn't involve loan sharks and thousands of rands, but spoke of a life completely out of control.

"One night I was with this girl in her car in front of a restaurant. She wanted to go and have something to eat. I wanted her to give me some money for the casino. She didn't want to. I tried to wrestle her bag from her. She held on. Then my other addiction surfaced, and I tried to pull down her panties as I was fighting with her for the bag. She struggled. Eventually her eyes closed and she just slumped behind the wheel, and I took her money. I went into the restaurant. I was terrified. I sat there for three hours, waiting for someone to come and arrest me. I didn't know if she was dead. When I left the restaurant when it closed, the car was gone. So I imagined she was okay. I walked home from Claremont to Plumstead."

By the time I heard the fourth story, I knew I wouldn't be back. These stories were better than any I'd read in a book, and the beauty of it was, the teller was completely unashamed. Finally, it was my turn. I had to say something.

"My name's Abby," I said. "I won't give the word compulsive any power. I play the slot machines, but I don't think I'm compulsive. I came here tonight to listen. Maybe next time I'll say more."

I saw the faces. Some of them smiled. They felt sorry for me.

There were five more stories. Achmat Samaai only gave his name, and said he didn't have anything to share that evening. He'd been there before. The meeting ended at nine-thirty with coffee and cake. I didn't stay to chat. I got into my car, and drove straight to the casino.

I lost the last five hundred rand on my Visa card.

The next morning I woke up late and didn't have the heart to go on my prayer mat. What could I say? Sorry? Again? I was exactly like those people at G.A. The amounts and the stories differed, but the behaviour was the same. I was as compulsive as the guy who'd wrestled the woman's bag away from her. I couldn't stop.

I sat on the edge of the bed berating myself. My life was a mess. I hadn't seen a psychologist in years, I didn't want to know what my problem was, but for all my fasting and praying, I was an addict, and hated it. Gambling had weakened my connection with God. It had eroded my soul. I would stand on my prayer mat, beg for God's Mercy, and hardly be finished before I started lusting after the slots again. The slot machine had become my other lover. My distraction. My comfort. You went, you lost. The ride home was always filled with remorse.

How could I let this continue? I would turn fifty in two months and was long past the mark where I should've grown common sense. Was I going to be one of those old women hanging about the machines, hoping that their last twenty rand would bring them luck? Were my sons going to get a call one day and be told that their mother had had a heart attack in the casino?

*You have a chance now, Beeda, it's not too late.*

*Just one more time.*

*You've lost all your money already.*

*I'll stop. I just want to win some back.*

*You never win it back. Cut your losses. Wet your feet and go on your prayer mat. You're a compulsive gambler. Admit it, and stop. You have no control.*

*I have.*

*You don't.*

*I do.*

*Stop having the conversation!*

Margaret came in from the yard to tell me that Mr Imran was just pulling into the driveway.

I was in my pyjamas. I didn't want to see him in the state I was in. It was two decades now, but I still couldn't look at him without a backwash of emotion. "Tell him I'm out," I said.

She looked at me, not understanding.

"Tell him I'm not here, Margaret. Ek is uit!"

"But Madam."

"Just tell him!"

I walked into the bathroom, and locked the door. I could hear voices in the kitchen. A few minutes later I watched from behind the curtain in my room as the jeep reversed out of the driveway. He had on sunglasses and a baseball cap. At forty-seven – he was two years younger than me – he was still great to look at.

I went into the kitchen. On the table was a tray with two casserole dishes. I lifted the lids. Snoek curry with chopped coriander, and basmati rice.

"Mr Imran say Madam must call him," Margaret said.

"Okay. Margaret, I have to borrow some money from you again."

"Dis okay, Madam. Ek makeer nie nou nie. Hoeveel?" How much? It's all right. I don't need it now.

"When my son gives me some money, I'll pay it all back. I need seven hundred."

Margaret went inside to her room and came out with the money. I felt bad that I had to borrow from her, and promised to increase her pay by a hundred rand. I would start a little business again, like in the old days, and she could help me.

I went to the shop, bought what I needed, and paid the accounts. When I got home, Margaret told me that my son had called.

"Which one?" I asked.

"Sound like the big one, Madam."

I called Zane at the shop. He told me that he had bought a whole sheep at the butcher, and had some meat to give me. Then he told me that his stepmother had gone to the breast clinic at Groote Schuur on Wednesday, and seen Zulpha there. Zulpha might have something in her breast.

"She would've told me," I said. "Are you sure?"

"I'm just saying what Daddy told me. Mummy knows how she is. Auntie Zulpha keeps everything in. Everyone's been saying how thin she is."

That was true, and I wondered whether that was what Imran had come by to tell me. He didn't come by on his own. It hadn't been easy, and the first years had been the hardest. The phone calls, the tears, the regrets. Then he and Zulpha went away for four years to Australia and had people look after the house. I hated him more for taking such a definite step to end things between us. But it was the best thing he could've done or we would've gone on forever punishing ourselves. He wrote letters, telling about their new home, their experiences, changing the tenor of the relationship. When they returned from Australia, he never mentioned again what had happened between us, and never came to my house alone.

But women have long memories, and mine never could get past his lips and his eyes and the way he moved inside me. I would cry the way he loved me. "This is how much I love you, Beeda," he would say into my hair, "With my toes, my legs, my arms. Every part of me loves you."

If I were a fool, no one knew about it. If I were sick to hold on to it after so many years, that was my own secret. The memory was mine. Entirely.

I said goodbye to Zane, and said I would drop by the house later on to pick up the meat. I transferred the food from the casserole dishes into two pots, got into my car and drove to Zulpha's house. Imran's jeep was in the driveway. I knocked on the door, and walked in.

Zulpha was at the picnic table in the yard reading a magazine. Imran was hosing the lawn. I kissed my sister, and put down the tray with the pots.

"Thanks for the food," I said. "That was thoughtful. How're you?"

"I'm fine," she said, not looking at me.

I noticed circles under her eyes. "I heard you were at Groote Schuur."

"Who told you?"

"Zane."

She looked down at the magazine she'd been reading. "I have to go back on Tuesday. They want to do a biopsy."

"A biopsy's good," I said. "Rhoda's sister had one, remember? The biopsy saved her. She never had to have surgery."

"She's dead."

"She died of a stroke. It's not the same thing. When are they doing the biopsy?"

"On Tuesday. At eight in the morning. If everything's okay, I'll be back home in the afternoon."

"I'll come with you," I said.

"Thanks. I'm not telling anyone until afterwards. So don't tell Toeghieda. I don't want everyone fretting over me."

"Is Zainap all right?" It had always bothered me that Zulpha had been friends with my ex-husband's wife.

"She has to have a mastectomy."

"Oh no." I was genuinely sorry to hear it. "When's her operation?"

"Next Thursday. She's going to be there for a while. She's quite worried about it." She looked at me. "You know, the daughters are all married. Two of them live in Port Elizabeth. The youngest one's in Canada. If anything happens to her, Braima will be all alone."

I hadn't thought of it that way. But it was true. And if anything happened to Zulpha? Imran would be free also. I realised suddenly that both these men stood to lose the women they'd chosen over me.

Imran shut off the water and joined us. "Some tea, Beeda? Coffee? Or something cold?"

"I'll have rooibos, thanks. One sugar."

He left for the kitchen. I took out my cigarettes.

"You have to stop smoking, Beeda. Imran quit two weeks ago. I'm so proud of him. Now he's eating chocolates. But rather chocolates than inhaling all that nicotine. He's put on a little weight."

"I see so."

"Don't mention it to him. I don't want him to go back to smoking. It's funny, at this age we want to give up our addictions."

"And some are harder to give up than others. I met a man the other day who's addicted to sex. He doesn't have to love them, and they don't have to be pretty. They just have to be hookers."

"Imran, did you hear that?"

Imran came out with a tray. "I heard," he laughed. "I don't know where your sister runs into these men."

I watched him put down the tray and bring out a plate of coconut tarts. An idyllic scene. The little tea party under the loquat tree. The smell of lavender. The tinkling of cups. I looked around the yard where I'd first played as a child. My father playing skipping with us girls, my mother watching from the window. My mother had been the vigilant one. My father had been the happy-go-lucky father every girl dreamed of. It was a different place now than the one I'd known. The guava and avocado pear trees were still there, but much bigger. Now there was a manicured lawn also, a kidney-shaped pool, and a white, stuccoed wall. The house itself had been transformed with an open kitchen, an additional bathroom, a pantry, and a spiral staircase leading up to a loft where Imran watched his soccer games. The two of them had weaved together this little nest. However convoluted their beginnings, it had worked out for them. They seemed the perfect couple. And in a way they were. Perfect had nothing to do with love, just about getting it right.

"My sister has her ways. She's been and she's seen."

"We ran into Rhoda at the Waterfront on Saturday," he said. "She's going on hajj next year."

"Really?" I was surprised, and wondered where she got the money from.

"You don't see her any more, do you?"

"No. She came to Reza's janazaah, but we're not in touch."

"We're thinking of going on pilgrimage also," he said. "We've been to

Egypt, Italy and Australia. We can't think of another holiday without performing our hajj first. If everything's all right with Zulpha on Tuesday, our niyyat is to go next year, Inscha Allah. You're the first to know."

"Insch Allah. Everything will be fine with Zulpha."

Zulpha had always had one ailment or another, but mostly it was a case of nerves and worrying too much. But she was the most blessed of the three of us. Toeghieda had a husband and a nice home too, but didn't think anyone knew of Mylie's philandering. The only difference between the way she handled an unfaithful husband, and the way Garaatie handled it, was that Mylie's clothes got packed for him and he got the boot. He'd spent many nights on his sister's couch. But Toeghieda kept up the bright side. She visited with him like they were couple of the month. I knew about the thirteen-year-old son Mylie had with a woman from Simon's Town. No one talked about it, but support payments went out every month. Everyone has his secret. My sisters have theirs, and I have mine.

When Zulpha and I were alone later on, I asked if she could lend me five hundred rand. I had never borrowed money from anyone in my family. I told her I needed it to repair my car, and would give it to her when I saw her on Tuesday. She was only too glad to help me out. I left her house and went straight to the casino. I was so anxious to start playing, I didn't even check the computer to see whether the machine had paid out already. I stuck my card in, lit a cigarette, and looked around for a waitress. I spotted one, and ordered a coffee, and another packet of cigarettes. I was down two hundred and seventy rand by the time she appeared. I lit a fresh cigarette, checked the computer, and saw that the machine I was playing on had paid out two thousand rand just an hour earlier. The same familiar disgust set in, and I knew I would lose the rest of the money, even if I went to another machine. You get that feeling, when you know you're doomed and that no matter how much money you have, you're going to lose. Still, I sat on, watching the last of the money disappear. I had no money at home. There was nothing in my savings.

I got up, and immediately moved away from the area. I didn't want to know who would win after I got up. I took out my wallet, and counted twelve rand in silver. I walked over to the cashiers.

"Can I have a ten-rand note?" I asked, putting down a handful of silver.

The cashier tried not to look at me. It was embarrassing to see someone scratching about for their last bit of silver to continue playing. She gave me the note. I headed for the first machine I came to, and stuck my card in. The ten rand disappeared. All around me the machines glittered and gloated. I looked about at the grins and the scowls, the looks of concentration, disappointment and disgust. I had no money left. An announcement came on that the casino had another grand winner!

I went to sit in the lounge and read the paper. I didn't even have change to buy coffee. I heard my name called, and turned around to see Garaatie standing behind me with Mahmood. I was shocked.

"Garaatie . . ."

She came over and hugged me. "What're you doing here?" I whispered. "And you're back with him?"

"Come with me to the ladies room," she said.

I greeted Mahmood and followed her to the toilet.

"Garaatie," I said, when we were out of earshot. "The two of you are back together?"

"Not quite," she said, looking a little sheepish. "I have some things to think about."

"What?"

"I have to think about whether I can accept his second wife and remain in the marriage."

"I see."

"Look, I know you would never go for something like this, but I don't like being alone. And maybe I can do all those things you said on the days I don't see him. It's not so bad, and better than being completely alone, having no husband."

I wasn't going to talk her out of it. Who was I to tell her anything? And polygamy was the answer for some couples.

"How come you're at the casino?" I asked. "You don't come any more."

"It was his idea. I suppose it's the one place no one would see us to go and tell Moena."

It was strange hearing her put it like that. She was the wife, and she had to be concerned about how the other woman would take it. And she could say the name. Moena.

"Is he staying over tonight?"

"No," she said, but there was a smile on her face, and she glowed.

I knew what that meant. They'd been at it already. I must say I liked this lustful side of Garaatie. She still had it in her for all this sex. I didn't know what it was any more to feel a man's arms about me. But Garaatie still had it in her, and she wasn't even on hormone replacement at forty-five.

"Have you got any money on you?" I asked suddenly.

"Yes. Do you need some?"

"I do. I'll give it back to you in the week. How much can you spare?"

"A hundred?"

"That's it?"

Garaatie opened her wallet and counted the notes. "I have four hundred on me. I can lend you three."

"Okay."

We talked for a few more minutes, then left the ladies room. Garaatie returned to Mahmood who was seated at one of the tables in the corner, drinking coffee. I immediately went to the machine where I'd lost. I asked one of the players whether the machine had done anything in the last twenty minutes.

"Yes," a short lady with grey hair and twenty rand on her card responded. "You just got up, and it paid one thousand, eight hundred rand."

The story of my life. I stood with Garaatie's three hundred rand burning a hole in my wallet, and decided not to be reckless. I checked the computer for pay-outs and discovered all ten of the machines had paid out except for the one at the end. I waited for it to become available and watched a young woman spend two hundred rand on it. I let another player take the machine after her. Except for ten and twenty rand here and there, the machine did nothing. When that player also got up, I took a seat. The machine took the whole three hundred rand while two of the machines which had paid out already, gave two more one-thousand rand spins.

The first year of my sister's marriage to Imran was the hardest. I had to go to birthday parties, anniversary parties. I had to see them together on Eid and family occasions. I had to smile when my heart bled, and listen to other people talk about them. Even though it was I who'd told Imran to go ahead with the marriage, he'd gone back too easily. How could you do that if you loved someone else? He wasn't suffering. He'd done exactly what he'd said he could never do. I couldn't understand this love he said he'd felt for me.

I hated him, and didn't know what I felt for my sister. She'd played the poor little chimney sweep, and hooked the prince. It was hard with all this hurt to remember the order of things. I was therefore not kindly disposed towards her when she sent him to my house one night with a basket of guavas. I almost believed that she knew, and was testing him.

It was raining. The boys were in their beds already with hot-water bottles, fast asleep. I was in my pyjamas, getting ready to go to bed myself. The doorbell rang. I was irritated. And there he stood on the stoep, with a basket of guavas. I hadn't spoken to him since that day after my thirtieth birthday when he'd called me and I'd told him to let go.

I opened the door for him. He followed me into the kitchen, put the basket down on the table, looked about for the children, and scooped me up in his arms. I didn't resist. He walked me out onto the back stoep, and closed the door. He had me up against the damp wall, pulled down my bottoms, and unzipped his jeans. We stood there, grinding and kissing under a dripping roof, crying into each other's hair. But it was over all too soon, and all too soon we were back to reality.

"Do you mind if I have a shower?"

"No," I said, already walking towards my bedroom. My anger had pushed up again. I'd vowed never to weaken, and I had. I wasn't a wife, not even a lover. Already he was concerned about washing away the evidence.

When he came into my room ten minutes later, I pointed to the keys on the bed. "Let yourself out," I said. "Throw the keys through the window."

"Please, Beeda."

"Just do it."

"Please . . . you wanted it as much as I did."

"Was this what it was? Wanting *it*?"

"No. I wish I knew what we could do without hurting anyone. Do you think I'm not suffering?"

"How are you suffering? You've gone on with your life. You sleep next to someone else. You can't fuck someone else when you're suffering. And you come here, you fuck me, you wash off the evidence, and you leave me. Am I supposed to bless this nice little life you're having? Don't come here again bearing gifts. Tell my sister to bring it herself!"

The visit set me back. All my hard work on my emotions had been for nothing. I went to see Abdul. Abdul had become much more than my madressah teacher. He was patient with me.

The heart was the culprit, he said. The heart was playful, a trouble-maker. The heart sought constantly to be satisfied. The brain knew the truth, but we didn't listen to our brains. We listened to the heart when we ought not to, and didn't listen to it when it spoke from the soul. He wrote out a du'ah to address the heart, to talk to the heart, to ask the heart to let go.

"I'm a fool for this man, Abdul. I make all these resolutions, and he just has to walk through my door and it's all over. I was good for months, and he came and disturbed me all over again. I'm angry. I'm angry that he came into my life, and I'm angry that he's with her. I know it's my sister, but I'm still angry."

"You have to overcome this, Abeeda. It's not good for you. You have to take responsibility for what happened. You responded to that letter, you're not a victim. You have to forgive him, then you have to forgive yourself. You have to end this in your head."

"What did I do that was so wrong? We shared our pasts, and found common ground. We fell in love."

"You fell in love with your sister's man. He belonged to her."

"You don't belong to anyone, Abdul."

"And in the same way, he doesn't belong to you. It's a matter of hon-our. You'll hurt yourself if you do this. Don't confuse what I'm telling you with religion, Abeeda. Religion is for feeling comfortable with your cir-cumstances, to accept the hardships in your life. What you have to do, is tap into your soul. Sometimes we ask God for help, and don't like the help that comes. Be still and find the source of your pain, feel where it is in your body. Focus on it, make friends with it. Articulate the sound of your pain. Maybe just a single word, or a scream. Then let go of it. You can do it in the shower when the water's rushing over you, or into a pillow. But let go of this energy and give it back. Take back your power, Abeeda. This is an old pain. That's why it hurts so much. When you peel back the layers and find your centre, you'll see that this need that you have to be loved, is the need to love yourself."

I went home and sat on the stoep with a lemonade and a cigarette to think. Abdul was right. It was an old pain with long tentacles. It was the need to be loved, to feel that I was worthy and desirable, to be a winner, that had undone me. But there were no winners. Zulpha hadn't won. She would always wonder what had made Imran end the engagement, and be insecure. And Imran would swing back and forth between love and loyalty, and never be truly happy. Or maybe he would. Men had a way of dealing with pain. Some took the fast route out. Rabia's uncle, Boeta Salie, had hardly taken forty steps from his wife's grave when he proposed to the sister-in-law, marrying her only one day after the hundred nights.

I thought about Abdul's advice. It *was* a matter of honour. Honour was a big thing with us people. I didn't quite know where to begin. I was conditioned to do the five prayers, and had never taken time out to sit by myself and meditate. I didn't know how to, but decided to give it a try.

I usually stayed up after faj'r in the mornings to get the children's sandwiches ready and to see them off to school, so it wasn't that I couldn't fit it in between my chocolate making and deliveries. I made a few changes. I still helped Iris in the mornings in the garage, then when Reza had his nap before noon, an hour before my midday prayers, I would sit in a pool of light in the corner of my living room on a thick rug with my eyes closed, listening to music of tinkling waterfalls and natural sounds. Sometimes I lay stretched out on the rug, pretending I was on the white sands of a beach with palm trees and emerald waters. After that I took my ceremonial ablution, and performed my prayers.

I felt good, and got used to spending this time by myself. I started to feel happy for longer periods of time. Two weeks, three weeks, four weeks. I became better at editing my thoughts, and planned my life in such a way that I never ran into him.

But I couldn't avoid sickness, anniversaries, celebrations, and it was to

Zulpha's twenty-sixth birthday party – I was thirty-one at the time – that I covered up completely for the first time.

The family teased me about my scarf and robe, saying that my madressah teacher was working miracles with me. It had little to do with Abdul. It had to do with not letting him have even a glimpse of my body.

He stayed away. There were no phone calls or visits. No contact. Zulpha delivered her baskets of fruit herself, and started to appear alone at some of the functions.

A few weeks before Christmas, she called to say that Imran's mother had had an ingrown toenail removed and had developed gangrene. There are things you can avoid, and things you just have to do. Imran's mother lived alone with a woman, Muriel, who looked after her. It was my duty to go and see her, and I went to her house on a Thursday afternoon.

I didn't see any vehicles in the driveway and was therefore surprised when Imran answered the door. His mother's sister stood at the end of the passage, having come to see who it was. I greeted her, and followed them into the room.

I sat with his mother, and listened to her tell me about the excruciating pain in her foot. I hadn't seen her in a very long time, and couldn't believe how sick she looked. The pills weren't helping, she said. A nurse came every second day. The pain had started to travel up her leg.

"The doctor wants to operate," Imran said. "My mother refuses."

She looked at him with half closed eyes, but said nothing.

"It's Mummy's foot or Mummy's life," he tried to persuade her. "Talk to her, Abeeda. Maybe she'll listen to you."

I looked at his mother lying in bed, and remembered the story of his father, the suicide, the other man in his mother's life. It was all such a vicious little world.

"Is Auntie Latiefa scared of surgery?" I asked.

"No," she said. "But I can't just let them take off my foot."

"The surgery will save Auntie's life. What if it affects the leg?"

"Everything is from Allah," she said. "I have to accept it."

"But Auntie doesn't have to just lie down and give up. Auntie must fight."

She didn't answer. She was from the old school. The foot had to go with her.

In the kitchen afterwards, Imran told me that if the surgery didn't happen soon, his mother was likely to lose her leg. I watched him as he talked;

the way his lips moved, the whiteness of his teeth, his pink gums when he smiled. He was leaning against the kitchen counter, the hardness of his thighs making it hard for me to look away. He seemed undisturbed by my presence, and had no idea what was going on with me. I sat calm and collected, but my heart fluttered in my chest.

"I must go," I said, getting up. "Thanks for the tea."

He walked me out to the car, and opened the door for me. I got in.

"You must visit us more often," he said. "Zulpha misses you."

I looked up at him through the window, starting the car. "And you?"

I didn't wait for an answer, and pressed down hard on the accelerator, shaking as I zoomed down Ottery Road.

*You fucking fool, Beeda. You just had to say it.*

When I pulled into my driveway, Iris told me that Reza had bumped into the table with his walker, and that half the chocolate and nuts mixture had toppled over. As I helped her clean up the mess, Zane came into the garage and told me that the teacher was waiting in the house to talk to me. Munier had been caught going through the teacher's satchel during recess. Marwaan was involved also. He had guarded the door. I walked grimly inside.

The teacher sat tight-faced in my dining room waiting for me. She made a ten-minute production out of it. I was shocked to hear what my twins had done.

"There was another incident involving stolen crayons not so long ago," she concluded. "I haven't reported it to the principal. I just wanted you to know that there's a problem. They're clever children. I don't think they really want to do this."

I thanked the teacher, and promised to take care of the matter. I didn't know anything about psychology and bad behaviour, and the negative consequences of a father's absence. I didn't know that a mother's troubles during pregnancy could result in trauma to an unborn child, and how this had accounted for my own feelings of abandonment when my mother was pregnant with me, and which I'd passed on to Reza when I was pregnant with him. Like me, Reza had suffered rejection in the womb.

But the twins had never given me any trouble. They got into mischief like everyone else, but were happy kids, always had each other, and there had been no signs that not having a man in the house had affected them. They were happy, bounce-back kids, I thought.

That same night Braima came by to deliver his child support. I had already given the twins a talking to, and warned them. I didn't read a book first or consult an expert on how to handle my children. I just looked them straight in the eye, and put the fear of God and their father into them.

As I sat in the kitchen while they visited with their father in the front room, I contemplated whether I should tell Braima about the teacher's visit. I was ambivalent about him. The divorce was still a hard thing for me to deal with, and my resentment had only been numbed by other distractions. It still flared up. I was toying with the idea of telling him when Zane came into the kitchen.

Zane was my quiet, introspective son. I knew immediately that something was wrong. I got up from my chair, and went to stand next to him at the sink. I had hardly touched his shoulder, when he burst into tears.

"What's the matter?" I asked, looking towards the front room where the twins were still with their father.

He had difficulty coming out with it. "They're going to have a baby . . ."

"What?"

"Daddy's just told us. He'd told us before that we would be his only children. He lied to us."

I put my arm around him, and drew him close. He cried into the front of my blouse. Any notion of having tea with Braima and telling him about the twins' escapades was gone now.

When he left, I made custard, and set out four bowls. Zane was in his room. The twins were in the front room watching television. I called them to come into the kitchen. When they were seated around the table and had finished their custard, I dished some more into their bowls.

"Your father's going to have a baby," I started to tell them. "Your father's married now. He has a new life. Having another baby doesn't mean he doesn't love you. You're his first children. He loves you."

"We know," Marwaan said. "I hope it's a sister." He had already forgotten the scolding I'd given them earlier that day.

Zane got up and kicked back his chair. I watched him leave for his room. I sat with the twins while longer, then went into Zane's room. He was on the bed, crying.

I sat down next to him. "I know it's hard for you to accept, Zane. Your father has children, and he wants more children. And he doesn't live with his own children. It's hard. I know that. But that doesn't mean that he doesn't love you."

"He lied to us. He told us that we would be his only children. He lied. I'll never believe him again."

"He shouldn't have said that to you. No one can make such a promise. I know it's a shock to hear you're going to have a brother or a sister, but you can't change it. The baby's on its way. I know you feel like he's betrayed you, but he's got a new wife. That wife also wants children."

"He *has* children. Why does he need more children when he has us? He shouldn't have said anything, then."

I lay down next to him and held him. After a while he quieted down.

"Do you want some Milo?" Milo was his favourite nighttime drink.

"No thanks. Can Mummy put off the light, please?"

The telephone rang in the kitchen. I went out and answered it. It was Imran.

"I can't get you out of my head," he said.

I stood with the receiver in my hand.

"Are you there?"

"I'm here."

"I love you, Beeda. This is the effect you have on me. I manage when I don't see you, but when I see you, I'm all weak again. You asked me if I missed you. I miss you more than anything."

I listened. I put down the receiver, quietly, and left it off the hook.

But I didn't sleep that night. I couldn't sort out my feelings. I felt anger at the same time as I felt love. Then there was a gleam of hope. Then came the despair.

In the morning, I drove straight to Abdul. "I was getting stronger, Abdul. The pain was getting less. And one call, and I come undone like an old jersey. 'I love you,' he said. What's the point of *telling* me? He can't *love* me."

"Don't be so hard on yourself, Beeda. You put down the phone. You didn't let him in. Feel proud of yourself. It took courage. You couldn't do that two months ago."

"Why doesn't he leave me alone?"

"Do you want him to leave you alone?"

"I'll be better off not hearing from him. He's not letting me get on with my life. This is taking too long."

He closed his eyes, and opened them slowly again. "Sometimes we're impatient for things to happen, but there's a time to act, and a time to do nothing. Wait for the spirit to speak. Pain is a gift, Abeeda. Remember, what I told you? Religion is the oyster shell. You want the oyster."

"This is all very abstract stuff when you're hurting, Abdul. I need something concrete to extinguish this misery."

"I know. And doing nothing seems like you're not doing anything. But doing nothing is doing something. Time heals. It's your enemy now because you're impatient. But you can't rush it. Nothing happens before its time. Do you know the story about the boy who tried to rush the process of the caterpillar turning into a butterfly, and widened the opening of the cocoon? The butterfly emerged, but because it hadn't struggled its way out, it's wings hadn't developed properly, and it struggled to fly. God lives outside of time, Abeeda. We live inside. The Lord is your shepherd, thou shalt not want, the Bible says. Let God deliver you in his own time."

When I arrived home, Iris told me that a man in a bakkie had been there. The man said he was coming back.

"Did he say what time?"

"He just said after supper tonight."

All afternoon I fretted. My feelings ranged from being light-headed and excited, to one of gloom. I washed my hair, put on some jazz, and sat on the back step with Reza. When my children arrived from school, I gave them spaghetti and meat balls, and told them Iris was staying to look after them. I was going out.

I didn't know where I was going, or what I was going to do. All I knew was that I didn't want to be home when Imran arrived. I ended up at Toeghieda's house.

"My word!" she exclaimed. "Look who's here, Mylie. Abeeda never comes here unless we invite her."

"I thought I would come and see how you were," I said, laughing. "You always accuse me of not visiting. Here I am."

"I just got off the phone with Zulpha," she said. "She wanted to know if Imran had stopped off here. He was coming this way to see a customer. She wanted him to bring back a litre of milk."

It was an interesting bit of information. Customer was the excuse for going over to my house. Only I wasn't going to be there.

"How are things with his mother?" I asked. "I went to visit her the other day. She didn't look good."

"She's going to hospital. I don't know the full story, but apparently she's taken a bad turn. Zulpha's going with her tomorrow."

"She's going to die with that foot, you know."

"I know."

I stayed for supper, watched an Al Pacino thriller with them, and went home at ten-thirty. My children were asleep. Iris had made a bed for herself on the couch, and told me that the man had come and left an envelope on the kitchen table.

"I'm sorry I came back so late, Iris. I can drive you home, but then there'll be no one here with the children."

"It's okay, Madam. I'll sleep here. I called home already."

I waited until the living room was in darkness before I brought the envelope to my room, and sat down with it on the edge of my bed. I wasn't in a rush to open it. I felt through the thin airmail paper. It didn't feel like a letter inside. To prolong my excitement, I put on my pyjamas first, brushed my teeth, and performed my prayers. At last I got into bed. I opened the envelope, and looked inside. A tuft of brown hair slipped out onto my palm. What an odd thing to send me, I thought. I recognised it as my own hair, remembering an afternoon in the yard when he'd first come to work on my house. I had taken a scissors and cut an inch off my hair. Zane had held the mirror. Imran had been busy painting the burglar bars. I had let the hair blow away in the breeze, not thinking any more about it.

I felt the silky strands between my fingers. I wanted to put it under my pillow and weave all kinds of magic in my sleep, but knew that dreams wouldn't bring me the answer. I had to forget him. I walked over to the bedroom window, and blew the strands out.

In the morning I was busy in the garage packing fudge into glass jars, when the bakkie pulled into the yard. It was Zulpha, in a strange mood, stomping up to the garage.

"Was Imran here?" she asked.

"What do you mean?"

"Last night? Was he here?"

I was sure Iris didn't know Imran's name as she hadn't met him until yesterday. "No," I said. "I wasn't here."

"Then how do you know?"

"I don't. Someone was here. Iris didn't take a name."

Zulpha turned to Iris.

Iris was a Worcester girl. She had little experience with madams and seemed a little intimidated. "The meneer that came yesterday had the same bakkie as that one," she said, pointing to the vehicle Zulpha had arrived in.

"What time was he here?" Zulpha asked.

"In the afternoon."

"That's strange," Zulpha said. "He said he was here last night."

I prayed Iris wouldn't say that the same man had been here in the evening also. She knew it was the same man and it wouldn't have been wrong of her to say so. But Iris said nothing. Which made me take a new look at Iris.

"I was at Toeghieda's last night so I don't know," I said.

"I know he visits you."

I didn't know how to take that, especially the way she said it. "The last I saw him was at his mother's house a few days ago."

"You went? Imran never mentioned it."

"Maybe he just forgot. He's got a lot on his mind. Toeghieda told me Latiefa's going to hospital tomorrow."

"Yes. It's not looking good. They're going to have to put her on something for the pain. She still doesn't want to have the surgery. But you know how they are at that age. She's from the old school. And some people get that feeling, when they know. She wants to go with her foot."

We went into the kitchen to have tea. She seemed on edge about something.

"I think Imran's having an affair," she blurted out suddenly.

"What?"

"There's this Christian girl who does his books, and answers the phone for him three days a week. She's calling a lot."

"That's your evidence?"

"It's just a feeling. Two nights ago, he thought I was sleeping. I came into the living room for my glasses and found him on the telephone, whispering."

I was glad my back was turned to her at the fridge. "Maybe he didn't want to wake you up."

"Maybe. And last night he went out, saying he was going to a customer in Toeghieda's area. He never got there."

"I know. I was there. You wanted a litre of milk."

"When he came home, I asked him where he'd been. He said he'd dropped by your house after the customer, but you weren't home. I don't know what to believe."

"It was him then that came here," I said.

"But your girl would've said so."

"She was probably asleep on the couch, and doesn't remember."

Zulpha became quiet.

"What's the matter?" I asked.

She took a tissue out of her bag. "I have nothing to base this on, but things don't feel right. He's very far away sometimes. I know I'm not making a lot of sense."

I looked at her face, shining like alabaster in the soft morning light. "You have a lot on your plate right now with his mother. Imran's devoted to you."

"Devotion's not enough. And maybe I am depressed, but you don't get depressed for nothing. Women know. And I know I'm not wrong."

Her words stopped me short, and made me more resolved to cut things with Imran.

I went to see Abdul.

"I'm not surprised to hear this," he said. "You can't be in love with one person, be married to another, and not slip up. You can play the role, but you can't force something that's not there. And she's sensed it. But Zulpha presenting herself is the solution for you. You asked for help, and here it is. Divine intervention. A way out."

"What do you mean?"

"She's come to you. Whether she suspects something or not, she's basically said there's a problem in my marriage. Help. This is your chance. You can hurt her now one time and take him, or you can walk away clean and for good."

"I *have* walked away."

"Have you? I don't mean the physical separation – putting down the phone on him, not being there when he comes. I'm talking about saying goodbye and letting go. Not waiting for something to happen."

He was right. I hadn't done that. "Tell me, Abdul, is it fair for two people to be together when only one of them loves?"

He gave a wan smile. "When was life fair, Abeeda? But things have a way of working themselves out. Remember what you said about honour? It *is* important."

"Is this the part now where you tell me I'll be blessed? I don't need any more blessings, Abdul. I'm so blessed, I don't know what to do with all this good fortune I'm carrying around."

He laughed. "See how fortunate you are? You're funny, and you can laugh at yourself." He walked me to the door. "What happened was an error in judgment, Abeeda. Not a criminal act."

"It was a cruel trick."

When I got home Iris told me that the telephone had rung three times in my absence. I went out directly to buy an answering machine. When I got back, I helped Iris pack in the orders, and let the machine answer my calls. It rang four times. A call from Toeghieda, one from Garaatie, and two from Imran.

I didn't return any of the calls. I went to see a movie. It was like I expected Imran to knock on my door at any moment, and didn't want to be there. The following morning, Zulpha called from the hospital to say that Latiefa was in intensive care. She was unconscious.

The morning after losing the last of my money, I wallowed in bed with disgust. It wasn't like I didn't know how I would feel, or hadn't felt this despair before, or hadn't vowed countless times that I would stop. But this was the end of the road. There was no way out of my predicament without actually going to my sons to help me out, I owed my sister and Garaatie money. I owed Margaret money. I was in arrears on my credit card. I had overdue accounts. And I didn't have a cent in the bank. My children would gladly give me the money, but would find it strange that I didn't have money to pay my accounts.

"Margaret!" I called out from my bed.

There was no answer. I looked at the clock. It was after ten. I realised it was Margaret's day off, and that she'd gone out. I stared up at the ceiling. There were no answers there. This other, confident woman of ten months ago with twelve thousand rand in a savings account had left the premises.

I got up and had a shower. I switched on the kettle and saw that there were only three slices of bread. I left them for Margaret. I had black coffee and a cigarette. I walked around the living room and formulated my plan.

*It's dangerous, Beeda. You could go to jail.*

*I'll be careful.*

*But God, Abeeda . . . what about God?*

I looked in the telephone book for a number, and wrote it down. I didn't want to call from the house, and walked to the public telephones at the petrol station. The man I was looking for answered the phone himself.

"Kwikstop Panelbeating."

"Is that Yusuf?"

"Yes."

"Yusuf, this is Abeeda Ariefdien. We met once when I came to your shop with my car for a quote. I drove a white Toyota at the time."

"I remember."

"We talked about – repairs, you know. You made some suggestions. I told you I wasn't interested."

"Yes. You have a problem? You were in an accident?"

"Yes to the first one. No to the second."

"I see."

"Do you understand?"

"Yes. What kind of car do you drive now?"

"A red Toyota. A year old."

"When can you come and see me?"

"This morning."

"It sounds urgent."

"It is."

"How much money are you looking for?"

"As much as I can get. It's practically brand-new."

"Where does the car stand at night?"

"In the garage."

"Park it outside for a night or two, and come and see me. We'll talk about figures after I take a look at the car."

I walked back to my house, feeling stomach cramps coming on. I made another coffee, but couldn't drink it. I wondered if it wouldn't be better just to go to Garaatie and spill my guts, and ask her to bail me out. I could go back to making sweets and pay her back. Garaatie would help me. She had lots of pennies saved up. But I was too embarrassed for her to know what the gambling had done to me.

"Forgive me, God, for what I'm about to do." I had the gall to go on my prayer mat and make God part of my scheme.

I lit another cigarettte, and went to see Yusuf. His garage was an old warehouse in Paarden Eiland. Two men with goggles were busy knocking out dents and spraying cars. Yusuf came out to look at my car, then took me into a small cement floor office with a table and chair.

"How much are you insured for?"

"Forty thousand."

He took a small pen knife, and raked the dirt out from under one of his fingernails. "Ten thousand is the best I can do."

"You must be joking. It's a new car."

"You'll get forty from the insurance company."

"I'll have to buy another car. I won't get the same car with that money."

"I understand, but it costs money to move the car. Plates, chassis number, a new spray. The car will go to Jo'burg or Durban. There's a lot of risk involved." He flipped the knife closed and slipped it into his back pocket.

"Fifteen," I said.

He looked at me, considering. "Eleven."

"Twelve. There's also risk on my side."

He pretended to think about it. "All right. We have a deal." He held out his hand for the key. I handed it to him, and watched him take an impression of it.

"Write down your address in the meantime," he said. "And listen carefully. This is what I want you to do. Tomorrow night, Tuesday, you'll go out, come home, and park your car in front of the house. The reason for leaving it outside is because it was late and you were too tired to park it. Someone will drive by the house after midnight to scout the area, and to see if that's where we want the car parked. On Wednesday night you'll park the car in the garage. On Thursday night, you'll go out and come home late again, and leave the car outside. On Friday morning, you'll know what to do."

"What if something goes wrong?"

"Nothing will go wrong. You have to work out where you're going on those two nights when you're coming home late. Visit people who can back up your story if the police or the insurance company comes calling. Your reason for leaving the car in the street must be believable. You were tired, you'd done it before, you didn't think the car would be stolen. That's why I want you to leave it out twice. If they check with the neighbours, someone will remember that the car had stood in the street a few nights earlier." He paused to look me dead in the eye. "I'm not saying any of this will happen, but just in case. Once the car's taken, there's no turning back. And we don't know each other."

*It's not too late, Beeda. Go to Garaatie.*

"When do I get the money?"

"It'll take about a week."

"I can't wait that long. I'm going to need half of it on Thursday, before you take the car."

He smiled at my boldness. "What proof do I have that after I give you the money, you won't change your mind?"

"And what guarantee will I have that after you've taken the car, that you'll pay me? You have to pay me half when you come for the car. I'm the one who must have the trust. You'll have the car."

"We're not going to make contact with you when we come for the car. The money will have to be paid beforehand. In the afternoon. You can still change your mind then."

"Well, Yusuf. I'm here. You have my word. I'm Muslim."

"Muslim?" He laughed.

"Okay, that was stupid. But you know what I mean." It was at that moment, standing there in a greasy garage conspiring to cheat the insurance company out of forty thousand rand, that I felt the true weight of my sin.

"Okay, Abeeda, I'm going to trust you. Six thousand before we take the car. Six thousand a week later."

"I want an I.O.U. for the six."

"You'll get one."

My ride home was miserable. I felt frightened, and had pains in my chest. How was I going to reconcile this in my heart?

*All you're doing is parking the car in the street.*

It was four in the afternoon when I got home. I went to lie on the couch. It was past my prayer time, but I was flat on my back, smoking cigarette after cigarette, until I had nothing left. I got up. Margaret wasn't home, so there was no asking her for a smoke. I got back into my car and drove to Zane's shop. The manager, Howard, was the only one there.

"Zane just left twenty minutes ago," he said. "I don't know when he'll be back."

I stood for a moment looking at the expensive cameras in the shop. I needed a cigarette.

"Listen, Howard, I'm at the shop down the road, I need some money. Can you let me have three hundred rand, and tell Zane about it? Tell him, I'll have it back to him by Friday."

Howard looked unsure, but knew he couldn't take the chance of offending his employer's mother. "No problem, Mrs Ariefdien. Three hundred?"

"Yes, that'll do fine. Thank you."

I went to the supermarket, and bought groceries and a carton of cigarettes. After a tuna sandwich and tea, I sat down and thought about who I was going to visit on the two nights I was supposed to come home late. Tuesday night was easy. I would go with Zulpha to hospital in the morning, then spend the rest of the day with her. Thursday night was another matter. I could visit one of my sons, but didn't want them involved in any questioning by the police or the insurance company, and didn't want to see Garaatie until I had her money.

I dialled Toeghieda's number. She had hardly recovered from the surprise of my last visit, and here I was calling again asking what she was doing on Thursday night.

"As a matter of fact," she said, "Mylie's invited this friend to supper. Actually, it's amazing that you've called. The guy lost his wife a few months ago. I don't know why I didn't think of it before. He's about fifty. Mylie knows him from work. Achmat Jacobs. Will you come? He's a love-ly man."

"I'll come, but you know I'm not interested. Don't tell him anything."

"Wait till you meet him," she said.

"All right. I'll take my be-nice pills."

She laughed. She knew from experience that I wasn't a good candi-date for a blind date. The last time I'd agreed to one, the man thought he could take me to Wembley for a drive-in steak sandwich, and park with me afterwards on Signal Hill. I'm too old for that take-out and a make-out stuff. That's how I ended up being pregnant with Zane and finding myself married to the wrong man. The blind date ended before it started, and Toeghieda never made me forget how poorly I'd treated the man.

The next morning, I got up early, left a note for Margaret on the kitchen table, and drove over to Zulpha's house.

"Imran will come with us to hospital," she said. "Then he'll leave and come back. Will you stay at the hospital while I'm in surgery?"

"Of course," I said, putting my arm around her shoulders. "I've set aside the day. And everything will go well, Insch Allah, you'll see. Are we going in two cars?"

"It's better," Imran said, "just in case."

I had no doubt at all that Zulpha would be out by one o'clock, and that all her fears would be laid to rest. After the forms were filled out and she was taken to the operating room, and Imran was gone, I took out my glasses and settled down with the book I'd brought along to read. An hour passed. I bought coffee, went outside for a smoke. Imran returned, and we went back inside to the waiting room. A little after eleven, Dr Spielberg came out in his green gown and cap.

"Your wife's in the recovery room," he said. "The surgery went well."

"She's all right, then?" Imran asked.

"I have to wait for the results before I can say anything. I don't want to speculate. But the surgery went well. I'd like her to come and see me on Friday."

Imran and I went to a nearby coffee shop. We ordered muffins and cof-fee, then he went up to the waitress to add something else. I looked at

194

him standing at the counter. He was a little more filled out than when he was younger, but still had the same hard physique and rugged look.

I had taken care with my appearance that day, and had on loose cream cotton pants, and a cream top. My bottle-green scarf was pulled back and tied under my shoulder-length hair. For all my covering up, I had a zestful look, and a heck of a body for my age.

Imran came back, and sat down across from me. "I hope Zulpha's all right," he said. "Sometimes they know when they open you up. They just wait for the results to confirm it."

I looked at him. "I don't think so in this case. She's healthy. She'll be fine."

"Do you have a cigarette?"

"You quit."

"I know."

I took out the pack. He lit cigarettes for both of us. A smile curled at the corner of his mouth as he handed one back to me.

"You look nice," he said. "The green colour suits you."

I felt my face go a little warm. "Thank you."

There was a moment's awkwardness. "How have you been, Abeeda?"

"I miss my son. Otherwise I'm fine."

"I know, and I'm not going to say you'll get over it. I don't know what that feels like, to lose a son." He paused. "Do you want to know how I am?"

"You can tell me."

He took a drag on his cigarette, then put it out in the ashtray. "Zulpha's a good wife." I looked out the window.

"She's been good to me."

I put my hand on his wrist. "Please . . . "

"You don't know what I want to say."

"It's been a long time, Imran. Let's not go there."

"No, Beeda, I want to. All these years I've watched you and never spoken. We're both sitting here, concerned about the same person. What happened was beyond our control. I met the right person at the wrong time. I did what was right, what you told me was right. You haven't forgiven me."

"I have."

"You've not been the same to me."

"Being the same to you would've destroyed us. I didn't trust myself. I couldn't be friends with you. I was angry for years, and sad, and a whole lot of other things, but I've freed myself from you the way you've freed yourself from me."

The waitress came with our order. We watched her place everything before us, and leave.

"I haven't freed myself."

"You're married, Imran. Your life has gone on."

"I've never stopped loving you. Zulpha and I get along, we even have some very good times, but we've never had what you and I had. Marrying your sister cheated me out of an intimacy I never will have with any woman but you."

I looked down at my hands. "Why tell me all of this now?"

"I've always wanted to. I love Zulpha but it's a deep caring. There's no fire."

"Fires get extinguished, Imran, and mine's out long ago. But tell me, how is it that men marry the women they say they just care for, but hurt the women they say they love? Is it duty towards the weak? Or is it that they think the strong woman doesn't feel pain and doesn't need love? I never could understand that. Do you think it's because the man himself is weak?" I got up and pushed back my chair. "It's a rhetorical question, you don't have to answer. Excuse me, I have to go to the loo."

In the ladies room, I sat on the toilet seat and cried. I hadn't expected all that pain still inside of me. When I emerged from the cubicle, I looked at my face in the mirror. I wasn't one of those women who looked pretty when they cried. My face was red, my eyes looked swollen. I took a stream of toilet paper, blew my nose, and dabbed myself back to respectability.

"You've cried," he said when I came back.

I managed a smile. "God puts mist in the heart of whomsoever He pleases. Do you know that saying? It's by the Prophet."

He smiled. "This is what I like about you. I know you didn't expect this, Abeeda, but we couldn't not talk about it forever. So many times I've thought of calling you and coming to see you, but I couldn't. I didn't want to disturb the life you were having."

"I'm sorry if I seem nasty. I just didn't expect it after all these years. Friends?"

"Yes. If things were different . . ."

"Please . . ."

"If things were different, Abeeda – would you?"

It took me a while to respond, and to do so honestly. "No. I would have to cry too hard before I could laugh again. I wouldn't trust it."

I used Imran's mother's death to help me deal with my own loss. The ambivalence in my life disturbed me. I no longer wanted an up-and-down, happy-one-day, unhappy-for-a-week kind of life. I wanted stability. I wanted every day to be the same. I wanted no sudden moments of fears and tears. On Abdul's advice, and after evaluating and re-evaluating my financial and emotional situation, I decided to go on pilgrimage. I was thirty-two, young for such a spiritual journey, especially as this wasn't about the culmination of the five pillars of Islam, but rather for the opportunity to stand on holy ground in front of the Ka'bah and ask God to give me hidayah and iman and put acceptance into my heart. I couldn't go to Mecca, come home, and return to my wicked ways.

Because I had no husband and needed a mah'ram – a man who could be my guardian and protector – to be able to enter Mecca, I had to find a family member who also was going on pilgrimage. Toeghieda's husband, Mylie, was accompanying his own mother to perform hajj, and it was decided that I would go with them. I started my preparations. Preparations started a good year ahead of the event.

I went for hajj classes one night a week, and started to learn what was expected of me on this journey. I toned down on the way I dressed, and started to cover up. I increased my customer base for my sweets business and hired another girl to help with the extra production so I could have enough money for the trip, and to leave behind with my sisters who agreed to look after my children. They would stay with Toeghieda on weekends, and with Zulpha during the week to continue their schooling.

My sweets business was so successful, it paid not only for my trip to the holy land, but also for a holiday in Egypt, Istanbul, and Jerusalem. This part of the trip I did on my own, and was away for two months. There were times during this journey when Imran would flit into my thoughts, and I would be reminded, and feel a little sad, and times when I was so involved in my environment and with what I was doing, that the people back home seemed very far away indeed. Mecca and Medina were two places where I thought of no one at all.

The experience started for me the day I arrived in Mecca and stood in front of the Ka'bah and looked at the House of God with the black silk *Kiswah* and gold embroidery. I was standing on the same spot where Abraham had once stood with his son, Ishmael, and smashed idols and placed the Black Stone – *hajar al-aswad* – believed to have descended from Heaven, as the symbol of the covenant made between God and Abraham, into the foundation of the Ka'bah thousands of years ago. In Abraham's time, the Ka'bah was only as tall as a man. In the Holy Prophet Muhammad's time, the Quraysh rebuilt the Ka'bah, and the Black Stone was removed, and again placed into the foundation of the House of God. I was standing on holy ground. The ground of the prophets. The ground where Abraham's wife, Hagar, had run to and fro between the hills of Safã and Marwah, looking for water for baby Ishmael. The sacred soil where the Holy Prophet himself had touched the highest part of his body to the ground, and prostrated himself before God. I was in the sight of God. If I made my tawãf after midnight, and closed my eyes, I could hear whispers of days gone by. On the Mount of Mercy – *Rahmãn* – Arafãt, on the ninth day of the month of pilgrimage, standing amongst millions of worshippers, performing *wuquf* – recitations of the Holy Qur'an – I was a grain of sand in a desert storm. If I died, I would be in the ground by the next waq't. The throng would press on. The next call to prayer would sound. I was as ordinary as the person next to me, and as insignificant. I cried as I thought how important I had made myself.

I returned home with a new mindset. Imran belonged to my sister, and that was it. I had to do nothing at all to encourage him. I had to let go. When they invited the whole family over for supper a few months after my return and announced that they were emigrating to Australia, I went home and cried, but knew that God had answered my prayers.

*You do love me, God. It's painful, but I know it's better for me.*

I spent a lot of time in Abdul's company. I clung to my experience in Mecca and Medina, for it was easy to get into a rut once you were back home. I was steadfast in my devotions. I never went out bareheaded, and never missed my prayers. Garaatie got me briefly involved with her work with street children in the Cape Town business district, and once a week I helped out. On the financial end, my sweets business was thriving. My children were also doing well at school, and involved in other activities. Their father was seeing them on a regular basis, and the twins sometimes spent weekends at his house.

One Friday afternoon everything came undone. Abdul came out of the mosque where he went for jum'aah prayers, and was shot by a man waiting in a car on the opposite side of the road. He died instantly. The man who'd shot Abdul was gay. It came out in the papers that he was a rejected lover. I was shocked. How could this be? A man who loved God and taught Islam? But of course faith has nothing to do with sexual preference, and it wouldn't have made one bit of difference. Garaatie, Rhoda, and I went to his funeral. We stood at the head of the katel and cried. Abdul had deeply touched my life.

At home, I recalled some of the advice Abdul had given me. *Be steadfast in your love for God, Abeeda. He knows what's in your heart.* He too, had been trapped in a situation where society would judge more harshly than God. I was crushed by his death. I had no mentor now, no madressah to attend. My friendship with Rhoda and Garaatie was new. I didn't discuss everything with them.

Watching television one Sunday morning, a program on spirituality caught my attention, and I listened to the speaker talk about the way to reach your higher self. There was a number at the end of the program, and I called it. Two weeks later, I sat with fifteen other people in a room in Claremont, meditating. There were exercises, drawing with crayons, serenity classes, and some of the sessions lasted up to six hours.

I made several new friends, but two in particular, a young Hindu girl, Lerisha, and a Christian man, Gregory, from the Cape Flats, with an earring in his left ear and a motorbike. We started to talk, and found that we enjoyed the meditation very much. We scheduled a session at my house on a Saturday afternoon.

After meditation, we had cake and tea. Lerisha talked about her mother who'd died ten years ago. How she missed her, how she wished there was a grandmother for her young daughter. She said prayers for her mother and talked to her.

Gregory seemed moved by her experience and also spoke.

"Four years ago my wife, Magdalene, and I lived in a house in Retreat. Our son, Jason, was eleven months old."

I knew from his tone that we were going to hear something painful.

"One Sunday morning Magdalene went out shopping for a few things we needed to prepare for her parents who were coming for lunch. I was with Jason in the yard. He was crawling about on the grass. I needed something from the garage, and went to get it. The telephone rang. I thought it was my wife and went to answer it. When I came out, I couldn't see Jason at first. Then I saw his legs sticking out of the bucket in which we used to carry the compost. The bucket was empty of compost, but it had rained the night before."

Inside of me I felt an ache. I looked at Gregory. His face was damp.

"She left me and went back to her mother in Athlone. I joined a group of bikers, and for a while I just drifted. Then one day on the street a Hare Krishna stuck a book in my hand, *Spiritual Warrior*. I can't tell you what's in the book, but it gave me something to hang on to."

He stopped talking. Lerisha stretched out her hand, and touched him. I was too moved to say anything. When he got on his bike to go home, I stood with him for a moment at the gate.

"If you want to talk about it," I offered. "Sometimes we have to speak."

Greg took to calling me on the telephone, and started to come on his own to my house. He spoke about his son, and his interest in Eastern and other philosophies.

"But Islam's a difficult one," he said. "I've taken a look at the Qur'an. It's not easy to read. Two of my cousins are Muslim. They fast and everything. What is the most difficult thing to understand about Islam, do you think, for an outsider?"

"Maybe that you see it as a religion where there're so many things to do. I like to say that in Islam, you're so busy trying to stay on the straight and narrow, that there's no time to sin. But of course, we make the time. If it had been up to me," I laughed, "I would've been born with a Muslim heart, a Jewish sabbath, and the Catholic confessional. Ten Hail Mary's and all's forgiven."

It was the first time I heard him laugh.

After four or five visits my own story came out, and I was surprised at the way I opened myself to him.

"Did you see it as a betrayal?" he asked.

"Not that I loved him. You have no control over that."

"You let your sister have him."

"He was hers to begin with."

"He didn't love her."

"He found a way."

"What did you do?"

"I turned to God. No human being could help me. I had a very special friend, Abdul. I lost him six months ago. He was shot."

Greg was a sensitive man, and in a way, gave me the friendship I missed with Abdul. The weeks passed, our conversations became more intimate. One night he asked if I wanted to go to a movie. I said yes, but we would go in my car as I refused to sit on the back of a bike. The movie was a comedy. What I liked best was the popcorn and that we laughed like kids.

On my thirty-third birthday, Greg gave me a book on Japanese cooking and a beautiful card which read, *Your friend Greg who'd like to know you better.*

I can't say that it was a complete surprise. But I didn't delude myself. I knew what I had to do. I had known what to do when Imran first gave me the letter, but had gone with my feelings. I wouldn't go with my feelings now. Greg was of another faith. He was vulnerable. And I was needy.

"Islam is my life, Gregory. And I won't marry again. A relationship with me can only lead to marriage."

He laughed. "I should make you an honourable woman, then."

"I am an honourable woman, but I know what you mean. And I don't know that I'm ready to think in that direction, or that you should give up your faith."

He took it well. "We can remain friends?"

"Yes. We can be friends. But nothing will change with me."

We stayed friends, and went out to movies sometimes. Sometimes he just called and asked if he could come and have supper with me. He was a great friend, and even met Rhoda and Garaatie who told me I shouldn't be stupid, I should go for him. "A Christian man, Beeda. Hy kan draai vir jou. Just think what Shariefa will have to say."

That alone would've been worth it, but of course, we were all just fooling around. I had four children. I covered up. I was Muslim. I wasn't going to even think what it would be like with this man. I had an idea, but I wasn't going to find out. Just because I'd been to the holy land didn't mean I didn't look where I shouldn't be looking. I noticed things like lips and legs and hard behinds. I knew if he had just a taste of me, he was finished. So, sometimes when he called, I said I had something else to do, and he didn't call again for a few weeks. But the friendship remained, and helped me through the years Imran and Zulpha were away. Then they returned from Australia.

I came home late from Zulpha's house that night. Imran's talk with me in the coffee shop had unsettled me. He'd cranked open a window I'd shut long ago.

I arrived at my house after ten, and left the car in the road. I had taken the first step. The car might actually be stolen by real thieves. I was still unsure whether to go ahead, but had until midnight to change my mind. If the car wasn't in the street when Yusuf scouted the area, they would know that the deal was off. At eleven I stood by the window and toyed with the idea of parking the car in the garage. But I owed too much money, and couldn't bring myself to do it.

On Wednesday morning I woke up nervous and irritable, and drew aside the curtain to look out. My car was still in the street. I went out for half an hour, just to drive around a bit, then returned and parked in the garage. But I was on edge, and couldn't settle down to do anything. I paced up and down, smoking cigarette after cigarette. The first part of the plan was complete. They had scouted the area. Still, I told myself, I had time to change my mind, and didn't have to leave the car out on Thursday night. There would be no turning back once I did that.

On Thursday morning, I woke up worse than the day before. I hadn't called Zulpha to find out how she was, and was scheduled to meet Yusuf at one to get the first half of the money. He suggested that we meet in front of the health food shop at Kenilworth Centre. It was becoming real. Once I took the money I was in over my head.

Garaatie called just as I was rushing out the door, to ask if I wanted to come for supper that evening. Mahmood wouldn't be there that night, she had some things to tell me.

"I have plans to go to Toeghieda," I said, "but I'll see you this afternoon."

I wanted to pay Garaatie what I owed her, and also sort Zulpha out. I didn't have time to think about Zulpha's test results, I was sure there would be nothing wrong.

I said goodbye to Garaatie and left. The postman was at the gate on his bike with a stack of letters. I took them from him. I didn't want to look at them. They all looked like accounts. White envelopes with cellophane windows. I threw them on the passenger seat, and drove off.

I arrived at the mall. Yusuf was where he'd said he would be, and was glancing at his watch already when I walked up. All he had to do now, I thought, was act like a hood in one of those cheap movies and hand me the money surreptitiously.

"Do you want to have a juice?" he asked, nodding his head towards the coffee shop.

"Okay. I can't stay long."

We sat down and ordered fruit cocktails.

"Everything looked okay last night," he said. "The car will be picked up around two or three in the morning."

*You can still walk away, Beeda. It's not too late.*

He waited for me to respond. "Do you still want to go ahead?"

Whatever I said – yes, no – I was in trouble. "I would do anything not to do it. That's the truth."

"Then don't. I have the six thousand on me, but don't do it if you don't feel right. I can leave and we can forget we met."

I was sure he could smell my desperation. "I'll take the money. But I might still bring it back to you before tonight."

"No, Abeeda. Once you take it, that's it. There're other people involved. This has to be it. It's on or it's off."

"Okay. It's on."

"Now about tonight. You are still going out?"

"To my sister's house."

"What time will you be home?"

"Ten or eleven."

He reached into his inside pocket and took out a brown envelope which he handed to me. "Count it."

We were at the back of the coffee shop. I took the money out of the envelope and counted the notes. "It's all there. Thanks. When do I get the rest?"

"A week from now. We can meet here again. I have the I.O.U." He reached into his pocket and took out another envelope, with a white sheet of paper with two lines stating that he owed me six thousand rand, which would be paid the following week. He handed it to me and got up.

"This is it then. I have to go. I'll be in touch."

I didn't want to walk out of the centre with him, and said that I had some shopping to do. I had six thousand rand. I could pay Garaatie, Zulpha, Margaret, Zane, and a big chunk towards my credit card. I would still have a balance, but I was out of the hole. I would start a small little business again to get on my feet.

But the six thousand rand burned a hole in my wallet. It was dirty money, dirtier than gambling money. And dirty money begot more dirty money. I had an urge to sit behind the machines again. I picked up a few items of groceries, got into my car and turned left onto the M5. I would go with five hundred rand and leave five thousand, five hundred in the car. If I won, I would drive straight back to Yusuf and give him back his six thousand rand.

I left the money under the mat in my car, and headed for the entrance. I was feeling good again. The glitter and hum welcomed me back. I headed straight for the wheel of fortune machines. As luck would have it, I got on the right machine, and won five hundred rand.

*Get up now. Give Yusuf's money back. You have five hundred.*

I played on. I won another three hundred. And then two hundred. And then five hundred. After only half an hour in the casino, I had one thousand, eight hundred rand on my card. It was the perfect time to leave. I had everyone's money to give back to them. This was my chance to terminate any criminal act I had planned. All I had to do was go to Yusuf and give him back his money.

I sat on. The waitress brought my third coffee. I had already smoked half a pack of cigarettes. The amount on my card was two thousand, four hundred rand.

I glanced at my watch. It was ten past four. I hadn't gone to see Garaatie yet, and I still had to go to Toeghieda.

But, I couldn't leave. The machine was paying, and was likely to pay out the jackpot. I gave myself fifteen minutes to see if I could go over three thousand rand.

Fifteen minutes later, my money was down to one thousand six hundred rand.

*Get up now.*

I checked the time. Four-thirty. I got up and went to the bank of telephones near the exit. Yusuf himself answered the telephone.

"Thank God you're still there," I said.

"Is that Abeeda? You sound out of breath."

"I am. I was so worried I wouldn't get you in. I don't want to go through with it, Yusuf, I want to give you back the money."

"You don't want to go through with it?"

"That's right."

"But I told you, once you take the money, that's it. I've set the ball rolling."

"Please, man, I'm begging you. I promise I'll never bother you with something like this again."

He was quiet for a moment. "You've wasted my time, Abeeda, really. Those guys are going to be upset. But all right. Bring me the money."

"I know you leave at five. Can I meet you somewhere at six?"

"Six is cutting it tight. Can't you come now?"

"No. I'm stuck where I am."

"Okay. Let's meet at the same place as this afternoon. No later than six."

"I'll be there."

I went back to the same machine. A man in his thirties was sitting there, thrilling at the five hundred rand spin he'd just got. I could see from the leisurely way he took out his cigarettes and lit one, that he wasn't going to get up. I took the machine that became available next to him.

By five o'clock I had five hundred rand left on my card.

*You can still leave a winner. You've only played with a hundred rand of your own money.*

I continued to play. The man next to me got another spin, and won a thousand. I deeply regretted having left the machine.

At five-thirty I had one hundred rand left, the one hundred I'd loaded into the machine when I first started to play. I had no winnings, but I hadn't lost. I could cash in, and would have the full six thousand rand Yusuf had given me, but I wouldn't be able to pay my debts any more.

I lit a cigarette to give myself time to think. I would just make it to Kenilworth Centre. But how could I give the six thousand back when I had no other money?

"Are you playing here?" someone asked behind me.

I turned to see who it was. A couple, waiting with cards in their hands. That decided me. I'd pumped over a thousand rand into the machine. They wouldn't get my winnings like the man next to me. But I knew if I pressed the button even once, I would be eating into Yusuf's six thousand.

I started to play. Nothing happened. The machine had gone cold. I lost the hundred on the card, and the four hundred rand in my wallet. It was five past six. Too late for Yusuf now who had gone to Kenilworth Centre for nothing.

*You're just a greedy little guts. Go to Garaatie and tell her what happened.*

But even if Garaatie helped me, how was I going to give back Yusuf's money? I had no idea where he lived.

"Are you playing, lady?" the woman behind me asked again. She was still waiting for my machine.

"Yes. I'm just going to the ladies room." Turning to the man next to me, I said, "Would you mind keeping an eye on the machine for me? I'll just be a minute."

I flashed the couple a look, then walked quickly out the casino to my car in the parking lot. I took five hundred from under the mat and returned to the machine I'd played on. The couple was still there, waiting. I took my time lighting a cigarette, then started to play.

At seven o'clock, the man next to me gave a sudden hoot, and I watched in stupefaction as all three wheels of gold locked into place on his machine. I had never seen anyone win the jackpot. Fifty-two thousand rand! I couldn't believe it. It was the machine I'd played on, a machine I'd felt instinctively was going to pay. Yet I'd left it to go and make a telephone call.

I thumped the button on my own machine with a vengeance. *Pay you motherfucker!* But as the machine next to me trilled like an old whore, my own machine stripped me. When I had lost the entire five hundred rand, my heart sat in my shoes. I lit a cigarette, trying to decide what to do. A thousand gone from the six thousand. Even if I wanted to give Yusuf back his money now, I couldn't do it.

"Excuse me?"

I turned. It was the same lady. "Are you finished now?"

"For God's sake!" I snapped, "Can you stop hounding me? Go find another machine."

The husband swelled out his chest. "Now wait a minute . . ."

"No, you wait. Is there a sign posted here that says how long I can play? Or can't you wait to get your hands on the money I've pumped into this machine?"

The man gave a smug smile. "We'll wait, lady, and we'll get it."

I wanted to spit in his eye. "If you don't stop harassing me, I'll call an attendant. Now stop standing behind me."

They gave me a look and backed off a little. I returned to the machine. But I had no money left in my purse. The man on my left was busy with the attendant and the photographer who wanted to take a picture of him and his cheque. I waited for the attendant to finish.

"I have to run to the ladies room," I said. "Could I ask you to keep an eye on my machine?"

"Not a problem," she said.

Five minutes later I was back from the parking lot with more money. I had to forget about visiting Garaatie, and it was getting late for Toeghieda.

I sat in the casino until ten that night, until the whole six thousand was gone. I couldn't believe it. I had taken out hundred after hundred rand in the hope that the machine would turn around, but the machine was a programmed predator. It had no conscience. I looked about for an attendant and called one over.

"There must be something wrong with this machine," I said. "I pumped six thousand rand into it. It gave me nothing. How can that be? The casino's supposed to pay back ninety-five percent. Not even a flippin' five hundred rand did it give me."

The technician was used to these laments. "The machine has a cycle, ma'am. It must be in a down cycle."

"It didn't pay anything to me. And how can you play six thousand rand and get nothing? How does it work out to ninety-five percent?"

He smiled. "It doesn't mean that you get back ninety-five cents for every rand you play. The machine may pay nothing for one or two days, then boom, it pays it out all at once. Over a complete cycle, and a cycle may take several days, it must pay out ninety-five percent. These machines can pay three or four mini jackpots in a day."

I understood what he said. The hardest part was getting up and relinquishing my seat to the couple who was still there, hovering about like two scavengers. The man took my seat with a look at me that said, fuck you lady, it's your money I'm going to get. I should've walked away, but made another, serious mistake. I watched. I wanted to see the machine continue its relentless greed, and take this man's money also. But it didn't. It was the first time in the history of the casino that night, when two wheel of gold machines next to each other paid out the jackpot. The man played forty rand, when suddenly all three wheels of gold symbols fell on the line, and he won forty-one thousand rand!

I went to the ladies room and sat with my face over the toilet bowl and threw up. I felt an actual pain in my heart. Not indigestion or anxiety, but heart pain. I became frightened. My knees shook against the cold cement floor. My body trembled. I had visions of fainting, and the casino people having to extricate me from the locked cubicle. I could see my sons standing over my body on the katel, disgraced by the fact that their mother had died in a casino.

At eleven-thirty that night, I found myself in front of Garaatie's house. The place was in darkness. I rang the bell anyway.

"Who's it?" a nervous voice asked from the other side of the door.

"It's me, Garaatie. Beeda."

She opened the door, and I practically fell into her arms. Garaatie walked me to the living room, and switched on the light. She brought coffee, and listened to the whole story. I started from the beginning and told her everything. When I came to the end, she was speechless.

"Don't ask me how it got this out of hand, Garaatie. It happened. But I'm in serious trouble now. I took Yusuf's money, and his boys will be in my neighbourhood anytime now – if they're not there already – to pick up my car."

Garaatie found her speech. "You need help, Beeda, you know that."

"I know. I need to be stopped. I know that. But right now I'm in real shit. What's the time?"

Garaatie glanced at her watch. "Quarter to one."

"Oh my God. They've been to my place. What am I going to do now?"

I could see from the frown on Garaatie's face that she was against the idea. "Listen, Beeda. I don't want you to go through with this. I can lend you six thousand to give to him."

I looked at Garaatie with her new teeth. Garaatie had taken almost a week to decide whether she should pay the hefty fee of a prosthodontist who used imported teeth to give a more natural look, or an Indian guy in Rylands who charged two-thirds less. In the end she opted for the natural look, which made a huge change to her face.

"You would do that for me?" I asked. "You have that kind of money?"

"You're my friend."

I hugged her. "Thanks, Garaatie. But it'll be some time before I can pay you back. I'll start baking or doing something again."

"That's okay. You can pay me off. But I want you to get help."

"Thanks. I will. Now, how am I going to get the money to Yusuf?

They're probably there now for the car."

"Don't leave it outside," she said. "And leave the light on in the house so they know they can knock on the door."

"What if it's not Yusuf? I can't give the money to strangers."

Garaatie got up and pulled a robe over her nightie. "I'll come with you."

"You'll stay with me the night?"

"Yes. Let me get the money."

"Are we going in two cars?"

"Better not," Garaatie said. "If your car's in the garage and mine's outside, just now they steal the Benz by mistake."

"You're right."

Garaatie and I left for my house with the six thousand rand in a brown envelope, and an extra five hundred rand for me to help me out until my children gave me some money, and I was also earning some money again.

We arrived at my house at one-thirty. There was a car parked on the corner, but I paid no attention to it. Except for the street lights, everything was in darkness.

"I have to go in to open the garage door from inside," I said.

"I'll come with you. I should've gone to the toilet at home."

Garaatie came inside with me. I switched on the light and the kettle to make ourselves something to drink.

The phone rang just as I was about to go into the garage. I went to the phone, and noticed that there were six messages waiting. I answered.

"Abeeda?" the voice asked.

"Yes."

"What happened to you at six o'clock?" Yusuf asked angrily.

"I'm so sorry," I said, "I had an emergency, and couldn't reach you. I just got home. I've got your money."

"It's too late now," he said. "When you didn't pitch with the money, I had to go ahead with the plan. My guys just called me. They're in front of the house. Don't go out there."

I felt the heat rush up into my face. "But I have your money. I don't want to go through with it."

"It's too late. It's out of my hands now. And you can't give *them* the money. They won't go without the car."

Garaatie came out of the toilet. "What's wrong?" she asked.

"They're outside," I said. "They're going to take the car."

Garaatie walked into the living room and peeped through the blinds.

"They're in the car already," she called. "Oh my God, they're driving off with it."

I returned to Yusuf on the telephone. "They've taken the car."

"Listen," he said. "There's nothing you can do now. It's done. You have half the money. I'll call you in a week to make arrangements to pay you the rest."

"I didn't want to do this," I said.

"I tried to accommodate you, Abeeda. You didn't pitch. Put off the lights, please, and go to bed. I want your place to be in darkness. Tomorrow morning call the police and your insurance agent. You came home late, you parked the car outside. In the morning the car was gone. Don't add any frills."

I replaced the receiver, and sat down. "I don't believe it . . . my car's gone."

Garaatie came to stand next to me. "It's all right," she comforted me. "You'll get through this."

"He told me my place should be in darkness."

Garaatie switched off the light and sat with me in the dark. "Beeda, how do these things happen to you?"

"I don't know."

"Rhoda can't know about this," she said. "And not your children."

"My children will know tomorrow morning. I'll have to call them. They'll find it strange if I don't call them after having my car stolen. Do you think it's a good idea for you to be here when they come?"

"No. I'll walk to the corner and take a taxi in the morning."

I held her hand in the dark. "I don't know what I would've done without you, Garaatie. At least I can give you your six thousand back. I won't need it now."

"You can keep some of it to pay your accounts if you want."

"No, the five hundred's enough."

"Did you leave anything in the car?" she asked.

"No. There were some letters, but I brought them in with me. Just some accounts."

Garaatie left my house at six-thirty in the morning. I waited half an hour, got dressed in tracksuit pants and a long T-shirt, then called the Athlone Police Station. Two detectives came to see me.

I had practised in the mirror what I would say, and was ready for them. "I got up this morning, got dressed, went outside for my car – I was going to join the gym at Kenilworth Centre – and my car wasn't there. I had parked it right in front of the gate."

"You don't park in the garage?" Detective Van Schalkwyk asked.

"I came home late last night. You have to come in to open the garage door from the inside. I was too tired. I didn't think anything would happen."

"Do you usually park outside?"

"Not really, but I do occasionally when it's late. You hear so much about car-hijacking in your own driveway. When I open the door from inside the garage, I'm quite vulnerable. From the garage you can go straight into the house. I don't like to open the garage door late at night, or when there're no neighbours about. I came home late one other night this week also, and left the car out. Nothing happened."

"Did you notice anything unusual when you came home? What time did you say that was?"

"After one. I didn't notice anything. Well, yes, there was a car parked near the corner."

"Did you see what kind of car?"

"No."

"Was there anyone in it?"

"I didn't pay attention. I just remember that there was a car. It may have belonged to the people in the house."

The other detective was busy making notes. "Were there valuables in the car?" he asked.

"Just some old tapes in the cubbyhole."

"Did you have a tracking device?"

"No."

"How many sets of keys?"

"Only the one I have. It's hanging on that hook right over there," I pointed to the spot above the microwave oven.

He finished writing, and looked at Van Schalkwyk. Van Schalkwyk nodded. "All right, Mrs Ariefdien. If you could take a look at this, and just sign here."

I read what he had written, and signed.

They got up. "We'll get on to it," he said. "In the meantime, you have to report it to the insurance company. They'll need a copy of the police report. You can give them my name and telephone number." He wrote down his details, together with the case number, and gave it to me.

"What are the chances of getting my car back?" I asked.

"I can't say. Sometimes we get lucky, and we find it within the next few days, and sometimes we don't. We'll let you know as soon as we have anything."

When they were gone, I took out my policy, and called the agent. Solly Horowitz was Zane's agent and took care of all Zane's insurance. He came over almost immediately. He listened to my story, made notes, and seemed more thorough in his questioning about the events of the previous night than the police. Did I owe any money on the car? Had the car been in any accidents?

I answered without showing my irritation. "No."

When he had asked all his questions and written a two-page report, he got up and put everything in his briefcase. "I'll get the police report from Detective Van Schalkwyk."

"What happens now?" I asked.

"We have to wait and see what they come up with. Let's hope it's just one of those overnight things, and the car's found. But there're lots of cars being stolen by syndicates, especially Toyotas and Golfs."

"I can't believe it's been stolen," I said. "It's going to be strange not having a car."

"We did talk about insurance for a replacement vehicle, remember?"

"I remember, but who would've thought something like this would happen?"

I felt quite dirty after that little performance. By one o'clock that afternoon, I had spoken to my sons on the telephone. Zane came to the house to see if I was all right, and offered one of his drivers in case I needed to go out. I told him about the money I'd borrowed from Howard at the shop.

"It's all right," he said, putting his hand into his trouser pocket and taking out his wallet. "I might as well give Mummy's money now before I forget." He counted out six hundred rand and gave it to me.

When he was gone, I called my eldest sister. "I know you're upset with me, Toeghieda," I started, "but hear me out. I couldn't make it to your house last night. I had to go and see Garaatie at the last minute. I couldn't get away."

"You could've called. We waited for you, and this man was so disappointed. I had told him so much about you."

"I told you not to tell him anything. I'm sorry. And to crown it all, when I got up this morning, my car was stolen."

"What? Your new car?"

"Yes."

"But don't you park it in the garage?"

"I do, but I didn't last night. It was after one when I got home. I was too tired."

"After one? Oh my. I didn't know you stayed out that late. It must've been a helluva time you had there with Garaatie."

"It was nothing like that. Anyway, I've called the police and the insurance agent and sorted it all out. Zane's driver will help me if I need to go anywhere."

"What are the chances of getting the car back?"

"I don't know. I'm insured for theft. I won't be able to get a new one, but maybe a 2000."

"I'm sorry to hear this," she said. "What a rotten thing to wake up to. Have you spoken to Zulpha?"

"Not yet. I know she gets the results today."

"She's got the results."

The way she said it made me defensive. "And?"

"She's got cancer. The left breast has to come off."

"What?" I sat down. Toeghieda had a way of breaking news.

"There's more," Toeghieda continued. "She's also pregnant. Can you believe it? Three months. After all this time. She's at home, not knowing whether to laugh or cry. Imran says she's keeping it all in. You know how she is. Mylie and I are going there later."

"Can you come around here and pick me up?"

"Sure. We'll be at your house around five."

I lit a cigarette and went to sit in the lounge for a few minutes before making a call to my younger sister. A mastectomy was a serious thing. Breast cancer killed, and Zulpha had got thin over the past year. Our mother hadn't had cancer, but our grandmother had died of it. And a baby now, at forty-three.

It was a confusing time. I hadn't had time yet to digest the events of the last twenty-four hours, but just the thought of the casino depressed me. And stealing my own car. That was the hardest. I finished my cigarette. I wanted to get up and call Zulpha, but my body ached. I had no energy. I would wait until Toeghieda picked me up, I thought, and have a nap in the meantime. I had hardly laid my head on the pillows, when the doorbell rang.

It was Garaatie, anxious to know what had happened after she left my house. I was fatigued, yet glad to see her. I'd told one lie after another all morning, and desperately needed to speak to someone I could be honest with. I made tea. We sat on the couch. I told her everything that had happened.

"You can be glad that part's over. Just hope they don't catch the thieves. Ya Allah, what a mess."

"I feel sick when I think of it. But you know yourself that I didn't want to go through with it."

She looked at me. I had an idea of what was going through her mind, but Garaatie wasn't one of those I-told-you-so kind. She already knew that I knew I had a gambling problem. I appreciated that she didn't lecture me.

"We can only hope that the police are too swamped to give this case a lot of attention," she said. "Yusuf could've called the thing off if he wanted to. Can you find out if everything went all right?"

"He doesn't want me to make contact."

"He still owes you six thousand rand. That piece of paper he gave you means nothing."

"I know. It's not as if I can go to the police and say, this man owes me six thousand rand for stealing my car."

Garaatie picked up a magazine from the coffee table, and started to fan herself.

"Do you still get hot flushes?" I asked, noticing her clothes and her hair. Garaatie had done something about her appearance since Mahmood took a second wife, and had grown her hair a bit and touched it up with a little henna. She no longer bundled herself up like a mummy, and wore a single muslin scarf, and had even taken to wearing loose pants and tops. She still wore too much polyester, but she was coming right.

"I'm hot all the time," she said, fanning faster, "even at night, with no one next to me. I throw off all the blankets. I have to go to the gynie."

"Just take the patches, they help. But talking about no one next to you, what's happening with you and Mahmood?"

She smiled. "I'm seeing him tonight."

"A Friday night? Oh my. That's a big night to give to you, Garaatie. You're scoring points."

"It's not big like a Saturday night, but it's still weekend."

I looked at her. The battle had been too hard, the stakes too great. "You've come to terms with the whole thing."

"I've decided just to let things be. At least when I see him the two nights, he's not running off anywhere. And we go out on Friday nights. We never used to do that before. He was always off on his own. And when he leaves to go to her on Saturday, he only leaves around five in the afternoon."

"Are you happy?"

"I'm not unhappy. On the days he's with her, I don't have to worry about cooking and I can do what I want. It's not bad, Beeda. I have time for myself now. I see just how much my life had revolved around his. It had been all about him. When I see him now, we actually spend time together."

"I'm glad, and if you're happy, I'm happy. And maybe Mahmood will settle down now. You look happier."

She became wistful. "I'm still hurt that I wasn't enough. He didn't say to me, when he married me, that one day he might want another woman. I still think of that. But I've put up with his arse for twenty-five years, another woman isn't going to take it all away from me. I like driving a Benz, I won't lie to you, and my monthly allowance isn't bad. He's unfaithful, but he's not stingy. In fact, the more he cheated, the more he gave. That guilt thing. And I've asked Bronnie to come and live with me permanently now. At least when I come home late at night, there's someone there. It was a nuisance anyway driving her to the station every day to go home, and she has no one really waiting for her there. She goes home on weekends now."

I saw Toeghieda's car stop in front of the house.

"Visitors?" Garaatie asked.

"Mylie and Toeghieda. I'm going with them to Zulpha's house. She's not well."

"What's wrong with her?"

"You're not to say this to anyone, Garaatie."

"You know I won't."

"Zulpha might have to have a breast removed."

Garaatie's hand flew to her mouth. "What?"

"I only heard this afternoon. I have to go now, but we'll talk later."

Garaatie walked out with me. I got into the car with Mylie and Toeghieda.

"How's Garaatie?" Toeghieda asked. "She looks different. Did she lose weight?"

"Yes. She's also growing her hair. And she wears pants and tops now."

"I heard her husband got married again, to a girl in her twenties."

"Yes."

"And Garaatie's okay with that?"

"What woman will be okay? But she's happier now, if you know what I mean. She has time for herself now. She's discovered this other person called Garaatie."

When we arrived at Zulpha's house, she and Imran were at the kitchen table having pizza.

"Sit down," Imran said, "I'll put another pizza in the oven."

Imran was good with sandwiches and pizza, and I was happy for something to eat. While he got out the olives and feta cheese, Zulpha poured coffee. I noticed dark circles under her eyes. A cream dress she'd worn just the previous week, seemed even looser around her shoulders.

"You got the test results," I said.

"Yes. I have to have surgery."

"How serious is it?"

"I have to have a mastectomy."

"She's not sure she wants to have the mastectomy now," Imran said.

"What do you mean?"

"They also discovered that Zulpha's pregnant. If she has the mastectomy, she has to have radiation or chemotherapy. She wants to hold off with the surgery until after the baby's born. I told her that her own life had to come first. We've lived all the years without a baby, she can't take a chance waiting half a year to have the surgery done. It's no use there's a baby, and no mother to look after it."

Zulpha stared down into her coffee cup.

"He's right, Zulpha. And a child now – you don't even know if . . . "

"If it will be normal?" she asked.

"Well, you have to think about it. I know how much you've always wanted a baby, but you've got to put your own life first. How serious does the doctor think it is?"

"He wants to operate next week."

Toeghieda spoke for the first time. "I think Zulpha must decide what's best for her. She knows the implications. And she just got the news. She needs time to think."

"Thank you. I'm still struggling with the fact that I have cancer. I need time. But if I do go ahead with the surgery, I won't have the treatment until after the baby's born. I'll take my chances. And in case anyone of you are thinking it, I'm not too old to have this baby." She said it with such finality, that no one dared to respond. I looked at Imran. His eyes told me that Zulpha was firm in her decision.

I sat in the kitchen with my sisters and their husbands until late. While Toeghieda talked about the dinner I'd missed at her house and the man she'd wanted to introduce me to, I thought of where my car might be at that moment, and whether the thieves had gotten away clean. I never thought once that a police van might roll up to my house to take me to jail. I was more afraid of the consequences to my soul, which already was in a stage of putrefaction. I had sold my soul for six thousand rand. Me, a woman who'd been to Mecca. A woman who until a year ago hadn't missed any of her prayers. That same woman had turned into a gambler and a thief.

On Monday morning Zulpha called to say that she was going ahead with the surgery, which was scheduled for Thursday. Imran also called to tell me what the doctor had said. The cancer was advanced, a pregnancy would complicate things. He had recommended a termination. Zulpha refused.

"I asked her to delay the surgery by a week so she could think it all out carefully, but she doesn't want to. A mastectomy's all she's going to have."

Imran's call made me think. I couldn't imagine what it was like to be told that your breast had to come off, but I did have an idea of Zulpha's desire for motherhood.

On Thursday afternoon, Garaatie picked me up to take me to the hospital. I didn't want Imran to fetch me. I felt vulnerable. The least provocation, and the whole rotten story of the stolen car would come pouring out.

Zulpha was out of surgery and in the ward already when we arrived. She was drowsy, and didn't really know that we were there. But I knew the moment I saw Imran's face that it was bad news.

"How did the surgery go?" I whispered.

He walked with me to the hallway. "The cancer's spread to the liver."

T

hree days after Zulpha's surgery, I got an unexpected visit from Rhoda. I was busy in the kitchen with Margaret rolling out pastries for pies, and there she stood at my back door in a black robe, peering into my kitchen, with a carrier full of guavas.

"Abeeda, how are you?"

I put down my rolling pin. "I'm fine. And you? Come in, please."

She came in and put the carrier bag on the kitchen counter. "I brought you some guavas from my tree," she said. "I'm going to Mecca, Inscha Allah. I don't know if you've heard. I thought it was time to come and see you."

She was coming to greet, and you couldn't go to Mecca without asking forgiveness of anyone you might've hurt.

I pulled out a chair for her, and put on the kettle for tea.

"You're baking," she said. "A function?"

"Not really. My grandson completed his memorisation of the Qur'an. He's graduating on Sunday."

"Marsha Allah. He's a clever boy. But then Rabia's always been one for reading the Qur'an."

She spoke for a few more minutes, then came to the point of her visit. "Well, Beeda, I know things haven't been the same between us."

"I'm not bad friends with you, Rhoda."

"I know, but it's not like before. And I know it's because of what happened at the casino."

I met her eyes. "What happened at the casino?"

"I played on your machine."

"That's it?"

"I played on your machine and I won."

"No, Rhoda. You *insisted* on playing on my machine, a machine I didn't want to get up from. You won ten thousand rand and you took it all for yourself."

She looked down at her hands. "I know. I feel dreadful about it. But I haven't done anything with the money. I came here to end this rift between us." She reached into her bag and took out a clear plastic wallet with a wad of rolled up orange notes.

"The money for our friendship," she said, putting it in front of me. "Take what you think is fair."

I looked at the plastic wallet. Could we have the old friendship back, I wondered? Could I take the money? I didn't know about the friendship, but I knew about the money.

"No, you do what you think is fair. This is your thing, Rhoda. I'm not going to help you."

She considered my words. "Half? Five thousand for you and five thousand for me?"

"That's fair."

She smiled. "I know money can't buy friendship, but I hope we can start again. I can't go to Mecca without your forgiveness."

"This is why you came here, for my forgiveness?"

"For your forgiveness, and to do the right thing."

I got up and hugged her.

"I said to Garaatie, holier-than-thou-with-her-twenty-rand, Miss Doesn't Gamble, then she insists on playing on my machine and she wins. Let's see her go to Mecca with *that* money!"

Rhoda laughed heartily. "That bladdy Garaatie wouldn't tell me anything. I kept asking her things, but she just evaded me. I missed you."

"Me too. I was pissed off, but I still missed you."

She became serious. "This can never happen again, Beeda. We've known each other since high school. And all over gambling."

"I know. I wouldn't have believed a year ago I'd get into such trouble."

"You're in trouble?"

"Yes. I'm not out of it yet, but I'm better. Garaatie stood by me."

"Are you going to tell me? You can't let Garaatie know and not me."

"I don't have the energy to tell you now."

"But you will tell me?"

"Yes."

She searched through her bag for her cigarettes. "Did you hear what happened to Shariefa's cousin, Ganief? The one with the chicken franchise?"

"No."

Rhoda lit two cigarettes and handed one to me.

"Shariefa always has a lot to say about other people, but you don't hear her talking about this. Apparently, Ganief was at Sun City a few weeks ago. Toyer was with him, and told me the story. Ganief played five thousand rand on a machine. The machine swallowed the whole five thousand without giving him anything. Ganief was convinced it was going to pay. It had taken his money, it had to give something back. That was his reasoning. Anyway, he sent Toyer to the hotel room for another five thousand. Toyer brought him the money and Ganief played on. The machine took that money also. Ganief sent Toyer back to the hotel room. Toyer returned with another five thousand. He lost that money also. By now, Toyer said, there was a crowd of people gathered around. He asked Toyer to get more money. Toyer didn't want to do it. Ganief insisted. The floor manager felt sorry for Ganief and had the waiter bring him a cola tonic. Toyer gave in and went to fetch the last five thousand rand, and watched in disgust, he said, as the machine took that also. Everyone waited to see what Ganief was going to do. Ganief got up. He didn't look left or right, and went to the hotel room, to the toilet. Half an hour went by, he didn't come out. Toyer knocked on the door. There was no answer. Toyer got the hotel manager. They found Ganief lying with his face on his arms on the floor. Next to him was an empty plastic container."

"Oh my God."

Rhoda took a long drag on her cigarette. "The family hushed the whole thing up, but you know how these things get out. They pumped his stomach, he was in hospital for three days. He's in therapy now at a clinic in Claremont. His wife went home to her mother."

It was a horrible story, but I had stories of my own I could tell. I could tell Rhoda about the people I'd seen at the casino. She knew some of them. Some of them came in robes and fezzes, and occupied lofty positions in the community. I could tell her about the hadji with the gold-trimmed medorah and thin cigarettes who'd actually asked me for money. She'd seen six hundred rand on my card and asked if she could borrow a hundred. Asking a complete stranger for a loan, as if there wasn't any responsibility to pay it back. I gave her a fifty-rand note and told her she could keep it.

I could tell Rhoda about the young mother who came with her housekeeping allowance and her eight-year-old son, and left the child alone for hours where he stood like a lost sheep in the foyer waiting for her to finish gambling.

I could tell her about the girl from Bishop Lavis who would play out her taxi fare home and then had to hang about the machines until the next morning when someone would come and collect her.

I could tell her about the four fifty-year-old fatties who came at eleven o'clock on Wednesday nights, after the draw, when the machines had been pumped full of money. They would go for their toasted cheese sandwiches and free coffee first, then go out on the floor. Each one contributed five hundred rand. With two thousand, they played with four white cards, and shared the winnings. They had numerous strategies, but hardly ever went home with anything more than heartburn.

I could tell her about the singer with the big hit who'd won a twenty-thousand rand jackpot, and played the whole amount out the same night. The woman was so distraught, she had a hyperventilation attack, and rolled around struggling for breath outside on the pavement. The security had to be called, and she was taken off in an ambulance.

I know these stories because in a casino the man next to you is your partner in chance, and you get to hear everything. You see the person throwing up in the toilet, you see the one crying behind the machine. And always there's a story of great gain and great loss. The stories would make Rhoda laugh and cry, but what story could be more tragic than the Muslim woman who arranged for her own car to be stolen to settle a gambling debt?

When Garaatie called later that evening, I told her that Rhoda had been to my house and given me five thousand rand.

"I don't believe it! She actually came to see you? My word."

"Did you know she was coming?"

"No, but I'm glad she did. It was time you guys had it out. Did you tell her about the car?"

"Only that it had been stolen. You're the only one who knows. When are you coming around? I want to give you your money. You won't believe what else happened. Remember those letters from the postmen I brought in with me the night they took the car?"

"I do, yes."

"One of them was from Reza's insurance company. I was one of two beneficiaries on his policy. I'd forgotten all about it. And if I'd looked at those letters before I ran off to see Yusuf, I would never have done it."

"Oh my word. God loves you, Beeda. You've been given another chance. You can't ever go back to the casino."

"I won't."

"And what about your money from Yusuf? The week's over."

"I'll call him tomorrow. He didn't want me to contact him, but that's too bad."

"Anything from the police?"

"No."

She was silent for a moment. "You'd better make a call to them and sound anxious. Ask about the car. People do that. I know I would if my car was stolen."

She had a point, but I couldn't bring myself to do it. I didn't even want to think about what I'd done, let alone continue the charade. I could only hope that the car wasn't found.

"Not today. I want to go and see Zulpha tomorrow. She's coming home from the hospital."

"How is she?"

"Very depressed."

"I'll come by and pick you up," she offered. "What time do you want to go?"

"Two o'clock. I want to give you your money. I don't want to have it in the house."

"Don't go to the casino, Beeda."

"Don't be silly. How can I? I don't have a car."

The next morning the telephone rang loud and shrill next to my ear on the bedside table. I glanced at the clock. It was just after 6.30 a.m. I wondered who would be calling me so early in the morning.

"Mrs Ariefdien? It's Detective van Schalkwyk, Athlone Police Station."

My heart jumped in my chest. "Yes?"

"I think we've found your car."

The car wasn't supposed to be found. It was supposed to be whisked out of Cape Town, resprayed and sold. "Where did you find it?" I asked, trying to sound happy.

"In Elsies River. It's been stripped."

"But why would anyone strip a new car? Are you sure it's my car?"

"It's a red Toyota. We can't be sure. The engine's been taken out. But we think it's yours."

I asked the question that I knew could alter the rest of my life. "Did you find the people who stole it?"

"Not yet, but we have some leads that we're working on."

I closed my eyes. I could see the two detectives walk up to my door to come and arrest me. "What happens now?" I asked.

"We'll make a full report after the investigation's complete. I just wanted to let you know that we've had some success. As I said, we can't be sure, but we're working on it. One thing I want to do, is send someone over to take your fingerprints. We'll look for matching fingerprints in the car. At least that'll rule out whether or not the car's yours."

My first thought was to phone Garaatie and tell her, but I remembered that Garaatie was coming later that day to take me to Zulpha. I was worried. If they caught the thieves, they would find Yusuf, and Yusuf would point his finger at me. I couldn't imagine what I would tell my sons.

I got up and had a shower. I stood under the spray until the water ran cold. I got dressed, but forgot to make salaah. Out on the street, I realised that the shops were still closed. I hadn't even had coffee, and was walking to the corner café to make a call. And why call Garaatie from a shop? I was thinking like a writer. No one was going to monitor my telephone to see who I'd called.

I walked back to the house, and called Zane. Rabia answered and told me that he had just left.

"Do you know if he's driving the Polo or the BMW today?"

"Does Mummy need a car? He's got the BM, but the Polo's here. I'm not going anywhere today, Mummy can use it."

"Thanks. I really would like to. I have some things I need to do. I can have it back to you this afternoon. I'm going to Zulpha around two. Garaatie will pick me up."

"That's fine," she said. "We can even pick the car up from there. I'm just getting Shaheed ready to go to his classes. I can bring the car over, and Mummy can drive me back."

"Thanks. I'll wait. Maybe you can take the pastry back with you. It's all ready in the fridge for Sunday."

Rabia brought the car to me shortly after nine. I dropped her off at home with the pastry and rolling pin and told her I could be there early on Sunday morning to help with the baking. One of them would have to fetch me. Then I drove to Garaatie. It had been Mahmood's night the night before, and he was there in the kitchen with her having a honeymoon breakfast of sausage and eggs.

"Is something wrong?" Mahmood asked. "You look like you've lost your best friend."

"Almost," I said, laughing. "I didn't know you were here, or I wouldn't have come barging in like this so early."

"It's not a problem," he said, "we're just having breakfast. Sit down, please. Have something to eat with us."

Garaatie got up to make more coffee. I looked at her standing at the kitchen counter. She was still in her nightgown. I knew this was a bed-to-breakfast-to-bed thing, and that I had come at the wrong time.

"You're off shopping?" he asked.

"Yes. I wanted to know if Garaatie wanted to come to Cavendish with me. As I said, I didn't know you were here." He buttered some toast. I winked at Garaatie.

"I would come with you," she said, "but I just have some stuff to do with Mahmood in town this morning. I'm still picking you up at two."

"Okay. But wait for my call. I have Zane's car. I might go to Zulpha directly."

"You don't mind that I can't come with you now?"

"Of course not. I'll see you later."

Garaatie gave one of those smiles. I must say, I hadn't seen her this happy in a long time. Garaatie had completely got used to her new situation.

She walked me out to the car. "I had a call from the police this morning," I said. "They found the car. Or they think it's my car they've found."

"Oh my God. And now?"

"That's why I came to see you. I wanted to call Yusuf. I don't want to go to the garage. What do you think? I don't know what happened, and I don't want to go there just in case the place is being watched. I'm scared."

She glanced back at the front door. "I don't think you should go to the garage. But you must make the call. He owes you six thousand rand."

I had her five hundred in an envelope in my pocket, and took it out. "Thanks for helping me out, Garaatie. It's all there."

She took the envelope from me and put it in her gown pocket. "Thanks. What are you going to do now?"

"I'm going to call Yusuf from a public phone, and pray that it's someone else's car that was found."

"It won't be your car, you'll see."

I hugged her and opened the car door. "From your lips, Garaatie, to God's ears."

I went to the bank and paid two thousand rand towards my credit card. Then I went to the shop to buy groceries. I had left Margaret's money at home, together with an extra three hundred for incidentals, and had a thousand rand left of the money Rhoda had given me, out of which I still had to pay Zulpha her five hundred rand. I had a call to make and three hours to kill.

I was on the highway coming up to the Jan Smuts exit. If I took the exit, I would go home. If I stayed on the highway, I could shoot all the way to Vanguard Drive, and hang a left. I had seconds to make the decision. The car continued along the highway. I felt heavy and depressed. I was in a mess, and was going all the way to the casino to make a telephone call. I would just make the call, take a look around, and come back.

I parked in the lot, took out Zulpha's five hundred rand, and left it under the mat in the car.

*Just a phone call, and a look.*

I didn't go to the telephone. The urge to see what was happening at the wheel of gold machines was too great. I checked the computer. I saw that two of the three machines I usually played on hadn't paid out since the day before. I chose one of them. Within five minutes, I hit a mini jackpot, and won two thousand, five hundred rand. The attendant came and gave me a cheque. It was ten-thirty. I hadn't even ordered coffee yet.

*Go make that call and go home.*

I saw a waitress and asked her to bring me a coffee. I went to the second machine that hadn't paid out. The machine took eight hundred from me, then suddenly went tick, tick, tick, and gave me a red seven and two wheels of gold. Three thousand rand!

I couldn't believe it. Several people had seen me win the earlier jackpot, and were standing there. I was still playing with my original hundred rand.

"Lady," a man with an earring said at my ear, "you really are the *king* of the wheel of gold. You're really fucking these machines, lady."

King of the wheel of gold, I thought. I could imagine myself standing in front of God one day, and God saying, "Aah . . . the wheel of gold lady."

While I waited for the attendant to sort me out, I inserted my other card into the machine next to it. I felt almost guilty when I got a spin and it landed on a thousand rand.

"Hell!" the same man exclaimed. "This woman's lucky! She's just won three thousand rand, and now she's won another thousand!"

"And two thousand, five hundred on the machine behind it," someone else added.

I took my cheques from the attendant and went to cash out. Back in my car, I counted out my winnings. Four thousand, six hundred, plus the money I'd come with. I was free now. I would never come back.

At Zulpha's house that afternoon, I couldn't apply myself to what was happening. Zulpha was depressed and Imran did most of the talking. The house had an oppressive atmosphere. Nothing I said cheered my sister up. Munier and Marwaan arrived with their wives to come and visit Zulpha. I made tea and sandwiches and thought over and over again about the wheel of gold machines. It was almost sickening that I could've won so much money. But just like I'd won it, I knew I could lose it all if I went back.

I called Garaatie from Zulpha's bedroom. "I'm sorry I didn't call you earlier," I said. "You don't want to know what happened."

"What happened?"

I glanced towards the door. "I went to the casino."

"You didn't."

"I won four thousand, five hundred rand."

"What?" Then her voice dropped and she sounded almost desperate. "You're never going to stop, Beeda. This thing with the car didn't scare you."

"It did. I never thought of going to the casino when I came to your house this morning."

"Oh, now you're going to blame me?"

"I'm not blaming you. I just had nowhere to go."

"For God's sake, Beeda, what did you do before this casino came to town? You had a life. Remember?"

I didn't want to continue this on the telephone. "You're right. I have no excuse."

"Agreeing with me doesn't absolve you. You have to *do* something about it."

"Keep on with me, Garaatie. I need to hear it."

"Did you call Yusuf?"

I felt a heaviness come over me. "Not yet."

"You have to make that call, you know that."

"I know. I'm scared of what I might hear. Anyway, I have a lift home, so you don't have to come and get me if you have something else to do. The

226

twins are here. Rabia and Zane are also coming later. One of them will bring me home. We'll talk tomorrow."

But tomorrow with Garaatie never came. Zane said I could use the Polo until Sunday when I came for Shaheed's graduation. I went home after nine and went straight to bed, but I couldn't sleep. I tossed under the sheets until it was time again for my faj'r prayers, at four-fifteen. I got up and made salaah and asked God to give me strength so that I never returned to the casino. I tried to go back to sleep. I kept seeing the machines, wondering if anyone had won since I'd left.

I got up, got into the shower, and put on my jeans and a loose top. It was dark outside. Mine was the only light on in the street. I switched on the kettle for coffee and counted out my money into four piles at the kitchen table while I waited for the kettle to boil. One hoepie for Margaret, one hoepie for the bank, one for household accounts and groceries, and one for me. The one for me was spending money to the amount of five hundred rand. This I rolled up and put into my purse. When the kettle boiled, I didn't make anything to drink. I would have coffee where someone could bring it to me on a tray. I was in the Polo heading down Klipfontein Road just as the first thread of light crept into the sky.

I was surprised to see five people at the wheel of gold machines already. From their pasty expressions, I could tell that they'd been there all night. I looked for a waitress and ordered a coffee, then went to check the machines on the computer. The machine that had paid me the two thousand five hundred the day before, had paid out another three thousand three hours later. But the machines that I hadn't played on, hadn't paid yet. I had a choice of seven, and chose one of the triple-diamond machines. They were better than the double-diamond ones on the end, but not as generous as the five-times ones I liked to play on.

I inserted my card and a hundred-rand note. It was just after six. By six-thirty, I was down four hundred and seventy rand. I was in a panic. I didn't want to go to the ATM machine and withdraw money that I'd just paid in on my credit card the day before. I played on. On my last six rand I got a spin. It was for a hundred rand, which allowed me to play on. I got another spin of seventy-five rand, then a combination of seven hundred and twenty. I had all my money back, plus a profit of three hundred.

*Okay, you've checked the machines, you've played. Time to go.*

I got up from the machine and went to sit on the one next to it. It took less than an hour for that machine to take everything. I stopped to light a cigarette. Was I going to sit here the whole morning winning and losing until I had nothing left? When was I going to stop? I was *not* going to the ATM machine for more money. I started to play again, and lost what was on the card. I got up, and went to the ATM and withdrew three hundred rand. I went back to the same machine. After playing out two hundred and thirty rand, I got a spin and won a thousand.

I lit another cigarette. I had the five hundred I'd come with and the three hundred from the ATM, and a two-hundred rand profit. I could go home and tell myself I'd had a grand time. I got up, and went to a third machine.

By noon, I was still sitting there. I hadn't had anything to eat, and still hadn't called Yusuf. I played on. One coffee. Two coffees. I glanced at my watch. Half past one. I had one thousand, four hundred rand on my card.

"Would you mind keeping an eye on the machine for me, please?" I asked the woman next to me. "I'll be right back."

I took out my card, inserted another one, and quickly went to the toilet. Before returning to the machine, I went up to the cashier and asked to cash out a thousand. I would play just with the four hundred rand profit, and take home the money that was mine. When I got to my machine, the woman told me that several people had wanted to play there. I thanked her for looking after it for me, removed the card, and inserted the one with the four hundred rand on it. Within minutes, the machine made that ticking sound and three diamonds locked into place. I watched as sixteen hundred rand went straight onto my card.

"Wow, lady, you're darem lucky."

The machine had done its duty by me, and I left it. I would have something to eat at the restaurant, call Yusuf, and go home. But I walked past the bank of cashiers, and left for the food court where I bought a packet of masala chips. I could bring the chips right to the machines where I could continue to play and not waste time in a restaurant.

And so I was still there, playing, at two-thirty in the afternoon. I had a thousand rand in my purse, and two thousand, three hundred rand on my card. Casino money. Dirty money. I was a professional. Compulsive. A compulsive professional?

*You're a gambler, and that's it.*

I saw an attendant with a striped jacket and a wire hanging out of his ear, and called him over. He came and gave that friendly smile.

"Yes, Ma'am?"

I looked at his name tag. Robin. "What a nice name, Robin. You know, Muslims don't have names like that. I like that name. It has a sense of spring about it. Freshness. God knows, Robin, there's no freshness in this place."

He looked at me, not sure where I was going.

"My name's Abeeda, Robin. I just want to tell you, that this casino has the right name. It's certainly a grand place, and I've had a great grand time coming here. But I've had enough, Robin. I mean it, it's all very comfortable and attractive with the lights and the buzz and the waiters bringing you your coffee while you smoke and play. It's a giant playground, who can resist it? But I want to stop."

"What do you mean, Ma'am?"

"I want to ban myself. I don't want to come here any more."

"That's quite a serious thing. Do you know what happens when you're banned?"

"No. I just heard about it."

"You won't be allowed to come onto the premises, not even through the gate."

"I believe so, and I want you to arrest me with both hands when you see me. I can't stop, Robin, and I have to."

I was standing behind my seat. The machine was playing on its own.

"Is that your card, ma'am?"

"Yes. I don't want to touch the machine. As you can see, it's on automatic. I have two thousand five hundred rand on it now. I just got another spin of two hundred. I can't handle it. I'm never going to stop. If I win, I'm back here tomorrow. I don't want to come back."

"May I make a suggestion, Ma'am?"

"Of course."

"Why don't you cash out and go home with the money?"

I laughed. "I don't want the money, Robin. I want the memory. I've made a lot of donations here. This one's my parting gift. If I take the money, I'm coming back."

I could tell from his eyes that he thought I was nuts. And maybe I was. I was in a heightened state of something.

"I'll come back for you then, when you're ready, and take you to security."

"Is it a big thing?" I asked.

"Let them tell you, Ma'am." He glanced at my card. "I'll come and check on you in an hour."

"Thanks, Robin. Make it half an hour. The machine would've taken it all by then."

But the machine had ears, and didn't want me to go. I got spin after spin, and several combinations. At six o'clock in the evening, I was still there, with three thousand rand on my card. I had been in the casino for twelve hours.

*Take the fucking money and go.*

*No!*

A crowd of people were standing with me now. I bought drinks for everyone with my points, they all knew that I was going to have myself banned.

An old man standing next to me nodded his head sadly. "If I were you, lady, I would take that money. Don't ban yourself. Just take the money and go home."

"Give it to us if you don't want it!" another woman said.

I could've been charitable and given it all away, but that wasn't the point.

At eight o'clock that evening, the money had dwindled all the way down to one hundred rand. A few people stood with me as we watched it go down. Ninety. Eighty-one. Sixty-six.

*Please, God, DON'T let me get a spin.*

Forty-five. Eighteen.

I got a mixed bar, and ten rand was added to my card.

I turned to the woman next to me, and smiled. "Believe me, I feel no pain."

Finally, all the money was gone. I took out my card, picked up my cigarettes, and said goodbye to the people who'd stood there with me. "Good luck," I said.

I found Robin near the roulette tables, and told him I was ready. He walked with me to the office where newcomers were busy filling out forms for cards. They were on the first leg of their misery. A truck full of angels couldn't stop them now.

Robin asked me to take a seat, and disappeared behind a door. I felt enormous relief. I had made my decision. A few minutes later Robin reappeared with a woman in a maroon uniform, who sat down and spoke to me. Her name was Maria. She wanted to make sure I knew what I was doing.

"I've never been more sure of anything. I don't want to come back. I can't stop, and I have to be stopped."

She too, I could see, thought I was on some kind of drug. "All right. We're going somewhere else to do it. We'll have to wait here for security."

"What actually happens with a banning?"

"We go into an interview room. We'll take your picture, and you'll be recorded. Security will explain it to you. They'll take you through the whole procedure."

The door opened and two men came out, both in black uniforms. One was big and menacing, with a gun on his hip. He didn't smile at all and let the other man, David, do the talking.

"Are you sure this is what you want to do?" David asked.

"I'm sure."

The big oke mumbled something into his mouthpiece, and asked me to follow them. We went through a side door, where we passed through several more doors, into the bowels of the casino. We came to a room no bigger than a cell, with a desk and three chairs.

The big man stood at the door. David sat down behind the desk across from me. Maria sat next to me. I figured out later that Maria was there in case I broke down and tried to hurt myself. The big guy was there in case this was something other than a banning. They were highly suspicious of this woman with the black scarf.

David took out a form that he said he had to read to me. "You'll be photographed. And everything you say will be recorded."

The big guy stood upright at the door. Not a word or a smile. He just looked at me, waiting. What was he waiting for? For me to burst out crying that I'd lost all my money? But it was my own behaviour I couldn't forget afterwards. The room became my confession room, I couldn't stop talking.

I looked up towards the camera with a big grin. "I bet the people who come into this room aren't smiling," I said. "I bet they're near ready to commit suicide. But this is my happiest day. I can't tell you how many times I've thrown my cards out the window as I passed the Epping market. Two weeks later I'm back signing up for a new card. I've had a grand time, I've won lots of money, but I've also lost lots. Today's the day it all comes to an end."

The big guy looked at me, waiting for some insane act. I turned away from the camera, "Okay, David, you can tell me now what I have to do."

David was young. I could see from his smile that he was in training. His demeanor revealed that he didn't know what to make of me. He was there to explain the rules.

"I want to read what is on this form to you," he said.

"Can't I just read it myself?"

"No, it must be recorded."

I looked up at the camera again and smiled. "Very clever," I said.

David read the whole form to me.

"So once I sign and give you my cards, you escort me out to the parking lot."

He smiled sympathetically. "Yes. You won't be allowed on the premises, not even in the other areas. You'll be trespassing. If you manage to get in, we'll ask you to leave. We take your card and your money, and give it to a charity of your choice."

"Do you arrest the person when they come back?"

"It's a self-banning. We just ask you to leave." He looked down at the form. "The ban is for one year. After one year you can come back."

"One year? Oh no. Scratch that out, please. Make it lifetime. How can you beat this if you make it for one year? After one year you come back and start all over again? It's a sick business, David. You guys should change the rules. People who end up in this room, can't come back. And don't send me any vouchers, please, or tickets for draws."

The big guy was getting gatvol. He glanced at David. David placed the form in front of me. I read it and signed.

"I have to take your picture now," David said, taking out a camera.

I gave a bon voyage smile.

"We'll take your card now," he said.

I opened my bag, and took out the two cards. He took the red one. "Keep the other one," he said. "You'll need it to leave through the gate. It won't be of any use to you after today."

I got up. "Thanks. This is a great day for me. I've really had a grand time."

Maria and David got up also. The big guy mumbled something into his walkie talkie, and opened the door. I stepped through and turned to Maria. "Maria, how many people have committed suicide as a result of gambling here – do you know?"

Maria looked quickly at the big guy. Still, the big guy played Boris Karloff. He didn't speak.

"I don't have that information," she said.

"Isn't it three?" I asked. "Wasn't there a guy who blew out his brains in the parking lot just last week?"

The ride home was euphoric. I was free. God had had his hand on my shoulder the whole time. Another day would've been too late.

When I arrived home there was a note in my mailbox. "Can we meet tomorrow morning at ten in front of the juice place?"

I got up for faj'r the next day, and thanked God on my prayer mat. *Thank you, Allah. Thank you for saving me. Thank you for another chance. Never again, I promise. Never.*

Yusuf was where he said he would be. There was no juice in the coffee shop this time.

"I didn't want to go through with this," I said.

"It's done now."

I took the money and said goodbye.

There was one thing left yet for me to do. I got back into my car and drove to Klipfontein Road and stopped at the Athlone Police Station.

*Don't think, Beeda, just do it.*

"Is Detective Van Schalkwyk on duty?" I asked a policeman at the counter.

"You're lucky," he said, "he was just leaving." He went behind a partition into another room. Van Schalkwyk came out.

"Mrs Ariefdien. What a coincidence. I just called you, but you weren't home."

I braced myself. "Listen Detective, there's something . . ."

He was interrupted by another policeman who told him that the call he'd been expecting had just come in. Van Schalkwyk excused himself and went back into the other room.

I waited. The minutes ticked by. I was ready to come out with the whole thing. Finally, he came out, and started to speak before I could say anything. "As I was saying to you, I called you, but you weren't home. I wanted to tell you that the car we found wasn't yours."

I wanted to fall down with relief. "Really?"

"I'm sorry that I gave you any hope. But the car wasn't in any condition to be salvaged anyway. I just wanted to tell you. I'll call the insurance adjuster on Monday. But there was something you wanted to tell me?"

"I was in the area," I said. "I just took a chance that you might still be here. I just wanted to know if there were any further developments. It's really difficult being without a car. I'm driving my son's car. You know how it is with family. I just wanted to know if you've heard anything."

Three weeks after the mastectomy, Zulpha started to become ill. She threw up, she didn't keep down all her food, and spent more and more time in bed. Imran employed a woman called Gloria to look after her while he was at work. Zulpha spent the day sleeping, and only got up to go to the toilet. The time came when she was too tired to do even that. She and Imran slept in different beds now. She was restless during the night. Imran didn't want to disturb her.

When she was seven months pregnant, the doctor told Imran that he didn't think Zulpha would last the term of the pregnancy. He could do a C-section and save the child, but Zulpha's life would be greatly compromised. Also, the child would be premature.

Imran was beside himself. He had watched Zulpha deteriorate and reject treatment in order to give this last gift to him, a gift he said he did not need at his age without a wife. Toeghieda and I sat with him at her bedside. Zulpha would drift in and out of sleep while her belly grew larger, hardly aware of who was there.

One afternoon, Imran and I were alone in the kitchen having tea. He was very depressed.

"In that room, there's a crib waiting, and in the other room, the mother is dying. How is this right, Beeda?"

I didn't want to go into a whole thing on what was right and fair. I could write a book about the unfairness in my own life. At that moment it's the pain speaking to you.

"You mustn't think you did anything wrong. It's not a punishment."

"Are you going to say to me it's a gift?"

"Perhaps. The child is a gift. An extension of Zulpha, a reproduction of your time together. Not many people get that. But you're angry now, and I understand. I lost my son. I was very angry. So angry I hurt myself."

"How did you do that?"

"I'll tell you another time. You don't know what's gone on with me."

"You haven't spoken to me. You've not shared any part of your life with me."

234

"That's true. I didn't want to."

"Are you okay now?"

"You have to be okay. You don't forget, but the pain gets less every day."

He was quiet for a while. "You will have to go through her linen cupboards, Beeda. She's bought things for the baby. I won't know what to do. She also bought her own kafan."

Even I hadn't been brave enough to buy my own burial cloth. But Zulpha had always been more practical. She was different from me, more observant, and never would've fallen victim to something like gambling.

"The doctor wants me to consider a C-section to save the baby," he said, coming at last to the decision before him. "But saying yes to the baby is hastening her death. A baby or my wife. It seems like such an unfair choice for me to make. The one needs the other right now to survive, but one is destined to die."

I didn't have any answers. We were all destined to die.

"You're not saying anything," he said.

"What can I say? It's a big decision."

He was quiet for another long time. He sipped on his tea. Then he looked up at me. "My heart tells me I must save the child."

I cried all the way home. What did it matter this silly little life I'd had with all its ups and downs, and things I'd thought were so important? It was insignificant when I compared it with my sister's. She was dying. She wouldn't live to hold her own child. And the man I'd wanted my whole life would be free. But did I want him now, twenty years later? And why was I thinking such things when my sister was still breathing?

The next day I arrived after Imran had already left for work and helped Gloria wash and change Zulpha. I had started to come every day during the week, taking charge of things, cooking, sitting with my sister and spending time with her. When she slept, I read or did some baking, or other things I needed to do. She had good days and bad days. That day she seemed stronger and we spoke. It was after lunch. She was awake.

"Imran asked me to look through your linen cupboards," I said, leaning over her in the bed. "You bought some things for the baby."

Her features softened as she tried to smile. "Yes."

"Have you thought of a name if it's a boy?"

"Shafiq."

"And if it's a girl?"

"Layla." I put my hand on her belly, and stroked it.

Her eyes closed. She was drifting off again. I looked around the bedroom. Zulpha had changed the furniture and the drapes in the last year, and the room was modern and bright. Not a sick person's room.

I lowered the wooden blinds a bit so she could sleep, and pulled up a chair to one of the cupboards. There were three linen cupboards on top. I stepped onto the chair, and opened the one on the left. It contained winter blankets and flannel sheets, and pillows.

The middle cupboard contained curtaining, towels, linen sheets and duvet covers. I knew this was the cupboard in which to look for the kafan, but couldn't get myself to take anything out. Why did I have to? My sister was here, she was alive. She might live longer than all of us.

I looked into the third cupboard. It was stacked to the top with jumpers and sleepers and bonnets and bootees and shawls and everything imaginable for a baby. I was amazed by the amount of baby things she had accumulated. I reached up and started to take them out.

Gloria came into the room with a cup of tea. "Thanks, Gloria. Can you take these things from me and put it in the room where the crib is?"

Gloria took an armful of baby things, and walked with it to the other room. I took out another pile. She came back and fetched this also. The cupboard was half empty now. I stood on my toes, trying to peer into the back. There was a box there. I reached in, and brought it out. It was my mother's old jewelry box. I remember Zulpha asking me at the time of my mother's death whether I wanted it. I'd said no. I lifted up the lid. The first thing I saw on top of some wooden beads and pearls and mismatched earrings, was a square of folded paper. My heart lurched in my chest. I picked up the small square and held it in my hand. I opened it. The writing was faded, but every word was as I remembered it.

*Oh God, Zulpha, you knew all the time. You knew.*

I folded up the letter and looked down at her. She had woken up again and was looking up at me. The jewelry box was still in my hand.

I stepped down from the chair.

"Beeda?"

"Yes?"

"What is that?"

"It's Mummy's jewelry box."

I sat down on the edge of the bed. The folded square was still in my hand. I opened the box and put it inside, and lifted out a string of brown beads. "Do you remember this?"

She looked at the beads. "It's Mummy's necklace."

"We used to fight over it. Remember?"

She smiled. "I know. Mummy would always let me have it."

"Yes. She always let you have things. Even my things. Do you think she had a favourite?"

"Yes."

"Who?"

She turned her face to me. "You. She let you drive her car at sixteen."

I had forgotten that.

"And you were allowed to go with a boy to a matinée. Remember?"

I did. And suddenly I remembered many other things our mother had allowed me to do, and not her. I looked at her now. Her eyes had closed again, but there was a contented look on her face.

"You must look after Imran," she said.

I held back my tears and sat with her until she was asleep. We didn't speak again. Imran came home early, and found me sitting in the baby's room.

He looked around. The crib was fitted with sheets and blankets, and cuddly toys. A basket next to it contained diapers, powder, and tissues.

"I've just come from the doctor," he said, standing in the doorway. "Surgery's scheduled for eight o'clock tomorrow morning."

When I arrived home that evening, there was an old silver Mercedes in front of my door. I saw immediately who it was.

"Patrick!"

"Mrs A." He got out of the car and hugged me. "How are you?"

"I'm fine, Patrick, and you?"

He looked sheepishly back at the car where someone was sitting in the passenger seat. "I won't say I was in the neighbourhood," he smiled. "But I just wanted to see you."

My eyes misted up. I knew what he meant. Seeing me, was making the connection with my son. He missed him. I missed him. The memories came flooding back.

"I've thought about you," I said. "I wondered how you were."

"I'm managing. It was hard in the beginning. That's not anyone new," he said, glancing at his friend. "He's a new cameraman."

I smiled. "We have to go on living, Patrick."

Patrick suddenly burst out crying. I held him.

"I loved him, Mrs A."

"I know, Patrick. Do you and your friend want to come in for tea?"

"Not today. Can I come and see you again?"

"Of course you can. I'm grateful to you, Patrick. What you did for Reza."

Patrick was a crier. He made sobbing sounds. "I found a diary," he said. "It was in a box in the cupboard."

He took a small little brown book out of his shirt pocket. "He was eighteen when he wrote it."

I looked at it. I couldn't speak.

"I thought you might like to have it," he continued.

I took the diary from him. "Thank you, Patrick." I squeezed his hand and kissed him on the cheek. "You go well, and come and see me. I'll make rootie and lamb curry."

His eyes brightened. "Thank you for everything, Mrs A."

"Bye, Patrick."

I never saw Patrick again, and that was all right. I didn't open the diary until many days later, and when I did, I laughed and I cried. I didn't tell my children about it, but I called Braima, and showed him. Braima was in my living room when he read the diary. His handkerchief was damp, I had to bring Kleenex. "Allah give him janaah," he said when he'd finished reading. "I miss him."

"Me too. It doesn't go away, does it?"

"No."

"That part about taking a girl to bioscope, wasn't it funny?"

He laughed through his tears. "Yes."

We sat for a few minutes in silence. "How's Zainap?"

"The surgery was a success, Alhamdu lilah. The mastectomy saved her life. I'm sorry about your sister. I liked your sisters, Beeda. I always liked them."

Layla weighed in at two kilos, and spent her first four weeks in an incubator. I went with Imran to fetch her, and held her in my arms; a tiny little thing with a sharp nose and a tuft of black hair. She didn't know about the life she was starting, or the mother she'd left behind. She spent her first week in her father's home. Then her crib was moved to my house, into the spare room, and Imran came every day to see her.

A few days after Zulpha's hundred days had passed, Imran stood with me at the crib in the nursery where I had just put Layla down to sleep. It was evening. I had just finished my prayers, and still had on my robe.

I felt his hand on my shoulder. He took off my scarf.

"Will you marry me, Beeda?" I came into his arms.

"We'll do it right this time," he said. "We'll wait."

"How long?"

"Saturday's in two days. After maghrib? Just the imam and the family."

"Yes."

He put his hand in my hair, and drew me close. "My Slamse meit."

I cried into his neck. At last, I was safe.

The next day I called my two friends. Both of them came to see me. I told them the news.

"I had no idea," Rhoda said, "that you had a thing for Imran."

I looked at Garaatie. "Should I tell her, Garaatie?"

Rhoda took off her scarf and threw it over the back of the couch. "What do you mean should you tell her? You mean Garaatie knows and I don't?"

"You were on a ten-thousand rand sabbatical, Rhoda. Remember?"

We laughed like old times, and I did tell her. The three of us took Layla bundled up like a babushka to Kirstenbosch Gardens in my new maroon Mercedes and had lunch under the trees. I told the whole story, but left out the part about finding the letter in Zulpha's jewelry box. I didn't want my friends to have any kind of feeling about it. I never told Imran about the letter either. There are things you keep from your friends, but there are even more things you keep from the man you love.

I'm happy now, and have the life I've always wanted, but one last thing I have to confess. About six months after my marriage, while having tea one afternoon with my friends, I said to them, "I feel like a James Bond adventure."

They looked at me. "This sounds like you want to do something bad," Rhoda said.

"Well, I don't know if it's bad, but I have the urge."

"The urge?" Garaatie looked worried. "Don't tell me you want to go to the casino?"

I laughed. "Don't worry. I'm cured."

"You're far from cured," Garaatie said. "Ons gaan nie weer nie. Look what happened."

"And you can't go," Rhoda added. "You banned yourself."

"That's why I say, an adventure."

The two of them looked at one another. "What if they spot you?"

"Well, let's see if they do. I'll go in disguise."

"Disguise?" Garaatie exclaimed. "You already have a scarf on your head. What kind of disguise?"

"I'll take the scarf off."

"O, ya Allah. You'll take your scarf *off* to go into a casino?"

"You guys are no fun. Is it you taking off the scarf? I just want that old thrill again."

"You haven't been there for months. I don't like this," Garaatie said.

"I promise you. It's not like before. I just want to see if I can get away with it."

"Ya Allah. Is ons nou weer op pad?" O God, are we on the road again?

And off we went to Auntie with Layla in the car, dropping her off first at Toeghieda's house for the afternoon.

We arrived at the casino and bought cards. We wouldn't play more than a hundred rand each. I led them straight to the wheel of gold machines, and checked the computer to see which ones hadn't paid. Two of the machines were available, and Garaatie and I sat down. The machines must've missed my touch, for I had hardly played out forty rand, when I got a combination and won eighteen hundred rand.

"Ya Allah!" Rhoda exclaimed. "You're lucky!"

"I don't want to play any more," I said.

"We just got here," Garaatie said.

"I know. Let's just wait for the cheque, and go to a movie."

The attendant arrived with a cheque and asked me to fill in my name. Garaatie and Rhoda accompanied me to the cashier. I handed in the cheque. The cashier asked for my I.D. I gave her my identity document. She checked it on the computer.

"Just hang on a minute," she said, walking over to someone on the other side.

I stood talking with my friends. We talked. We waited. It had never taken this long to get a cheque cashed. Then something about the security guy in the black suit talking into a walkie talkie a few feet away, caught my eye. And I knew. I saw him coming towards me.

"Mrs Ariefdien?"

I turned to my friends. "In the James Bond movies it never happens like this." I turned to the guy. "Are you coming to tell me I shouldn't be here?"

He smiled. He had a nice smile. I noticed his white teeth. "Mrs Ariefdien . . . you've been a naughty girl."

c1/1

su 3.19.14    rc 9. 2 .14
ha 4.29.14    bk 11.4.14
hu 7. 16 .14    HF 1. 5 .16
              ba 5.16

NNS                         NC